THREE TO FALL

SAINT VIEW SLAYERS VS SINNERS
BOOK 3

ELLE THORPE

Copyright © 2024 by Elle Thorpe Pty Ltd

All rights reserved.

No part of this book may be reproduced in any form or by any electronic or mechanical means, including information storage and retrieval systems, without written permission from the author, except for the use of brief quotations in a book review.

Editing by Studio ENP

Proofreading by Barren Acres Editing

Cover photography by Michelle Lancaster

Cover model: Chad Hurst

Original cover design by Elle Thorpe Pty Ltd

Discreet cover design by Emily Wittig Designs

V: 1

To Bagheera, my favourite alpaca. Because after 30 books, I'm running out of people to dedicate my books to. Clearly I need more friends.

1

HAYDEN

Anger swirled in the air. One person's hate and greed spread to the next like wildfire, until normally sensible people were dragged under by the tide of evil that Josiah's podcast stirred up.

One hundred thousand dollars to the person who captured his wife and returned her to him. He'd painted a target on her back in bright-red paint, impossible for the underprivileged people in this town to ignore.

The crowd swarmed, engulfing me, an angry mob all shouting for Kara's capture.

Or her blood.

Every cell in my body demanded I run toward her. Hurt these people who wanted to take her from me. Pull her into my arms and put my body between her and the very real danger surrounding us.

But then she'd signed Hayley Jade's name.

And in the same sign language we'd been learning so we could communicate with her nonverbal daughter, Kara told me she loved me. Signed it with her fingers through the glass window of the security door, barely hanging on against the barrage of chairs and fists thrown at it.

She needed to run, but she wouldn't while I was standing here.

Wouldn't until she knew her daughter was safe.

I wanted to scream for how stubborn she was.

Just nights earlier, she'd made me promise I would always put Hayley Jade first.

Now I needed to hold up my end of the bargain. Trust that she was strong enough to save herself while I went for the daughter she'd die for.

With every muscle in my body screaming to protect her, I turned and ran in the opposite direction. Leaving Kara to save herself.

I burst out into the daylight, bellowing out my frustration and fear.

My shout faded away, and I muttered to myself, "Get it together." If something happened to Hayley Jade because I was standing here falling apart over Kara, then I was no good to anyone.

The streets from the hospital to Hayley Jade's school felt a million miles long, and yet they flew by outside the car windows. In a blur, I called nine-one-one, shouting down the line that the hospital needed help before gunning my truck toward the gates of Hayley Jade's school.

They were wide open.

No security guard in sight.

No sign of Ice or one of the other prospects Hawk had assigned to stand guard every day Hayley Jade was there. Dark figures scattered throughout the schoolyards, fighting to make their way inside, shouts and cries breaking through the screaming siren of the school's panic alarm.

The mob had made its way to the school. A bounty on Hayley Jade's head, the same as the one on her mother's.

My blood ran cold at the sight of the Slayers' club van, abandoned a few feet away from the gate, engine still running.

No one inside it.

Suddenly, I wondered if Kara had sent me after Hayley Jade.

Or after Hawk.

"Dammit, Kara," I swore beneath my breath, realizing it was probably a combination of both. The woman was too damn selfless for her own good, always putting others first.

Bile rose in my throat at the sight of three men at the office administration door.

"Where is she, bitch?" one shouted. He smashed his fist against the wood. "Open this fucking door and tell us, then we'll be on our way!"

"We've called the police!" the terrified woman on the inside called back. "Just leave!"

That only pissed the men off more. One picked up a large terracotta potted plant and hurled it at the window. It hit the reinforced glass with a splintering crack.

The window didn't break, but the pot did, falling to the concrete in shattered pieces. Despite the failure, the other men followed suit, the three of them trying to break through with anything they could find.

The women's screams imprinted themselves on my brain, a trauma to process another time, because the thought of Hayley Jade in a classroom somewhere, screaming like that, was too much for me to bear to stop and try to help.

I stalked my way through the school, trying to think clearly, trying to calm my breath while knowing I probably only had minutes before the cops would arrive and that minutes might not be enough to get Hayley Jade away.

"Repent! Repent! Repent!" men shouted as the doors gave way and a cheer went up, a group storming into a long hallway.

Panic lit up inside me, and I twisted and turned, getting swept along with the pack, no idea which way to go or where Hayley Jade's classroom was.

A hand grabbed me, slamming me up against the wall.

On instinct, I shoved the guy back before realizing it was Hawk.

In the next instant, he was putting something into my hand. "Where the fuck is Kara?"

I didn't want to answer that. I didn't even want to think about where she was or if she was okay. I couldn't. If I let my brain go there, I'd lose it.

Instead, I stared down at the knife he'd given me, and then back up at him. "Are you fucking insane? Are you trying to terrify these kids?"

His fingers gripped his gun, mostly covered by the sleeve of his jacket. "They're already terrified. Those Josiah-loving assholes are all carrying. You want to be the only one who's not if it comes down to it?"

I didn't want any of this. This was the life I'd tried to leave behind. The life of violence I didn't want for me, or for Kara or even for Hawk. His chest heaved, his eyes alert, ears listening for danger.

He glanced at me as the panic alarm and warning sirens echoed back from somewhere outside. "There's a lot more of them than there is of me. I don't know where my guys are. Or how long it's going to take the cops to do their goddamn fucking jobs, especially when we'd be lucky if there's more than one car on their way. Fuck this town and their useless police force. Do you have my back or not?"

His green eyes stared into mine.

That was insulting. Of course I did. I took the knife, praying I wouldn't need it, shoving the sheathed weapon into my pocket.

When Hawk took off, his run purposeful through the huge elementary school, I followed. It was three more turns before he stopped in front of a classroom door and tapped his gun against it.

I breathed hard, watching the hallway for any sign of life, covering his back.

"Miss Winters? If you're in there, it's Hawk. Hayley Jade's..." He swallowed hard, glancing at me, but then a look of determination dropped over his expression. "Hayley Jade's dad. We've met a few times when I've picked her up. Don't come out. Just tap twice if she's with you."

There was a moment of pause, before two tiny taps came from the other side of the door.

"And once more if you're all okay."

There was another quick tap.

I slumped a little, relief kicking in. "They're better off staying in there." I kept my voice low so no one but Hawk would hear me. "We can't get her out safely with these pricks still lingering around and all hopped up on the thrill of the hunt."

"Agreed." Hawk's gaze flickered up and down the hallway, constantly assessing the situation. "Better off just standing guard until the cops get in here." He closed his eyes for the tiniest of seconds, shoving the heels of his hands to rub at them. "I hate this so fucking much. Hate she can't just go to school and be safe. Hate that Kara is..."

"Stop," I ordered quietly. "Kara is just fucking fine." I jerked my head toward the door. For all I knew, Hayley Jade was right on the other side of it listening to every word we were saying. She didn't need to be scared for her life, as well as her mother's.

Hawk swore softly and nodded.

A commotion from somewhere down the hallway had us freezing. A clatter of something being knocked over.

"What was that?" he murmured.

"Hopefully nothing."

But both of us had our gazes trained on the end of the hallway.

When three men rounded it, the two of us groaned quietly.

I scraped a hand through my hair, every muscle tensing. "Damn. Not nothing."

It was the same three guys I'd seen trying to break their way into the administration office.

"What's doing, fellas?" The leader had a cocky saunter to his step, like he had all the time and right in the world to walk these hallways, terrifying children as he went. "You're blocking that doorway, you know." He leaned on the wall a few paces away. "I used to be a hallway monitor, and that, my friends, is a fire hazard. So we're going to have to ask you to move on."

"Over my dead fucking body." I spoke more to Hawk, but clenched my fingers into fists.

"Play it cool," Hawk murmured. "We're just taking a break from the hunt. No need for them to pay us any attention."

I shook my head, my hair falling in my eye. "Not gonna fly." My gaze dropped to the papers clutched in the leader's hands. "I'll bet anything those are the classroom assignments. I saw them trying to break into the administration office."

Hawk let out a huff of irritation and rolled his head to one side, loosening the tension in his neck. "Damn, I hate when people get smart. You remember how to fight?"

"Been awhile."

"You gonna use that knife if it comes down to it?"

I answered honestly. "No. But it won't come to that."

Hawk glanced at me, then nodded.

He clearly didn't want to leave a dead body on the floor of an elementary school either.

The leader's eyes darkened. "You aren't having that kid. I need that fucking money. So unless you want to die today, I suggest you move the fuck over and let us through."

"Can't do that, brother," Hawk said casually, though the fighter's stance he was slowly moving into said he was anything but relaxed. "That little girl you want is our daughter. So you can imagine why we aren't too keen on letting you in there."

I glanced at him in surprise.

So did the other guy. "Your daughter? Both of you?

You two fags?" He spat on the floor at our feet. "That's fucking disgusting."

I cracked my knuckles, letting anger float its way to the surface of my emotions.

Hawk stiffened beside me, then shook his head, staring at the wad of spit on the floor. "I fucking hate germs."

I continued the conversation between us, loud enough for the other guys to hear, but not speaking directly to them. "I remember."

"You know how many germs are probably in the air right now 'cause this fucking moron has no manners?"

I shrugged. "A lot, I would think." I glanced at the three men. "He's into medicine. He finds germs personally offensive."

The guys stared at us like they had no idea what was going on.

In unison, without a word, Hawk and I let punches fly. Hawk's landed on the spitter, his head twisting sharply sideways beneath the force of Hawk's swing.

My fist connected with the jaw of the skinny white guy with straggly hair and two missing front teeth. The third guy was shorter, and heavier, and reacted so fucking slow I was also able to deliver a punch to his gut before he even realized what was happening.

Hawk threw a blow that sent his guy spinning backward and flat onto his face. He didn't get up.

Which left Hawk free to kick the knees out from the skinny guy, sending him to the floor too. My short guy took one look at his friends on the floor and held up his hands in surrender, walking backward down the hall, stumbling when his foot slipped on the admin papers these assholes had stolen.

Skinny followed after, crying out as he tried to put weight on his knees, and then crawling after his friend when he couldn't get his legs to work fast enough.

Hawk and I instinctively moved back to guard the door, both of us eying the thug leader still on the floor.

He rolled to his side and groaned, spitting out blood. "Fucking faggots. Fuck you, goddamn queers."

Hawk leaned back against the door, watching him. "Why don't guys like him ever just learn to shut up? He's literally just had his ass handed to him, and instead of just politely running away like his friends were smart enough to do, he has to run his mouth and piss me off all over again."

I shrugged, watching the guy struggle to his feet. I allowed it, but only because he was zero threat by himself.

He touched his fingers to his face, the tips coming away with blood from the stream trickling out of his nose. He spat again, this time his saliva red. He smirked at Hawk. "There's some more spit for you. Why don't you use it to coat my dick? You want to suck my dick, cocksucker? Since you like it so much? You want it in your ass, you fucking pansy?"

A low growl rumbled from Hawk's chest, anger flashing in his eyes, his fingers moving for his gun. Suddenly, I was really afraid that this guy's homophobic slurs mixed with the danger Kara and Hayley Jade were in was going to be the thing that pushed Hawk over the edge.

I didn't want a bunch of five-year-olds hearing

gunshots outside their classroom or watching in horror as a pool of blood seeped beneath their door.

I stepped in front of Hawk, just a tiny bit, so my shoulder brushed against his. "He's not worth it."

The leader's smirk turned on me. "You don't want your boyfriend sucking my cock? What about your little girl then? Bet she—"

I threw my fist into his face so hard I barely had a chance to register his look of surprise. A red haze dropped down over my eyes, and I kept punching, slamming my knuckles into the piece-of-shit's face, not feeling any pain, but knowing he was. His bones crunched beneath my fists and his blood spurted across my shirt.

Hawk didn't try to stop me.

Soft cries from the other side of the door started up, and Miss Winters's quiet voice tried to soothe the frightened kids. "Hawk," she said quietly. "Are you still there?"

"Yeah," Hawk answered, voice choked with emotion. "You all doing okay?"

"She's crying," she admitted. "They all are."

It gave me a second of pause, but the leader laughed through the blood filling his mouth. "I like when they cry the best. Crying 'cause my dick is so big."

Hawk glanced up and down the hallway. "No cameras."

That was all I needed. I pulled the knife from my pocket, unsheathed it, and used it to cut through the leather of the man's belt.

His eyes widened, and he tried to fight me off as I yanked his pants down, slicing through the fabric of his underwear. "Wait. No. What are you doing?"

Spotting a bathroom, and not wanting to do this

when there were kids around, but knowing it needed to be done, I dragged him toward it, hissing in his ear, "You just told me you molest little kids, you piece of shit. You think I'm just going to let that go? You think I'm going to let you walk out of here with your dick intact?"

"I didn't mean it!"

But a man didn't say things like that as a joke.

Crying from inside the classroom got louder, as well as Miss Winters trying to shush them.

Hawk's gaze met mine as he slid down the wall, sitting on the floor guarding Hayley Jade and the rest of the kids inside the classroom.

When he opened his mouth again, it was to sing the opening lines of "Hotel California" by the Eagles.

The same song I'd heard him singing to Hayley Jade at night through the walls of the clubhouse.

He nodded at me and raised his voice up loud enough to drown out the screams as I locked myself in the bathroom with a pedophile and did what needed to be fucking done.

2

GRAYSON

I clenched my fingers, channeling all the pent-up rage inside me into choking the steering wheel. When what I really wanted was to wrap them around my brother's neck and end his life the way he'd ended my wife's.

Whip sat in the passenger seat as stonily quiet as I was, lost in his own thoughts. But X poked his head through the gap, bouncing impatiently in the back, too full of energy to sit still.

"Where do you think Trig's been all these years?" X asked. "Somewhere awesome, for sure, right? Surfing in Australia? Trekking the Amazon jungles? Sailing the highest seas?"

Whip glanced back over his shoulder. "Yeah. And I flew to the moon on a rocket called *The Delusional*. Maybe you've heard of it?"

Torch and Ace both sniggered from their spots either side of X. If their laughter bothered him, he didn't show it. Just prattled on a million miles an hour with his usual rambling bullshit.

Normally I had all the time in the world for it. It was how I'd gotten to know him. How I knew what made him tick.

Today, all I could think about was getting back to my place to see if Trigger was there.

He'd been the one to call the meeting of this little psychopath support group he and I had started years ago. Back before he'd betrayed me in the most heinous way possible.

Putting a noose around my wife's neck and pulling it until she couldn't breathe was one way to end a relationship with a bang.

My chest tightened. I remembered finding her body. The blue of her lips. The pale, waxy sheen of her skin, the usual pink in her cheeks absent. The lifeless way she'd lain on the floor, unable to be revived.

I'd spent years thinking about how I'd get my revenge on the man I'd once called brother. How I'd make him suffer the same way she had, cutting off his oxygen and watching him fight until he had nothing left. I just hadn't known where he was to do it.

Now I did.

I put my foot down harder on the accelerator, knowing in my gut that he was waiting for me.

"Aw. Doc is so excited to see his brother. It's going to be the reunion of the century!" X had no idea of what had gone down between me and Trigger. He smoothed his hands over his T-shirt and jeans. "Dammit, I look like a slob. A blood-speckled one at that. Should have worn an apron while we were torturing that guy, I guess. If I'd known Trig was back, I would have worn my prettiest dress underneath."

Whip rolled his eyes. "Does your mouth ever stop?"

"Only when it's on your mama's pussy."

Whip took out a gun so quick all I saw was a flash of black.

But X was just as psychotic. He might have had Whip's gun pressed to his forehead, but X's knife was barely an inch from Whip's jugular.

Their reflexes had always impressed me. But when you had as many kills under your belt as the two of them did, I guess you got good at drawing a weapon in a timely manner.

I huffed out an impatient sigh. "Can you two murder each other some other time, please? Whip, your mother isn't even alive. Why let him get to you like that?" I glanced at the older man, knowing I was more likely to get through to him than X, who was like a firecracker on speed at the best of times. He was way more unpredictable than Whip, who was deadly but generally not as impulsive.

Whip gave X a cold stare. "Don't ever fucking talk about my family. Ever."

X grinned, dropped his knife, and folded his hands behind his head, leaning back against the seat. "Fine. Want to talk about mine? I was born in Massachusetts to parents Belinda and Edward, at eleven past one in the morning. It was a Friday, dark and stormy…"

Whip turned back around and pinched the bridge of his nose, like X's constant verbal diarrhea gave him a headache. "Drive faster, Doc. For the sake of my sanity, please fucking drive faster so I can get out of this car."

I was already pushing the gas pedal to the limits, taking corners too fast, tires screeching while trying to maintain contact with the road. I didn't need his encouragement. I had adrenaline flooding my system and nowhere else for it to go other than out through the vehicle.

Finally, the buildings outside changed from the shitty Saint View shacks, to nicer suburban homes, and then eventually to the mansions that were popular on the Providence side of the border. My apartment was the penthouse in an expensive building, one with private parking and security codes I did not have the patience or time for in that moment.

I jerked the car to a stop out front, one tire on the sidewalk, zero fucks given about the fine I would probably get.

I slammed the car door, practically running for the entrance to my building before Whip caught me, hauling me back with a heavy hand on my shoulder.

"Chill the fuck out. I know he's your brother, but we have no idea what kind of state he's in. And you're clearly in a state yourself."

I shrugged his grip off. "I'm fine."

But he was right. I had all the medical training to know it. I sucked in a few deep breaths and tried to calm myself as we all piled into the elevator that was barely big enough for two people, let alone five big men.

"Okay, who touched my butt?" X asked.

I leaned across him and hit the button for the penthouse apartment and used every calming technique I'd learned in my years of med school. My fingers shook, and I pressed them into the sides of my thighs, fighting the adrenaline buildup inside me and forcing myself to think clearly.

The elevator *binged* when we arrived, and I paused at the door to my apartment.

It was already open.

For once in his life, X went quiet.

I kicked the door wider. Blinding midmorning light streamed through the floor-to-ceiling windows on the other side of the room but did nothing to conceal the broad-shouldered man standing there. Even with his back to me, I recognized my psychopathic brother. The thick thighs and biceps, his back corded with muscle, his clothes always a tiny bit too tight because he was such a big man.

I was no slouch in the size department. I was over six feet. I had the sort of muscle that regular gym workouts gave you. But I was nothing compared to Trig.

And I didn't give a fuck.

All I saw was red.

Before I could even think about it, I was lunging for one of the kitchen knives.

And then toward the man who'd wrecked my life.

Trig had the same sort of reflexes the rest of the guys did. He turned around, a slow, dark smile spreading across his face.

I stopped dead, the blood draining from my face and the adrenaline replaced with a fear so bitterly cold it was ice in my veins.

No.

"I didn't expect a warm welcome. But you aren't even going to say hello to your pretty girlfriend?" Trigger twisted his fingers in the cord he had wrapped loosely around Kara's neck. "Hey, little brother."

The knife fell from my fingers. Clattered to the tiled floor with a clang.

Kara's huge, terrified eyes focused on me, wet with unshed tears. Her fingers gripped the cord around her neck, still loose enough for her to breathe.

But the threat was clear.

"Let her go." The fear built in my throat, forming a ball that tried to choke me.

"She looks like Annette."

My wife.

I swallowed hard. "I know. But let her go."

Kara blinked in surprise, but the only sound she made was the too-fast breaths she sucked in, like she was preempting the air she wouldn't get if Trig pulled that cord more than an inch.

Trig brushed her hair off her face and tilted her head back to peer down at her. "That why you like her? 'Cause she reminds you of your bitch?"

I shook my head. "No."

"But you do like her, right, Brother? She came here, all upset about something, saying there were bad people after her and searching for her knight in shining armor." He grinned. "Which she found in me, of course. Because you weren't here. Isn't that right, Annette Number Two?"

I didn't want to give him another weakness to use against me. But Kara's eyes stared into mine, and I knew deep inside me, if Trig wanted to, he could kill her in an instant. All it would take was one snap of her neck and she'd be done.

If that happened, I didn't want the last thing she heard to be a lie.

So I spoke the truth. "I think I'm in love with her."

Kara's bottom lip trembled.

I knew what it would look like to an outsider. I could feel the surprised gazes of the other guys. Though I'd never been stupid enough to tell a group of psychopaths about the woman I was falling for. Sharing my personal life with them had already ended badly once.

Plus, Kara and I had barely even kissed.

But the connection I felt to her wasn't just physical. It was so much more than just wanting my lips on hers, or to take her out of those clothes and worship the curves beneath.

She was the first thing I thought about in the mornings. And the last thing before I went to bed. She was who I dreamed of when I slept.

I didn't know why I felt the way I did. If I could have palmed it off as a crush, I would have. Except everything about her kept drawing me back in. Every time I saw her caring for a patient. Every time she laughed at one of my stupid jokes. I had no business falling for a woman who already had two men. It should have been simple to walk away from her.

And yet I hadn't. Because I couldn't.

I couldn't explain why I loved her. Just that I did. I wouldn't have voiced it this soon if Trig hadn't forced the issue, but now I needed her to know.

I wanted so badly to reach out and touch her. To rip her away from Trig. To apologize for the danger I'd put her in by selfishly inserting myself into her life. "I'm in love with you."

Her tears spilled over, falling down her rounded cheeks.

Trig shook his head at me, like I was completely and utterly pathetic. "You'll never learn, will you? She's Annette all over again. Got you so damn pussy-whipped you don't see anything else."

"Grayson," she whispered, the terror in her voice so tangible I could barely stand it.

"Ah, fuck," Whip spoke up from half a step behind me. "What are you doing, Trig? Let the woman go. This is cruel."

Trig eyed the gun in Whip's hand, his grip on Kara tightening enough that she winced. "Or what? You and the rest of your murder squad are going to hurt me? Shoot me in the leg maybe? Cut me up with that knife of yours?"

X cracked his knuckles. "If that's what Doc wants, we will."

But I knew Trig better than they did. And guns and knives weren't the way to get him to do what we wanted. "He can't feel pain."

Trig sighed dramatically, shaking his head. "There you go again, just telling all my secrets. Whatever happened to doctor-patient confidentiality? Or even just family loyalty?"

"Like, seriously?" Torch asked, the flick of his lighter the only sign he was agitated. "He can't feel pain at all? I could set him on fire right now and—"

"Wouldn't feel it." Trig's gaze dropped to Torch's lighter. "Wouldn't recommend trying it though." He glanced down at Kara with anger in his gaze. "This one probably isn't as lucky to be blessed with my condition, is she?"

He tightened the noose.

Kara gripped it fiercely. "No! Please! I have a daughter."

Her voice, so laced with fear and panic, was a knife cutting right through me, slicing open every organ and leaving me to bleed. She still had room to breathe. But barely. One more tug and she'd be fighting for her life.

"You think I care about your daughter?" Trig seethed. "Another little bitch in the making, no doubt. One the world will be better off without. You're all the same."

I wouldn't lose another person I loved at my brother's hands. I refused to let it happen. But I also knew him. And that more than anything, his twisted mind loved a game of cat and mouse.

I undid my buckle on my belt. Withdrew it from the loops on the suit pants I'd worn to work that morning.

"Uh, odd time to be getting naked, Doc," X whispered. "Guarantee mine is bigger anyway."

Ignoring him, I put the belt around my neck. Slid the end through the buckle. And then turned to Whip. "Pull it."

Whip blanched. "What?"

"You heard me. Pull the fucking belt."

"Grayson, no!" Kara fought against Trig's grip, trying to get to me with no success against the bruising grip he had on her arm.

Trigger's eyes darkened, focused on mine. "Don't be an idiot."

X screwed up his face. "But, Doc, if Whip tightens that belt, you'll…"

"Choke?" I asked him. "Suffocate painfully? Yeah, I will. But see, what Trigger here isn't telling you is that while he doesn't feel physical pain, he does feel emotional pain."

Trigger's mouth twisted into an irritated line. "You think pretty highly of yourself if you think you suffocating would cause me to feel anything remotely like pain."

I nodded at Kara. "Let her go, and we won't have to test the theory."

Trigger's upper lip curled. "I let her go and you and your boys kill me before I say what I came here to say."

A murderous rage rose inside me, taking the place of everything else I was feeling. It twisted through my muscles, fighting to be released. I wanted to throw myself at him. Hurt him the way he was hurting her. Punish him for taking every single thing I'd ever cared about. "You think I care what you have to say, Trig?" I roared. "You self-centered, narcissistic psychopath! You think I give one tiny fuck about whatever pathetic excuse you have for the way you took the one good thing in my life? And now you're doing it again. I've barely had a chance to know her, and now you're taking her away."

"Everything I do is for you." Trigger glared at me. "You don't see it, but it is."

Oh, that was fucking rich. That might have been true when we were kids. He'd taken a vicious beating the day at the beach when our foster dad had tried to drown me. It was Trig, older and bigger than me, though still no match for a fully grown man, who'd thrown himself at my attacker, giving me enough time to get out of the water and away from his vicious temper. It had been

Trigger who'd taken the beating when we'd gotten home, and who'd spent days in a cage afterward, learning his lesson for questioning our foster parents' discipline.

But that boy who'd loved his brother wasn't inside him anymore. He'd disappeared the day Trig had killed my wife. Clearly, nothing had changed. His blind hatred for women as blisteringly strong as it had been the day he'd killed Annette and her sister.

"Just let her go," I begged him. "She's done nothing wrong."

Trig shook his head. "Don't take orders from you, little brother."

I pulled the belt tighter around my neck, feeling the burn of the leather when it closed around my throat. I shoved the end of it into Whip's hand. "Do it."

Trig chuckled darkly. "He ain't gonna do it. You're an innocent. Whip never could kill the good ones."

Whip's eyes narrowed at Trig's arrogance, his voice deadly cold, no sign of any emotion. A peep into what he must be like when he buried the bodies of the men and women he killed. "You've been gone a long time, Trig. You don't know half as much as you think you do." He tightened his grip on the belt.

It flattened uncomfortably against my skin. Made swallowing difficult. Fear rose inside me, but I stared my brother down, refusing to budge when Kara was in exactly the same position.

He'd let her go. Or he could watch me die.

It was the only way I knew to hurt him the way he was hurting me.

Trig eyed Whip. "You were loyal to me once. I helped you."

Whip shrugged. "You walked out and left us. Doc didn't."

"You ain't gonna kill him."

Trig's taunt held the barest hint of worry. One you wouldn't have noticed unless maybe you'd been his therapist for years.

Or if you were his brother.

I glared at him. "He will if I tell him to. You care so much about me? Prove it. Whip can let go of the belt as soon as you've let Kara go."

Trig stared me down, his lips mashed into a hard line. "Whip is a fool who doesn't know his ass from his elbow."

I took a deep breath and gave Whip the tiniest of nods.

He didn't give me a chance to back out.

He yanked the belt hard. Cutting off my air.

Kara screamed. "No, please! Stop! Grayson!"

Trigger's grip on her arm tightened as she fought against him, trying to get away. But there was no chance of her going anywhere. Trigger was huge. Easily one of the biggest men I knew, up there with Rebel's partner, Fang, who had to be at least six foot five and two hundred and sixty pounds of solid muscle.

Trigger shifted his weight to one side and eyed Whip over my shoulder. "We really going to do this? I thought you and Gray were friends? You know he's an innocent. What happened to your morals? You were always mister 'no killing innocent people when there's plenty of bad ones in the world.'"

Whip didn't loosen his hold. If anything, he only planted his feet harder, using leverage to keep the belt from slipping. "We are friends. But it's not me killing him, is it? I might be the one pulling it so he can't breathe, but it's you who's killing him. Let the woman go, and I'll let go too."

The belt squeezed around my neck, so painfully uncomfortable I wanted to tear at it until my fingernails bled. But I didn't flail. Didn't fight against the hold Whip had on my throat, refusing to give in to the panic coursing through my body and the way instinct told me to do whatever it took to save my life. It took every self-calming technique I'd ever learned in med school to just stand there and let another man try to kill me. I stared my brother down in a deadly game of chicken that dragged out, every second a lifetime.

Kara's frightened gaze bounced around the men standing like soldiers at my back. "Help him!" she screamed at them. "Why aren't you doing anything? He's dying!"

In the reflection of the window, my face paled until it was almost white, a bluish tinge spreading across my lips. Black danced at the corners of my vision, while my lungs screamed for air I couldn't give them.

Kara's panic turned to desperation. "He's not dying for me!" She grabbed the cord around her neck and yanked it hard.

Tightening it. Drawing it closed around her throat until her eyes bulged.

I shook my head violently and tried to lunge for her, but my muscles all felt like they'd gone to sleep. Whip kept me up by my neck, my body weight only putting more pressure on my throat.

We were both going to fucking die. And my brother was just going to stand there and let it happen. A lifetime of memories flashed behind my eyes, so many of them featuring younger versions of me and Trig, back when he'd been known by his legal name, Kingsley.

I hadn't called him that in a decade. My gaze met his.

Something flickered in his eyes. Something I recognized from every time he'd saved me as a kid.

Trigger sighed in defeat. "Oh, for Christ's sake. Fine. Take the girl. She's not who I came here for anyway. I was just having some fun. You all need to lighten up." He loosened the cord around Kara's neck and shoved her away carelessly, pushing her toward me.

Whip let go of me at the same time, swapping his grip on the belt for the gun at his hip, raising it until it was pointed directly at Trigger's forehead.

Kara and I sank to the floor, our nooses loose, both of us sucking in deep breaths to replace the ones we'd lost.

Kara recovered in seconds, but I didn't. I'd been without oxygen so much longer than she had.

I coughed and spluttered, groaning in pain. I dragged the belt away from my throat, eyeing Trigger who seemed completely unbothered by my murder squad, as he'd called them, surrounding him, weapons drawn.

Kara ignored them, putting her fingertips to my neck, dancing over the damaged skin. "Oh my God. Grayson, your neck."

I was sure it wasn't pretty. But my lips tingled, blood rushing back into them, and my chest heaved painfully, finally filling with air again after being deprived for too long. My head ached like I'd been hit by a truck.

Kara rubbed at my arms. "Tell me what to do," she begged. "What can I do? Should I call nine-one-one?"

"No!" all the guys shouted in unison.

She blinked up at them, like she'd forgotten they were even there.

She was so damn selfless, not even seeing the danger she was in because she was so focused on me.

Weakly, I drew her into my arms and tried to smile. "You could kiss me."

She pressed her lips to mine without hesitation, half falling onto me in relief. The kiss wasn't soft or gentle. It was hard and desperate, a needy grab of her hands into my shirt, holding me close, trembling in my arms. "I thought you were dead," she whispered.

I kissed her back, ignoring the danger around us because just moments ago I'd been so sure I was never going to get to do this again. I kissed her until one thought surfaced through the fog the lack of oxygen had created in my brain. I was done wasting another second pretending this woman wasn't important to me. When she so clearly was.

"Aw!" X shouted. "Gray has a girlfriend!"

I didn't know if that's what she was. But in that moment, I knew I wanted her to be.

Her gaze flickered over my face, and her eyes watered. "You just nearly died for me."

"It would have been worth it."

She melted, coming down off the adrenaline high into tiny trembles that showed how scared she'd really been.

I hated it. I pulled her close again and kissed the top of her head tenderly, murmuring reassurances into her hair that I was sorry and I'd never do it again.

Even though I would have died for her a hundred times over.

Because I was so stupidly in love with her.

Behind me, Trigger groaned. "Jesus Christ, I leave for a few years, and this is what you turn into? You were never this sappy with Annette."

I blinked at the mention of how I'd been with my wife. Her name was like a bucket of cold water being thrown over me.

He was right. Annette might have looked like Kara, but she was different in every other way. She hadn't been warm and sweet the way Kara was. Annette hadn't liked public displays of affection, so we'd never kissed or hugged. Not even at home. I'd fallen for her because I was attracted to her and the sex had been good, but we'd never been affectionate with each other. We'd both been too busy for that. Me getting my degree and working long hours at the hospital. Her and her sister running their business and often away on trips.

I'd enjoyed her ambition, the money, and the curves of her body.

But she was nothing like Kara. She had none of Kara's softness. Her sweetness. Annette had been selfish.

I had been, too, so it had worked.

But I wasn't that man anymore. The work I'd done in Saint View, volunteering at that clinic every week and seeing how much people suffered, had put things into perspective for me.

If I was sappy now, it was a good thing. Not the insult my brother seemed to think it was.

But it didn't mean I could just let him go. He might have given Kara back to me, but he'd still broken the one rule we'd set in place a lifetime ago, back in foster care when he'd killed his first victim and realized he liked it.

He and I had made a promise that day, and it was one each member of our group had sworn to as they'd come to us over the years. No one wanted a life in prison. Or an institution. So we'd vowed that if one of us got out of control, the others would put him in the ground.

Trig had killed innocent people. My wife. Her sister. Alice. All three of their deaths had been by strangulation, which had always been Trig's weapon of choice. His name was written all over them.

He'd left me no choice.

"Whip, I need a gun."

The words hurt to get out around my bruised throat. My voice was barely more than a hoarse whisper, but there was no staying silent. I'd been quiet for years, never getting my chance to look my wife's killer in the eye and tell him exactly what he'd taken from me. I hadn't even told the guys what he'd done. I'd kept every detail to myself, knowing that it needed to be me who ended him.

Trigger rolled his eyes when I got to my feet and Whip put his gun in my hand, silencer already fitted to the end, which was unexpected but probably shouldn't have been, considering who Whip was.

A stone-cold killer. All the men in this room were. And I was just the idiot who'd wanted to help.

I'd always known it would come back to bite me. I raised the gun, pointing it at Trig.

He leaned on the window, looking about as bothered as if he had a fly buzzing around his head. "Well, this is dramatic. You even know where the trigger is on that thing, Gray?"

"Why Alice?" I knew Kara needed closure before this could end.

Trig tilted his head to one side. "Who?"

Kara's voice trembled from behind me. She moved slightly to the side, so I wasn't completely blocking her from Trig's view. "My sister. She was killed in an alley outside a nightclub in the city." She flicked the cord that hung round her throat like a necklace. "A cord just like this one wrapped around her neck and the life strangled out of her."

Trig shrugged. "That wasn't me. That cord is sold in every hardware store from here to Texas."

"Bullshit!" I shouted, wincing again at the pain in my throat, but an anger so thick and strong spreading through me it couldn't be ignored. "It was the exact same way you killed Annette and Portia. The way you kill all your victims."

Trig folded his arms across his thick chest. "I take full responsibility for Annette and Portia. Those bitches deserved to die. And while I'm confessing my sins, there were another two, a set of twins I caught up with just recently once I got back here. Acquaintances of your wife. Left them in the woods for the animals because they didn't deserve a burial."

Whip swore under his breath. "One of them was a curvy brunette? Strangled in the woods?"

Trigger nodded. "Caught up with her sister a few days later."

Whip mused over that. "Probably the woman I found."

Her twin sister would have been the woman my contact at the morgue had texted me about.

Trigger cocked his head to one side. "But neither of them were named Alice. And I didn't kill no woman in an alley. And outside a nightclub in the middle of the city? Ew. No. There are fucking rats there. You know how I feel about rats. I hate the city."

I blinked, remembering the rats that had crawled over us during the nights our foster parents had kept us in cages in their filthy basement. How Trig had woken screaming one night after being tied up and left for the rats to bite at when he couldn't shoo them away.

My fingers trembled remembering the horrific abuse that had turned him into the man he was.

And me into...this. A man forced to murder his own brother in cold blood.

If I could kill my foster parents all over again, I would. But Trig had already taken care of that.

"Gray," he said softly, honestly. "I swear, I didn't kill this Alice woman. Why would I lie about that when I just admitted to killing your wife?"

My fingers shook, and I squeezed the gun tighter.

Trig didn't even blink. "Kill me if it'll make you feel better. But we both know it won't."

I fucking hated he knew me as well as he did. "I made you a promise."

Trig nodded slowly. "You promised you'd end me if I killed an innocent."

"You agreed. No, not even agreed!" Anger rose inside me, boiled through my blood, and bunched my muscles painfully. I stepped forward, closing the distance between us. "You made me swear, Trig! You wanted this! And then you went and killed them without giving a shit about how I would feel, knowing I had to put a bullet through the brain of the one person who was always there for me."

He nodded. "That's still how I want it."

"Then why?" My voice dropped to a low, miserable tone. "Why Annette? Were you just jealous I had someone else in my life?"

Trig shook his head. "I was happy for you."

"And yet you took it away so fucking carelessly."

Whip sighed, folding his arms across his chest. The other guys just watched on silently, X still for once in his life.

Trig's eyes darkened. "You didn't love her."

"I did." Except even as I said the words, I was no longer sure I believed them.

Kara's fingers interlaced with my free hand, a silent support.

I glanced over at her, filling with a warmth I'd only ever felt when she was around.

I'd never felt like that with Annette. I'd wanted her body. Enjoyed verbal sparring with her. Drinking. Partying.

I'd never wanted to take care of her or protect her the way I did with Kara. Never wanted to spend all night holding her, reciting a list of everything I loved about her. Annette and I had gotten married because she'd said people expected it. Not because of some undying desire to be together forever.

If I put aside the anger over her death and really studied what we had, it wasn't very much.

Not compared to the way I felt when Kara was around. An internal war raged inside me.

Trig narrowed his eyes. "Want to know how I know you didn't love her? Because you didn't even know her, Gray. You know what she and her bitch of a sister and their friends were doing when they said they were 'working'? I know you don't because I know your bleeding fucking heart and you would have never loved her if you'd truly known who she was."

My head spun. I wasn't sure if it was because of the lack of oxygen or the realization that maybe he was right, and I'd been holding on to anger for the past five years rather than love.

"They were trafficking women. Actually, I wouldn't even call half of them women, because most of them were so young they should have been called girls."

I recoiled sharply. "What? That's bullshit. Annette would never."

But pieces clicked together in my head. The way she never really talked about her day, always diverting the conversation to mine. The way she and her sister were regularly out of town on business trips. The way she spent all of her time at the 'office,' but I'd never even known where it was.

The way she told me their business was 'importing and exporting goods.' And I'd been too wrapped up in myself to question or even care what that meant. I'd just enjoyed the money and lifestyle it had given us.

A trickle of fear skated down my spine. "That's not true."

At least, I didn't want it to be.

Trig pulled a thumb drive from his pocket. "I knew you wouldn't believe me. I always trusted you, but I knew it never fully went both ways. So I brought receipts. All the proof you need to understand why I killed all four of them. None of them were innocents." He swore low under his breath. "I fucking loved you. I would have never hurt your wife just for fun. Or because I was jealous. But good to know how fucking little you thought of me."

He tossed the small electronic rectangle at me, and I caught it easily.

Thing was, I did believe him. I just didn't want to. I so desperately wanted him to be a liar, even though I knew he wasn't capable of it. At least not with me.

"Why disappear? You've been gone for so long."

He pressed his mouth into a tight line. "I never meant to. Trust me, after I killed Annette and Portia, the only thing I had on my mind was getting to the twins they were working with and the rest of their crew. I only meant to stay away long enough for you to calm down and listen to me without shooting me on sight. Got picked up by the cops on a break-and-enter charge while I was down south. Spent the last five years doing time down there."

I gaped at him and then glanced over at Whip and the others. "Did you know?"

They all shook their heads.

Whip ran his fingers through his hair. "He would have come up on the release lists we check if he'd been local. But if he'd been out of state..." He glanced over at Trig. "Seriously. Five years?"

To men like them, five years was a life sentence. It was worse than death. The beatings. The rape. The solitary confinement. They'd all done time in the past. They'd all agreed never to do it again.

Guilt swamped me. Poured down over my head like a bucket of cold water.

I'd unknowingly left my brother to rot in a prison cell

for years. I hadn't even considered he could have been caught. He'd always seemed untouchable.

I'd made assumptions because I'd had my head too far up my own ass to see what my wife had been doing right under my nose.

When I'd thought about how selfish I'd once been, I really hadn't even touched the truth.

"For what it's worth," Trig said, voice softer than I'd probably ever heard it. "While I'm not sorry she's dead, I am sorry her death caused you pain. I didn't want that."

I didn't want my brother to have spent the last five years in a cell. When he'd spent half his childhood in a cage. My own PTSD flashbacks screamed through my head, and yet I'd been walking around, a free man for the past five years, while Trig…

I'd left him to suffer, the exact same way our foster parents had.

"I don't think it's you who needs to apologize," I croaked out. I lifted my gaze until it met his. "I'm so fucking sorry I didn't know."

He shrugged. But then his gaze darkened, focusing on Kara. "I just don't want you making the same mistake again." He shook his head. "Should have just fucking killed her before you got home, but then that didn't work out so well for me last time, did it? But now look at you, all over her like a fucking rash. You sure can pick 'em, Gray."

I bristled, not liking the way he glared at her. "She's nothing like Annette."

"Her boyfriend works for Luca Guerra. Just like Annette did."

X let out a low whistle. "Plot twist!"

I blinked and gazed down at Kara. "Is that true?"

Kara bit her lip. "Luca is Hayden's business partner. He knows full well he made a deal with the devil and he's not proud of it. But he's not trafficking women." She glared at Trigger. "And neither am I. You've clearly been watching us, so you'll know that's the truth. Am I right?"

Trigger lifted one shoulder. "Didn't kill you, did I?"

Kara glared at him. "Do you want me to say thank you?"

A tiny smile pulled at the corner of my mouth at her getting fired up. It was so unlike her, but I kind of liked it.

Trigger glanced at me with a shrug. "I might like this one."

I might as well.

3

HAWK

I'd never been a guy who sang. I didn't even really sing along with the radio while I drove. My voice was shit, and nobody needed to hear it.

Except Hayley Jade.

I sang that fucking song over and over while I stood guard at her door, and Chaos took care of the piece of shit who'd dared to open his mouth and admit the truth of who he really was. It was all I could do to comfort her.

These were the men Josiah and his bullshit attracted. Barely closeted pedophiles and rapists who were drawn in by promises of power and position. Something they'd never found in the outside world. Damaged men who couldn't function within normal society. The bottom feeders, those too weak to do anything but follow a liar who promised them the world.

Whatever Chaos was doing to that prick in the bathroom was deserved.

When he emerged, his face was clean of blood spatter, his hands washed too. His workpants were black and didn't show the blood.

But his plain white tee was a mess of red, and he grimaced at it.

I got onto my feet and stopped singing mid-verse. "You gotta get rid of that shirt. The cops are going to be in here any minute now."

"And what? Walk out of here shirtless?"

I screwed up my face. That was just as likely to draw attention. I shrugged out of my jacket and tossed it at him. "Put that on."

He caught it but just stared at it.

"What?" I asked, irritation creeping into my tone.

"It's your club jacket."

I was well aware of the Slayers' logo on the back. It was pretty fucking hard to miss. "Don't make it into something it ain't. You need something to cover up the blood. I have a jacket. Just put it on."

"Well, since you asked so nicely." He rolled his eyes as he shrugged into it.

I tried real fucking hard not to notice how well it fit him.

Or how I felt looking at him in it.

I turned away while he zipped it up so he wouldn't notice the effect it was having on me.

"That guy in the bathroom gonna die?" I asked. "We gonna have a body to deal with?"

"Nah. Not if the cops get here soon. He won't be using his dick properly ever again though."

"Good. He gonna rat?"

"Not if he wants to keep the one ball I left him with."

Running footsteps from the other end of the hall had

us both whirling around, and my upper lip curled in a snarl when it was Ice and the new prospect we'd brought on after losing Ratchet. Couldn't remember what the kid's name was. No point until he'd been here long enough to be sure he wasn't going to run home to his mommy the moment things got dicey.

So many of them did. Thought they wanted this life, only to realize they only knew some sort of TV, glamorized version of it and that it actually wasn't all that fucking great a lot of the time.

The smart ones left.

The dumb ones, like me and Ice, stayed and just let it make us fucking miserable.

The thought was weird. It wasn't the first time I'd thought about getting out. But it was maybe the first time I'd thought about how much I didn't want this life anymore.

Seeing the way Chaos had turned his life around might have had something to do with it.

"Where the fuck have you been?" I growled at Ice. "You were supposed to be on the gates!

He stared down at his feet. "I know. Colin's bike broke down on his way here. I just went to help him."

"Colin? Who the fuck is Colin?"

Chaos rolled his eyes and pointed at the other prospect. "He's been living at the clubhouse for two weeks now."

Oh, for fuck's sake. "Seriously? You've been at the club two weeks and you're still running with the name Colin?" That was fucking embarrassing. "Get a road name already. Quit being so lame."

But that was beside the point. I didn't give a fuck

about where Ice had gone. Only that I hadn't been able to rely on him to do one simple fucking task.

And this was why he was still a goddamn prospect. Everyone liked him, sure. Everyone gave me a hard time because I kept refusing to patch him in.

But liking someone didn't mean they were right for the club. I doubted either of these idiots were. I refused to make the same mistakes Riot had, patching in prospects before they'd truly proved themselves.

Look where it had gotten Riot. In an alliance with a cult and dead members on his hands.

Ice, to his credit, clearly knew he'd fucked up. He was also smart enough to know not to apologize to me, because fuck knows I didn't want to hear it. Instead, he offered up information.

"Cops have a bunch of guys in custody. We had to slip in the side entrance. They don't have enough men out there to cover that yet. We can get Hayley Jade out that way. I think."

I glared at him. "You think? Or you know? You've already put my kid in danger once today, so trust me when I say you do not want to make that mistake again."

It was weird how "my kid" was starting to roll off my tongue so effortlessly.

Ice nodded. "It's clear."

"Then let's get the fuck out of here. Go get the van and meet Chaos and me at the side exit."

Ice and Colin, whose name was so fucking ridiculous I couldn't even think it without wanting to roll my eyes, ran off, boots thumping on the linoleum floor.

Chaos stalked to the other end of the corridor,

checking it was clear, and when he nodded at me, I tapped on the classroom door again.

"Miss Winters? It's clear. Can you open the door?"

There was a moment of hesitation, and then the locks disengaged. The handle turned, and the woman's huge, terrified eyes peeped around the door. "Are you sure?"

I nodded. "But stay in here until the cops come to get you. Get the kids to pull their hats over their eyes as they walk out, okay? It's a bit of a mess out here." I cleared my throat. "And nobody goes into the bathroom. I don't care if someone pisses their pants. No one goes in there, okay?"

She agreed shakily. "Okay."

"I need to take Hayley Jade."

She bit her lip, then nodded, opening the door wider.

From a huddle of kids, Hayley Jade flew to her feet, sprinting across the room and launching herself at my legs.

In a heartbeat, I had her up in my arms, closing my eyes and inhaling the familiar scent of her hair. I let the smell calm my nervous system and crushed her to my chest. "Hey, shortie."

She didn't even squirm, hugging me right back, just as hard.

Miss Winters grabbed my arm before I left. "Please don't let this stop her from coming back to school. She's been doing so well."

I wanted to tape the kid up in bubble wrap and never let her leave my sight again. But I knew I couldn't. She needed to be here. It wasn't school that was the problem.

It was fucking Josiah.

I nodded at the teacher and then closed the door, reminding her to lock it again.

Hayley Jade spotted Chaos a step behind me and reached her arms to him, signing something with her fingers.

"What did she say?" I gave her to him and moved my hand back toward my gun. I didn't trust Ice and Colin as far as I could throw them, but we did need to get out of here before someone found our dickless friend.

I had a feeling Miss Winters wouldn't run her mouth to the cops. At least I hoped not. But I couldn't worry about that right now.

Chaos cradled the back of Hayley Jade's head, holding her close and jogging beside me. She laid her head down on his shoulder, her big dark eyes watching me quietly, red-rimmed from crying. "She said she was scared."

I fucking hated that these men had come into her school and tarnished something she loved.

"We'll get you back here," I promised her. "Back with your friends, and with your teacher. Just as soon as it's safe."

She didn't sign anything, and I cursed fucking Josiah to Hell beneath my breath. I'd had hope we might have her talking again soon. She'd been loving learning signs with Chaos and Kara every night, and then teaching them to me. This felt like a huge step back.

At the side entrance to the school, the Slayers' van waited with the prospects in the front seats. I covered Chaos while he made the short run to the back door with Hayley Jade and then I followed them in, slamming the sliding door shut behind me.

I banged my fist against the window. "Drive, prospect. Take them home."

I'd make sure they were safe. Then I was going after Kara. I had no fucking idea where she was but I would find her, even if I had to scour the entire town street by street.

Chaos, wearing my jacket, sat with Hayley Jade on his lap, his fingers stroking through the soft strands of her hair.

Something inside my chest tightened. Swelled to a point where I couldn't breathe.

I could have lost her today.

I could have lost him.

The feeling only intensified just thinking about the fact Kara was still out there somewhere.

I put the gun down on the seat beside me and dropped my elbows to my knees, leaning forward and sucking in great gulping breaths that didn't feel like enough.

The panic attack swamped me hard, a vise around my chest, suffocating me with its strength.

Hayden's hand fell to the back of my head, his fingers stroking over my short, spiky buzz cut. He didn't say anything. Didn't try to fucking hug me. Just comforted me the same way he was with Hayley Jade.

If anyone else had tried, I would have thrown them out of the fucking van.

But because it was him, I let him soothe some of my ragged edges, knowing the second this van stopped, so would the connection between us.

A smaller hand rasped over my hair, and I glanced up, battling to keep it together.

Hayley Jade smiled at me and trailed her fingers down my cheek.

"I love you," I told her quietly, not knowing I was going to say the words until they fell out of my mouth.

Hayley Jade made signs with her fingers. I looked to Hayden for interpretation. He was the best out of all of us at signing.

A small smile flickered at the corner of his mouth. "She said she loves you too."

I pulled her little head in and kissed the top of it. "You're my girl now, you know that, right?"

She made more signs.

Chaos interpreted without me asking. "She said forever."

This fucking kid was going to be the death of me. A lump lodged itself in my throat, and like Chaos knew I couldn't talk, he repeated the sign so I could copy it.

She might have been named for him, and he might love her just as much as I did, but she was my kid. And fucked if I was letting anyone take her from me.

We approached the compound with emotion getting to me. Fang stepped out from behind the wrought-iron gates and opened them for us.

"See, Ice?" I called to the man driving. "That's what guarding a gate looks like."

Ice nodded once, looking suitably abashed. And so he fucking should. He could have gotten Hayley Jade killed today. Taking some shit from me was the least he deserved.

We rolled our way down the hill to where the compound sat nestled between the trees. Grayson's car sat in front of the club, and I frowned at it. "What's Gray doing here?"

"No idea." Chaos followed me out, turning to help Hayley Jade climb out behind him.

The door to the clubhouse flew open so hard it slammed back against the brick wall.

Kara stumbled out the door, running at us. "Do you have her? Where is she?"

I caught her as she stumbled again, tears streaming down her face, my heart cracking open with both pain for the fear in her face and relief for the fact she was here and unhurt.

I wanted to wrap her in my arms. Hold her all night. Remind myself over and over again that she was okay.

But she needed her daughter more.

Chaos stepped aside. "Hey. It's okay. She's here. She's safe."

Kara stared down at her daughter, like she was a mirage she couldn't quite believe. Then she dropped to her knees in the gravel lot, kneeling at Hayley Jade's feet and wrapping her arms around the little girl's middle.

Kara sobbed against Hayley Jade's tummy, pressing her ear to her chest, listening as if she needed to hear the beat of her heart to assure herself her daughter was still alive.

It broke my fucking heart. Smashed it into pieces.

Chaos seemed equally destroyed, turning away with a shuddering breath he tried to hide.

"You're okay?" Kara asked, pulling away to run her gaze all over her daughter. She checked her head to toe and then looked to me and Hayden. "She's okay?"

"Not a scratch on her," Chaos murmured.

Kara squeezed Hayley Jade again, relief slowly replacing the trembling fear racking her body.

Hayley Jade stroked Kara's hair, the same way she and Chaos had done to me in the car.

I crouched at Kara's side, rubbing a slow hand up and down her back, trying to comfort her. "Let's go inside."

It took a few more minutes of convincing before Kara would let Hayley Jade go, but eventually she got back up on her feet and guided her inside.

Chaos and I followed.

Grayson sat on the couch, his head tipped back, his eyes closed. A gigantic red mark marred his neck, and I stopped, staring at it.

"What the fuck happened to you?"

He hadn't even been at the hospital when the mob had formed. He'd left earlier to take care of something personal.

Apparently, that personal thing was getting himself half choked to death. There was no other way I knew of to get that sort of damage to your throat. What the fuck?

Gray opened one eye but just shook his head, waving his hand toward his throat, indicating he wasn't speaking.

I winced at the fresh mark. Within hours it would probably be purple with bruises. The side of my brain that couldn't get enough of medicine was intrigued. I leaned over him, peering at the injury. "I'm not fucking surprised you don't want to talk. That's nasty."

Kara glanced over at him worriedly, but then down at Hayley Jade and gave a small shake of her head. "Long story. But he's okay." She stopped at the doorway to Hayley Jade's bedroom and glanced back at us. "Thank you. All of you."

All three of us shook our heads in unison. That was probably about all Gray could do with his throat all messed up the way it was.

But Chaos took the words out of my mouth. "No need." He brushed the back of his fingers down the side of her face. "You look exhausted."

She covered her mouth politely to hide a yawn. Her face was lined with worry and weariness. "I feel like I've been hit by a truck. Multiple times."

I studied her carefully for signs of injury. I had no idea what had happened with her and Grayson, but it seemed like he was the one who was worse for wear. "Shock will do that to you."

Hayley Jade wandered into her room and made a beeline for her bed, tucking herself into it, despite the fact it was the middle of the day, and she was really too old for naps.

"I think I'm going to lie down with her for a little while," Kara said quietly. "Some sleep will do us all some good." She cupped my cheek and then pressed her soft lips to it. "We'll share war stories later, okay?"

As much as I wanted to know every detail, so I knew who the hell to go hunt down, I nodded, seeing the weariness in her eyes and knowing she needed some time alone with Hayley Jade to assure herself she was okay.

Kara sank down onto the bed with her and wrapped her in her arms.

They'd both be asleep within minutes.

And I'd spend the next few hours watching them on the baby monitor, making sure they were okay.

Grayson looked like he needed a nap of his own.

I offered him my hand and hauled him up off the

couch. "Come on. I don't know what the hell happened, but you've clearly got some resting to do, and this thing is shit to sleep on."

"He can have my room," Chaos offered.

The two of us helped him in there, even though Grayson gave us silent death stares like he was perfectly capable of moving himself around.

I ignored him, checked his vitals before I left while he rolled his eyes at me, but I knew I wouldn't get any rest if I was worried about his fucking throat swelling closed or something.

When I was done with my poking and prodding, he flipped over and was asleep before we left the room.

Chaos let out a long, slow breath on the other side of the door. "He looks like shit."

I nodded. "So do you. You can use the shower in my room." I headed for it, moving past the spot I'd sucked Chaos's dick quickly, and then past the bed where he'd gone down on me. My cheeks heated at the memory while I rifled through the bathroom cupboard, searching for a fresh towel for him to use.

When I stood, we were face-to-face, both of us in the one small space.

Him still wearing my motherfucking jacket and looking way too good in it.

I couldn't stop staring at him. Couldn't help the way my dick sprang to life.

Something sparked in the air between us. That fucking attraction I couldn't deny. The one I'd tried to bury, so many fucking times, but it just kept coming back, forcing its way between us, determined to make itself known.

His gaze flickered over my face, his breaths a little too quick, like his body was still reacting to the last of the lingering adrenaline we'd both been running on for hours.

Kara and Hayley Jade and Grayson had all come down from their adrenaline highs with a jarring and exhausting crash.

Mine only made me desperate. Wild. Fucking needy for someone to touch me so I didn't feel like I was spinning out of control.

The look on Hayden's face said he felt the same.

The now dickless prick's gay slurs rang in my head, and yet I still found myself fingering the zipper on my jacket and drawing it down Chaos's body.

His gaze burned across my skin as I shoved it off his shoulders, letting it fall to the bathroom floor at our feet.

The blood-soaked T-shirt did nothing to quell the rising desire inside me, that adrenaline swirling into need and an all-consuming idea of getting my hands on him. Grounding myself in touching someone else.

Forgetting this whole fucking day had ever happened. Forgetting Kara and Hayley Jade were in danger. Forgetting Josiah even existed.

I fisted his shirt, dried blood making the fabric crunch, but I didn't give a fuck. I dragged it over his head, leaving his chest bare.

I didn't question what I felt. Didn't want to think about what it meant if I let myself do what my body was begging for.

I didn't fucking care.

I just wanted him.

I dipped my head, pressing my lips to the hollow

where his throat met his collarbone. I trailed my fingers over his abs, tracing the ridges of his muscles and the swirls of his tattoos until I got to the button on his pants.

I only paused for a second, and he was on me, dipping his head so his lips could capture mine.

He kissed me hard, the touch branding, rough, exactly what I needed. I couldn't do soft or tender right now. My heart had already been splayed open once today, I needed time for it to mend itself, so it didn't feel so raw. So fucking vulnerable.

I kissed him back with just as much demand, running my hands up into his hair, pulling out the tie at the nape of his neck so his hair fell around his shoulders.

His fingers went for his pants, undoing the button, drawing down the zipper.

I reached for the shower, flicking the handle upward so the water rained down. We toed off our shoes, him diving for the fly on my jeans while I yanked down his pants.

I released his dick from his boxer briefs, stroking it fast and groaning when he did the same to mine. I pulled my T-shirt off with my free hand, hating that I had to stop kissing him to get it over my head. But then his lips were back, trailing off my mouth and down my neck, sucking and kissing and biting me there while he walked me backward into the shower.

I hissed at the too-hot water, and he flicked the handle to the right.

We both cussed when the water turned ice cold, drenching us both.

But neither of us stopped. His body crowded me up against the solid shower wall. Water splashed all over the bathroom, the two of us too big to close the curtain around us, but I didn't give a fuck if we flooded the place.

All that mattered was the feel of his fingers wrapped around my cock and an aching desire for more than just a fucking hand job.

"Your soap good for jacking off?" he asked between rough kisses I shouldn't have liked but couldn't get enough of.

"What do you think?"

Every man had a soap that didn't sting while jacking off in the shower. Jesus fuck, if you found one that did, you got rid of it pretty damn quick.

He slicked his hands until they were slippery, coating his cock before sliding his fingers around mine.

I hissed at his touch, groaned at the grip and rhythm he set.

Wrapped my fingers around his dick and copied what he was doing.

We groaned, jerking each other, kissing in between hard, labored breaths, and fighting to get the other to the finish line, both of us desperate to reach it ourselves.

This wasn't enough. The feeling inside me was too fucking big. The dickless prick's words kept ringing in my head, calling me a faggot. But it didn't cripple me the way it would have in the past.

It only made me realize I didn't care. Not when it came to Chaos. There was no denying what this was. What I wanted. No denying his body turned me on just as much as Kara's.

No denying I wanted so much more than just his fist wrapped around my cock.

"Want to fuck you," I groaned out, water getting in my mouth as I licked it off his skin.

He moaned, not hesitating, switching our positions, taking up the spot by the wall and then turning around. His face twisted to one side, leaning on one arm, and he reached between his legs, fisting his cock and pumping it.

My dick immediately took up residence between his legs, sliding between his thighs, rubbing at his taint and his balls. My abs melded against his back, my hips connecting with the tight, rounded globes of his ass.

My head spun, desire and need and a rush of pleasure filling my brain, getting off on him letting me have this, feeding on him wanting me as much as I wanted him.

"You done this before?" I asked, reaching around him for the soap, even though my dick was already slick with it.

"Once or twice."

I groaned. That was so fucking hot. I pressed my fingers between his ass cheeks, skating over his rear hole.

He groaned, driving back at my touch, taking the tip of two slicked-up digits.

I forced him to still, pinning him to the wall with my body, slowing the pace. He and I might have fought like cats and dogs, but I wasn't into hurting him. I liked it rough. Liked finding other people who liked it the same way. But I wanted him to enjoy it.

Wanted him to come.

To scream my fucking name when I filled his ass.

He panted, heavy breaths, taking my fingers inch by inch, letting me warm him up so he could take my cock.

He groaned, closing his eyes, pausing the assault on his cock so he wouldn't come. Instead, he reached behind, grabbed my dick, and guided it where he wanted it.

Between his cheeks. Pressing against the star of his asshole while he moaned, returning his hand back to his cock. "Jesus, Hawk. What the fuck are you waiting for? A personal invitation?"

I paused, then told the truth. "I don't want to fucking hurt you, okay?"

Chaos laughed. "Wouldn't have picked you to be a gentleman."

"Wouldn't have picked you to be a bottom."

He glanced back at me. "Just 'cause I let you fuck me once doesn't mean this is how it's always going to be." His gaze connected with mine. "Fuck me and make it good. 'Cause when I fuck you, I'm not going to hold back."

My dick ached at the thought of our positions reversed, his thick cock sliding inside me, filling me the way I filled Kara. My balls drew up, aching, desperate to come just thinking about it.

I wanted it. Wanted him to have me like that.

I gave him an inch of my cock, fighting to keep still while he adjusted, but losing the battle all too quickly because he felt so fucking good. So tight. His ass clenched around my cock as I slid all the way inside.

He muffled his moan of pleasure with his arm, his ass rocking back on my hips, encouraging me to keep going.

I pulled out, then drove in again, fucking him slow, sinking my top teeth into the back of his shoulder while my hips worked.

"Don't stop. That feels so good." Chaos reached a hand back, his fingers digging into my thigh.

"Guess I'll find out when you fuck me."

He raised an eyebrow. "You want that?"

"You're moaning like a bitch in heat, so yeah, I fucking want that." It was the truth. But it was also fucking terrifying.

He sniggered, like he could read my mind. "Just come, Hawk. I'll fuck you another day, when you're balls-deep in Kara and so blissed out from me rimming you, you beg me for it."

Jesus fuck. I envied his confidence. I talked a lot of shit, I knew that. But Chaos had a quiet confidence that was admirable. A deep-rooted knowledge of who he was and zero need to prove himself to anyone.

I had no doubt he would take me in the middle of the Slayers' clubhouse or at Psychos or at Sinners and not give a flying fuck if anyone saw.

While I was still hiding in closets.

I fucked him harder, all gentleness gone, and his body responding to every thrust so I knew he was taking as much as I was. I groaned into the muscles of his back. Reached around him and took control of his cock, working him hard and fast, building him up until he was leaking over my hand.

"Fuck," he groaned. "Gonna come."

It was barely a warning, his dick squirting hot, thick liquid over my fist. His ass clenched around my cock, his entire body spasming with the force of his orgasm, sending me barreling into my own.

Inside him, I came with a shout, my legs shaking, fighting to hold my weight, an orgasm ripping its way through my body.

I rode us out, my dick in his ass until I went soft. My fingers sliding over his cock until he was brushing my hand away, telling me to fuck off and quit torturing him.

We stood there in the shower, the water falling over us, my chest pressed to his back, the two of us breathing in time.

"You okay?" he asked eventually.

"Fine. Why wouldn't I be?"

"'Cause you just fucked a man for the first time and maybe you have feelings about that?"

I shoved off him and rolled my eyes, grabbing the bar of soap to start cleaning up. "If you're hoping for an 'I love you,' you ain't getting one."

"Do I look like I need that from you?"

I grinned. "You look like you need my dick in your mouth, actually."

He snorted. "Do I?"

"After I wash it. Of course."

He shook his head, but his dick was already getting hard again. "You fucking wish. Get on your knees, Hawk."

And fucked if I didn't find myself down there in a heartbeat, his cock in my mouth, not knowing what this thing was between us but suddenly wanting to find out.

4

KARA

I held my daughter while she slept. Cried silently into her hair with a mixture of relief and adrenaline release, while silently thanking the two men in the room next door for bringing her back to me.

I smiled at the muffled sounds of their lovemaking in Hawk's shower. The walls might have been thick here, but they weren't magic.

They were done when Hayley Jade woke up from her nap, and she smiled sleepily at me, blinking her long lashes as she cleared her eyes.

"Are you okay?"

She nodded.

But I didn't want her just agreeing with me because she'd been trained to be sweet and meek and mild. I wanted her to tell me how she really was.

"A really scary thing happened to you today. You don't have to be okay."

Her bottom lip trembled, and I gathered her up, holding her to my chest.

Josiah was never going to leave us alone. He was just going to keep coming back, trying again, finding new ways to get to me.

I'd thought not giving him a child was my biggest sin. But the real sin was in embarrassing him. My lack of a child, my disobedience, my failures, my leaving, all made him look weak.

If he had no control over a lowly woman, then how could he be God's chosen one? How could he be the man to lead Ethereal Eden into His light?

He couldn't. That's what the other men would see, and Josiah knew it. Getting me back would be his only way to save face.

I knew all too well how smart he was. You didn't get to be in his position by being unintelligent. Every move he'd ever made since the moment he'd first stepped foot on our land had been calculated.

Nothing had changed. I was wife number one and while Josiah was still a free man, there was no getting away from that.

I needed to go back. Give myself up. That plan hadn't changed just because of what happened today. It couldn't. If anything, it had only reinforced that I was right. I wouldn't be the reason Hayley Jade couldn't go to school. And I wouldn't let Hawk and Hayden go there to kill him. It was too dangerous. They were already well and truly on the police radar. If Josiah suddenly turned up dead, they'd be the first suspects on the list.

All I'd ever wanted was a life of freedom. But I wouldn't exchange my freedom for the two of them being locked behind bars. If I could go back, maybe I could find some evidence that Josiah had been responsible for

Alice's death. Getting him put behind bars was the only way I could ever see me being truly free and out of his clutches and the men I loved all being free.

Hayley Jade pulled away a couple of inches, and I let her wriggle back, respecting her need for personal space. I twisted onto my back on her single bed and gazed at the ceiling, listening to the now familiar sounds of the clubhouse outside, as all the different people who lived here went about their lives. Ice or one of the other prospects had a Hoover going. Amber sang along with the radio. Queenie and Aloha laughed from the couches. Somewhere farther down the hall a baby cried, so I was pretty sure Bliss and War were here with Ridge.

They were all sounds I'd come to rely on. To enjoy. I wondered how on earth I was going to walk away from this place that had become my home.

Hayley Jade tapped my arm, and when I rolled over to my side, her big eyes watched me carefully. And then she tapped her thumb to her chin twice, the rest of her hand splayed open, fingers straight and spread apart.

I froze at the sign.

"Can you do that again?" I asked her quietly.

She repeated the motion, and my heart swelled. "Do you know what that sign means?"

Every part of me prayed she did.

She nodded. She pressed her lips together, and at first, no sound came out.

But she was trying. Oh my God, she was trying.

I nodded encouragingly. "Mmmm."

She screwed up her face in concentration and forced out the same sound.

But then her face fell, her eyes pooling with tears again.

"Oh hey!" I grabbed her and hugged her tight. "No tears! That was amazing! It's been a really long time since you tried to talk. It probably won't feel right at first. But it'll get easier. I promise."

She pushed me away and tried again, tapping her chin and making the Mmm sound. Frustration tightened each muscle in her little body until she hit out at the wall, her tiny fist barely making a sound but the agony in her eyes there all the same.

"Mommy," I translated for her, making the sign again. My throat clogged up with emotion. "You called me Mommy."

Hayley Jade grinned and nodded, clearly pleased to be understood.

While I just wanted to break down and cry. How could I leave her? How could I walk away and potentially never see her again? There was no guarantee I would find the proof the police would need to lock Josiah away. I was risking being stuck there forever.

But how could I stay, knowing that every minute I did put her and everyone else I loved in danger?

I made the sign for daughter. One I'd practiced so many times, just hoping I'd get to say it to her. I pointed at her. *Daughter*. And then at me. *Mother*.

She practiced both signs over and over, more and more pleased with herself each time we added in more family signs. Brother, father, grandmother, and grandfather.

When Rebel turned up with Remi and Madden, we researched the signs for aunt and cousin as well. I filled her in on everything that had happened while the kids excitedly babbled in signs, and my heart swelled at Remi and Hayley Jade actually trying to have a conversation. Madden, with way more energy and more limited attention span than our quiet girls, declared he wanted to go outside.

"How about the park?" Rebel asked but then quickly changed her mind when she saw the anxious expression on my face. "Oops! You know what? That's closed. How about we go get the swing sets and the trampoline out of the storage shed?"

Remi screwed up her nose.

Rebel cocked her head at her eldest daughter. "No? How about a nature walk around the complex then?" She glanced at Madden. "Or a nature run for you because you have too much energy. We can go find some big sticks and build a fort!"

I wasn't sure if Rebel or the kids were more excited by that idea. I got up to follow them, but Rebel stopped me.

"I'll watch them. You rest. Today sounds like it was a lot."

I nodded. "If you're sure? I should check on Grayson. He's hurt."

She hugged me but then pulled back at arm's length to study me. "It'll get better. You know that, right? This isn't going to be your life forever. I promise that."

She was right. Because as soon as I could, I was leaving. Going back to Josiah. And putting an end to this once and for all.

I waved off Rebel and the kids, the two girls carrying bags Queenie had given them to fill with flowers, sticks, and rocks they might find while out wandering around the compound. Grayson's car still sat in the parking lot beside the usual row of bikes and the club van, so I knew he had to be here somewhere.

I was fairly confident he wasn't hanging out with Hawk and Hayden, who hadn't surfaced from Hawk's bedroom.

Queenie and I walked back inside together, shoulder to shoulder, and she squeezed my fingers. She didn't say anything, it was just a silent show of support and affection.

I returned it, so grateful she was here. "Do you know where Grayson is?"

She pointed at Hayden's room. "Pretty sure they took him in there."

I thanked her and headed in that direction. I knocked, but there was no answer, which had kernels of worry beading in my belly. Those marks around his throat could have swollen in the time I'd been lying with Hayley Jade. I pushed the door open and breathed a sigh of relief when he was just asleep on the bed, his chest rising and falling regularly.

The bruises around his neck had already started forming though, the angry red marks already deepening. His throat was going to be a mess for a while.

Despite knowing I shouldn't, I crawled onto the bed with him and laid my head down on his shoulder. There was no doubt in my mind he'd saved my life today.

Risking his own in the process. My heart couldn't ignore that.

His breathing changed from the deep, slow breaths of sleep. His arms came around me, and his lips touched my head. "Hi."

"Don't try to talk. It must hurt."

His voice was croaky and soft. "It's not too bad."

I lifted onto one elbow so I could gaze down at him. "I've heard doctors make the worst patients."

He winced on a laugh. "Probably true. But I really am okay."

Despite his reassurances, I couldn't stop staring at his neck. "I thought you were going to die," I whispered, matching the quiet tone of his voice. Relief swirled inside me, climbing its way up my throat and turning into a ball of emotion. "Dammit, Grayson. Why would you do that? What if he hadn't backed down? What if you'd actually died? You didn't know for sure he was going to let me go."

"No. I didn't. But what was the alternative?"

"The alternative was you stay safe."

"And just let him kill you?" He breathed out softly. "That was never an option, Kara. Not for a single second."

The emotions of the day got the better of me, the remaining adrenaline mixing with relief and fear and so much more. I couldn't help myself. I pressed my lips to his, kissing him gently, until gentle wasn't enough. My tongue stroked against his lips, seeking an entrance, that ball of emotion in my throat disappearing little by little, every moment we touched. Wrapped in his arms felt safe and warm, and intoxicating. I basked in every trail of his fingers, every shift of his muscles against me, my body unconsciously seeking out his until I was lying on top of him, kissing him until we were both breathless.

A pool of need opened up inside me, an aching, greedy desire to have all of him.

But it wasn't right and it wasn't fair. I forced myself to sit up, legs straddled either side of his hips. My voice was breathless. "I'm so sorry. You just found out a lot of things about your wife, and you need time to grieve her." I realized I was essentially sitting over his dick and was horrified by how forward I was being. It didn't matter what he'd said to me in the heat of the moment earlier in the day.

Trigger had opened up a portal to his past and dumped a whole load of secrets out on the table for everyone to see. Grayson would need time and space to work through that. I swung my leg, trying to get off him.

He caught it, his fingers digging into my thigh as he settled my knee back where it had been, digging into the mattress beside his hip.

His gaze locked with mine.

He slid his hands up my legs, and to my hips. His eyes turned molten, and his chest rose and fell too quickly as he guided my hips, rocking them over his private area.

I let out a tiny murmur of pleasure when he got hard beneath me, the ridge of his erection rubbing at my clit through my panties.

"Everything Trigger said about my wife makes sense. I just didn't want to see it. We brought out the worst in each other. All she ever cared about was money and position and power. I don't know why I didn't notice what she and her sister were doing right beneath my nose when Trig did. All I can blame that on was that I was young, and so focused on making something of myself so I never had to live in a shitty house in Saint View with no food, and rats crawling over us while we slept," he shared softly and closed his eyes. "I can't even think about the women my wife hurt because I was too selfish to see what she was doing. How many lives did she destroy, just because she wanted to drive a nice car and live in fucking Providence? She was a foster care graduate as well. Came from nothing. We were so fucking proud of how far we'd come. I hate myself for wanting those material things too. Jesus fuck, Kara, I enjoyed the money she made! Until I was licensed, all our nights out, all our belongings, everything was funded by her."

The pain in his eyes was unbearable. He gave up rocking my hips and used his hands to scrub at his face.

I tugged his hands away, hating he was beating himself up over something that hadn't been his fault. "Her choices weren't yours."

His gaze changed from heat to anger. "I'm not mourning her again. I've spent years doing that, and she doesn't deserve it."

I leaned forward and kissed his mouth. "No, she doesn't. But nobody would blame you if you mourn her anyway. She was a big part of your life. And the woman you knew wasn't the woman she actually was."

He shook his head and then grabbed my hand, pulling my fingers to his mouth. "I put you in danger, trying to avenge a ghost. I'm so fucking sorry."

I shook my head. "You have nothing to apologize for."

"Kara, he had a noose around your neck!" His gaze shifted to my left and fixed, like he wasn't really seeing anything. "I've never felt anything like the fear that filled me when he tightened that cord around your throat. That was the moment I realized Annette and I had never been real. Because the idea of losing her had never felt like losing you... Shit, I don't have the right to say that. You aren't mine."

"What if I want to be?"

The words were out of my mouth before I could stop them. They were words I didn't have the right to say. But I didn't want to take them back. Leaving Saint View without ever truly being his felt like a fate worse than death.

I'd always be left wondering what he felt like. What he tasted like. What I would feel if I just let him in.

The look in his eyes burned with heat. "I don't want to wreck anything between you and Hawk and Chaos." But his hands were back on my thighs, skimming up beneath my skirt, settling on my hips while his moved beneath me.

God, he felt good. Thick and hard beneath his pants. He was so attractive, in a completely different way than Hawk and Hayden. Where they were rough, Grayson was polished. Where they were leather jackets and dirty jeans, he was suits and scrubs. Where they were messy hair and stubble, he was strong, clean-shaven jawline and piercing eyes.

"You aren't wrecking anything. Only making it better."

He lifted one hand to my cheek, and I leaned into his touch. When he snaked his hand to the back of my neck and dragged me down so he could kiss me, my body responded eagerly, falling onto him, bracing myself on his strong chest while his mouth moved on mine.

Our tongues came together, exploring, deepening the kiss until he rolled us, so he was on top. He lay between my widespread legs, grinding over my pussy and kissing me until my nipples beaded and I was making desperate little moaning sounds, needy for more.

But Grayson took his time, never stopping the friction between us and then adding to it when he slid a hand to my breast, groping and fondling me there, above my clothes, checking my reaction to everything he did.

"More," I begged, reaching for the buttons on his shirt, knowing what I wanted and needing him to get there faster. I pushed the shirt off his shoulders, revealing his warm skin and the solid expanse of his chest. Surprise flickered at the smattering of tattoos on his chest and shoulders. Nowhere near as many as Hayden and Hawk had, but I hadn't been expecting any. My fingers roamed across them greedily, flicking his nipples with my thumbs, then trailing my hands lower over his abs.

He only let me get a tiny touch before he was rearing back, lifting me up on the bed so he could take off my top.

I shivered, the cooler air hitting my heated skin. But it was instantly chased away by the desire in Grayson's eyes, his gaze roaming my body.

I reached behind me, undoing my bra and letting the cups fall away. My breasts were heavy and full, aching for his touch, my nipples tightly beaded and desperate for his mouth.

I realized with a start I didn't feel self-conscious. How could I when he stared at me like he'd just unwrapped the most perfect of gifts?

"Lie back, Kara," he murmured. "Let me see all of you."

I fell back against the pillows, anticipation roaring through me when he tugged my elastic-waisted skirt down my hips, taking my panties with him.

His gaze burned, staring at my body for the first time. "I've thought about getting you naked so many times, Kara. Not one of those daydreams even came close to the real thing." He trailed a finger from the hollow of my neck, down between my breasts, and over my stomach, where he flattened his palm to go lower, brushing over my mound. "God, you're beautiful."

His compliments would have once made me feel uncomfortable. But now I drank them in. Accepting them for the truth I could hear in his voice. He had no reason to lie to me. No reason to tell me I was beautiful if he didn't think that was the truth.

The thing was, when he looked at me like that, I felt beautiful too. Desired. Wanted. Hayden and Hawk had reminded me time and time again that Josiah's taunts had no place in this clubhouse. No place in my head. Every day they'd been erasing them with the truth, and now Grayson's touch did the same.

I was worthy of their touch. Of their admiration.

They didn't want me just as a place to put their dicks. I was worthy of more than what I'd always been led to believe.

All women were.

And the three men I'd found knew it.

I reached for his pants. Unbuttoning them, needing to see him as much as he wanted to see me. He helped, tugging them down, getting off the bed to remove them completely, his erection straining behind his underwear.

His hand trailed to his package, palming it slowly,

rubbing it through the fabric while he stared at my body laid out for him on the bed. "Tell me you want me like I want you. Fuck, Kara. I need to hear you say it."

His hand slipped beneath the elastic of his underwear.

My heart beat faster. I copied his movements, brushing my fingers over my mound and then lower to rub my clit.

He groaned at my leg falling to one side, giving him a better view of my fingers at work and the gleaming slit of my pussy, already wet and needy from the dry humping we'd been doing.

With one hand he dragged off his underwear, the other fisting his cock and stroking it slowly but deliberately.

He was thick. Hard. A perfect length so I knew when he was in me I'd feel it in exactly the right spot. I ached at the thought, needing him there, spearing deep inside me, filling the void. "You can have me," I whispered. "I'm ready."

But he didn't come closer. The corner of his mouth flicked up in a sweet smile. "I just can't stop looking at you. I don't think you have any idea how gorgeous you are like that, your fingers on your clit, your pussy wet for me. Fucking hell, Kara. I want you so bad right now. But watching you finger yourself wasn't on my bingo card, and now I really want it to be."

I burned with a mixture of pleasure and desire at his dirty words, wanting to please him further. I slipped two fingers inside myself, coating them in my juices and pumping them in and out a few times to ease the ache.

His eyes flared with heat, watching me put on a show

for him, one I never would have had the guts to do if Hayden and Hawk hadn't walked into my life and taught me that I was more than just a vessel for producing babies.

They'd taught me pleasure was my right and that there was no shame in taking it. Even if it was at my own fingers.

I worked my pussy, doing all the things I liked, touching myself the way they touched me, stroking my G-spot, rubbing my clit. It wasn't the same, nowhere near as good, but an orgasm built inside me anyway.

I couldn't stop watching Grayson. He moved his hand up and down his shaft at what had to be a torturously slow pace. His dick gleamed with need, and he swiped his thumb through the precum, using it to lubricate his grip.

I pressed my legs together, then opened them, feeling the delicious clench of muscles in my whole lower region every time I squeezed. My breaths got quicker with every swipe of my fingers until I was panting, desperate, needy to come.

I raised one hand to my nipple, tweaking it and rolling it between my fingers, desperate for his mouth. I wasn't going to be able to get myself all the way over the edge when what my body really wanted was him.

He moved between my thighs and dropped his lips to my ear. "Going to fuck you. But I need you to know that was the hottest thing I've ever seen in my life. And that I want to watch you finger yourself like that every morning and every night. Maybe every lunch time too. I have an office at the hospital and now all I can think about is you coming in there every shift and doing that on the desk."

I laughed softly. "And getting us both fired in the process?"

He kissed my neck, his dick hard against my thigh. "Just means I'll have to smother your moans with my mouth so no one hears."

"Or with..." I reached between us, gripping his cock.

He groaned so loudly I was sure Hayden and Hawk would probably hear it from Hawk's room. Grayson sucked my neck hard, flicking over the slight sting with his tongue. "Did you just say you want my cock in your mouth?"

Heat roared through me at the thought of his thick length driving past my lips, stretching me wide while I stroked my tongue against the ridged underside of his erection. "Yes." It was more of a moan than a word.

His groan mingled with mine. "Only if I can lick your pussy at the same time."

"I..." Heat flushed through me as I tried to understand what he was saying.

Grayson lay back on the bed, his erection jutting from his hips. I lowered my mouth to the gleaming tip of him, flicking my tongue across his head, licking off the precum and sucking him into my mouth.

Grayson hissed when I slid my mouth down his length, taking as much of him as I could before lifting back up again. Our bodies made a T-shape, his straight up and down the length of the bed, me on my knees at a right angle to his.

I sucked and licked him, but it was only seconds before he was reaching for my leg, dragging me around so I was facing his feet.

I loved the feel of his dick in my mouth. Didn't want

to stop, so I just kept sucking. He maneuvered me around, going wherever he wanted and I gasped when he pulled one leg across his body so I was kneeling over his head. "Grayson!"

I was so open to him it was embarrassing. He could see every inch of my body from that angle. My ass. My pussy. My breasts hanging, nipples brushing over his lower belly while I worked his dick.

But his hands massaged up the backs of my thighs, and he used his thumbs to open my pussy lips, swearing beneath his breath. "You're so fucking wet for me. Need to taste you, Kara."

He banded one strong arm around my thigh and dragged me down so my pussy landed on his mouth.

I shouted at the feel of his tongue in such a private place. But he muffled it with a slow thrust of his hips, pushing his dick into my mouth again.

I closed my eyes, finding my rhythm on his erection, using it as a distraction from the onslaught of feelings he was creating between my thighs.

He licked through my folds, spearing me with his tongue. Within minutes I was practically bouncing on his face, taking his fingers deep inside me while he assaulted my clit with his lips.

His hands encouraged me every second, rocking me over his face, never stopping, refusing to let me back off, even when my orgasm threatened to unleash.

"Oh!" I deep-throated his cock, needing the distraction to keep myself from shattering into pieces. But it was too late. He was too good. His fingers speared inside me, and an onslaught of feeling rocketed to the surface. I ripped my head away from his cock and threw my head back, grinding over his face. "Grayson!"

I came in pulsing contractions, squeezing and fluttering around his fingers, flooding his lips with fresh waves of arousal he licked up like it was honey.

"Oh God." My movements were uncoordinated. I was lost to the pleasure, just moving in any way that felt good, every nerve ending tingling with pleasure.

I wanted to keep going with his dick, make him come the same way I had, but my body was too blissed out, too overwhelmed to get it together. A pleasurable, fuzzy feeling came over my body, one I associated with the best kind of orgasms, and I let him guide me down onto the bed.

"Play with your nipples," he murmured.

My fingers came to my breasts, cupping the aching mounds, squeezing my nipples like they were clamps.

Grayson knelt between my legs, fitting himself at my entrance. His eyes met mine, a silent question in them, despite the fact I'd so clearly already given him permission.

But after all the times a man had entered me unwanted, him checking and checking again that this was still okay only made me want him more. I bent my knees, wrapping them around him, locking my ankles at his back and pulling him down so his cock drove inside me, landing in the place I wanted it most.

We both stilled, me full of his erection, him buried completely to the hilt.

And for the longest moment we just stared at each other, his gaze full of something I wasn't sure I was ready to see, even though my heart beat unevenly and my breath hitched at just the idea that this was so much more than just a casual thing.

This felt like a coming home. Like somewhere I was always supposed to be. When he slowly lowered his lips on mine, it felt like kissing a man I never wanted to leave, because being apart from him would be like tearing off a piece of my soul.

I didn't know the man he'd once been. But the man he was now was stealing my heart.

"What I said earlier," he murmured, drawing out slowly and pushing in just as gently.

Our gazes locked. He'd said he was in love with me. I shook my head. "It's okay. Emotions were high. I know you didn't mean it."

He stilled. Stared down at me. Breathed out slowly. "I meant every word of it, Kara. I'm in love with you."

I didn't know what to say. Or how to feel. I opened my mouth, and he silenced me with his.

"I know you aren't there yet. I know your feelings aren't as strong as mine, but I had to shoot my shot. I couldn't go another day just pretending that friendship is enough. I want to be your friend. I do. I want laughter and fun and companionship. But I want more than that. I want your body." He slid in again, harder this time, like he was proving a point. "I want your heart. I want every little part of you, just the way you are. I know you can't say it back, and that's okay. Just don't tell me no. Don't say you don't want me the same way. Just say nothing and let me kiss you."

He was wrong. His words dredged up emotion and feeling that threatened destruction if I hid it. A feeling too big to keep inside.

And yet letting it loose wouldn't be fair. I was already so selfish, using his body, fulfilling a need to have him, all while knowing this couldn't last.

I couldn't have this happiness until I was truly free.

That freedom couldn't be found here, in the arms of three men who'd built me up so high that losing them was going to be the worst fall of my life.

So I did as I was told and said nothing. But I let him kiss me, and I kissed him back, silently trying to explain how complicated my life had become, and wishing it could be different. He reached between us to stroke my clit between gentle thrusts, and when I came again, setting him off as well, it was quiet. Both of us holding on to the other, like we were scared the first time would be the last.

5

GRAYSON

"And then I cut off each of his fingers...but only the tips. Because I'm not a monster. Guy needs to be able to jack off, after all."

I paused with my hand still on the doorknob and wondered why I was even surprised to find my apartment a mess and five big guys sprawled out in various positions around the room.

X, the considerate one who'd left his last victim with most of his digits, waved a lazy hand from the rug where he was laid out amongst empty pizza boxes. "Hey, Gray!"

Ace and Torch nodded in my direction from the card game they were playing at the kitchen counter, but then went back to it like it was any other Tuesday.

Whip glanced at his watch, and then out the floor-to-ceiling windows, blinking when he noticed the time. "Shit, Gray. Sorry." He kicked X. "Help me clean up. This place is trashed."

X rolled his eyes. "Do I look like I do buckets and mops?"

Whip didn't miss a beat. "Do I look like I'll think twice about putting my size twelve up your ass? Don't be a fucking pig."

X grumbled but flipped onto his stomach and pushed up onto his feet. He picked up a pizza box, and when it gave the telltale noise of a single piece sliding around, he flipped it open. "Ooh! Pineapple! Mine!"

Whip cringed, watching X shove the entire piece of cold, fruity pizza in his mouth. "Yours because pineapple on pizza is nasty and nobody else would touch that with a ten-foot pole."

X winked at him, shoving more into his mouth. "Trig agrees with me, don't you, Trig?"

My brother sat on the couch, arms spread across the back of it as if he owned the place, knees widespread and posture relaxed.

Like twenty-four hours earlier we hadn't been in a standoff, Whip's belt around my neck, his noose around Kara's. Like he hadn't confessed to killing my wife.

Like he hadn't revealed every truth about her life, and mine, and ripped me out of the false sense of security I'd built up around myself for years.

"Gray eats pineapple on pizza too." Trig watched me carefully, his sharp eyes focused, despite the table full of empty beer bottles in front of him.

Despite pretending to do other things, my murder squad were all watching me, waiting to see how I reacted. It was clear they'd quickly forgiven Trigger and had spent the last day catching up with him.

Now they were waiting to see where I stood.

"Used to," I corrected, sitting beside him. "Don't eat pizza at all anymore."

Trig raised an eyebrow. "No shit? Why not?"

"Became a doctor. Saw what food like that does to your heart. Would prefer not to go out like that."

Trig leaned forward and plucked his beer from the coffee table; despite the fact it wasn't even ten in the morning. He took a slow swallow. "Some of us probably ain't gonna live long enough for that to be a problem." He tipped the bottle in my direction. "But good for you. You always were the smart one." He pointed to the cooler at his feet. "You want one?"

I stared at the man I hadn't seen in five years. I'd spent so long blaming him. So long hating him. Used those feelings to hide the truth of who my wife had been and the unspeakable things she'd done.

I'd accepted Trig's story as truth so easily that I knew, from a psychiatric perspective, some part of me had known all along. I'd ignored the middle-of-the-night phone calls and hushed conversations with her sister. I'd ignored the money rolling in, which was way too much for a legitimate startup business. I'd ignored the way she could never look me in the eye.

I might not have known exactly what she was doing, but that was only because I hadn't wanted to know.

I wasn't the smart one.

Trig had seen through my wife's lies and deceptions all along. He'd been the one brave enough to do something about it, even though it had cost him. He'd lost five years of his life. His friends.

His brother.

I dropped my keys and phone into a bowl on the table. "Give me a beer."

Trig grinned and flipped the lid on the cooler,

plucking a cold can from the watery ice inside. He handed it to me, and I cracked the tab, the beer fizzing softly.

Trig eyed me, wiping water off his hands on his jeans. "So you want to tell your big brother all about this woman you're so willing to die for?"

Things weren't fixed between us. That could only happen with time and patience and learning to trust each other again. But that could only start by making an effort. By wanting it to happen.

In Trig's eyes, I could see the hope. He thought he was hiding it, but I knew him better than anyone.

I took a sip of the beer. "Her name is Kara."

"You're in love with her." It wasn't a question. It was a statement of fact.

"Yes."

"You know I'm going to run a full background check on her, right? Dig into every little skeleton in her closet."

I raised an eyebrow. "Wouldn't expect anything less. But you'll be surprised by what you find."

He eyed me. "In a good way?"

I shrugged, swallowing down another mouthful of cold liquid, even though what I really wanted was a bowl of cereal and a coffee. "Cults. A kid. Two other boyfriends."

The room suddenly went as silent as a tomb.

Whip stared over at me like I'd grown a second head. "What the fuck?"

A sharp knock on the door had all five pulling weapons and pointing them at the peephole.

I frowned and waved a hand at all of them as I put the beer down and stood. "We're going to need to talk about knee-jerk reactions to stressful situations. And drinking as a way of coping with negative feelings. You're all triggered. Put those away. It's probably my neighbor, asking for a cup of sugar, and you've all got guns and knives out like you want to make chop suey out of her."

"A cup of sugar? Seriously? Who fucking bakes at this time of the morning?" Ace grumbled, lowering his gun half an inch.

X spun his knife between two fingers. "You do know most bakers actually start at like two in the morning, right?"

Ace gaped at him. "That's the middle of the night. Why the fuck do they start so early?"

X launched into an explanation of how to bake sourdough with a starter that nobody had asked for. I just shook my head and went to the peephole.

Hawk and Hayden stood on the other side.

I glanced over at the guys. "It's not my neighbor. But I know them."

I paused, not having any idea how to introduce the two of them to the men who'd taken over my apartment.

This is my brother and his psychopath friends. Don't worry about them. They're harmless...unless they're out stalking men from their hit list. Don't worry. You're probably not on it...

Shit. Maybe I should check that.

Trig waved his hand around impatiently. "Just open the door, Gray. We aren't going to hurt your little friends."

Someone calling the ex-leader of the Sinners street gang and the vice prez of a notorious MC my "little friends" would have been completely and utterly laughable…had it come from anyone but the five men in this room.

Hawk and Hayden might have taken a life or two. They might have run guns or drugs. Gotten in fights. Even done a stint or two in prison.

But neither of them was a psychopath.

The men in this room had done and seen things that Hawk and Hayden couldn't even dream of.

I knew, because they told me everything, and even I found some of it hard to stomach. The murder squad made the Slayers and the Sinners look like boys playing make-believe.

I shot Trigger a look. "Be nice, okay? You fucking owe me, and they're important to me."

I opened the door.

Hayden and Hawk both stiffened on the other side, surveying the men in the room.

Hawk's hand hovered toward his hip where I knew he kept his gun.

Hayden elbowed him sharply and cleared his throat. "Bad time?"

I gave them both a smile. "Nope. Great time. Come in. You can meet my…friends." I turned to the guys. "This is Hayden and Hawk. They're my…"

I glanced at the two of them for help, 'cause fucked if I'd know what we were to each other. I wouldn't exactly class us as friends, considering this was the first time I'd ever seen either of them without Kara around.

But I wanted them to be. They loved Kara. And so did I. That was only going to work if the three of us could get along as well.

X widened his eyes. "Wait. Wait. Are these your

lovers, Gray?" He rushed to shake Hawk's hand, literally lifting it from his side and pumping it up and down. "Bro! I am an LGBTQ+ ally. I just want you to know that. I put a rainbow flag in my window every pride month and I'm on the lookout for a gay best friend. You could be it!" He slung his arm around Hawk's shoulders. "BFFs! BFFs!"

Hawk did a double take and gave me a "what the fuck?" look as X dragged him into the room.

I just shrugged. "Just roll with it. He's harmless."

Sort of.

"Come in," I told Hayden, making room for him to step inside so I could shut the door behind him. "Don't let X scare you. He's overexcitable. Like a golden retriever."

Except golden retrievers didn't generally kill you slowly and painfully. But that conversation could probably wait for another day.

X had already gotten distracted taking ingredients from my cupboard because apparently the talk of fresh bread had made him feel like baking. Hawk and Hayden did the rounds, shaking hands with the other guys and introducing themselves before perching on the couch facing me.

Hayden smoothed his hands over his jeans. "We just wanted to come by and make sure you were okay. You left before we could catch up."

I rubbed a hand across my throat absentmindedly. "Nothing but a few bruises. I'll be fine."

Hawk cleared his throat. "Kara didn't tell me what happened exactly. Just said you saved her life."

I could feel Trigger watching on, his body tense.

But Kara hadn't said anything to Hawk and Hayden

about who her attacker had been. And I suspected that considering Trig hadn't actually hurt Kara, that maybe it was better if Hawk and Hayden never knew exactly what had gone down in this room twenty-four hours earlier.

I'd only just gotten my brother back. I didn't want to lose him again because Hawk kept trying to kill him. Especially because there was a very good chance it wouldn't be Hawk who won that fight if it ever came down to it.

I couldn't imagine anyone taking on the murder squad and living to tell the tale.

Kara had been smart not to say anything. It was for their own safety.

And so Trigger and I had a shot at being brothers once more.

God, I loved that woman.

I swallowed hard. "I love her. I'd do anything for her."

I waited for Hawk's expression to cloud over. For his fingers to bunch into fists. For him to take a swing and my face.

But all that happened was he shrugged. "Yeah, well. I think she loves you too. So that's probably a good thing."

I really fucking hoped so.

X watched the interaction with interest, his head swiveling back and forth between us like we were at a tennis match. "So all three of you are poking that Kara chick? I mean, I get it. She's got a banging body. All tits and ass..."

Hawk, Hayden, and I all turned to stare at him. Hawk's low, protective growl was all Doberman to X's golden retriever energy.

Whip clamped a hand on the back of X's neck. "You

know what? I just remembered we left a man tied to a table at my house! Time to go back there and see if he's still alive! Right, X?"

X propped his chin up on two hands, elbows resting on the countertop, and shrugged Whip off. "Not yet! I want to hear more about Gray's boyfriends."

Whip shoved him toward the door, nodding for the others to join them. "Come on. The guy on the table at my place still had his eyeballs. You can remove them. You know you love that."

X perked up at that and trotted down the hallway after the others, leaving me, Hawk, and Hayden staring after them.

I grimaced at the two men. "So...that's my friends..."

Hawk cocked his head to one side. "Have you introduced them to Scythe and Vincent? I think they'd have a lot in common."

6

KARA

For a few days, we laid low at the clubhouse. Hawk hovered like the bird he was named after, never far from me or Hayley Jade. Hayden fell into the habit of calling from Sinners multiple times a day, apparently just to talk, but we all knew it was because he was stressed out over what had happened. Grayson took time off work to hang around until the lure of the Friday free clinic drew him back. They needed him there, but even he found his way back to the clubhouse each night, crashing on the couch or crawling into bed with me if one of the other guys didn't beat him to it.

I was never alone. Not even for a minute, and while some might have found it claustrophobic, I enjoyed every second of having the people I cared about close to me.

It meant I couldn't do anything about leaving.

And that was a quiet relief.

I didn't want to go. But we couldn't live in this little bubble forever either. As the days wore on, things settled down, and I knew it was time to put my foot down about the coddling and get Hayley Jade back to school.

Hawk and War both went to talk to the principal, and she allowed them to bring in a new team of security specialists. Only after they'd installed cameras and sensors, and the hype from Josiah's podcast faded, did they decide that it was safe for Hayley Jade to return.

My heart overspilled with gratefulness that so many people loved my daughter enough to make sure she was safe.

She would be happy here. Loved by these people, even if they weren't her blood. Tears dripped down my face every time I thought about it.

I let myself bask in my last few days in Saint View, knowing the bubble needed to burst. Sucking up every ounce of determination inside me, I snuck down to Kyle's cabin and knocked on his door.

He opened it, blinking in surprise when he saw it was me. "Kara. Hi. Um, what are you doing down here? Does Hawk know?" He stuck his head out the door and glanced both ways, like Hawk might jump out of the trees and shout boo at any moment.

I squinted at him. "He doesn't bite, you know."

Kyle didn't seem convinced of that. "I promised to lie low down here, so that's what I'm doing."

I sighed, realizing what I was about to ask wasn't going to work. I'd planned for him to take me to the bus station tomorrow morning after Hawk took Hayley Jade to school. The Slayers' compound was in the middle of nowhere; the access road that led to the main intersection where the buses ran would take me hours to walk. I needed a lift, and Kyle and his truck were my only options. "Could you take me for a driving lesson tomorrow?"

Kyle hesitated. "I thought Chaos was teaching you?"

"He is, but I want to get all the practice I can, and he's busy with the restaurant. Plus, I thought you might like some company. You've been down here by yourself pretty much twenty-four seven since you arrived."

"I don't mind," he said politely. "I'm just grateful to not be living out of my truck." He cleared his throat. "I don't know if I ever actually said thank you for bringing me here. People have been nicer to me than I probably deserve."

I sighed, knowing he hadn't even seen the tip of the iceberg when it came to how good these people's hearts were. They were keeping their distance from him, as instructed by Hawk who clearly had trust issues. But I knew from watching him with Hayden that people had to earn his trust and respect. I couldn't begrudge him for just trying to keep his family safe. "You deserve their kindness, Kyle. They'll see that. And when they do, they'll welcome you in. If you want it."

He ducked his head, not meeting my eyes. "I do. I have no one else."

I knew how that felt. And knowing Kyle was taken care of felt like another thing I'd crossed off my mental to-do list. The one I needed to complete before I could get on that bus and go back to Ethereal Eden tomorrow.

Guilt swamped me at tricking Kyle into taking me to the bus station, but I didn't have much other choice. "So that driving lesson tomorrow. Please?"

He nodded. "Of course."

I breathed out a sigh that wasn't really one filled with

relief. It should have been. My plans were coming together, and I needed to go back. Find proof that Josiah had killed Alice. But I knew the cost. Knew that after months of living here, I was walking myself back to a man who would hurt me. Rape me. Starve me. Abuse me in every way he knew how.

Fear trickled down my spine, but I straightened it, knowing I was no longer wife number one. I wouldn't be able to stop him physically abusing me, but he couldn't touch my mind. Not when in my head I'd be here in this compound, with the people I loved.

I thanked Kyle, told him I'd see him in the morning, and mentally planned how I'd need to pack, and then somehow get my backpack into his truck without him noticing. I had no idea how I'd get him to leave me at the bus station. It might have to be something I figured out in the moment.

I was so in my head I practically ran smack into Bliss coming out of the clubhouse. I grabbed her arm, steadying her so she didn't topple over with baby Ridge in her arms. "Oh my gosh, I'm so sorry! I didn't even see you there."

Bliss smiled brightly. "I'm surprised you didn't hear us. He's been making quite the racket. I'm just taking him out for some fresh air and crossing my fingers a change of scenery helps his colic."

I remembered all too well what having a colicky baby was like. "I'll leave you to it then. The stars are pretty tonight. Hopefully they lull him to sleep."

I went to continue on inside, but Bliss tapped my shoulder. "Actually, Kara, wait, I was wanting to talk to you about something." She shifted the baby to her other arm. "I was wondering if you'd planned anything for Hawk's birthday?"

I blinked. "His birthday? When is it?"

"Next week. War's is tomorrow, and Hawk's is not long after. They're only about ten days apart."

"Oh. I didn't know. Gosh, that's really terrible of me." It dawned on me I had no idea when Hayden's or Grayson's birthdays were either. I really only had the faintest recollection of birthday celebrations back when I was a kid, before Josiah had come into our lives and convinced everyone that birthdays were vain and drawing attention to oneself in that way for simply existing was a sin. But I remembered a day when I was about Hayley Jade's age, where friends from my kindergarten had come to my house, and there'd been balloons and games and gifts. It was a fuzzy image, more an emotion than a true, clear picture. But it was one of the few nice memories I had, and so I'd held on to it all these years.

I hoped Hawk and Grayson and Hayden would throw her parties when I was gone.

Bliss smiled at me sympathetically. "No one expected you to know. So I actually thought that maybe we could throw them a joint party? This weekend. Something big. I think we should go all out."

My stomach sank, knowing I wouldn't be here for it. But I couldn't admit that to Bliss. So I nodded. "That sounds great. What did you have in mind?"

Bliss's smile widened. "Something a bit nice, maybe? A chance for everyone to get out of their jeans and jackets. Selfishly, I want to wear something other than a nursing bra and a puke-stained T-shirt, though the little vomit king here will probably ruin anything I wear. Won't you, Ridge?"

The baby gurgled at her in agreement.

Bliss glanced back up at me. "I know it's late notice but I was wondering if Hayden might consider hosting it at Sinners? And do the food?"

I gaped at her. "You want to have War's party at a rival club to your own?" Bliss' club, Psychos, was Saint View's version of Hayden's Providence-based Sinners. But the two towns were too close together for Psychos and Sinners to not be competition for each other.

Bliss shrugged. "I don't want to have it here at the clubhouse. We have parties here all the time, and I want this to be something different. Something special. Our house is currently overrun with baby bottles, toddler toys, and Lexa's art and craft supplies. I don't want people sitting on a chair and ending up with Play-Doh stuck to their behinds. Which only leaves Psychos, and I'm not too proud to admit that we are not a perfect venue. Our food sucks. We throw a good sex party, and if you just want somewhere to have a beer and play pool, we have that covered. But if I have it at Psychos, then we're eating fries and burned sliders unless I get caterers in. And Nash, Vincent, Rebel, and I will all have to work it."

"Doesn't sound like much fun for War if his entire family is working instead of having fun."

"Exactly. I just want one nice night with my men. I just want to feel like someone other than a mom for a little bit. I want to eat a nice dinner. Do some dancing. Have more than one glass of wine." Her cheeks went pink. "This is starting to sound more like a party for me than a party for War, isn't it?"

I chuckled. "Any night that makes you happy is going to be what War wants for his birthday. I can ask Hayden."

"Ask Hayden what?" Hawk asked from behind us.

We both glanced over to find both him and Hayden emerging from the trees. Hayden had a leaf in his hair, and both their clothes were rumpled.

I hid a smile, and Bliss's gaze bounced between them, eventually turning on me. "Are they...?" she mouthed silently.

I wasn't about to give away their secrets. But the thought of them out there in the darkness, doing whatever they'd been doing, had me tingling from head to toe. I wasn't too sure on where Hawk stood with publicly coming out of the closet, though, so I pressed my lips together, and Bliss, never one to pry, quickly got the message.

She glanced at Hawk. "I was just asking if Hayden could host your birthday party at Sinners on the weekend."

They both paused, Hayden looking over at Hawk warily. "Uh, I mean, I can, if that's what Hawk wants..." He cocked his head to one side. "Are you a birthday party kinda guy? I can't really imagine you wearing a paper hat and standing there proudly while people sing to you."

Hawk scowled at him.

But Hayden had a point. I couldn't really imagine it either. Hawk liked a Slayers party when it was just beers and pool and sex. I couldn't imagine him at any other sort of party, even if I squinted really hard.

Bliss jumped in before Hawk could put a pin in the idea. "Please just say yes. All you have to do is wear something nice and turn up. If you don't want birthday songs or cake, we can play AC/DC and eat Jell-O."

Hayden crinkled his nose. "Please don't make me serve Jell-O. I'm trying to run a nice place."

Bliss ignored Hayden and pinned all her hopes on Hawk. "War is way more likely to be on board with this if you are. He probably won't want a cake or a fuss either."

"But you want to make one anyway?" Hawk cracked his neck as he eyed her.

She shrugged. "I love you both. You both deserve to be celebrated."

He groaned and scrubbed his hands over his face. "Jesus Christ, Bliss. How am I supposed to say no to that?"

She grinned and pressed up on her toes to kiss his cheek. "You aren't. Thank you, thank you, thank you! And to you too, Hayden." She let out a girly squeal. "I'm so excited. I'm going to go tell the others."

She trotted back inside, calling over Queenie and Rebel, the three of them chattering excitedly about decorations.

I turned back to my men and plucked the leaf out of Hayden's hair. "How was the sex?"

Hawk's grin was wide, but it was Hayden who drew me in and kissed my neck. "Would have been better with you in the middle of it."

Hawk closed in from behind me. "Agreed." He kissed my neck and ground against my behind, his fingers gripping my hips. "We could go a second round, all three of us right now if you want?"

Hayden groaned and leaned back. "As much as I would love that, apparently, I now have only three days to sort out the food for your party. That takes a little more effort than just pulling some frozen spring rolls out of the freezer. I need to go talk to Bliss about the menu." His gaze turned hot as it ran all over my body. "But later, when I come to your room, be naked. Both of you."

Hawk rolled his eyes. "And what are you going to do if I'm not?"

Hayden glanced around, making sure there was no one else watching, then gripped Hawk's chin, drawing him in, kissing his mouth. "Undress you myself."

Hawk shoved him off, and Hayden grinned at me while he walked away.

I eyed Hawk, who might have actually been blushing just a tiny bit beneath his stubble. "You can just admit you're into him, you know?"

Hawk shrugged, dragging me into his arms. "I like arguing with him. I can't even explain why. I just do."

I laid my head against his chest, listening to his heartbeat in the quiet night. "Are you mad about the party? I can try to talk Bliss into something more casual if you really hate the whole idea."

But Hawk shook his head over the top of mine. "I don't hate it. I've never had a birthday party before."

I pulled back to stare up at him. "Never?"

"Never. Nobody gave a shit about my birthdays when I was a kid. My mom tried giving me a party once, but my dad was a jealous fuck, never wanted her thinking about anything but him. And that even included me. If I got too much of her attention, he'd get jealous. The one time she planned a party, he packed her bags and whisked her off to some shitty hotel by the beach for the weekend to remind her why all her attention should stay on him."

I gasped. "He hurt her?"

"Nah. He probably just made her come until she saw stars. He did it regularly, reminding her she was never going to get it better anywhere else, even if he was a jealous prick. At least he treated her right. Shame he didn't give a fuck about me, but then he was an ass, so I didn't really want any more of his attention. Never cared much about birthdays after that. It was just another day."

"That makes me sad for you. Bliss is right. You should be celebrated."

"Don't be sad. What happened in the past doesn't matter. Only that this birthday will be different, because I'm with you." He buried his face in my hair and inhaled deeply. "All I want is you and Hayley Jade by my side. I don't need fancy food or a cake or gifts. Just you being there. That's the only thing I want."

He wrapped his arms around me and held me close, whispering how much he loved me.

And in that moment, I stupidly, selfishly convinced myself I could stay another week. That being there for him was important and everyone I loved would be safe, even though a monster stalked the streets, hunting us down, just waiting for his chance to ruin any happiness I'd found.

7

KARA

Despite what happened at the hospital the last time I'd been there, when Friday rolled around again, a nagging feeling settled in the pit of my stomach and wouldn't leave me alone. I anxiously cleaned anything I could find at the clubhouse, wiping down the kitchen, even though Hayden did that religiously. I washed sheets and blankets. Scrubbed bathrooms, and when I checked the clock and it was only ten, I wanted to scream.

Hawk seemed equally lost. He grouchily snapped at everyone who looked his way and complained loudly about the fact no one had fixed the wobbly leg on the pool table and then stomped off to the shed to find some tools to fix it himself.

After a few minutes of tinkering with the tools, he slammed the toolbox shut, the metal on metal making a painful screeching sound. "I fucking hate this!"

I paused in the middle of wiping down the communal

room walls. "Maybe you should take a walk. Or a ride? You haven't done that for a while."

He paced across the room, perhaps considering the idea, and then stopped to stare at me, a sort of helpless expression on his face. "I want to be at the hospital clinic."

"Me too," I admitted.

He groaned, scrubbing his hands over his closely cropped hair. "Fuck it. Let's go."

I smiled for what felt like the first time since everything had happened. "Seriously?"

"Seriously. People there need us. Gray said security has been insane at the hospital after what happened. They're checking IDs of every person who walks in, and the cops have a whole team stationed down there apparently."

That was surprising. "Seriously? Providence Police Department actually did something proactive?"

"That new chief is on the warpath about gang violence. Maybe it had something to do with them."

I frowned. "Not sure Josiah's followers count as a gang."

Hawk shrugged. "Maybe not an officially branded one, but calling together a mob of people with the intent to hurt or capture might be worse. Clearly, it was enough to get them to get off their asses and do something. I'm not gonna look a gift horse in the mouth."

Neither was I.

Hawk's party was tomorrow night, and there was a midnight bus out of town leaving the terminal just down the road from Sinners. I knew I needed to be on it. The pieces had fallen together too easily. Last week I'd tried to come up with ways to leave, and all of them had involved elaborate schemes and lies.

But tomorrow night, while everyone was enjoying the party, I'd just slip out. Walk the block to the terminal and get on the bus before it left.

I knew nobody would be happy with me. But I'd written letters for them all, explaining why I was doing it, asking them to respect my decision and not come after me.

I expected Hawk and Hayden to ignore it completely, but if I could get a couple of hours' head start, then I'd be inside Ethereal Eden's gates before they could intervene.

But if today was going to be my last day in Saint View, while Hayley Jade was at school, I wanted to be at the hospital. I owed Willa a thank you, and there was nowhere else I was more needed than with the underprivileged patients the clinic served. I kissed Hawk's cheek, knowing he'd spend the entire shift hovering over me, making sure he was never more than a few feet away, but I was okay with that. "I'll get my purse and meet you in the van."

Hawk paused and then shook his head. "Wait. I got you a present."

I paused halfway to my bedroom and glanced back at him. "What do you mean? I'm not the one with a birthday coming up in a few days."

"I know. But I got you a gift anyway. I was going to give it to you tomorrow, before the party, but I changed my mind. I don't want you leaving the house without it."

I frowned, following him into his room and leaning on the doorjamb while he plucked a package clumsily wrapped in brown paper from the top of his closet.

It was soft, but heavier than I expected. I shook it as a joke.

He grinned lazily at me, nodding. "Go on. Open it."

I perched on the edge of his bed and ripped the paper.

The smell hit me before my eyes registered what it was. A familiar scent now, after burying my face in his jacket on more than one occasion.

A gasp slipped out of my mouth as I pulled the jacket out and stared at it. "What?...Is this..."

"Your old lady jacket? Yeah."

I stared at him and then down at the jacket that I'd only seen on a couple of other women. Bliss and Rebel. War's mom, Fancy. Queenie. The Slayers' emblem covered the entire back of the jacket. The skeleton figure holding a scythe a demonic and intimidating figure, but one I'd come to associate with safety and kindness and the love of the people who wore it with pride.

On the front, where Hawk's jacket had patches that showed his title of vice president, this jacket had a patch that read "Old Lady."

I ran my fingers over it. To the outside world, it wasn't exactly a complimentary term, but in here, it was the ultimate sign of respect. It was a commitment.

It was as good as a marriage proposal from whichever man gave it to you.

"It's amazing," I whispered. It truly was. It was so intricately made, the stitching neat and precise. The design complicated and beautiful, though I wasn't sure others would see it the way I did. "I don't know what to say."

Hawk plucked the jacket from my fingers and moved

in behind me, holding it up for me. His head dipped to my ear, and he kissed me just below it. "Say you'll wear it. Say you'll be my old lady, Kara."

My eyes filled with tears. A "yes" sat hot on the tip of my tongue. I wanted to blurt it out. Shout it from the rooftops. Tell everyone how much I loved him and wear his jacket with pride, everyone knowing I was his.

My reckless heart had me slipping my arms through the sleeves before my brain caught up and shouted I couldn't do this.

I froze with the jacket half on, but he didn't notice, he'd already twisted away to rifle through his drawers. When he turned back around, he held two small patches, identical strips to his VP patch but blank.

I peered at them. "What are those?"

He flipped them over, revealing the writing on the back.

One read Little Mouse. The other had Hayley Jade's name.

My heart swelled so much I was sure it was going to suffocate me.

"I had them made when I got your jacket done. They go here, on my sleeve, so you're always with me."

The lump in my throat was enormous. I couldn't even speak.

All I could do as a tear slipped silently down my face was let him pull the jacket up on my shoulders and zip it up.

It fit perfectly and was by far the most beautiful thing I'd ever owned.

His gaze drank me in, molten eyes tracking every curve of my body now encased in leather. He groaned. "If we didn't have somewhere we need to be, I'd have you naked apart from that jacket and riding my tongue until your legs don't work."

I wasn't all that sure they were working right now.

But if Hawk noticed, he didn't say anything. Just guided me outside, passed me a helmet, and told me to get on the back of his bike.

I did. I slid on behind him, wrapping my arms around his middle and feeling the tight warmth of his body against mine. All while wondering how I was ever going to walk away from this man, when he'd so totally and completely stolen my heart.

The new hospital security was intense. We had our hospital-issued ID badges checked before walking through metal detectors. There were new security doors in place of the ones that had been destroyed by Josiah's groupies. We'd taken off our jackets so as to not draw attention, but Hawk attracted it anyway, getting himself a pat down from a police officer before we were admitted to the clinic.

I nudged him as we made our way behind the nurses' desk. "That was very big of you. You didn't even complain about that officer getting up close and personal."

"Why would I? He's here to help keep you safe. If I have to have my junk groped by a dozen cops to make sure no one brings a weapon in here that could hurt you, then I will."

I pressed up on my toes and kissed his cheek. "You're

a much sweeter man than you let others believe. You do know that, right?"

He took a sneaky handful of my ass and wiggled his eyebrows. "Still think I'm such a nice guy?"

I rolled my eyes and pushed him away. In the female locker room, I hung my new jacket with care and grabbed a pair of scrubs to change into.

Hawk waited for me outside, dressed in scrubs of his own, and matching Grayson, who leaned on the wall beside him.

Grayson's smile met his eyes when he saw me, and I fought to keep my gaze on his face, instead of letting it wander lower. Knowing that he had all those tattoos beneath his clothes was a distraction I hadn't anticipated.

He moved toward me, then paused, glancing back at Hawk. "Uh, I don't know the protocol here." He turned back to me. "I really want to kiss you right now. But..."

Hawk let out a low, menacing growl from somewhere deep in his chest.

Gray and I both swiveled to stare at him.

The purring rumble cut off, flipping into a wide grin, showing off his white teeth. "Just messing with you. Kiss her. I won't hurt you."

Gray leaned toward me.

"Much," Hawk added.

I glared at him.

Grayson sniggered and tipped my chin. "Hey."

I melted, staring into his eyes. "Hey."

His mouth on mine was so sweet. He kissed me slowly, lightly at first, his mouth playful until his tongue was seeking entrance, and I was leaning into him, loving the feel of his hard body against my softer one.

"I shouldn't find this hot," Hawk muttered. "Can we do this somewhere else? When we don't have patients to help, maybe?"

Both of us looked over at him in surprise. Blood rushed to my face at the very thought of being sandwiched between him and Grayson.

Gray cleared his throat. "Uh, did you just hit me up for a threesome?"

"No. That would be super inappropriate. You're our boss."

My hopes fell.

Grayson's cheeks went pink with embarrassment. "Right. I'm sorry."

Hawk raised an eyebrow. "I was thinking more of a foursome. Chaos will want in."

Oh my God.

Hawk laughed, walking backward down the hallway toward the clinic. "Don't act like the two of you haven't been thinking about it. We all know what this is. We all know it's happening at some point. Question is, when?"

He disappeared around the corner into the clinic waiting room, leaving Grayson blushing and me practically panting.

I glanced up at him, trying to decipher his expression. "You don't have to—"

"I want to."

The words came out his mouth so quick there was no denying he meant them. My heart thumped hard. I didn't even know how the four of us together...like that...would even work.

But I so wanted to find out. "Do you want to come over tonight?"

"I want to, but I can't."

"Tomorrow morning?" I asked.

He frowned. "We'll be getting ready for the party. Hayden asked us to come in early to help decorate, remember?"

I nodded. "Right. Of course."

He took my hand, sliding his fingers through mine. "Maybe I could come back to the clubhouse after the party tomorrow night? No pressure. We just see what happens?"

Except I'd be gone by then. On a bus back to a life I didn't want.

For a second, I convinced myself I could stay and that everything would be okay. That this calm I felt right now wasn't the eye of the storm.

But I couldn't forget being locked in that coffin. I couldn't forget being chased down by men with evil, soulless eyes. I couldn't forget they'd brought knives and guns into my child's school and if Hayden and Hawk hadn't gotten to her in time, I might not have her at all.

Josiah was never going to stop. He was just planning his next move.

I had to make mine before he could.

I forced a smile for Gray. "Sure. Tomorrow night sounds great."

It wasn't the first lie I'd told. And it wasn't the first one I'd regret.

8

KARA

The next morning, before the sun rose, I packed a bag with a handful of belongings I knew I'd probably never see again once I was inside Ethereal Eden's gates. But I put in some of the clothes Hawk had bought me when I'd first arrived, some body lotion I'd come to love, and my hospital ID. I tucked a photo Hayden had printed of me and Hayley Jade into my pocket, wanting it close. If by some miracle they weren't all confiscated, they'd be all I'd have to remember this time on the outside.

I'd already been through this once before. When I'd left Saint View last time, all I'd had was memories to keep me going.

Those had never faded. I hadn't let them. I'd lived in my head more than I'd lived in the real world. Until I could find some proof that would put Josiah away for what he'd done to my sister, then I would do it again.

It was still dark when I snuck outside and lifted the cover on Hayden's truck. I pushed my bag in, fitting the tough black fabric back in place and hoped he wouldn't have some reason to check the back before we left for Sinners.

I hurried back inside, right as Hawk wandered out of his room, rubbing at his eyes sleepily. He stretched so his T-shirt rode up, giving me a flash of his perfect abs. "Where were you?"

I had to fight to keep the drool in my mouth. "Just went outside to watch the sun come up. It's pretty." That part wasn't a lie. The sunrises here were my favorite. They'd been the one thing I loved about Ethereal Eden, watching the sun rise and splash the fields in pinks and golds.

But the sun peeking between the trees here at the Slayers' compound was better. Sitting outside with a warm cup of tea with the air fresh and cool around me and knowing my family was safe and happy inside the walls was my new favorite.

It nearly broke me realizing I didn't know when or if I'd ever get to see it again. I suddenly wished I'd stood out there every morning. Regretted all the sleep-ins I should have forfeited just to see the sun.

Hawk flopped down on the couch, looking like he was going to nod off again. But Hayden came out of the kitchen, startling both of us.

I put my hand over my heart; it beat too fast with panic he might have seen me slip outside. "I didn't know you were awake."

He shoved Hawk's feet off the couch and sat next to him. "I've got a million things to do before tonight. But I wanted to talk to you about something." His gaze focused on me. "I think we should talk to Hayley Jade's teachers about going into her classroom one day a week and teaching the kids to sign."

I blinked. "Really?"

He nodded. "Obviously, I'm not an expert, but we've all picked up the basics. Kids learn so quickly, and I think it would be really good for all of them. What do you think?"

I loved he wanted to give up his time to make Hayley Jade's life a little better. "I think it's a great idea."

He leaned forward, resting his elbows on his knees. "So if they okay it, you'll run the class with me?"

My mouth dried at having to tell yet another lie. But they were both staring at me, waiting for a response. I had no choice but to nod.

Hayden clapped his hands and pushed to his feet. "Great. I'll call the school about it on Monday then. I'll see the two of you over at Sinners this afternoon."

Hawk waved a sleepy hand in his direction, and Hayden squeezed the back of my neck on his way past me. "Love you."

"Love you too." But my voice got lost in the sound of the door shutting behind him.

I frowned, but then Hayley Jade was tumbling out of her room and needing breakfast, and the day quickly filled up with tasks that needed to be taken care of before we left to go set up the restaurant.

Hawk and I dropped Hayley Jade off at Rebel's place, where she was spending the afternoon. We'd determined that this party would be child friendly, at least for the first few hours, despite where it was being held. The doors to the maze would be securely locked when kids were in attendance, and I'd be double-checking them myself.

But Hawk had wanted Hayley Jade there, and War had wanted his kids as well. Hayley Jade was going to meet us at the party, driven in with Rebel and her family.

When we got to Sinners, Grayson's car was already parked outside, right next to Hayden's.

Hayden had closed the entire restaurant for the night, but we ignored the sign and let ourselves in, finding Grayson manning a vacuum. He turned it off as I wandered over, and he pulled out headphones I hadn't even noticed him wearing. He stopped in front of me. "I have news for you. Both of you, actually."

Hawk raised an eyebrow. "Backing out of our foursome tonight? That's not news. We all knew you'd chicken out."

I gaped at Hawk and elbowed him sharply. "Stop it. He doesn't have to do anything he doesn't want to do."

What was I even saying? There wasn't going to be a foursome. At least not with me in it.

The thought of the three of them being mad enough at my leaving to have a foursome with someone else left me feeling sick.

But that's what would happen when I left, wouldn't it? If they read the notes I'd left back in my room and did as I asked, I could be back at Ethereal Eden for months. Years. I had no idea how long it would take to find the evidence I needed.

They'd move on with their lives.

They were smart, attractive men who would have no shortage of women to pick from once I was gone. My stomach rolled at the thought.

Grayson pointed the vacuum at Hawk. "Nice try, but that was not what I was going to say. What I wanted to tell you both was I got a phone call last night, offering both of you a paid position at the hospital."

My mouth dropped open. "What do you mean? I'm not qualified for anything. Why would they pay me?"

Grayson grinned. "Willa and I have been talking with the hospital board about a sort of paid apprenticeship. You'd study to get your nursing degree—" He glanced at Hawk. "Or your EMT and paramedic qualifications, while getting hands-on experience at the hospital on the days you aren't studying. It'll take a little longer for you to complete your degrees but is more fitting for adults who can't afford to go for long stretches without being paid." He grinned. "All while the hospital gets slave labor!" He winked. "Okay, cheaper labor."

"You serious?" Hawk asked. "You actually want to pay us? For what we're already doing for free? How did you sell that to the hospital board?"

"By telling them you're a special snowflake."

Hawk flipped him the bird.

Grayson chuckled and leaned on the Hoover. "We need more staff. You've seen how it is down there. And you two actually are special, in that you give a huge amount of your time. But most people can't do that. And the thing is, we want to keep you, and we know we won't be able to if we don't start paying you at some point. The volunteer program never worked. What Willa and I need it to be is an entry position into the medical field. We've known that for a long time. We just didn't make it a priority to get it approved until we had the two of you." He glanced back and forth between us, his eyes brightly shining with excitement. "So? Are you in?"

Hawk's smile widened, zero hesitation in his voice. "Yeah. I'm in. Absolutely."

I wanted to cry with frustration. Why now? Why did everything have to fall into place when it was just inches out of my grasp? "It's an amazing offer," I hedged.

But that clearly wasn't enough for Grayson. His gaze felt like it burned right through me in the same way Hayden's had earlier. "An offer you're going to accept, right? If it's not what you want, I'll go back to the board—"

"It is!" I blurted the truth out like my lips couldn't contain the words. "What you and Willa have done for us is amazing."

Grayson was like a dog with a bone. "So you'll come in on Monday and we'll talk through the details? Sign contracts? You'll need to get your GED so you can enroll in the other courses you'll need to complete, but that was already the plan anyway."

They were both looking to me for an answer. Guilt swirled in my gut, but there was nothing else I could say. I nodded weakly, knowing I'd have to lie again. "Okay."

"We'll be the three amigos permanently!" Grayson said gleefully.

Hawk screwed up his face. "Please don't ever call us that."

Grayson sobered. "Fair enough."

"And if you make me a celebratory glove balloon animal, I'm quitting. I hate those things."

"Noted." He glanced at me. "Any special requests from you?"

"No. Just...thank you." It was the very least I could say. I really hoped they found someone else to take my spot.

Hawk and I made our way to the kitchen where Hayden and two of his staff members busily bustled around, preparing various types of food for the party tonight. Trays filled with the beginnings of sliders, potatoes being peeled and chopped up for I had no idea what, and chicken wings marinating in a dark sauce.

He looked up when we entered, and relief washed over his face. "More hands. Excellent. Can you both set tables? I'll show you where everything is."

He wiped his fingers on his apron and led us to the maître d' standing desk and knelt to open a cupboard not visible from the customer side. "Tablecloths are in here. Cutlery and anything else you might need should be behind the bar. If you need—"

The front door swung open.

Four older men walked in like they owned the place, not even acknowledging that we were standing there.

"Uh, guys?" Hayden called. "We're closed right now."

A fifth man, younger than the others, followed them in. One I unfortunately recognized.

Luca clapped his hand against Hayden's cheek. "Not closed anymore. Get someone to bring us menus, yeah? The guys and I have some business to take care of."

Hayden grabbed his arm, not letting him pass. "No. Not here. Not now. I'm preparing for a private party. I told you we were closed today."

Hawk silently moved himself into position at Hayden's back. While simultaneously putting himself between me and Luca's friends. His muscles tensed, clearly preparing for a fight.

Luca darted a peek at the table full of older men, then lowered his voice so it wouldn't be heard above their shouts and laughter. "Look, I'm going to be straight with you. I don't want to be here any more than you want me here. But my father and his friends don't ask permission, and they're all carrying. Are the two of you? You really want to turn this into a thing? Or do you want to just serve us some food and some drinks so you all can go on with your party and I can be anywhere else?"

Hawk glanced over at the table and sighed. "He's not lying. I count three guns, and that's only the ones that are visible."

Luca cracked his neck to one side, his agitation clear. "Please, Hayden."

I blinked in surprise. Luca didn't strike me as the sort of person who ever asked for anything nicely.

Hayden shook his head, and his teeth mashed together. But his eyes softened just a little. "An hour. One. You'll get fed and have a drink and then you'll leave well before any of my guests get here tonight."

Luca nodded. "I promise. Thank you." He went to sit with his father and the older man's friends.

The one to Luca's left, who I suspected might have been his father or at least an uncle, as there was a strong family resemblance, tapped his hand on the tabletop. "What kinda place do you have here, Luca? We can't get no menus?"

Luca shot Hayden a pleading glance.

"I've never seen Guerra this rattled," Hawk mumbled.

Hayden sighed heavily. "I don't even have any of the waitstaff or the bartenders here until five."

Hawk pressed his mouth into a grim line. "I'll do it."

"Me too," I said quickly.

"No," all three men said in unison.

I rolled my eyes.

"I worked my way through med school at a bar," Gray offered.

Hayden didn't look happy about it. "This probably won't end well."

"Probably not," Hawk agreed. "But what choice do you have?"

None. We all knew it. What Luca wanted; Luca got.

And he very firmly had Hayden in a spot none of us knew how to get him out of.

9

HAYDEN

I'd never chopped vegetables as aggressively as I did while watching Luca and his father and their friends on the restaurant security cameras. I resented every slice of my knife, and the sharp blade took chunks out of the chopping board because I wasn't being careful.

I needed to settle down before I took a slice out of my finger and ended up with yet another round of Hawk's stitches. But Luca's presence always got under my skin.

Especially with him and Kara in the same room.

I didn't want her anywhere near him. But it seemed that was inevitable today.

I just needed to cook quicker. Get them out of here faster.

Kara came over from the sink where I'd basically hidden her, busying her with washing dishes, and I relaxed an inch at having her close to me. She rubbed a soothing hand up and down my back, not saying anything, but just knowing her presence was all I wanted.

"They'll be gone soon, and then we'll get the party back on track. Luca said it's just an hour."

She had a lot of faith in Luca's word.

I did not.

Kara's hand pausing on my back should have been the first sign of trouble, but it was Luca's shadow falling over me before I realized there were other people in the kitchen.

His father and his friends all stood behind him.

Luca cleared his throat. "So this is where all the action happens..."

I glared at him. "What are you doing back here?"

"Just giving my father and his friends the grand tour of the place while we wait for our meals."

"Kitchen's off-limits," I snapped. I nudged Kara toward the back of the room, away from Luca's friends and their leering stares.

An older man narrowed his eyes at me disapprovingly, but his words were directed at his son. "You let your staff speak to you like that?"

"I'm not his staff," I bit out.

Luca changed the subject. "Chaos is an amazing chef. The food is getting rave reviews..."

Luca's dad wandered into the kitchen, peering into the frying pans on the stove and strolling about the place like he had every right in the world. He paused behind Kara and cocked his head to one side, studying her. "And who's this pretty thing? Too pretty to be hiding away back here if you ask me." He glanced at his son. "What have I told you? You put the pretty ones out in front where we can see them. Nobody wants to be served food by men." He offered me a fake smile. "No offense."

Anger bubbled up inside me, but Luca stepped between Kara and his father and gave me a 'I'm handling it, settle down' look. Which only made me want to hit him more.

Luca cringed, getting my message loud and clear that neither he nor his family were welcome in my kitchen. "Come on. Let me show you the sex club side. That's where all the action really takes place."

His father nodded and went to follow, but then he paused, bending over to pick something up off the floor. He opened the folded piece of paper and then looked at Kara again.

"Is this your daughter?"

The man flashed a photo of Kara and Hayley Jade. One I'd had printed for her that usually sat on her bedside table.

Kara dried her hands quickly and reached for the photo. "Yes. Thank you. That must have fallen out of my pocket."

Luca's dad moved the photo out of her reach. "Pretty runs in your family." He showed Luca the photo. "She'd go six figures at an auction."

The blood drained from my face. I lunged for the man, but Luca stepped in front of me swiftly, cutting me off before anyone else noticed I was moving.

He snatched the photo from his father's fingers. "That's not funny. She's a child."

But his father clearly wasn't joking. "Yeah. A pretty one. Big market for that if you want to stop being such a princess and do as you're actually fucking told for once."

Luca lowered his voice, eyeing his father and the

other older men all watching on curiously. "We're in the way of my staff. Let them do their jobs. Tour's over."

Luca's dad eyed him in challenge, neither of them budging an inch, the standoff real in their rigid postures. Father against son.

Luca was an inch taller, and I knew he had a gun at his hip, currently hidden beneath his suit jacket.

But his father had a domineering presence that couldn't be ignored. As well as three friends ready to back him up if it came down to it. They all watched him, taking their cues from the elder Guerra.

Seconds felt like minutes.

Until he smiled and put his hands up in mock surrender. "Of course. Of course. It's your business now. You get to run it as you see fit." He turned to his friends. "Let's go see if our drinks are ready, yes?"

They all relaxed visibly and walked out of my kitchen as a pack.

Luca let out a long sigh tinged with relief and leaned his elbows on the metal countertop, breathing hard.

All of us left in the kitchen stared as Luca's shoulders shook silently.

I jerked my head at Jonie and Mitchell, my kitchen staff. "Take a break. Out in back somewhere. Go through the maze. You go nowhere near those men. Got it?"

They nodded quickly, pulling off their aprons and scurrying out.

Luca sucked in a deep breath and lifted his head. "Thanks." He turned to Kara. "I'm really sorry."

Her mouth dropped open. Then closed. Then opened again. "You are?"

She took the words right out of my mouth.

He straightened, clearly trying to get himself under control. "What he said about your daughter…that's…I'm just sorry. You shouldn't have had to hear that."

I went to say something, but she cut me off, obviously needing to say some things of her own. "So you have a physical reaction to the idea of a child being sold but zero care when that person is a woman?"

Luca scrubbed his hands over his face. "At least they're adults."

"Not consenting ones." Her voice was sharp. Unforgiving. "Don't go thinking you're some sort of hero just because you drew a wobbly line in the sand about not trafficking children. That doesn't forgive your sins."

Pride swelled inside me, watching her stare Luca down and confront him with the truth. She was so different from the quiet, meek woman I'd once known.

I'd loved her then. But I loved this version even more. She was brave. Bold. Unafraid to stand up for others, even if she didn't always stand up for herself.

I'd never seen Luca so rattled. It wasn't just Kara's words getting to him. Something else had to be going on.

I folded my arms across my chest, waiting for some sort of explanation.

"You know my sister is married to one of those guys? My baby sister, I should add." The bitterness in Luca's tone filled the kitchen like a frost had just rolled in. "Their wedding was last weekend, and I had to sit there in the front row and watch it." He shook his head. "She's barely ten years older than your kid now."

"That's horrible," Kara whispered. "Fifteen is still a child."

Luca nodded. "It was. It is. My sister cried through the

entire ceremony. But my father determined she was available, and Lorenzo made the highest bid." He swore softly beneath his breath. "You know my father didn't even react to Isabella's tears. He just sat there, completely unmoved, even when she begged him to stop it. And when Lorenzo got pissed off and backhanded her to stop her crying, my dad put a gun to my head because I dared to reach for mine."

All I could see in my head was an image of a slightly older Hayley Jade, dressed in all white, crying while a priest bound her in holy matrimony with a man old enough to be her grandfather.

"I think I'm going to be sick," I muttered.

But Kara held Luca's gaze. "My world wasn't so different to yours. My marriage was arranged and not one I ever wanted. Nobody stood up for me either."

I couldn't stand hearing any of it. Didn't want to think about the horrors that child had suffered for the past week at her husband's hands.

Anger swelled inside me rapidly. I stared at Luca, unable to understand him. "What are you doing, man? Is this really the life you want for yourself? For other people?"

Luca lifted his head wearily. "What exactly do you expect me to do? I tried—"

Oh, he was a piece of work. "You tried? Is that seriously how you're sleeping at night, knowing that old man is raping your sister? Could you look her in the eye and tell her you truly did everything you could to save her?"

Luca stared at me. "You and I aren't all that different, you know. Once upon a time, you were just as involved in this world as I am."

Except we were different, and we both knew it. "I was a twenty-five-year-old kid with no money, no prospects, and no direction. I was desperate. But that still doesn't excuse what I did to Kara, and to the other women we held all those years ago. I made mistakes. I owned them. And I grew the fuck up. I made a choice to get out. Don't kid yourself into thinking you can't do the same if you wanted to. You have a choice to make. And it's yours."

Luca pulled back his shoulders, buttoning his suit jacket, but his eyes still showed the raw vulnerability of his true feelings. "Choices like that are a luxury, Chaos. Not one all of us get to make." The guards came back over his eyes, darkening them as he built his walls up around himself once more. "Get our meals out. We'll eat and then we'll be gone. I won't bring them back here. This place is yours."

Kara watched him walk away. "What did he mean by that?"

I didn't know but there was one thing I did. That nothing Luca said or did was ever as it seemed. "Probably nothing good."

10

KARA

*S*inners was packed with bodies from one end of the restaurant to the other. Music played loudly, people danced in any spot they could find, and kids ran about underfoot, completely getting in the way, but everyone indulged their energy, smiling at them as they zoomed by or even adding to the chaos by charging around after them.

We'd sung "Happy Birthday" and cut cakes. Drinks flowed. Hayden's waitstaff wandered around with overloaded trays of finger foods, trying to palm them off onto anyone who'd take one, even though all our stomachs had been filled hours ago. Hayden had even managed to get out of the kitchen, ditching his chef blacks for jeans and a T-shirt and leaving the kitchen cleanup to his staff.

Everyone was having a good time.

Except for me.

The clock on the wall counted down the minutes and then the hours to the time I'd need to leave to catch my bus, each second becoming one I dreaded.

Rebel wandered over sometime around eleven with a hand rubbing across the swell of her baby-number-five belly. "I'm beat," she admitted. "I'm too old for partying all night anymore." She groaned when she looked at the clock. "Is it seriously only eleven? I'm pathetic."

I smiled at her. "You're growing a baby. That takes a lot of energy. Not to mention chasing around after four kids under five."

"This is why I volunteered to have all the kids tonight. I'm ready to ditch. Do you mind?"

I shook my head. "Of course not. All that's left now is the drinking part, and you can't do that anyway."

"I swear, between being pregnant and breastfeeding, I haven't had a drink in five years. Forever the designated driver."

She sighed, but I knew she didn't really mind. I wouldn't have picked her as the type to love being a mother. But my sister was one of the best ones I'd ever seen. Her kids were lucky to have her.

As was Hayley Jade.

I swallowed hard and hugged my sister. "I love you. Thank you for everything."

She leaned back, her eyebrows knitting together. "What do you mean? I didn't do anything."

I cleared my throat and made up a lie. About the fiftieth one I'd told that night. "For taking Hayley Jade home with you all tonight."

Her frown smoothed out. "No problem at all. She's not the crazy one." She grimaced at Madden, who was running around the room with his T-shirt over his head like he was a soccer player who'd just scored a goal. "I don't know who let him eat all that candy, but hopefully the sugar crash will knock him out for the night before we get home. Do you want to say goodbye to Hayley Jade before we go?"

I nodded, following her over to where Fang stood with Lavender asleep on his shoulder, Remi and Hayley Jade at his feet, poking paper straws into an uneaten piece of cake and giggling.

Fang immediately slipped his free hand to the back of Rebel's neck, and she gazed up at him. "Take me home."

He leaned down and kissed her mouth. "With pleasure."

She was so happy. And I was happy for her, that she'd found three men who loved her so well. I knelt at their feet and tapped Hayley Jade on the arm. "Aunty Rebel is going to take you home now for a sleepover with Remi."

She grinned and nodded, brushing cake crumbs off her icing-smeared fingers.

I didn't care that she was sticky. I pulled her into my arms and held her close, closing my eyes to stop the tears pricking behind them. "I love you so much. I hope you know I'd do anything for you."

She nodded against my chest and squeezed her little arms around me tight. Panic rose inside, and I held her longer than I should have, just trying to memorize everything about how it felt to have her there. What she smelled like. How soft her skin was.

"Hey!" Rebel patted us both on the head. "It's just one night. You'll be back together in the morning. Right, Kara?"

I could barely breathe. "Right." I clutched Hayley Jade's arms, drawing back to look her in the eye. "It's not goodbye. Just a see you later."

Hayley Jade nodded happily, no idea anything was wrong, and ran off with Remi. Fang led the way to the exit while Kian and Vaughn rounded up their boys.

"You good, sis?" Rebel asked with a final lingering stare.

I looked down and wiped my eyes quickly. "Sure. Of course. I'm just being silly. I probably have PMS."

It was a plausible excuse, one Rebel accepted. "Okay. If you're sure..."

I was. "Go. Love you. Thank you." I walked away to the corner of the room to compose myself before I could cry.

Something cold pressed against my arm. "Cocktail? Made it myself."

Grayson put the pink drink into my hand, and I smiled gratefully at him, taking a sip of the fruity liquid. I blinked in surprise. "You made this?"

He nodded, sipping on his drink, though his was a much less interesting cola concoction. "I've been helping Steve behind the bar all night." He gazed around the room. "Your friends drink a lot."

I laughed but then sobered, picking out Queenie and Aloha dancing in the middle of the room. Ice and the other prospects sitting at the bar. Bliss and War making out in a corner since their kids had been picked up by their sitter. "They're not friends. They're family," I corrected, feeling it all the way to my toes.

Grayson put his arm around my shoulders. "I'm glad you found them. And they're lucky to have you. We all are."

I peered up at him, trying to fight off the urge to cry again when he put his arm around my shoulders.

I wasn't ready to say goodbye yet.

We hadn't had enough time.

I didn't want to waste another second of it.

I slipped my fingers between his. "Come on."

He didn't ask where we were going. I led him through the crowd, weaving between people I loved, and collecting Hayden and Hawk along the way.

None of them said anything.

My intent was clear as I followed the hall to the solid door with Sinners engraved in the wood.

Hayden took the key from his pocket and stepped up to fit it to the lock. He glanced at me and turned it. "Lock it behind us? Or leave it open for others to join? All the kids have been picked up."

These people might have been no strangers to public sex. And there was a part of me that got hot every time I thought about the night we'd come in here to watch Grayson. But tonight, I just wanted it to be us. I shook my head. "Not tonight. I want the three of you to myself."

We slipped through the doorway and Hayden flicked on a combination of lights that lit the pure-black room gently. Taking his phone from his pocket, he tapped the screen a few times, then peered up at the speakers hidden in the corners of the high ceiling, until sultry music came from them.

I faltered, need for them getting me this far, but then not having the experience to know what to do next. I had no idea where to even begin or what was expected of me. I had no idea how to please three men at once, but I wanted to.

Hawk saw the flash of indecision in my eyes and took the hand that wasn't holding on to Grayson's. "Come on."

He led us through the maze, retracing the steps we'd taken the last time we were here, until we stood in front of a huge bench, big enough for all four of us.

"Tell me what to do." I practically begged for his guidance.

He glanced at the others.

They said nothing, and Hawk seemed to take that as some sort of permission. He stepped forward, pulling me into his arms and dropping his mouth onto mine.

He was so warm, so familiar. He was the man who'd taught me what sex was supposed to feel like, and so he was the man I went to for direction.

His lips brushed over mine. "What's your hard limit, Kara? What don't you want to do tonight?"

"I don't have one. I want all of you. Everything." They were the words I said out loud.

The ones I said in my head were: *I don't want regrets. Give me something to remember when I'm not here. Show me you love me, so I have something to hold on to when everything feels lost.*

I half expected an argument. Expected him to disagree or say I wasn't ready.

He kissed me instead, carefully, his mouth worshipping mine until I was breathless.

Hayden moved in behind me, kissing my neck, his hands gliding down my sides to stop at my hips. One reached out farther, hooking into the belt loop on Hawk's jeans and drawing him in, sandwiching me between them tight.

Hawk's mouth slid to my ear, kissing the sensitive spot just beneath, and my eyes fluttered open, searching for Grayson.

His gaze connected with mine, and slowly, he pulled off his jacket, tossing it beside an armchair opposite the bench bed.

He lowered himself into it, watching the others kiss me, which was the exact purpose of that chair and clearly the whole reason it had been placed there. He rolled his sleeves to his elbows and undid his top button, loosening it from around his throat.

"We're going to get you naked," Hawk whispered against my skin. "Then I want you to go ride Gray. He's on the outside of the three of us. If this is going to work for you, he needs to be comfortable too."

It was an unexpectedly polite thing for Hawk to say, when his usual demeanor was guttural and harsh and probably even a bit selfish. But I knew there was a fondness between him and Grayson. A mutual respect, not born of attraction, like the one between Hawk and Hayden, but a friendship and loyalty that had started when we'd begun working together and cemented itself when Gray had put his life on the line for me.

I slipped my feet out of my ballet flats, and Hawk's fingers came to the sides of my gauzy shirt. It was new, prettier than any of my others, though still in the subdued tones I think I would always prefer. It was loose and flowy, and when Hawk dragged it over my head, it came away easily.

He stared at me in the lace and silk bra Bliss had bought with me yesterday afternoon, when I'd confessed to her I had nothing nice to wear tonight and no idea where to buy it from. I was still living off the money my sister had given me when I'd first arrived, had barely even made a dent in it because my needs here had been fully taken care of by these men and the other members of the club.

But this had been something I didn't want them to know about. And Rebel had encouraged me wholeheartedly, determined I should feel like a queen for my first foursome.

It felt ridiculous even thinking that in my head. I'd been such a wallflower for so many years. And now I was wearing pretty underwear and feeling confident enough in my own skin to have sex with multiple men all at once.

Hawk's fingers traced over the lacy, see-through cup of my bra. "What's this, Little Mouse?"

I shivered when his fingers pinched at my nipple through the sheer fabric. "Do you like it?"

His gaze burned hot, holding mine. He lowered his mouth to my breast and sucked my nipple through my bra. His other hand cupped me, thumb rubbing over my tip until both nipples were beaded, taut and needy.

Hayden's lips trailed along my shoulder. "He likes it."

I twisted my head, needing to see his expression.

He lowered his mouth to catch my lips, kissing me softly. "And so do I. So much harder to take it off you when you look this good in it."

Despite the voiced hesitations, his fingers seemed to have no problem finding the clasp at my back and undoing it. The straps slipped down my shoulders, and Hawk moved his mouth just long enough to let it fall to the floor before he was back, sucking on my nipples.

With him ducked and at work, it gave me a better view of Grayson. His erection pressed hard against the fabric of his suit pants, the outline thick and long, even concealed the way it was.

He breathed too fast, and I stood in front of him, naked from the waist up, while two other men put their hands and mouths and tongues all over me.

There was nothing but heat in his gaze. No jealousy.

A little part of me relaxed at his expression.

He undid another button on his shirt, and then a third, the rest falling away quickly to reveal his abs and pecs, and the tattoos across them. My gaze danced across the ones on his forearms, normally hidden by his shirt-sleeves.

But it was his fingers undoing the buttons on his pants that drew my attention. The slide of his zipper. The slight lift of his hips as he dragged his pants and underwear down just far enough to release his erection.

Hawk and Hayden followed, Hawk getting my fly undone, while Hayden tugged down the neat black jeans I'd purchased. I couldn't remember ever owning a pair before this. It was an odd change from the long skirts I'd grown so used to.

All I was left with was the panties that matched my bra.

"Go to him, Little Mouse," Hawk whispered in my ear, ending with a flick of his tongue. "Let him decide if he has you with those still on, or if he wants them on the floor."

He stepped aside, making way for me to walk to Grayson.

He let out a low hiss of breath and snaked his fingers around his cock, stroking it up and down, torturously slowly while he waited for me. "Come here, Kara."

I did as I was told, a rush of heat taking control of my body.

He reached for me, fingers hooking in the elastic waist of my panties and then swiping side to side, brushing over my lower belly and my mound. "Take them off. I don't want anything in the way of getting inside you."

My breath caught, heat flooding me at his commands. It never failed to turn me on when they told me what to do like this. It was like they knew how to turn off the switch to all my worries and just be in the moment, here with them.

Nothing else existed outside of this. I had no child to worry over. No husband hunting me down. No sister dead in a morgue.

I just got to be me.

I slid my panties down my thighs, leaving myself fully naked and on display for him, waiting for my next instruction.

Grayson stood, dropping his pants and underwear to the floor and kicking them aside.

I went to touch his skin, but he caught my wrists and spun me around so my back was to his chest.

He was warm behind me, his dick prodding at my lower back as his arms wrapped around my middle, one taking a handful of my breast, the other trailing over my tummy rolls and then lower, between my thighs to rub my clit.

I gasped at him touching me there, the tiny bud instantly responsive to his touch.

Or maybe it was responsive to the show Hayden and Hawk had started up on the bench, the two of them laid out on their sides, making out, their kisses deep and strong and powerful in the dim light.

"They're hot together," Grayson murmured in my ear. "I wanted you to see them."

There was no denying that. They were both ridiculously attractive men, and it was only multiplied when they were together. Hawk grabbed at Hayden's shirt, impatiently lifting it so he could get his hands on his skin.

"Watch them while I make you come." Grayson nudged my thighs wider, forcing me to turn my foot out so I was opened up for him. His finger moved from my clit to my entrance, coating himself in the arousal pooling there before pushing it up inside me.

I let out a little moan at the intrusion, loving the way it felt and instantly wanting more. He pumped his fingers in and out of me, watching the two men just as much as I was.

Hayden reached one hand over his shoulder and fisted the back of his shirt, helping Hawk out by pulling it off entirely. His hands came to rest on the back of Hawk's head as he ran his mouth down the length of Hayden's body, his tongue running over every ridge of his abs before stopping at his belt.

Hawk got up on his knees. "Undo your belt."

Hayden raised an eyebrow. "Giving orders to me now as well?"

Hawk rolled his eyes. "I am if you want me to suck your dick. Otherwise, feel free to stay fully clothed. I can always go suck Grayson's."

Grayson paused in surprise. "Uh...I know I said you two were hot together, but I didn't really mean I was into you like that..."

Hayden chuckled good-naturedly. "He's full of shit. Don't worry. He doesn't want anyone's dick but mine. True, Hawk?"

Hawk shot him a dirty look. "Just fucking take your pants off, would you? God, I wish I didn't like you."

Hayden caught his arm and drew him back down until they were face-to-face. "You do though. So stop denying it." He pressed up on his elbows, dragging Hawk down by his neck to kiss him and then pushed him down his body.

Grayson returned to my clit and Hawk undid Hayden's fly to get his pants off. His mouth was on him a second later, and I couldn't turn away. He bobbed up and down over him, taking Hayden's dick deep into his mouth and gripping his balls none too gently.

Hayden groaned; his head thrown back as he thrust up into Hawk's mouth.

My core clenched pleasurably at the erotic show they put on, Hayden pulling Hawk's shirt off when he took a moment's break to work Hayden's cock with his hands.

Grayson fit his mouth to my neck, placing open-mouthed kisses there while he added a second finger to my core. "You're so wet."

I blushed at his dirty words, feeling the arousal between my thighs, my body gushing for him every time his fingers hit my G-spot. My knees wobbled, and I was sure I was drowning his hand in my juices.

His free hand groped my breasts, squeezing and pinching the nipples, then matching those movements on my clit.

Hayden groaned and grabbed the back of Hawk's head, his voice deeply guttural. "Gonna come."

So was I.

As Hayden's hips jerked off the bed, Hawk not pulling away, my own orgasm barreled down on me. My head swirled, my legs threatened to give way, and my pussy clenched hard around Grayson's fingers. More than two of them. I was so wet I couldn't even tell how many of them I'd been able to take.

"Oh God!"

The spasms focused themselves around my core, but a blissful, pleasurable feeling spread out farther, taking over each limb and spreading warmth across my skin in a hot flush. I dropped my head back on Grayson's shoulders and let him prolong the orgasm, too lost to the feeling to be aware of Hayden and Hawk any longer.

"Need to be inside you," Grayson whispered, sitting in the chair again.

With one hand on his dick, the other on my hips, he guided me down on top of him so I was impaled on his erection, facing away from him.

I groaned at the delicious stretch of my body around his. And then again at the instinctual need inside me to move, to bounce on his cock and ride out the last morsels of my orgasm.

He gripped my hips, thrusting up into me from beneath me. My breasts bounced while I ground on top of him, gasping when Hayden settled himself on the floor in front of us and spread both of our knees wide, getting in between.

I shouted when he put his mouth on my clit, sucking me there and making me lose any rhythm I'd found. I went boneless, flopping back against Grayson's chest while Hayden licked me and Grayson thrust into me from beneath.

Hayden's gaze caught mine, and I stared down at him, fascinated with how hot he was there between my thighs while another man was inside me. He didn't care his tongue was an inch from Grayson's cock, all he cared about was throwing me into another orgasm.

One I had no hope of denying when he looked at me like that.

"Need to come, fuck," Grayson groaned.

"Need Chaos to lick your balls for you?" Hawk asked lazily from the bench, stroking his erection while he watched. "He's real good at that."

"Shut up, Hawk," all three of us groaned in unison.

He sniggered, but I was too lost to the feel of the two men to care. I took two handfuls of my breasts, and that added friction got me over the line for the second time. A dam burst inside me, my orgasm flooding free again, this one even more powerful than the first since every nerve ending was already sensitive.

Gray shouted from beneath me, coming hard, his fingertips gripping my hips.

I pushed Hayden away, knowing he'd stay there between my thighs all day, even though my body was spent and he clearly wanted to give me another orgasm to add to his tally.

He laughed softly. "You need a minute?"

"Maybe a few." My vision was blurry, and I floated on a cloud of bliss, Grayson still deep inside me, though neither of us moved, both of us too boneless with pleasure to budge an inch.

Chaos kissed the top of my head, lips gentle on my hair. "Rest for a minute while I take care of Hawk. But, Kara?"

"Mmm?"

"We aren't done."

11

HAWK

I jerked my cock slowly, not wanting to come, though watching Kara fall apart with Gray's dick inside her and Chaos licking her pussy had made it real hard to keep a grip on my orgasm.

My gaze had traced every curve of her body, every heave of her chest. I was sure I'd memorized every little sound she made, but I still wanted more of them.

But with her taken care of, my attention came back to Chaos. Fuck, he was doing it for me. All tight ass, perfect skin, tatted up and muscular. But it was the confidence pouring off him that really made him hard to look away from.

He'd had his mouth a mere inch from Grayson's cock, and it hadn't bothered him in the slightest. He walked around the room now, naked as the day he was born, with zero shame. He went to a rack of sex toys, studying the selection, while all I could do was stare at the muscles that bunched and moved across his back.

I didn't know if I was bi, or just really fucking into

him. I liked Gray. Could see why Kara was attracted to him, thought it was hot watching them fuck, but I didn't want to get down on my knees for him the way I kept doing for Chaos. He was an addiction I couldn't stop. Didn't *want* to stop.

He picked something, and then to my surprise, bypassed Kara who had been fucked so good she was practically passed out with pleasure and tossed his finds onto the bed with me.

"What's that?" I asked him warily, paying attention to him rather than whatever he'd picked out.

"Wouldn't you like to know?"

"If you're going to put it in my ass, I do."

Chaos shook his head and laughed. "It's an ass plug. A teeny-tiny baby one that even you can take."

I had my doubts.

Chaos clearly saw them written on my face. His expression gentled, and he leaned down to kiss me, softer than he ever had before. "You don't have to do anything you don't want to do. But, Hawk?" He kissed my neck, open-mouthed, sucking until I was sure I would have a hickey.

I didn't care. His mouth there only had me stroking my cock faster, thrusting into my own grip, desperate to get closer to him. "Mmm?" He smelled so damn good, a combination of scents that was so him I was now sure I could recognize it anywhere. It spun my head until all I could think and see and smell was him.

"I can't fuck you if you've had no practice."

I groaned, rolling onto my side and dragging him down so I could kiss him. I thrust my tongue into his mouth and kissed him hard, fumbling on the bed until I found the plug. I put it into his hand. "I want you," I murmured honestly, drunk and horny enough not to have a filter.

"Want you too. And look. I picked out a super manly plug for you. No diamonds or jewels on the base. It's just black."

"Like your eye is going to be if you keep talking instead of sucking my dick."

He laughed, and I was pretty sure I heard chuckles from Kara and Grayson too, but then Chaos's mouth was on my cock, and I couldn't think of anything except the wet slide of his tongue, and the undeniable desire inside me that really did want more from him than just blow jobs.

Fucking hell.

"Stop stressing," he coached quietly. "This doesn't have to mean anything."

Except it did to me. And it was more than just me trusting my body to him.

I squeezed my eyes shut tight and breathed, concentrating on sucking in deep breaths of air and filling my lungs instead of worrying about the warring thoughts inside my brain.

Chaos bobbed his head up and down my shaft, sucking and licking me perfectly, building me up, only to back off when I thought there was no return. Except he knew exactly where my limits were now, knew how to read my body, and he gripped my balls in just the way I liked.

The slide of the lubed-up plug between my ass cheeks had me freezing, but Chaos held his position, continuing his onslaught on my dick until I relaxed enough for him to push it toward my asshole.

He didn't try getting it in, just rubbed me there with it, over and over, the sensation adding to what he was doing with my cock and balls. I didn't dare open my eyes. I knew Grayson and Kara were still here in the room, watching. It wasn't that I wanted them to leave. I wasn't even near to done with Kara yet. But I was scared of what I'd see in their eyes. My brain told me that neither of them were judging me for being into this. And yet a lifetime of homophobia had conditioned me to feel like this was something that shouldn't happen. Or if it did, that it should be hidden.

Fuck that. I didn't want to hide.

"Little Mouse." I fought to get a grip on the rising pleasure. "Get your sweet pussy over here and ride my face."

There was movement from her side of the room, I was aware of it, even though I still had my eyes closed. I didn't open them until I felt her thighs settle across my face and her sweet scent filled my nose.

She was wet from fucking Grayson, but he'd used a condom, so her taste was all her. I licked her slit, feeling the soft warmth of her thighs around my head and using it as a distraction from the increasing need inside me for Chaos to do more than just tease me with that plug.

I widened my legs, giving him more room, and a clear signal I was ready for more.

He plunged his mouth over my cock, deep-throating me while giving me the tip of the plug, and then more and more, until I was groaning and taking the entire thing.

I let him fuck me with it, knowing it was barely half his size but no doubt in my mind that what he was doing felt good, and that his warm, thicker length would feel even better.

"Fuck," I groaned into Kara's pussy, gripping her thighs and digging into her flesh to hold her where I wanted her. "Don't make me come. I need her pussy."

Chaos gave the plug one final slow, delicious thrust inside me, and then left it there.

I stilled the rocking of Kara's hips and held her in place while I slid up the bed, until my dick was lined up with her pussy.

She plunged down on it with no instruction from me, and we both shouted, my entire body tightening, balls sucking up, threatening to unleash, my ass clenching around the plug, too pleasurable to stop.

She watched me carefully, all dark hair flowing down her back and over her tits in wild, messy waves. Her tits were well more than a handful, heavy and full, so fucking beautiful as she rode me, moving slowly because the entire room would have to be deaf and blind to not know how close to coming I was.

But I didn't want this to end. I couldn't stop looking at her, the curves of her hips more intoxicating than any of the drinks I'd consumed earlier in the night. She was a better high than flying down an open freeway on my bike while the sun rose. She was the thing that made my heart beat. The reason I wanted to get up in the morning and why I slept solidly at night.

She would never understand what I felt for her because there weren't words big enough for me to explain how utterly I'd fallen in love with her. "Kiss me, Little Mouse."

She leaned forward, pressing her lips to mine, slowing herself down to slip her tongue into my mouth, her kisses sexy and wild, and so unlike the timid thing she'd been when she first arrived. She took what she wanted from me, and I wanted to fucking crow with pride over her owning her own pleasure like this.

"Hayden." Her voice was so soft and gentle, but no less powerful than my barked-out commands.

He moved in behind her, settling either side of my legs, the same way she was. He took two handfuls of her ass, massaging her cheeks. It was hard for me to see more than that, but Chaos was proving to be an ass man, and I was sure from the increasing moans from my girl that he was playing with her rear hole the same way he'd just prepped mine.

Except I wanted more. Wanted his dick touching mine. She'd always been such a good girl, taking as many fingers as I could give, getting so wet for me I was sure I could fist her if I hadn't been worried about scaring her.

But she was ready for more than just me. Her dripping pussy, the easy slide in and out of her body told me she needed more than just one cock.

My gaze met Hayden's over Kara's shoulder. "She needs both of us in her pussy."

12

KARA

I moaned at the guttural command Hawk gave Hayden. My nipples rubbed against his chest, and he kissed me hard, tonguing my mouth, his fingers tight on my hips, keeping my motions steady and rhythmic while the torrent of feeling inside me threatened to get free.

Hayden's finger rimmed my rear hole, rubbing lube onto the starred opening, thrusting just his fingertip inside, enough to have me wetter than I'd ever been and desperate for another orgasm, even though I'd already had two.

There was no limit on pleasure. The longer I stayed here, lost in the feel of their fingers, tongues, and cocks, the longer I didn't have to think about getting on a bus and this never happening again.

I kissed Hawk to shut up my inner thoughts, and then shouted in surprise at Hayden's dick pressing inside me too, right alongside Hawk's, my body opening to accept them both.

My eyes rolled back, and I arched, angling myself so the thickness of the two of them combined hit me just right. Stars floated behind my eyes as they stilled, letting me control how fast and how much I took of them.

They groaned when I slid my hips back, taking them to the hilt.

Hayden squeezed my ass cheek, and I looked over my shoulder at him. He stared down at the place the three of us were connected, watching intently. Back and forth, in and out, I kept the rhythm going, loving every little noise they made, my pussy squeezing tight around the both of them together.

My orgasm started gradually, kept at bay by the others I'd already had perhaps, but a small, consistent nagging feeling that quickly grew the longer I kept the rhythm. I slowed down, dragging it out, wanting more. "Grayson."

He was sprawled out on the armchair, so entirely delicious. There was no trace of the professional doctor I knew he could be. That whole persona had disappeared, and in its place was a man whose eyes burned with desire, never looking away from me, never asking for more, even though I wanted to give it to him.

My gaze met his. "I want your dick in my mouth when I come."

Hawk chuckled from beneath me. "Little Mouse talking dirty. Fucking hell. All my Christmases just came at once." He glanced over at Grayson. "You gonna sit there jacking off or you gonna give the woman what she wants?"

Grayson jerked his head at Hawk. "Stop worrying about me and make her come already."

Hawk's chuckle turned into a laugh. "Don't worry. I've got that covered."

He slipped his fingers between our bodies, seeking out my clit and rubbing it in just the right way.

"I need to come," I moaned.

But I wanted Grayson in my mouth when I did.

All three men connected to me in some way. Taking something from each of them in the same way they'd all taken a piece of my heart. I pushed my weight up onto one hand, moaning as Hawk took the opportunity to suck on the breast in his face. His free hand slid up from my hips so he could play with both, alternating his mouth between nipples and driving me wild with a combination of licks and sucks and nips of his teeth.

I wrapped my free hand around Grayson's base and drew him close with it, stroking his erection, getting him fully hard again in seconds.

His fingers speared into the long lengths of my hair, and he scraped it back from my face, twisting it into a ponytail and then wrapping it around his fist. "This what you wanted, Kara?" he murmured, putting his cock to my lips. "You like sucking cock?"

There was no doubt in my mind that I did. And that his harsh, unromantic words did nothing but turn me on more.

Grayson pressed his dick past my lips, and I opened wide for him, drawing him in deep, taking him as far as I could, and loving the way he felt.

Hawk rewarded me with a long squeeze of my nipple. "That's my good girl. Taking all three of us. Fuck, Kara. You have no idea how beautiful you are."

But the thing was, for maybe the first time in my life, I think I did realize. I felt beautiful between the three of them. I was desired. *Wanted*. These men had done nothing for months but make me feel loved outside of bed, and now I was feeling it inside. They were giving me the space to explore what I liked, while guiding me gently, worshipping my body, and praising me every step of the way.

Grayson thrust in and out of my mouth, matching my rhythm, his grip on my hair getting tighter and tighter as he fell into his own pleasure. His abs constricted, the muscles there so delicious, his V lines a tease that drew my gaze lower. I worked him with my hand and my mouth, until his precum spread across my tongue, salty and tangy all at once.

Knowing he was close seemed to be the thing that dislodged my hold on my orgasm. I let feeling barrel through me, until I was panting, gasping, going blind with the need inside me.

"Fuck," Hayden groaned behind me. "You're so damn tight around my cock."

I was so full of all of them I couldn't even respond. Didn't need to. The way I moved had to tell them all that I was just as close.

Hayden gripped my hips, drawing me back, making each thrust punishing in the best way. Each slide of my hips had me grinding on both of them, every inch of my skin so sensitive it was impossible to keep going, and yet my orgasm taking hold demanded I didn't stop.

"Come for us, Kara." Hayden's command had me splintering apart, spasming around the two of them and moaning around Grayson's dick. His cum spurted across my tongue, and my knees shook.

Hawk and Hayden shouted out their own releases, groaning beneath and behind me, filling me with their liquid, while I swallowed down Grayson's.

Lights flashed across my vision, my whole body on fire in the best kind of way. Every inch of my skin had been touched, licked, stroked. Every fiber of my being responded now to the pleasure inside me, my blood sending the feeling around my body, creating a perfect storm of emotion and an experience I would never forget. I cried out as it all came together, muscles clenching and releasing, the orgasm taking hold and sending shock waves through all four of us. I moaned and gasped and shouted, all of it coming out a muffled mess of noises that made no sense because my brain was short-circuiting.

Spent, Grayson pulled his cock from my mouth and leaned down to kiss me, surely tasting himself on my tongue but clearly not caring. When he flopped back on the bed, I collapsed on Hawk, Chaos coming down on top of me, all three of us still connected, until they were soft enough to drift out of my body.

Chaos rolled to one side to avoid squashing me, but I had nothing left in me to give. I just breathed with my head on Hawk's chest, listening to his heart, one hand reached out to stroke Grayson's arm, my foot against Hayden's leg.

"That was perfect," I whispered sleepily. "Thank you."

Grayson rubbed his fingers across the back of my hand.

Hawk rolled us over so I was on my back and he was

hovering above me. "I love you, Little Mouse. You and your sweet fucking pussy." His dick nudged me there, but neither of us had the stamina to go again. Hawk didn't seem put off by that though. "Give me twenty minutes and I'm going to go down on you again."

But I knew I couldn't. It would be almost midnight by now. I needed to get my things and get on a bus.

"I need a break first. You guys stay. I need to go get some water."

Grayson shook his head. "I'll get some for you."

But I pushed him back down. "I need the bathroom as well. And I want to check my phone and make sure there are no messages from Rebel."

That was yet another lie, but I needed them to stay here, so I could slip away. I hadn't had a chance to say goodbye to Queenie and I just couldn't leave without giving her one last hug. She was important to me, and I needed her to take care of them all while I was gone.

I stood and put my clothes on, taking one last look at the three of them, before slipping away into the darkness.

I hurried through the maze, knowing the way now, and letting myself back inside the restaurant.

If anyone had noticed us missing, they didn't say. The party was still in full swing, with drinks flowing and everyone dancing. I spotted Queenie at a standing table, chatting with Ice and the other prospects. My heart squeezed. I really loved this woman. She was the kind of mother I wanted to be, despite not having any children of her own. She'd shown me and Hayley Jade nothing but kindness and care, in a way my own mother never really had.

At least not since Josiah had come into our lives.

Queenie's gaze met mine, and I raised a hand, motioning for her to come to me.

She squeezed Ice's arm and walked away, threading through the crowd to my side. Her expression fell the closer she got, clearly feeding off the negative energy I was surely putting out. "What's wrong, sugar? You good?"

I shook my head, suddenly battling to keep it together.

She sighed, like she could see right into my head, and led me back down the hallway to the ladies' room, which was miraculously empty. She slid the lock in place so nobody else could come in.

"Someone might need to use the facilities," I whispered, barely able to keep the tears out of my voice. This goodbye was going to be as hard as the one I'd just said with my body to my men. Maybe harder, because I didn't have an orgasm to distract me from how much leaving this club hurt.

"They're just going to have to use the men's room then. Or pee their little panties. Because clearly you need this space more than they do."

I swallowed hard. "I'm leaving."

Queenie sighed.

I cocked my head to one side. "You don't seem surprised."

She took my hand, leading me away from the door. "I'm not. Because I know you. Child, you think I'm blind? I've seen the agony in your face ever since Josiah put that reward out for your return."

"I have to go back. Not just to keep Hayley Jade safe,

but to find the evidence we need to put Josiah away for Alice's murder. That's the only way I get to be free."

Queenie pressed her lips together. "A lot have things have changed about you since you came here, Kara. But your selflessness isn't one of them. And I don't know that it's a good thing in this case."

But there was no choice. If I let Hawk and Hayden deal with it, they'd be the ones in prison. If I stayed, everyone I loved was in danger and I'd always be looking over my shoulder.

That was no way to live.

It was me who needed to end this. On my own terms. I drew my shoulders back and stared the older woman in the eye. "I need you to take care of them for me." I swallowed hard, shoving away the lump in my throat so I could speak. "Please. Don't let them come after me. I won't come back with them. Don't let Hayley Jade forget how much I love her. That I never stopped. Never will."

Queenie brushed tears off my face. I didn't even realize I'd been crying.

Eventually, she nodded. "I'll do that."

Surprise lit up inside me. "You will? I thought for sure you'd argue with me. Try to convince me there was another way—"

Queenie held up one finger and then unzipped the purse at her hip. She rifled through it, clearly searching for something. "I didn't finish. I'll do that, if you do one thing for me first."

I nodded quickly, ready to agree to anything. I just needed to know someone would be looking out for them when I wasn't here. "Whatever you want."

She placed a familiar stick in my hand. One I'd seen

only once before, around six years earlier, not long after I'd left Ethereal Eden for the first time. I snapped my head up in surprise.

But Queenie's eyes were all knowing. "I'll pick up the pieces after you leave. Love Hayley Jade like she's my own damn daughter. You know I will. But only if you can prove to me right now you aren't taking another child back into that hellhole."

I stared down at the pregnancy test. "I'm not pregnant."

Her eyes scrutinized me. "Then prove it. I've had that in my purse for a week now, knowing this moment was coming, and knowing this would be the only way to stop you from being a fool and sacrificing yourself."

"I can't get pregnant," I insisted, pushing the test back at her. "My husband and I tried for five years, and never once..."

Queenie's eagle-eyed gaze wouldn't let up. "Don't be dumb, Kara. You're too smart for that. You have a child. You can get pregnant. Maybe the problem was never you but him."

I shook my head. "His other wives have children. Hayley Jade's birth was so traumatic, I must have damaged—"

"Or those other women saw what was happening to you and found other ways of getting a baby in their bellies."

I stared at Queenie. "They would never..."

She shook her head. "People will do anything for self-preservation. If I'd been one of those women, watching you get beat and raped and punished for not giving that man a child, then I would do whatever it took as well. Or maybe it's just the combination of you and him that didn't work. I don't know. But what I do know is I will not stand by and watch another child go through what Hayley Jade did. And I know you won't either." She handed the test back to me. "Take the test, Kara."

13

HAYDEN

The Sinners door closed behind Kara, and I sat up quickly, not wanting her out of my sight. "It's tonight."

Hawk blinked sleepily and twisted his head, stretching his arms over his shoulders. "What is?"

"I found her backpack in the back of my truck when I went out to get some supplies earlier. She's going to do it tonight. I'm sure of it."

Hawk jerked up off the bed. "Are you for fucking real? And you wait until now to say something?"

"Where exactly do you think she was going when she was impaled on our cocks?"

Hawk glared at me, and I rolled my eyes, dragging on my shirt. "I didn't want to ruin your party, okay? And I've been watching her."

Grayson got to his feet in a rushed scrabble. "Shit." He searched around the floor for his clothes, tossing us articles that didn't belong to him. "I really didn't want it to come to this. I really hoped she wouldn't do it."

Hawk yanked up boxer briefs that I actually thought were mine, but I wasn't going to complain about in the moment. Wearing his underwear was hardly the worst thing to happen, considering I'd had my mouth all over him just minutes earlier.

"She's not fucking leaving," he swore bitterly. "I should have just said that to her."

I shook my head. "And make yet another decision for her? We did everything we could. Gave her all the reasons to stay."

"Well, apparently that wasn't enough, was it?" Hawk was visibly stressed, and I was sure my expression was nearly identical.

Panic coursed through me at the idea of Kara walking out those doors and never coming back.

Gray shot both of us stern doctor sort of looks. "You both need to keep your shit together. You can't just demand she stays."

"Yes, I fucking can." Hawk shoved one foot into his boot.

Grayson bumped his shoulder hard enough to get his attention. "Drop the hothead act. It's not helping."

"Well, neither is your shrink bullshit! This was the worst plan ever!"

Hawk was spiraling because of how in love with her he was. We could all see it, but Grayson didn't have the connection with him to stop it.

I did.

I caught Hawk's arm as he stormed toward the door, pulling him to a stop against the wall.

He tried to shove me off, but I wouldn't let him, pinning him again and again. "Settle the fuck down."

"We're wasting time!"

"You're panicking."

His gaze finally settled on mine. "I can't have her back there."

I understood the feeling. It had embedded itself deep in my bones.

Gray was the one who spoke up though. "None of us can. But short of tying her up, which frankly, I'm not willing to let any of you do, we need to let her decide that for herself."

The fear inside me swelled until it was a roar in my ears. I needed to get out there. Find her. Beg her not to go, because clearly us subtly giving her reasons to stay wasn't working. The ASL classes at the school. The hospital job offer. Grayson had been the one to come to us and voice concerns that he thought she was planning to run. And as soon as it had been pointed out, it was all I could see, each of her actions preparing herself and the rest of us for her departure.

We'd all agreed we'd let her come to her own decision, but now time was up.

All we had left was begging. I wasn't above getting down on my knees and pleading for her not to walk out of my life.

The three of us stormed out of the maze, back into the party.

"I don't see her," Gray murmured, panic seeping into his voice. "Shit, what if she already left?"

I checked my watch. It was still twenty minutes before the last bus out of town. I'd looked at the timetable the minute I'd seen her bag in my truck. "She still has twenty minutes, and that bus stop is only a few yards down the road. She surely hasn't left yet."

Hawk grabbed War's arm. "Have you seen Kara?"

War shook his head, but Bliss rolled her eyes. "Men are so unobservant. I saw her and Queenie go down to the bathroom just before. They haven't come out yet, I don't think."

All three of us turned on our heels and rushed for the bathroom door.

Hawk leaned on it, but when it didn't give way beneath his weight, he smashed his fist against it. "Kara!"

There was no reply from inside, and his panic eventually got to me, despite me telling him just seconds before he needed to keep it together. I joined in with the banging. "Kara! Are you in there?"

She needed to still be here. I needed to tell her I loved her. Tell her I couldn't live without her. Tell her we could take Hayley Jade and move to another goddamn country if we had to, but running back to Josiah wasn't an option.

I loved her too much. Wanted a life with her. To marry her. Have babies with her.

I'd wanted all of that from the moment she'd put her trust in me five years ago and let a stupid street thug deliver her baby into a world that wasn't good enough for either of them.

Gray paced the hallway behind us, quieter than me and Hawk, his expression pained.

"Kara. Please," I begged.

"Yeah, yeah, hold your damn horses!" Queenie shouted from the other side.

The lock clicked, disengaging.

I had to grab Hawk to stop him from slamming open the door and hitting the women standing behind it.

Queenie came out first, one eyebrow raised, and shook her head, like the three of us were utterly ridiculous. "You're all so damn pussy-whipped."

I didn't care if I was. I would happily claim that title.

But then she grinned and nudged me. "Looks good on all of you. She deserves that sort of devotion."

I already knew that. Kara just needed to accept it.

Queenie moved aside, and Kara was standing behind her, her eyes huge as she took in the three of us crowded around the door.

God, she was so effortlessly beautiful. With barely any makeup, in simple jeans and a top, her hair a mess, I'd never seen anyone more stunning. I couldn't even speak. And clearly Hawk was having the same troubles, trying to get his emotions under control enough to talk.

Grayson spoke for us. "You can't leave."

If it were even possible, Kara's eyes got even wider. She opened her mouth but didn't get a word out.

Grayson cut her off. "I think you know we're all in love with you. And we know you think you need to go back to him. But I'm begging you not to. I wanted to give you the space you needed, hoping you'd change your mind, but all I have left is asking you not to go. For me." He cleared his throat. "And if not for me, for them. For Hayley Jade. For your sister and all the other people here your leaving will destroy."

She glanced at me. "You knew I was going to leave?"

"Yes."

She turned to Hawk; her surprise written all over her heart-shaped face. "But none of you said anything?"

There was a low growl in his voice. "That wasn't my choice. I wanted to chain you to the bed and give you orgasms 'til I wore down your resolve, but I was told I couldn't make decisions for you. That it needed to come from you." He glared at Gray. "That was a shit call by the way."

He threw up his hands. "It was the right call! She's a grown woman. You can't take away her agency."

Hawk reared back. "Her agency? What the fuck does that even mean? Quit using your doctor speak and talk English."

I ignored their bickering, cupped her cheek, and pressed my forehead to hers. "Don't fucking go, Kara. Just don't."

She pressed something into my hand.

I glanced down at it.

A pregnancy test. Two faint lines and the word positive on the display.

My fingers shook. My head snapped up to meet hers. "You're…"

Grayson and Hawk both realized something was going on and quieted, their gazes swiveling in our direction. I silently held out the pregnancy test.

Hawk squinted at it. "What is that?"

Grayson just stared at it; his body frozen.

Kara's voice was barely more than a whisper. "I'm pregnant."

The two of them stood stock-still, shock written all over their expressions.

But warmth kernelled inside me. A sweet, slow, perfect feeling creeping its way through my limbs until it wrapped itself around my body. It pulled at my lips, turning them up into a smile, and then a grin. I stared at her, down at her belly that was no different than it had been earlier but somehow just was. I put my hand there, stroking over her shirt with my thumb. "You're pregnant?"

Her fingers shook, but she covered my hand with hers. "Yes."

Hawk looked like he was about to pass out. But he grabbed her chin, tilting her head in his direction, and claimed her lips. He kissed her hot and hard, a branding, demanding kiss that was all him. Bossy. Arrogant. So fucking in love with her it was killing him.

He pulled back an inch, his lips barely hovering over hers. "You aren't going back there with a baby in your belly."

She shook her head. "No. I'm not."

The relief shattered the air around us. Hawk slumped back against the wall and pressed the heels of his hands to his eyes. I doubled over, breathing hard, not even realizing I'd been holding my breath, waiting for her answer.

Grayson moved in and gathered her into his arms, cradling her head as she began to cry, tears rolling down her face while her shoulders shook. "What are we going to do?"

He kissed the top of her head. "Live. Have a baby. Love it."

She smiled through her tears. "I want that. I don't know how we can have it, but I want it."

"We'll get it for you." He smoothed a hand down her back as he made the promise. "We'll work it out."

Kara buried her face in her hands. "I don't even know whose baby it is. None of us have been very careful." Pink flushed her cheeks.

I shrugged. "Gotta be either mine or Hawk's, right? Grayson's only been around for five minutes."

Grayson cleared his throat. "First time we were together was two and a half weeks ago. That's plenty long enough for it to be mine. Depends how far along she is."

Hawk scoffed. "It's mine for sure. I was planting those seeds long before either of you came along." He grinned, twisting her hips so she was facing him. "Can't wait to see that baby stretch your belly. Fucking hell. I'm gonna be a dad."

"Or I will be," I interjected. "Kara better hope he's not yours. If your ego is genetic, this kid's head is going to be ginormous."

Hawk gave me his favorite middle finger.

Kara glanced nervously between each of us. "Will it matter? Whose baby it is, I mean? Does this..." She glanced down at the floor.

But I'd seen the fear in her eyes. I knew exactly what she was worried about. I put my fingers beneath her chin and tilted her face up to meet my gaze. "It changes nothing for me. I'll love any baby we have because he or she is a part of you. If it's Hawk's or Grayson's, it doesn't matter. I'm still in."

"Me too," Hawk said without hesitation. "It'll be better looking if it's mine though."

Kara laughed and wiped her eyes as she turned to Grayson. "What about you? If I have a baby by another man—"

"Then I'll love it just as much as I love Hayley Jade." He cupped her cheek. "I want *you*, Kara. When I told you I loved you, I meant it. That doesn't suddenly change because you're pregnant."

She shook her head quickly, pressing up on her toes to kiss him. "I don't want to lose you. I want you to be okay with this. Them. Me. The baby. All of it."

He kissed her gently, then grinned against her mouth. "I'm having a baby." He glanced at Hawk and me. "Holy shit, *we're* having a baby! I can buy the baby her first stethoscope! Oh, her first pair of baby-sized scrubs! Crap, I need to learn how to make new glove balloon animals. She's going to get sick of the rooster pretty quick, isn't she?"

All three of us stared at him, knowing the odds of him being this baby's father were probably on the slim side.

But Grayson didn't care. He shrugged. "What? I can't want my kid to be a doctor too?"

Hawk rolled his eyes. "Fine by me, as long as he can still ride a bike."

"And make a decent meal," I added.

Kara just smiled softly, and in her eyes, I knew this baby had just saved her.

Saved all of us.

14

KARA

Hayden kissed my neck and fit himself behind me, waking me up sweetly and gently, morning sun streaming through my bedroom window.

I ground my ass back against him, loving the feel of him hard behind me, and his warm hands trailing over my bare skin. He flattened his palm on my belly and rubbed slow circles there, while his breath misted across my shoulders. "I can't believe you're pregnant."

I shook my head. "Me neither. Last night feels like a daze." I reached for the test on the nightstand and checked the little display window again. I held it up so Hayden could see it over my shoulder. "It still says pregnant."

He chuckled and plucked it from my fingers, putting it back where I'd found it. "How many times during the night did you look at that thing?"

I laughed softly. "At least three. Sorry. I tried to be

quiet about it. Will you take me to get some more pregnancy tests today? Just in case that one is wrong?"

A sick fear swirled in my stomach at the very thought that maybe it was a false positive. If I hadn't peed on the stick myself and watched it react, I would have accused Queenie of rigging it, just to get me to stay.

But I'd been there. That test was so very positive it was impossible to deny.

I put my hand over Hayden's on my belly, pressing his hand tight to my skin. "I so want this to be real."

He rolled me over so I was facing him, his beautiful eyes focused solely on me. "Hey. It is real. You aren't dreaming. You're having a baby." He grinned. "Not sure how I didn't notice your tits are bigger."

I stared down at them excitedly. "Seriously? Do you think so? I have no pregnancy symptoms. No morning sickness or tiredness." I just wanted some sign to tell me the test hadn't gotten my hopes up for no reason.

Hayden slid down the bed to bury his face in the plump swells of my breasts. "Trust me, I spend a lot of time every day memorizing each curve of your body. I can see the differences."

I was sure he was pulling my leg. I was probably very early pregnant, and that was the most likely reason why I hadn't noticed. In a few weeks I'd probably have my head over the toilet bowl every morning.

I grinned at the thought. I couldn't wait.

Something inside me was so victorious. Healed by this tiny baby growing inside me. I'd spent five years feeling so incredibly broken and sad. Robbed of the chance to ever be a mother, first by men who took my child from me, and then by my own body.

I allowed myself a tiny bit of hope. A quick daydream of bringing this baby home to an extended family who loved it, and men who would fight tooth and nail to keep me and my children together.

Everything about the first time was so wrong. Wrong man. Wrong time. Wrong place.

And yet I wouldn't be here now, with my beautiful daughter, three men who loved me, and a second child on the way if it hadn't been for all the heartache.

Suddenly, I knew I wouldn't change my past, even if I could.

How could I, when changing something back then would mean I wasn't here right now?

My mind whirled with everything that needed to happen next. "We need to go to the doctor. Get scans done. Blood tests."

Hayden nodded. "First thing Monday. But until then, while Hayley Jade is still at Rebel's place..."

His dick slid between my legs and slowly up inside me.

I murmured a sigh of pleasure and hooked my leg over his, opening myself up and drawing him closer.

Thumps came from the door. "Quit fucking and get out here. Grayson's here. Says we have to study for the GED."

I groaned, Hayden buried inside me to the hilt and my pussy throbbing around him, not nearly satisfied. "Tell him I'll be there in a minute."

Hawk's voice was practically a growl. "No minutes. I need you out here now because if I know what you're doing in there, I'm going to come in and join you. We all know I'm lasting a whole lot longer than Hayden 'limp dick' Whitling. We don't have time to fuck all day. The GED isn't waiting for your libidos to be satisfied."

Hayden flipped off the door, but his gaze and words were for me. "As much as I'd love to keep you in here, tied to my bed until the sun goes down, he's right. With the baby coming, you're both going to need to get as much studying done as you can. It's going to be harder when he's here and so fucking cute we just want to snuggle him all day."

"Him?" I asked with a gentle smile. "Grayson seemed pretty convinced it was a girl last night."

"Hayley Jade has been my girl since the day she was born. It needs to be a boy. I can't imagine loving another little girl the same way."

I kissed his lips softly. "You would."

"Mmmm. But I do think it's a boy. Do you have a preference?"

I shook my head quickly.

Except in my heart, I knew that was a lie.

There was a tiny part of me that was terrified of having a boy for the sole reason that if Josiah ever found out, it would give him all the more reason to come after me.

If this baby was a boy, he could try claiming it as his. His followers wouldn't ask for a paternity test. All they would care about was Josiah's first wife had finally born his heir.

I didn't voice my fears. Didn't want to burden any of the guys with the dangerous thoughts rattling around inside my brain.

It was trauma talking. Fear. Anxiety.

I pressed my hand to my belly harder.

Nobody was taking this baby away from me. Not this time. Not for one minute.

Showered and dressed, Hayden and I emerged from his bedroom twenty minutes later to find Grayson, Hawk, and oddly, Kyle, sitting at the big common room table in the Slayers' clubhouse.

Papers, textbooks, and laptops were spread all over the tabletop in a messy array, pens and highlighters everywhere the eye could see.

Kyle stood as I entered the room. "Hi, Kara. How are you feeling today? Can I get you a tea?"

Hawk eyed him lazily. "She's feeling like you should quit brown-nosing and keep writing out those study notes." Then he leaned back on his chair to reach out and grab the long fabric of my flowy skirt. "Hey, Little Mouse. You want a tea?"

I giggled and nodded, rolling my eyes when Hawk shouted for one of the prospects to bring out a mug rather than getting up to get it himself.

"What?" he asked when he saw the look on my face. "I've got studying to do. And so do you. Don't give me a hard time for using the resources I have. That's just good time management."

I raised an eyebrow. "Oh. Time management, huh? That's why Kyle is writing notes for you?" I leaned over the table and kissed Grayson sitting beside the younger man. "Hi, you."

He cupped the side of my face. "Hi, beautiful."

Hawk glared at him.

I squinted. "Really? After last..." I remembered Kyle was in the room and didn't need to know every detail of what Hawk, Hayden, Grayson, and I had done last night. "After everything, you're getting cranky with him for touching me?"

Hawk shook his head. "I'm not cranky. I'm pissed he didn't stick up for me and tell you Lyle here isn't taking notes for me."

Kyle cleared his throat. "Um. It's Kyle..."

Hawk glared at him. "I think now it's Pile. As in pile of shi—"

I gave him a disapproving look. "Be nice. For once."

He rolled his eyes and patted Kyle none too gently on the back. "*Kyle* has decided to take the GED with us."

"You have? That's great, Kyle!" I raised my hand for a high five.

He slapped it back super gently, with a fearful glance at Hawk, like if he hit me too hard Hawk might have his head.

Which to be fair, was probably not far from the truth.

I doubted Hawk was ever going to lose his overprotective ways, even if we had let other men into our bed.

I settled into a chair, and Grayson ran over some of the material with all three of us. To Hawk's credit, he took the study session way more seriously than I thought he would, and I smiled, watching him ask Grayson for help with one question, and the two of them with their heads together, talking through the problem together.

They figured it out and my heart squeezed at the bright smile that lit up both their faces.

Grayson was a natural-born teacher, excited and

eager to help us, and Hawk had found a focus I'd never seen in him before.

I could practically see the daydreams of becoming an EMT or a paramedic dancing in front of his eyes. Having a real ability to help people when they were at their lowest.

I wanted that too, but without the pressure of an emergency situation. Hawk would thrive on that. But I didn't need that level of stress.

Hours passed with me diligently taking notes on a notepad because I didn't have much experience with computers, and it felt like more hassle than it was worth to try to learn right then and there. Smells wafted from the kitchen, and we all started getting distracted as they grew stronger.

Hawk grumbled beneath his breath. "Ugh, he's making chili, isn't he? If he tells us it's for the restaurant tonight and not for us to eat right now, I'm going to have to end this relationship."

Grayson put his highlighter down. "Very dramatic of you."

"You haven't tasted his chili. It's the best fucking thing I've ever eaten. He made his own recipe, and I swear, the thing should have earned him at least two Michelin stars, it's that delicious. And he does this side of mashed potatoes with rosemary and garlic and..."

Gray listened with a small smirk lifting the corners of his mouth.

Hawk finally quit going on about Hayden's food and threw an eraser at Grayson's face. "Shut up."

Gray laughed. "I didn't say a word."

"You didn't have to. Your face said plenty."

"I'm just glad the two of you got your shit together enough to be happy."

"Me too," I added. "You and Hayden are really good together."

A blush crept up Hawk's neck, but he tried covering it by dragging me onto his lap. "Not as good as me and you. Should we show everyone exactly how good we are together, Little Mouse?" He rocked me over his lap just enough for me to feel the slight hardening of his cock. "Show everyone here how hot it gets when you ride my cock with your tits in my face."

Kyle's chair scraped back over the polished concrete floors, and he stood, gathering up his papers in a hurry. "I should go. I can finish studying in my cabin."

Hawk grinned around me. "Sit, Kyle."

Kyle sat back on the seat like a well-trained dog. "Yes, sir."

I elbowed Hawk behind me. "Stop. You're traumatizing him."

Poor Kyle looked like a deer caught in the headlights, no idea which way to turn.

Hawk leaned back in his chair, taking me with him so I was leaning on his chest as Hayden wandered out with big plates full of food.

Kyle gratefully pounced on a bowl, but Hawk wasn't done teasing him. "You got a girlfriend, kid?"

Kyle shook his head. "No, sir."

Hawk rolled his eyes at the sir title but didn't correct him, clearly more interested in digging into Kyle's personal life. "You're out in the big, wide world now. Don't you want to...sample a little of what's on offer?"

Kyle shook his head quickly. "I'm fine here."

"You're hiding."

I slapped Hawk's leg. "You told him he had to stay here until you trusted him! He hasn't left the compound once since he arrived!"

Hawk tilted his head to one side. "Did I?"

Everyone else nodded.

Hawk grinned. "Oops. My bad. Damn. So what, you haven't gotten laid in like, weeks?"

A blush crept up Kyle's neck. "I haven't gotten laid ever, sir."

Hawk sat up straighter. "Wait. What? You're a virgin? Aren't you like twenty?"

"Nearly."

Hayden put a bowl of food in Hawk's hand. "Leave the kid alone. It's not a big deal to be a virgin at twenty."

"Like hell it's not!" Hawk protested. "Kyle. Seriously. Do you have any idea what you're missing? The sweet heat of a pussy wrapped around your cock. Your woman's clit on your tongue. Her screaming your name while you bend her over a table and take her hard and fast from behind..."

His dick was so hard beneath me, I had to fight to keep my breath even at the very thought of having him bend me over a table.

Grayson leaned back and smiled at Kyle, whose face was starting to resemble a tomato. "Being a virgin at your age is nothing to feel ashamed of. If you aren't ready—"

"I'm ready," Kyle cut in quickly.

Hawk laughed, slapping a palm down on the tabletop. "Kid is horny as fuck. Don't worry, we take care of our family here. We'll get you a girl." He twisted around toward the hallway. "Amber! Kiki! Fancy!"

My mouth dropped open. "Fancy! Hawk, she's got to be sixty years old! She's War's mother! Are you trying to get Kyle killed?"

Hawk was clearly finding himself hilarious. And I had to admit, the expression on Kyle's face was funny. I'd come to learn this sort of teasing was normal within these walls. All the men did it, paying out on each other for laughs. I'd begun to realize it was how they showed affection. Though Grayson with his PhD in psychiatry would surely have something to say about how unhealthy that was.

Thankfully, none of the women appeared to be home, and Hawk held up his hands in mock surrender. "Okay, okay. Probably a bit much for one of the club girls to be your first. Or War's mom."

Kyle's face was pale. "I don't mean any disrespect to Ms. Fancy, but..."

I squeezed my eyes shut at Kyle and just shook my head. He just needed to be quiet right now and not give Hawk any more fodder.

Hayden cleared his throat, a hint of understanding in his tone. "Kyle, if you want to find someone, you aren't limited to the women who hang out here. Get on one of the dating apps."

Hawk didn't try to hide his groan of disgust. "Whatever happened to going to a bar and just going home with some smokeshow? Or not even getting that far? Just fucking her right there in the parking lot..."

I raised an eyebrow. "Really? Is that how you want your future son-in-law to treat Hayley Jade when she's old enough?"

Hawk's eyes darkened. "I will gut and kill any man

who even peeks at her in a bar. Or on the street. Or... Ever."

I rolled my eyes. "Great, so we'll just be blindfolding the entire male population once she turns sixteen, will we?"

Grayson paused with his spoon halfway to his mouth. "It's not a bad idea."

Hawk nodded in agreement. "I see no problem with that."

"Me neither, just saying." Hayden seemed like he was in pain at the very thought of Hayley Jade dating someday.

Poor kid. With the three of them in her life, she was never going to be able to meet a boy.

But it was also a little bit cute.

"Can we get back to the idea of Kyle dating?" I changed the subject. "One of those dating apps doesn't seem like a bad idea. It's hard to meet nice people."

Hawk snorted. "I'm laughing at you thinking you might meet 'nice' people on one of those apps. Nice for a night, maybe."

I ignored him and focused on Kyle, who really was looking at me like I was a lifeline. He was clearly lonely, and I felt awful for not seeing it sooner. I'd been so wrapped up in my own problems, I hadn't even noticed he'd been isolating himself, not even coming up to the clubhouse. He'd spent his last few teenage years inside one prison, and we'd basically locked him in another with no one else his age. He didn't know a single person in this state, other than the people inside this clubhouse. "Ignore them. Download an app. Meet some people. You don't have to…um…do more with them if you don't want to."

Kyle pulled his phone out of his pocket and ran his thumb over the screen, scrolling. "I don't even know which one is good."

Hawk shrugged, leaning over to peer at his screen. "Fuck, why are there so many? Just download any of them. Wait. Just use that one. It says it's already on your phone."

Kyle screwed up his face. "No, it's not."

Hayden took a peep over his shoulder when Kyle held it out to him. "App store says otherwise."

Kyle's eyebrows knit together in confusion as he stabbed at the screen. "I swear, I've never seen that app before. It's not on my phone."

He'd piqued my interest now too, and I got off Hawk's lap to peer over Kyle's shoulder. There was no dating app on the main screen, but there were a number of folders. I pointed at the search bar. "Just search the app name. Maybe your phone came preloaded with it."

He nodded, putting in the app name in the search bar.

It popped up instantly.

Hawk slung his arm around the back of Kyle's chair. "Who have you been swiping right on?" He squinted. "Or is it swiping left? I don't know."

"I haven't been swiping on anything, I swear." Kyle shook his head, clearly thoroughly confused.

Hayden patted him on the shoulder. "Then why do you have an account already logged in?"

We were all crowded around him by this point. But Kyle seemed completely bewildered.

"I honestly have no idea. There's a bunch of chats here and everything, but they're all usernames. No legal names." He held the phone out. "Here. Look. It's weird."

Hayden took it, scrolling through the pages of private messages. "You aren't TulipRose1254?"

Kyle made a face at him. "Last I checked, no."

Hayden passed the phone to Grayson with a shrug. "I don't get it then. What is all this?"

Grayson raised an eyebrow. "And you think I get dating apps?"

Hawk sniggered. "There's a doctor, two ex-cult members, a biker, and an ex-gang leader sitting at this table. Out of all of us, who do we think is going to be most likely to understand a dating app?"

We all turned to stare at Grayson.

"Yeah, okay fine. Let me see it." He took the phone, glanced at the screen and then back at Kyle. "You definitely have an account set up under the name TulipRose. If that's not you, then someone has been using your phone. Your mom maybe?"

Kyle screwed up his face. "Oh, absolutely not. Come on. She's one hundred years old and married."

"She's maybe forty-five, Kyle," I corrected. Though I totally understood how much older parents seemed when you were a teenager without any kids of your own. Having a baby and getting older yourself changed that mentality. Fact was, forty-five wasn't even close to old, and Kyle's mom very well could have been using his phone to contact a lover on the outside. She'd allowed Kyle to keep a secret phone, even though they were banned at Ethereal Eden. She clearly wasn't as devoted to the rules as they made out.

But Kyle adamantly shook his head. "My mom wouldn't do that to my dad. And she never had my phone that I know of. But..." He glanced at me.

"What? I didn't take your phone."

"No. But Alice did. A lot."

Shock punched me in the stomach, but at the same time, this suddenly made a lot more sense. The day we'd fled from Ethereal Eden in Kyle's truck, Alice had asked Kyle to use his phone. She'd known the password, and it was clear to me even then that it hadn't been her first time using the device. She'd been too familiar with it, putting in the code and tapping her fingers across the screen confidently.

I took the phone from Grayson's hand and scrolled through the pages and pages of texts. Here and there were messages from random usernames, but mostly, TulipRose talked with one other user.

I tapped on one of her chats with GoldenDreams and skimmed over the paragraphs of text.

In my head, it was Alice's voice I heard reading them out loud. "Alice wrote these. They sound just like her."

My gaze snagged on one message, dated the same day we'd left Ethereal Eden. The message opened up.

Alice's message stopped me dead, the phone tumbling from my fingers and crashing onto the tabletop face up for everyone to see.

TULIPROSE:

We're here. I'm so excited. I can't wait to meet you.

GOLDEN:

> Sneak away as soon as you can. Meet me at Sixth Street in the city. It's a club. I can't wait to meet you either.

I stared at the phone in horror and then up at the men sitting around me. "She was meeting someone the night she was murdered."

Grayson swallowed thickly. "What are the odds of being murdered by someone you know?"

Hawk pressed his lips together. "Way higher than being murdered by a complete stranger." He glanced at me, but I already knew what he was going to say before he said it.

"We might have the text messages Alice sent her killer."

15

KARA

I read my sister's texts in every spare minute for the next few days. In between helping Hayley Jade take a bath and cooking her dinner. On every break from the hospital. At night before I went to bed and in the mornings as soon as I woke up.

There were hundreds, if not thousands of them, dating back around a year. And they quickly became an obsession I couldn't quit.

As I read through each of them, I watched my sister fall in love.

And my heart broke, knowing it was all a lie. That every message she received was one that brought her closer to her death.

Gray rolled over in my bed and propped himself up on one arm, hand beneath this head. "What's Golden gaslighting her with today?"

I glanced over at him. "Sorry. I didn't mean to wake you."

"You didn't. But I'm getting worried about you. Did

you even sleep last night or were you up all night reading their texts again?"

I'd slept a little, but it was hard when they were all I could think about. There was just so many of them. Kyle had admitted Alice had borrowed his phone for at least an hour a day, for a very long time, and that she'd had a spot out in the fields, away from prying eyes where she liked to go with it.

Kyle had apologized a thousand times. He'd thought he was being a friend. He was so in love with her, he would have given her anything she'd asked for. Not that he'd admitted that, but it was clear to the rest of us.

I twisted onto my side, facing Gray, Kyle's phone in my hand between us. "I just need to get through them all so we can go to the police. I know they'll confiscate the phone as soon as we report this, but I need to read them first."

He kissed my lips softly. "No one is blaming you for wanting to read them. You have every right. I just don't want you making yourself sick over them."

I swallowed hard. "I should have paid more attention to what she was doing."

He sighed. "You've been saying things like that for days. But it wasn't your job to keep tabs on her."

"I was so self-centered. Always focused on myself."

He snaked a hand to the back of my neck and held me tight so I couldn't look away. "You were fighting for your life. You were imprisoned by a man who beat you, belittled you, and withheld basic needs. You were in survival mode. Nobody is blaming you for what happened to Alice."

Nobody but me.

Nothing had even changed since I'd left Ethereal Eden. I'd spent more time focused on myself and the danger and drama I seemed to attract, rather than finding the person who'd murdered my sister.

I'd failed her in so many ways.

Reading these texts was agony, each one ripping away a piece of my heart, but it was a pain I deserved for not being the sister she needed when she was alive.

GOLDEN:

Hey, sweetheart. Missed hearing from you this morning. Hurts my heart when I don't wake up to messages from you on my phone.

TULIP:

I'm so sorry! Had a really busy night. My hands are killing me today after typing all day yesterday. Was working right up until my head hit the pillow. Couldn't get the phone from Kyle until now. I missed you too. What are you up to today?

GOLDEN:

Who's Kyle?

TULIP:

A friend. It's his phone. I told you, we aren't allowed phones here, so I have to borrow his.

GOLDEN:

You can't have a phone but he can?

TULIP:

Well, neither of us can, but he's a rebel like that.

GOLDEN:

So are you. My little badass. Wish I could see a photo of you.

TULIP:

I barely get enough signal out here for texts.

GOLDEN:

Can't you just connect to the Wi-Fi? I really want to see you.

TULIP:

I wish it were that easy. The only Wi-Fi here is locked, and we aren't allowed to know the password. Josiah says the internet is what got the world in the state it's in now and it's rotting our brains.

GOLDEN:

He's probably not wrong. The world is fucked up.

TULIP:

My world is. But you're out there, with the freedom to do anything. Go anywhere. Josiah keeps us in a prison.

GOLDEN:

Sounds like he's just trying to protect you. You have it better than you think. Having someone who cares about you and keeps you safe. Having a community who all works together and shares to provide for all members. People who protect you. Those are all good things.

TULIP:

> I guess so. I just want to explore the world though. I don't want to be kept safe. I want to get out and experience things. Travel. Eat foods I've never tried before. Learn...

TULIP:

> Meet you.

TULIP:

> Kiss you.

TULIP:

> I'm sorry. That was very forward of me.

TULIP:

> I've made this into something it's not, haven't I? This is so embarrassing.

TULIP:

> Don't mind me, I'll just be throwing myself into oncoming traffic.

GOLDEN:

> How will I kiss you back if you've been smushed by a semi-trailer?

I sighed when Grayson plucked the phone from my hand and pushed his finger at the space between my eyebrows. "That frown is going to end up permanent."

I kissed his mouth. "I know a doctor. He can probably hook me up with some Botox."

He kissed me back, pulling me into his arms. "That doctor thinks you're perfect just the way you are. Frown and all. But you know what that doctor doesn't want?"

"To stop talking about himself in the third person?" I suggested cheekily.

He grinned, his smile warm and sweet and turning

his face boyish. "That doctor doesn't want you giving yourself an ulcer from stress. Let's leave this for today. Hayley Jade is at school. We both have the day off from the hospital. Hawk too. We should go do something."

I traced my fingers over his chest. "We should probably study."

Grayson squinted at me. "That's very responsible."

"'Responsible' is my middle name. And I think it's yours too."

He groaned. "It is. Fine. But I really do think you need to get out of this clubhouse and into the fresh air. It's a nice day outside. We can pack your books up and hike up to this spot I know. It'll be quiet, since it's a weekday, and we can pack a picnic and study in the sunshine." He pointed at the phone. "No signal out there, so you won't even have a reason to take that thing. Nothing but sun, exercise, and learning."

It actually sounded really nice. And Grayson was right, I definitely needed a break from obsessing over Alice's texts. "Deal. You go have a shower and get ready while I tell Hawk."

Grayson saluted me and walked backward, naked, to the shower.

I grinned at the sway of his dick and his goofy expression, all while appreciating the fact he always watched out for me.

Hawk was just walking back in the front door and tossed the van keys onto the bar top. He made a beeline for me, sweeping me into his arms. "Just the person I wanted to see."

His tongue was in my mouth a second later, his kisses always dirty hot compared to Grayson's sweeter ones.

Both had their place and spun my head in different ways. But I pushed him away. "Hayley Jade get to school okay?"

Hawk nodded. "Yep."

It was their little routine, the two of them. Hawk took her every morning, often stopping for hot donuts and coffee first, the two of them chatting together about anything they had the signs to communicate about. Sometimes I went too, but I instinctively realized this time was special to them, and that letting them have it was important. All the guys had fallen into these routines with her.

Grayson liked to be here in the afternoons to help her with homework or to just sit on the floor and play. He was desperately trying to encourage a love of hockey in her, and more than one puck had been shot across the concrete floors of the clubhouse. Not that anyone minded. Anything went here.

Hayden had thrown himself into the deep end, learning as many ASL signs as he could, and Hayley Jade ran to him every evening when he got home from the day shift at Sinners, ready to learn.

I pushed up on my toes and kissed Hawk's stubbled cheek. "Grayson wants to take our study session outdoors today, since it's nice out. Hike to some spot he knows then have a picnic."

Hawk glanced down at his standard uniform of faded jeans and motorcycle boots. "I don't hike. I don't even own a pair of shoes I could hike in."

"You and Grayson are the same size...I bet he has a spare pair."

Hawk screwed up his face. "That's like asking me to wear his underwear."

I laughed. "How is that the same thing?"

"I don't know, but it is! Ugh, his foot fungus germs coating themselves around my socks..." He shuddered.

I gave him a fake pout because he was being a princess. "Please?"

He rolled his eyes. "Fine. I'll hike. But only because I'm gonna watch your ass sway all the way up the trail."

"Deal." I would have agreed to anything to get him to come. But I liked the idea of his gaze on my body while we walked. I'd be thinking about that all the way up the track. "Go get ready. I'm just going to see if Kyle wants to come." I walked backward toward the door. "Don't change your mind while I'm gone."

Except I knew he wouldn't. Because he'd proved time and time again he would do anything for me.

That was a heady feeling. Having his devotion. His love. His protection. The sun was unusually warm, and I practically skipped down to Kyle's cabin to ask him if he wanted to come with us.

Kyle peeped his head out from beneath the blankets and blearily told me he didn't feel well and would skip today's little adventure. I didn't like that he didn't feel good, but I promised to bring him back some cold and flu tablets, got him a fresh glass of water for his bedside table, and left him to sleep.

Kiki and Ice were both sitting in the common area when I got back, Kiki scrolling her phone, Ice listening to something playing on his through a set of headphones. I liked Kiki. She wasn't as brash as Amber was, and I put my hand on her shoulder. "I'm going out, but Kyle isn't well. Are you home today? Do you think you could keep an eye on him for me? Just check to see if he needs anything once or twice. I worry about him, out in that cabin alone."

She gave me a bright smile; her lips painted a magenta purple that caught the light from overhead. "Of course! I'd be happy to. Poor thing. Maybe I'll make some chicken soup for him. Do you think he'd like that?"

I smiled. "I do. He's used to homestyle cooking. That's all he ever got at the commune. It's lovely of you to offer. Thank you."

She skittered off to the kitchen, clearly happy to have a project for the day. I watched her go, wondering what she did with her time when she wasn't here. I realized I had no idea. I hoped she had something more than just waiting around here for bikers who might never see her as more than a club girl.

Maybe I'd talk to her about volunteering at the hospital. She seemed excited by the idea of caring for Kyle while he was sick. Maybe she'd be interested in doing it more often.

In my room, I got dressed quickly, pulling on a T-shirt and a pair of shorts that were hemmed mid-thigh. I paused for a second, noticing the cellulite on my legs that the shorts did nothing to hide.

For half a second, I thought about putting longer pants on. Hawk had promised to be staring at my behind the entire way up the trail. He'd see every dimple and bump in these shorts. But it was hot out. I'd be sweating like a pig if I put on longer pants, and I'd spend the day miserable and self-conscious about butt sweat.

But then Grayson walked out of the shower, and his

gaze lit up, like a kid on Christmas morning. "Why don't you wear those more often?"

I smoothed my hands over them. "I never wear shorts. I don't like my legs."

He skimmed his hands over the curve of my behind. "But hear me out. How often do you look at your legs during the day?"

I shrugged. "I don't know. A couple of times I guess, though not with any purpose for the most part."

"Right. But I look at your legs approximately eleven billionty times a day. And your hips. And your ass. And your tits. And your face. And your pinky finger..."

I giggled. "I get the point. You look at me."

"I like your legs. In anything. Shorts. Pants. Skirts. Scrubs. Hessian sacks." He sniggered, but then he sobered. "Wear the shorts, Kara. Erase the idea from your head that nobody wants to see you. I do."

A slow warmth trickled through me. I loved the way he stared at me, the way he saw me and built me up when my self-confidence had a wobble. I'd come a long way from the broken woman I'd been when I'd first arrived in Saint View, but I was far from completely healed.

His words helped though. Little by little, they mended the holes Josiah had punched through my heart.

"I love you," he murmured. Then clapped his hands together, not waiting for a response from me. "Let's go hike!"

Some part of me wanted to say it back. But there was another part that just wasn't there yet. I loved he wasn't pushing me. He was so content, so sure of himself that he could happily tell me he loved me and not need me to say it in return.

I knew I would eventually. But when I said it, I wanted to truly mean it with every ounce of my being. Anything else would be a cop-out, and he deserved more.

The man deserved the world for all the good he put into it. Just last night he'd gone on a house call, just to sit with a patient who'd been having a tough time. He might have made light of some of the more trivial aspects of his job, but when it came down to it, Grayson cared. He was there when someone needed him. No questions asked.

He also looked really good in shorts.

"Did you plan to go hiking today?" I eyed his muscular legs, nicely tanned, despite the fact the weather had been cold lately. "Or do you just carry your hiking gear around with you in case someone wants to ogle your legs?"

Like I was doing right now.

He glanced down at himself. "They're just gym shorts. They're all I had in my car." He winked at me. "But you're not going to be self-conscious, and neither am I. Right?"

I made a face at him. "Your legs look like they could do modelling campaigns."

"Your legs look like they need my face between them. So shall I do that to stop this little spiral of self-doubt? Or can we go hike?"

I fought a smile. "We can go hike."

For now. But later, I might consider taking up his generous offer.

16

GRAYSON

I stared at Hawk, who was apparently ready to go hiking. "What are you wearing?"

He scowled at me. "That's it! I'm not going." He shot Kara a dirty look. "I told you this was a bad idea."

She caught his hand. "Stop it. You're fine." She glared at me. "Isn't he?"

The corner of my mouth quirked up. "Sure. Just never thought I'd see you in anything other than denim, white tees, and leather."

Hawk flipped up his middle finger. "You saw me in my birthday suit the other night, and I didn't hear you complaining."

I sniggered. "But you weren't wearing neon-pink shorts then, so I really had nothing to tease you about. Wait!"

I held my phone up and snapped a photo of Hawk's outfit then quickly forwarded it to Hayden before Hawk could stop me.

He scowled as his phone beeped with an incoming

message, and he turned it around so Kara and I could see the laughing emojis Hayden had sent him.

"Where did you even get those?" I wiped at my eyes quickly, trying to disguise my tears of laughter.

He shrugged. "I don't know, actually. They might be Scythe's." He tugged at them, trying to pull them down over his muscled thighs. "Yeah, not happening. I'll hike in jeans and fucking boots."

I couldn't help but think that might be a good idea. What I'd said to Kara about wearing clothes you were comfortable in went for men too. But ribbing him was too hard to resist. "Bring the shorts anyway!" I called loudly through his bedroom door. "If we get lost, they'll be a beacon for helicopters to spot us!"

"I think I hate you more than I hate Chaos," Hawk grumbled back through the door. "You both suck."

I laughed beneath my breath, but his grumbling couldn't kill my good mood. Too many things were going right this week, and I just wanted to bask in the glory of being happy. Facing what had happened to my wife and having my brother back in my life had settled some angry part of me that hadn't been coping. Sleeping in Kara's bed at night and smelling the soft scent of her hair was something I'd dreamed about for months, but now I got to actually have it. Knowing she had a baby in her belly, who could very well be mine, even if the odds probably were stacked against me, felt like a grounding I hadn't knew I needed.

It wasn't so much that the club felt like home.

But she did.

And building a world around her was easy.

I was well aware I was stupidly head over heels in love

with her and that she hadn't said it back, but I couldn't help what I felt. It was too strong to keep inside, and I could see her falling a little more each day.

I didn't need to rush her.

There was no finish line in this thing between her and me. I wasn't going anywhere. If she could never say it back, then I would accept that. But I'd still be here. Loving her, until she told me she didn't want it anymore.

With Hawk back in his regular clothes, I drove us toward the bluff. I was familiar with the many trails that snaked their way from the parking lot through the trees and along the edge of the coast.

We all got out, shouldering backpacks full of food and study supplies. I stood in front of the information board that directed to different walks, where they ended up, and highlighted each walk's difficulty.

But there was one in particular I wanted to do, so I led the way, taking a track marked in yellow on the map, that led through the woods and out along a path with a tree-restricted view of the ocean. "It opens up farther down here," I called back. "The view just gets better and better the further we go."

After some gawking, and commenting on how calm the ocean was today, we fell into a comfortable silence, me setting an easy pace, the other two following single file along a well-worn trail.

Hawk spoke to Kara quietly from the back of the line, but I couldn't make out his words. The trails were quiet with it being the middle of the week, and this being one of the harder, non-toddler-friendly routes. There'd been a small number of other cars in the parking lot, but we hadn't seen another person since setting off. I knew from hiking these tracks regularly on my weekdays off, it would be unlikely for us to stumble upon anyone else. The crash of waves and the gentle roar of the breeze against the cliffs wrapped around me, calming my nervous system, clearing my head of anything but me and nature.

And Kara moaning.

I stopped and glanced back at them, eyebrows furrowing together. "You hurt?"

Kara was so pink I couldn't tell if she was sunburned or blushing as she passed me. "I'm fine. Let's keep going."

But then Hawk smirked at me. "We should stop soon. Somewhere private. If you catch my drift."

I gawked at him. "Out here?"

"Why not?"

"Do you ever just do it in a bed?" I grumbled, following him.

He glanced back over his shoulder with a grin. "Not if I can help it."

I just shook my head and called ahead to Kara, who was now leading. "Take the trail to your right. It turns inland a bit, so you lose your view of the ocean, but it's worth it. Trust me."

Kara raised her arms above her head in a thumbs-up and followed the path I'd indicated.

A few minutes later, they both saw why I'd wanted to come this way.

A waterfall trickled from the rock face high above our heads before opening into a freshwater pool with sand at the edges and then a grassy embankment, perfect for picnics. If you followed the pool far enough, it eventually narrowed into a stream, finding its way downhill to the ocean below, but this pool was the real highlight of the walk.

"This is amazing," Kara breathed, taking in the pretty sight.

Hawk interlaced his fingers at the back of his head and breathed deeply, catching his breath. His T-shirt was plastered to his back with sweat. "I didn't even know this was here."

"A lot of people don't. But it gets busy on the weekend. Not so much during the week. As you can see." We had the entire place to ourselves.

Hawk took off his shirt, tossing it to the grassy bank beside the backpacks we'd discarded. His boots followed, until he was barefoot at the edge of the natural pool. "My feet are killing me. This feels like bliss." He dug his toes into the rocky sand, letting the gentle water sit around his ankles. The ragged hem of his jeans darkened with the water kissing it, but if Hawk noticed, he didn't care.

Kara was still bright pink, flushed either from the unusually warm day, the exercise, or maybe a combo of Hawk mumbling dirty things behind her for the entire trek. Or it could have been the fact he was now standing shirtless at the edge of the water.

She busied herself, spreading the blanket out and pulling textbooks from her backpack, setting everything up to study.

But every time she bent over, I wanted to grab her ass. Press my lips to the pink of her skin and taste the salty sweat beading there. "Hot?"

She glanced up. "Very."

"Want to swim?"

"I didn't bring my suit. And it will suck to walk back in wet clothes." She shuddered. "So much chafing."

I laughed and pulled my shirt off. "So swim naked."

She paused. "Uh. No. It's the middle of the day, and anyone could come by at any minute."

Hawk caught wind of our conversation and gave me a grin that was full of mischief. "Is Mr. Straighty One-eighty stepping outside his comfort zone?"

"I had a foursome in a sex club. Not sure how you thought that was *in* my comfort zone."

Hawk shrugged. "You got a little inner kink beneath your doctor's scrubs. You know you do."

Didn't everyone?

I didn't think public sex was mine, but there was no denying that water looked good, and I was hot, sweaty, and maybe some part of me wanted to show Hawk that just because I was a doctor, didn't mean I was uptight.

I could be spontaneous.

Hawk hollered from the water's edge, "Take it off!"

I kicked off my sneakers and socks, and then gave Kara a wink before pushing my shorts and underwear off my legs.

This was a completely different experience than getting naked with them in a sex club, when alcohol had been flowing, the lights were dim, and the music was sultry. There was nowhere to hide here. It was the bright light of day, and there was a tiny voice in the back of my head reminding me random hikers could appear and catch my dick just swinging in the breeze.

But the water was so damn inviting, and I felt gross after walking for the last hour.

I strolled past Hawk, who chuckled at me, but I ignored him and waded into the water.

"How is it?" Hawk asked when I was hip-deep.

"Cold," I admitted honestly. But it didn't stop me from dunking my head under and enjoying the cool rush of water across my entire body.

"I'm in," Hawk announced, unzipping his jeans and pulling them off, tossing them back toward Kara on the edge of the picnic blanket. "Get naked, Little Mouse. We're swimming."

She gaped at Hawk strolling into the water. "No way. It'll be freezing."

"It's great." He walked into the water, his back to her.

I sniggered because I got to see his expression, and he silently mouthed a string of cuss words, wincing at the less-than-pleasant water temperature.

After he was deep enough to dive, he slid beneath the water, and when he surfaced, he muttered to me, "Jesus fuck, does this thing run off a glacier?"

It was so not even close to that cold. He was such an exaggerator.

I flicked some water in Kara's direction. "I'm naked with Hawk. Don't let that be a thing. At least give me plausible deniability with the hope of a threesome."

Hawk rolled onto his back and floated, zero fucks given about exposing himself. Kara eyed him, and then me. I could see the indecision on her face. She wanted to come in. But she kept darting little glances toward the trail, like a group of fifty tourists might appear at any moment, take their cameras out, and start snapping photos like she was the wildlife.

"Take your gear off so your underwear isn't wet and

then put my T-shirt on. I'll hike back without one. No biggie."

She frowned at me. "Your shirt will be like a second skin on me. And it's white. It'll be completely see-through when I get in the water."

I winked at her suggestively. "I know."

She laughed.

"You know, either way, as soon as we get out, we're getting you naked too. You might as well get cool first."

Hawk chuckled from his position deeper in the pool. "You know he's right. You think I'm not getting inside you after staring at your ass the whole way here?"

She rolled her eyes and shrugged out of her T-shirt. Then those little shorts that barely covered her thighs. Her bra was next, and with a final glance at the trail, which was of course still completely empty because I really had been telling the truth when I'd said no one ever came down here during the week, especially at this time of year when only crazy people would swim, she lowered her panties.

Hawk let out an obnoxious catcall, but it was clear from the heat in his gaze that she had his whole attention. His gaze dropped low and then slowly glided back up, and when I turned back to her, I couldn't help but do the same.

She was so much more beautiful than she realized, even more so just standing on the edge of the water, bare-ass naked, like some sort of water nymph.

"I don't know about you," I said to Hawk softly, unable to take my eyes off her. "But my dick is no longer interested in studying."

"Mine neither. Fucking hell." His words were a

guttural groan of need that only intensified when Kara waded into the water and squealed as it hit the sensitive spot between her legs.

"Oh my God, it's freezing! You two are horrible!"

But she dived beneath the water quickly, coming up spluttering and jumping up and down, trying to warm herself.

Her tits bounced, and it was all I could do not to reach beneath the water and stroke my cock.

She turned and ran back to where we'd left our things, the world's shortest skinny-dip apparently over.

I didn't even need to look at Hawk to know he was following her out of the water, predator stalking its prey, just like I was.

She stopped at the edge of the picnic blanket. "We have no towels."

Hawk flopped down on the picnic blanket and fit his hands behind his head. "Come lie down here and I'll lick the water off you."

She frowned at him. "Not sure that would get me dry."

Hawk opened one lazy eye. "If me licking you ever gets you dry, I'm clearly doing it wrong."

"Sun's warm," I suggested more helpfully. "If we lie here long enough, we'll air-dry." I dropped down onto the opposite side of the blanket from Hawk, mirroring his position, and patted the spot in between us. "Room for three."

She put her hands on her wide hips, only accentuating her curves, and reminding me how badly I wanted to get my hands on them. "If I get down there naked, things are going to happen."

"I can behave," I promised, though every part of me wanted to do anything but.

Hawk lifted his head. "I can't." His hand wrapped around his semi-erect cock and stroked it.

Her eyes flared, watching him jack off, then drifted to my erection. "You're hard."

"That's what happens when you're naked." I couldn't drag my gaze off her. Her nipples were tight buds, straining in my direction, just begging for my mouth.

She lowered herself so she was kneeling on the blanket between us. And then tentatively, watching like we might have some sort of negative reactions, she reached for both of us. Her fingers wrapped around Hawk's dick at the same time she gripped mine.

Hawk and I let out groans of need and encouragement the moment she touched us.

Her hands slid up and down, working both of us in the same, torturously slow rhythm, getting us fully hard while she was all tits and belly rolls and thick thighs with her hair escaping the messy bun she'd tied it up in.

"Spread your thighs, Kara," I instructed. "I want to see what's between them."

She rocked back, supporting her weight by digging her toes into the soft dirt beneath the blanket and creating a little groove there to give herself leverage.

Then she opened her legs, giving me just a tiny glimpse of her gleaming slit between the softness of her thighs.

"Such a fucking good girl," Hawk muttered, gaze glued to the arousal shining over her clit and opening.

She let out a moan at his dirty praise, clearly turned on by being told what to do.

So I kept going. "Need your mouth, Kara."

Without stopping her rhythm on Hawk, she lowered her mouth over my cock, bobbing her head low to take me all the way to the back of her throat. Her warm wetness encased me, and I was sure this was what heaven felt like. My fingers fell to her head, taking out her bun so I could stroke my fingers through the long lengths, scratching my nails gently over her scalp.

She moaned around my dick, so I kept going, massaging her head while she blew me and jacked Hawk off with her free hand.

After a while, I stopped her, and she looked up at me with huge eyes, her lips still wrapped around my dick. I groaned, "Suck him too."

She switched, pumping me, blowing him. We took what she offered, until Hawk needed more control than he was getting lying flat on his back. He got to his knees, gripped the back of her head, and fucked her mouth in slow, gentle thrusts that had her quivering.

On her hands and knees, she pulled her mouth away from his erection and glanced over her shoulder at me. Her lips were swollen. Her eyes unfocused, but there was only lust and need and desire floating in the cloudy haze.

She didn't need to say what she wanted. The desperation was written all over her face, and her pussy was dripping when I fit myself behind her.

I was already so hard, and she was already so wet that I slid inside her with no resistance, filling her and burying myself to the hilt in soft heat.

She moaned around Hawk's cock, arching her back, angling her body so my thrusts hit her just right, each one jolting her forward so she took Hawk's cock deeper and deeper until she was deep-throating him.

She stared up at him, and he praised her every step of the way, encouraging her, telling her she was beautiful. I added my own, telling her how good she felt, how turned on she got me, how I wanted her, needed her, loved her, until we were both showering her in the positive words I knew full well she'd never heard from her husband's lips.

Somewhere along the way she'd lost the timid little mouse persona Hawk had first nicknamed her after. There was none of that here. She was a fucking goddess, taking two men, owning every minute of her pleasure and ours, no hiding her body from the sun or from us.

She took a breather from Hawk's dick, and I pulled her upright, wrapping my arms around her from behind, and whispering in her ear, "Confidence looks good on you."

She moaned, slipping her fingers between her thighs to rub her clit while I slowly pumped into her from the back. Hawk lowered his head to suck her nipples, alternating between them, licking and nipping at them, squeezing them between his fingers until her moans echoed around in the quiet air.

With her breathing turning into short pants of desperation, she pushed him back and devoured his cock again, blowing him fast and slamming back to meet me, encouraging the same pace.

I gripped her hips, fingers sinking into the softness there and rode her hard, thrusting fast, strong and powerful into her body. My abs flexed; my balls drew up.

But I refused to come until she had.

"I want you..." she moaned, pulling off Hawk's cock to look back at me.

"You already have me, Kara. In every way."

Hawk's tone was as dry as ever when he sniggered. "She means in her ass, Gray."

Oh.

My gaze met Kara's, seeking her permission. Her cheeks were pink with embarrassment. But when I fit my finger to the small rear hole, she rocked back, moaning loudly, taking my finger like she'd just been waiting for the opportunity.

"Fucking hell," I muttered, watching my dick and fingers fuck her all at once.

She shouted, shattering apart, spasming around my cock like a vise, her internal muscles gripping and releasing me while she moaned around Hawk's cock. He came too, with a guttural groan, grabbing her hair and coming in her mouth while she swallowed him down.

I wanted her to come again. And again. Just so I could hear those sounds of pleasure fall from her lips and feel her body tremble beneath my fingers.

I pulled out, barely hanging on to my orgasm, and pressed the tip of my cock to her ass.

She gasped, her voice a sharp "Oh!" of need when I thrust inside her.

Hawk, his dick softening now he'd come, slid beneath her body while I filled her

She was so fucking tight I couldn't move without coming. And I didn't want it to be over.

From beneath her, Hawk sucked her nipples, her tits hanging in his face and just begging for his touch. But he didn't stay there long, sliding farther down on his back so she was kneeling over his face, her legs either side of his head.

They were in the perfect sixty-nine position, just with the added addition of me fucking her from behind as well.

Hawk probably had a super attractive view of the underside of my balls, but he was fully concentrated on licking Kara's clit and getting her to come again, rather than the fact I could teabag him in the eyeball with one wrong move.

The thought had me battling back a laugh.

It was a good distraction from the fact I needed to come. I let the thought of Hawk staring up at my ball sack distract me enough to fuck my girl the way she deserved. Slow. Purposefully. All attention on her.

I refused to come until her body shook again and her loud cries of pleasure scared birds away. Only then did I let myself fall over the edge with her, coming hard, thrusting in and out of her tight ass.

My head was still spinning when I pulled out, breathing hard.

Kara's wobbly legs gave out, and she collapsed down on Hawk, her head resting on his thighs, her throbbing pussy still at his mouth.

I got up and went back to the water's edge to clean up, watching Hawk lazily lick her, even though she'd already come twice and was too spent to even move off him.

When I flopped back on the blanket beside them, Kara sleepily rolled off Hawk and lay squished between us, too blissed out to care any longer about being naked in a public place.

"This is not teaching us anything we need for the GED exam."

I twisted onto my stomach and kissed her mouth. "You're smart enough for today."

She raised an eyebrow. "Smart enough to get you to go down on me before I get dressed?"

Hawk and I both stared at her in shock, so unused to her just coming right out and asking for what she wanted.

And then shoved each other out of the way while she laughed at both of us trying to get back between her legs.

17

KARA

Hawk, Grayson, and I picked up Hayley Jade from school on our way home from our hike. Hayley Jade climbed into the back of Grayson's car from the school pickup line and waved at all of us, a delighted grin on her face.

"You had a good day, sweetheart?" I twisted around from the front passenger seat to check her over.

Her hair was a mess, and she had a tiny smear of paint smudged on one cheek, but she nodded.

Grayson steered the car out onto the road, but in the opposite direction of the clubhouse.

I frowned at him. "Where are we going?"

"Hayley Jade seems like she needs a..." He glanced at her in the rearview mirror. "Milkshake?"

She smiled widely.

"Candy too," Hawk added, ruffling her hair. "She definitely looks like she needs some candy."

I gave all three of them a disapproving frown, but it

was mostly playful. She'd be on a sugar high for the rest of the afternoon, but I was on a high of my own and I wasn't quite ready to come back down to earth yet.

Kyle's phone full of my sister's texts was waiting for me back at the clubhouse, along with the stress and grief of needing to read them all.

I could stand living in the bubble of happiness I'd found here with two men and a little girl for a few hours longer.

Hayden met us at a café not far from his work, and we all ate a ridiculous amount of sugar considering we were having dinner in a couple of hours.

But I couldn't stop watching Hayley Jade. The way her eyes were bright. The way she lit up when Grayson asked her about her friends at school and she was able to make a few simple signs to tell him she was friends with two girls and one boy.

Hayden and Hawk both frowned at the mention of a boy, but I elbowed Hawk and kicked Hayden under the table, and both schooled their "overprotective dad" expressions into something more neutral.

But my heart saw it. The way all three of them were with her. Grayson had taken on more of a friend and teacher role, rather than a fatherly one. And that was okay with me, and clearly with Hayley Jade as well. I didn't expect any of them to be her dad and I didn't want to pressure their relationships in any way.

They would develop in their own time.

But Hayden, and especially Hawk, were gazing at my daughter like she'd hung the moon, and I knew in my heart while Hayden had loved her since the day she was born, Hawk had fallen for her as much as he'd fallen for me.

I smoothed her hair back off her face tenderly, and in that moment, made peace with the fact she might never speak again.

Even if that were true, I wasn't to blame. I wasn't the one who'd taken her from me. I wasn't the one who'd made threats against her life, forcing us to run.

All I'd ever done was love her.

By the time we got back to the clubhouse, after a day away from the place and some time with the people I cared most about, I felt more ready to deal with the texts on Kyle's phone. Hayley Jade tugged on Grayson's hand, holding up a book Hawk, Hayden, and I had already read a hundred times each, but Grayson trotted after her into her bedroom, the two of them settling side by side in pink beanbags so he could read the story to her.

With Hayley Jade taken care of, I picked up Kyle's phone, and yet again, lost myself in my sister's whirlwind affair with a man who had probably killed her.

> GOLDEN:
>
> You ever just feel like you don't belong anywhere?

TULIP:

> Every day. I don't fit here. Never have. My sister is married to our spiritual leader. So she's obviously the golden child in our family these days. The way my parents brag about her to every other member of the community is so gross. My other sisters aren't much better. They all have their heads stuck up their asses, their only interests in marrying a man of the Lord and bearing his children. Yawn. I can't think of anything worse. I need to get out of here before I end up in front of an altar, marrying a man three times my age.

GOLDEN:

> You have no idea how lucky you are to have a family. People who respect you. Care about you enough to want you married to a man who can take care of you.

TULIP:

> Did you miss the bit about me marrying a man I don't love? Or even like?

GOLDEN:

> I didn't. But I focused on the good things about your family so I wouldn't type words I know I shouldn't.

TULIP:

> Don't be cryptic now. You know me better than that. You can tell me anything.

GOLDEN:

> You could marry me.

I nearly dropped the phone. My fingers shook.

Hayden, with his arm around my shoulders and a cat on his lap, noticed my trembling and looked down at me. "Hey. What is it?"

I showed him the screen.

He swore low under his breath and pressed his lips to my head. "Just remember everything you're reading is in the past. This isn't happening right now, and this isn't something you can save her from. That responsibility wasn't ever yours."

I nodded. "I know."

But it didn't stop me wishing she'd come to me. Told me what was going on. Wishing I'd been more available for her instead of so wrapped up in my own problems.

All I could do now was find this man and make sure he paid for his crimes.

I laid my head on Hayden's shoulder and stroked my fingers through the soft fur of the cat on his lap, drawing comfort from both while I kept scrolling.

TULIP:
Are you serious? About marrying you, I mean?

GOLDEN:
Don't freak out.

TULIP:
I'm not. Much.

GOLDEN:
In a good way or a bad way?

TULIP:
Is it crazy if I say good? Is it even crazier if I say I would marry you in a heartbeat?

It was like watching a train wreck in reverse. Knowing the inevitable impact and being able to do nothing to stop it.

GOLDEN:

You would? You don't even know me.

TULIP:

> We've been talking every day for months. I know you better than some grumpy old dude who's a friend of my father's and needs a young wife to give him babies. If I married you, I couldn't marry him!

GOLDEN:

You don't even know my name.

TULIP:

> You don't know mine either. That didn't stop you from asking me to marry you. And it won't stop me from saying yes.

GOLDEN:

That's crazy.

TULIP:

> Maybe. But if I could get out of here and come to you, would you do it? Would you marry me?

TULIP:

> Please. I don't want to marry a man I don't know or love. I can be a good wife to you. I can cook and clean. I can get a job somewhere to help support us. I just need somewhere to go when I leave here. I just need you to say yes. Please don't leave me here.

My eyes welled with tears for how desperate she'd been to get out. I knew the feeling all too well.

GOLDEN:

I want to marry you. But you don't have to get out. I can come to you. Ethereal Eden sounds amazing.

TULIP:

No! I know you want a family who accepts you. I know you've never had that. But I can't stay here. I want to travel the world. I want to see things. Meet people.

GOLDEN:

People and things are overrated.

TULIP:

Not to me.

TULIP:

I'll come to you. Somehow. I'll figure something out. And then we'll get married. Have babies. Create our own family. Together.

GOLDEN:

Okay.

TULIP:

Okay? Really?

GOLDEN:

I'm Xan.

TULIP:

Alice.

I scrolled right through the rest of the messages that were dated right up until the day we left the commune. My fingers shook violently as I opened the last few threads of Alice and Xan's conversations.

TULIP:

> Xan! You are never going to believe this, but stuff went DOWN during the night. BIG HUGE STUFF. I'm out. Oh my God, I'm so giddy I can't even talk. If there's typos in this message, I'm sorry, I can't even blame my sore fingers. They're all because I'm currently flying down a freeway, getting the hell away from Ethereal Eden. FOREVER.

GOLDEN:

What? Are you serious?

TULIP:

> SO serious. Josiah threatened Hayley Jade, so now I'm on the run with her, Kyle, and my sister. We'll be in Providence in hours. You said you live near there, right?

GOLDEN:

Yeah. Just across the town border in Saint View. I can't believe this. Can I see you when you get here? Tonight?

TULIP:

> YES! Where? Can we go somewhere fun? Somewhere where I can dance on tables and drink alcohol?

GOLDEN:

You aren't twenty-one.

TULIP:

> Shit.

TULIP:

> If I can steal my sister's ID, we can still go? Please? I am so full of adrenaline right now I can't even sit still. I'm trying so hard to play it cool so my sister doesn't suspect anything. She'd never understand if I told her about all of this. She's so scared of everything out here. Even her own shadow, it seems. I thought she was going to hold my hand to cross the road when we stopped at a gas station. I just want to stick my head out the window like a dog and scream that I'm free.

GOLDEN:

> Don't do that. I've got some things to take care of in the city tonight. Can you get there?

TULIP:

> YES!

GOLDEN:

> Text me when you get to your sister's place.

TULIP:

> Oh my God. I can't wait to hear your voice.

GOLDEN:

> Alice?

TULIP:

> Yes?

GOLDEN:

> I love you.

TULIP:

> I love you too, Xan.

TULIP:

> We're here. I'm so excited. I can't wait to meet you.

GOLDEN:

> Sneak away as soon as you can. Meet me at Sixth Street in the city. It's a club. I can't wait to meet you either.

Tears flowed freely down my face, my heart breaking.

Hawk squished onto the couch with me and Hayden and took the phone from my fingers. "Stop. It's over. We give this to the cops and let them handle it."

"It might not mean anything," Hayden said softly. "It still could have been Josiah or one of his guys who killed her. She might have gone to meet this guy there and been intercepted before they could meet."

"But if that's true, why are there no more messages from this Xan guy? Why do they all stop that night? If she hadn't turned up, wouldn't he have called her? Texted her?"

Hayden looked as hopeless as I felt. "Maybe. But Hawk's right. We need to give this to the police so they can handle it."

There was nothing else I could do.

The clubhouse door swung open, and Kyle and Kiki stumbled through, their arms around each other, both of them a disheveled mess. Kyle had a hickey on his neck the size of a small planet.

We all stared at them, and they straightened up.

Kiki pulled at her short skirt so it stopped riding up her long, toned thighs. "Oh. Hi, everyone. Good to see you. Did you have a nice day?"

Hawk sniggered. "Maybe not as nice as you and Kyle seem to have had."

Kyle grinned at him. "I got laid."

Kiki slapped at him playfully, but her giggle was cute, and she clearly didn't mind he'd just advertised their business to everyone.

Hawk raised an eyebrow. "Kiki popped your cherry, huh?"

Hayden pointed at the refrigerator behind the bar. "Grab yourself a beer. Losing your virginity should be toasted."

I glanced at him and whispered, "Seriously?"

He shrugged back. "Just trying to make him feel included. It's tough being on the outside around here. You wanted him to fit in, right?"

Hawk sniggered. "He fit his cock right on into Kiki's pussy."

"I did!" Kyle called, raising his beer into the air in victory.

Kiki laughed and dragged his hand back down. "Sweetie, I know you're riding a sex high right now, but you lasted all of two thrusts. Don't get too braggy."

I couldn't help my laugh, and it mixed with those from the guys.

Kiki slapped Kyle on the cheek. "Don't worry. You'll get better with practice. You're cute, so you can practice on me anytime you want."

Kyle's cheeks went pink, but he dropped onto the opposite couch and pulled Kiki down onto his lap, pleased as punch with himself, even if Kiki had just brought him down a peg or two with her honest assessment of his skills.

I was happy for him. He sipped his beer, seeming more at ease than I'd maybe ever seen him. He was a nice kid. If only my sister had seen that in him. If she hadn't gone out that night to meet this Xan guy, maybe she'd still be here with us now. A ball of emotion lodged in my throat, considering all the what-ifs.

"You know what I don't understand about Alice's texts?" I mused out loud to distract myself from the tears pricking the backs of my eyes. "She mentions multiple times that her hands are sore."

Hawk shrugged. "Lotta physical labor on a farm."

"The men do most of the hard, manual labor at Ethereal Eden." Kyle ran his fingers absentmindedly over Kiki's bare thigh. "The women do a bit of gardening and feed animals. But mostly they're cooking or at the women's center. Maybe she did a lot of bread kneading or hand-washing on the days she mentioned having sore hands?"

I shook my head. "No, she specifically mentions typing. But Josiah confiscated all computers and devices years ago."

Kyle shrugged. "Maybe it's just a woman thing? My mom always complained about having sore hands at night too."

I glanced over at him. "She did?"

"Sometimes she had to ice them. They got so bad at one point Dad asked Josiah if he could get in a wrist brace for her."

"Did he?"

Kyle's face clouded over. "No. He told my father a woman's pain was necessary to bring new life into the world or some rubbish like that."

Hayden squinted. "Was she giving birth at the time as well? For fuck's sake. I can't even think about that prick without wanting to stab something."

Something clicked in my head. "Kyle, what did you just say about a women's center?"

He frowned, his brown eyebrows pinching together. "You know, the big building where all the women who don't have young kids go."

I shook my head. "I don't know anything about that."

Kyle's frown deepened. "I guess because you only ever came out of your house for church. But it's the big building they erected a year or two ago at the back of the property so Josiah would have an office."

Something wasn't making sense. I knew Josiah had an office because it had been a blissful relief to have him out of the house. But him allocating a whole building to women, who were the lowest rungs on the totem pole at Ethereal Eden, didn't compute in my head. "What do the women do in there?"

He shrugged. "Honestly, I have no idea. I assumed they were knitting or playing cards or something—"

That didn't fit at all. "Josiah isn't that generous. He wouldn't give women a place of their own just to congregate and socialize. He believes a woman's place is in her house, ready to serve her husband at any time."

Kyle paused. "What are they doing in there then? My mom goes there every day."

I didn't want to guess in front of him for fear his mother's job at the commune was similar to the service I'd seen Shari performing the night we'd left. She'd taken men into the woods so they could use her body however they saw fit. A command from Josiah who was recruiting new members by showing them what they could have if they joined him.

But Kyle must have seen the expression on my face. "You think Josiah is having them do something bad in there?"

"I don't know," I said honestly. "I hope not."

Kyle pushed to his feet, pacing the room, his face twisted in agitation. "She never wanted to join the stupid cult. It was my dad who dragged us there. That's why she let me keep my phone and snuck me recharge cards whenever she went into town to sell vegetables at the market."

"You need to call your parents," Grayson said softly, coming out of Hayley Jade's room. He glanced at me. "She's watching something on her iPad."

I nodded, but my head was too full of questions to be too concerned about the amount of screen time Hayley Jade was having right before bed.

She was safe. That was more than I could perhaps say for the women at Ethereal Eden.

Kyle paused in his pacing, leaning against the wall and considering Grayson's words. "I haven't spoken to them since I left."

Hayden shifted his weight, his mouth pressed into a concentrated line. "You think they won't take your call?"

Kyle shook his head. "No. They will. I deliberately didn't call them because I didn't want them to have to lie for me if the police questioned them about where I was. But if she's being forced to do...something...against her will..." He squeezed his eyes shut tightly and dug the heels of his hands in on top. "I feel sick."

I picked up the phone and went to him, pressing it

into his fingers. "Stop. None of this is your fault. We don't even know if anything has happened just yet. Let's not get ahead of ourselves. Let's just call her and see if we can get some more information from her."

He bobbed his head in agreement, taking the phone. "What do I do if my dad answers? It's his phone."

Men were the only ones allowed any sort of technology in Ethereal Eden, and even then, it was strictly limited to men higher up in the ranks.

"Just tell him whatever you think he needs to hear." Grayson perched himself on the armchair. "Just get him to let you talk to your mom."

Kyle's face was still a mess of doubt, but he pressed his thumb against the screen a few times, and then the ringing tone came through the speaker for all of us to hear.

"Hello? Who's calling, please?" It was a man's voice, deep and rumbly.

I didn't recognize it, but then I'd barely spoken to Kyle's dad. How could I when I was locked in my house most of the time? I was beginning to realize I knew very little about what had been going on around me.

We all turned to Kyle as he sucked in a breath. "Dad? It's me. Kyle."

Mr. Baker let out a large breath of air that sounded a whole lot like relief. "Kyle! Really, it's you?" His voice cracked with emotion. "Son, your mother and I have been so worried about you. Where are you? Are you safe?"

Kyle ran his fingers through his hair. "Yeah, I'm safe. I'm staying with some friends."

Like the initial, guttural response to his child making

contact had passed, or maybe it was the reminder there was a whole other world outside of Ethereal Eden, Mr. Baker suddenly went cold. "You need to come home. Immediately. Josiah wants to speak with you urgently."

Hawk rolled his eyes, but Kyle remained composed, keeping his focus on Grayson, who nodded at him, encouraging him to agree to whatever his dad wanted.

"I will, Dad. Soon. I promise. Can I talk to Mom, please?"

Mr. Baker paused, and I knew exactly what he was thinking. That it was a sin for women to make contact with the outside world without Josiah's permission. Some of the women were allowed into town once a week to sell vegetables and homemade baked goods at the local market. Josiah always made a big show out of bringing them up to the altar on Sunday mornings during church and giving them special blessings to protect them while they were outside the Ethereal Eden gates.

"John! Is that Kyle?"

The woman's voice came down the line, screechy and panicked.

I held my breath, hoping Kyle's dad wasn't as brainwashed as all the others and he would have enough heart to let a mother speak to her child.

"He's fine. He's—"

"Kyle?"

Kyle's face crumpled at the sound of his mother's voice. Despite the fact he might have just lost his virginity, he suddenly looked like a kid who'd had a lot of bad things happen and his mother was the one person who could make them better. But just as quickly, he glanced at the guys all staring at him, and Kiki watching on from the couch, and he pulled himself together, straightening his shoulders. "Mom." His voice only held the barest of cracks. "I need to talk to you, but I need Dad not to hear it. Can you get away from him?"

There was a pause. Then she said to his dad, "The line is crackly. I need to go outside, I think, where the reception is better."

"I'll go with you."

We all winced.

But his mom had it handled. "I have dinner on the stove. I don't want it to burn, someone needs to stay here and stir the sauce. I'll only be a minute and I'll make sure nobody sees me with the phone. I promise."

That would have never flown with Josiah. He would have backhanded me in an instant for so much as thinking about asking him to do a menial job like stirring a sauce.

But Kyle and his parents hadn't been a part of the cult as long as some others had been. His dad had risen through the ranks quickly, as a lot of men his age did, but maybe there was still some part of him that remembered his life pre-Josiah and he wasn't mortally offended by cooking.

Or maybe he actually loved his wife enough to give her something she desperately needed.

Josiah didn't love anyone but himself, so he would never.

Mr. Baker sighed. "Just for a few minutes. I need to leave for the council meeting soon."

We didn't hear a response, but a moment later there

was the sound of a door closing and then his mother's hushed voice came down the line. "I'm alone. What's wrong? Where are you?"

"Mom, I'm good. I swear, I'm safe, and I'm with friends. But we need to know something. What happens at the women's center?"

She paused. "What? The women's center? Why do you want to know that?"

"Kara and I found—"

"You're still with Kara?"

He grimaced at me apologetically. But there was no point worrying about it now.

I racked my brain, trying to think of her name, and eventually it jostled free in my head. "Joan, hi. Kyle is good. He's safe. But we really need to know what happens in that center. My sister said her hands were sore from whatever goes on there, and Kyle says yours are too."

Joan breathed heavily into the phone. "We're forbidden from telling anyone. Even our husbands."

I eyed the others, realizing we might have stumbled onto something big. Maybe even something that could help us get Josiah locked up. At this point in the game, I didn't even care what he went to jail for. If he wasn't the one responsible for Alice's death, he still deserved to be locked away for life for the abuse he'd inflicted on me, and for the countless other crimes I was sure he was committing within the cult. His hands weren't clean in any capacity. It was just finding the proof and taking concrete evidence to the police so he couldn't charm his way out of it.

"Please, Joan," I begged her. "I need to know what my

sister was involved with before her death. Anything you can tell me helps."

Her voice dropped until it was barely more than a whisper. "We just do needlework..."

"No, you don't."

"He'll kill me if he finds out."

I let out a long, shaky breath. "He might kill you anyway. Look at what happened to Alice."

I could see Joan's face in my head, long brown hair always tied neatly off her face. Warm brown eyes, the same as Kyle's. She was a tall, slender woman, one who blended into the background, just how the men of Ethereal Eden expected their women to be. I understood what I was asking of her. It went against everything she'd been brainwashed to believe.

But Joan was strong enough to fight it. "The women's center is filled with computers. We type all day, every day, except for Sundays. Hours and hours of typing."

That fit with what we knew from Alice's messages. "Typing what?"

"Josiah calls it spreading the word. We use chat and dating apps to create relationships with people on the outside."

I squinted, mulling that over in my head until it made sense. "So you're like the people who come to your front door to talk about God?" I'd had some conversations with people like that when I'd first left Ethereal Eden. Two women had knocked on my door and wanted to speak about the Lord. They'd handed me brochures and told me I should read them. I'd quickly thrown them in the bin and hadn't answered the door the next time they'd come calling.

"I wish that's all it was. I could get on board with that." Joan's voice shook.

"Mom, please. Tell us. We need to know what Alice was involved with. If this is something to do with what got Alice killed, then you and all the other women are in danger too. I have friends out here. We can help you. Get you out."

His mom's breaths increased. "You can't do that, Kyle. He'll kill you. He'll kill all of us. He gives us scripts. We form relationships with men or women, it doesn't matter. We lie, make them think we're people we aren't. I've been an older man, a younger woman, whatever character I need to play in order to gain the other person's trust."

"For what purpose?" I interjected with a sinking stomach.

"Money, mostly. We trick them into sending us cash. Often this is how new members find Ethereal Eden. If the conversation starts seeming like the person might be open to joining, we push in that direction, filling their heads with ideas of how accepted they'd be within our community. How women would be looked after and men would be powerful. Everything depends on the target and what they might be lacking in their lives."

"It's a honeypot scheme," Hayden muttered. "Fucking hell."

I didn't know what that was exactly, but it couldn't be anything good. From what Joan had described, what Josiah was making them do was fraud at the very minimum.

There was a noise on the other end of the line, Kyle's dad calling for his wife.

Joan whispered into the phone, "I have to go. But Kara, are you still there?"

My stomach swirled with a sick feeling. "Yes."

"Your sister is involved."

It didn't surprise me. "Which one? Naomi or Samantha?" They were both such good, Ethereal Eden women who worshipped the ground Josiah walked on. It didn't even surprise me they were involved with this. If Josiah had told them it was the Lord's will, then they would have offered themselves up in a heartbeat.

"No, not them. They were both wed in a marriage ceremony a few weeks ago and are in their honeymoon seclusion period."

The three-month period where a wife was not permitted to leave her home for any reason other than church. It was where she was expected to get pregnant with her husband's child, and was therefore expected to be ready to receive his seed every day until that baby was conceived.

I shuddered at the memory of my own. Though unlike the other women, who mostly got pregnant during that time and could then live a more normal life, I'd been basically living five years of honeymoon seclusion hell.

Joan's voice whispered down the line. "Jacqueline."

My youngest sister's name cut through my dark memories.

"What about her?" I asked, not making the connection, my brain triggering dark images through my head and making it hard to remember what was right here in front of me now.

Kyle's dad shouted for her again.

"I'm worried for her safety. Something is going on. I

see the way Josiah and his circle stare at her, and there's nothing holy or respectful about it. They're planning something, and she's at the center of it..."

My heart thundered. "She's a child!"

Joan's voice was rushed, barely above a whisper. "That's not the worst part. They use images of her to draw men in. Naked—"

I slammed my eyes shut, squeezing them so tight they hurt. "No!"

Joan stopped. "I have to go. I'm so sorry, Kara. None of us want this, I assure you. I was horrified the first time they gave me her photos to use, but there's nothing we can do. If you can do something...anything to get her out... Kyle? I love you."

The call ended before any of us could reply.

I couldn't breathe. My skin crawled like bugs were covering it, and I scratched at my arms, fighting the horrible feeling.

Arms came around me, all three of my guys surrounding me, reminding me I was safe.

Reminding me I didn't have the luxury of falling apart again. I'd come here a shell of a woman, and they'd built me up into something more than I ever could have dreamed of.

Now it was my turn to stand on my own two feet and fight alongside them.

She was only thirteen. Barely a teenager. Definitely not yet a woman. And my husband was abusing her.

There was no time for berating myself. For beating myself up over not taking her with me in the first place. I'd tried, and I'd failed.

I couldn't do that again.

"We need to go get her," I said quietly, but with a strength I didn't think I'd ever heard in my own voice. I sounded like Rebel. Like Bliss. Like Queenie. Like a woman who had power and wasn't going to let a man take it from her ever again. "We're going back to Ethereal Eden. We're getting my sister, and any other woman who wants to be free."

18

HAWK

I couldn't stop the sick feeling swirling in the pit of my stomach. I stood in the doorway of Hayley Jade's room, watching her sleep, her hair all spread out across her pillow. Her eyelashes fanned across her cheeks, and her chest rose and fell in deep, relaxed breaths, her body at rest because she knew she was safe here within these walls.

I couldn't stop thinking about Kara's little sister. About how she was barely older than the child sleeping in front of me now.

I'd done some shit things in my time. I hadn't always treated women well.

But I sure as hell hadn't come close to the level of fucked-up Josiah and his cult of freaks had shown. Being an arrogant prick was bad enough, but I wasn't in the same league as Josiah.

Someone stepped in behind me, and I instantly knew from how big he was and how close he stood that it was

Chaos. Nobody else would be all up in my space like that, but for once, I didn't mind. I found myself leaning until his chest was brushing my back.

His voice was soft so he didn't wake Hayley Jade. "What's the plan?"

I sighed. "Other than go get her sister, while leaving enough men here to keep Hayley Jade and everyone else safe, I don't know."

"We don't have enough guys, do we?"

I shoved my hands in my pockets and closed my eyes, wishing I hadn't already come to that conclusion. "No. I don't think so. From what Kara has said, Josiah has more than a handful. And probably even more now, after his fucking podcast went viral. The men we dealt with at the school and the hospital were all armed. I just can't see Josiah not having a stash of weapons himself. He has to have a way of protecting his turf. It's one thing for us to protect our own grounds. We have the upper hand here. But if we have to split up, half of us here, half of us there... We don't know his grounds. Don't know what we're facing. It could end up a fucking shit show in a matter of seconds if we play this wrong."

"Kara knows Ethereal Eden."

I spun around and stared at him. "You are not seriously suggesting we take her? We'll take Kyle."

"We should take them both."

I shook my head stubbornly. "No fucking way."

"She's not going to take no for an answer. I saw the look in her eyes just now. It's the same one I've seen in her every time she has to protect Hayley Jade. Or me. Or Grayson. Or you."

I swore beneath my breath. "She has zero sense of self-preservation."

"She cares about people."

"Why can't she use some of those feelings to protect herself?" It seriously fucking killed me how she was always willing to sacrifice herself.

"Would you?" Hayden asked, so fucking sensibly I wanted to smack him in the nose. "You just said yourself we don't have enough men to do this safely. There is a real risk we might not come home. Is that going to stop you?"

"No." The answer came so quickly and easily and felt so right I didn't even have to question it.

A grin pulled at the corners of his mouth. "So the two of you are exactly the same then, aren't you? Actually, you're probably worse, considering you've never even met Jacqueline. And yet you're willing to die for her."

"She's important to Kara. So she's important to me."

"Ditto. But all I'm saying is don't give Kara a hard time for not wanting to sit here on the sidelines when you couldn't either."

I scowled at him. "Fuck, you're annoying."

He brushed his lips over mine. "Yeah, well, you're an asshole."

Couldn't deny that.

Couldn't deny the way my dick kicked at each brush of his mouth either. Or the way my fingers acted as if they had a mind of their own, tucking themselves into the waistband of his jeans and tugging him closer so I could fucking kiss him properly.

He kissed me back, mouths opening, tongues joining, the kiss turning hot fast.

My dick ached, straining toward him, but I pulled away with a groan. "Can't do this right now. I need to call the Louisiana chapter. See if they can help."

Hayden's eyes darkened, and he stepped away as if I'd slapped him. "What the fuck? No. They're in with Luca."

"So are you."

His face went cold. "That was a cheap blow, and you know it. I'm not trafficking women for Luca. The Louisiana Slayers were expecting an entire van full of them. One of their guys fucking buried Kara alive."

"Or one of ours did. We don't know for sure because both Ratchet and Thunder are buried six feet under."

"Why are you standing up for them?"

I sighed. "I'm not. But we fucking need help, and I don't know where else to get it."

Grayson cleared his throat from the other side of the room, and both Chaos and I jumped a mile. I glared at him, feeling slightly stupid for having a lover's tiff in front of him. "Fucking hell, you stalker. Where did you come from?"

"Been here the whole time, you were just too wrapped up in each other to notice. But that's beside the point. How many guys do you think you need?"

I shrugged. "I don't know. The more the better." I eyed him. "But if you think I'm letting you and your doctor buddies have guns..."

He gave me a deadpan stare. "Funny. They aren't my only friends, you know. You know those guys you met at my apartment?"

I remembered them. Five big motherfuckers who'd had Chaos and I hovering fingers over our guns, even though one of them had been baking bread and trying to make me his gay BFF. Or something. "The ones who were joking about tying a guy up and scooping out his eyeballs?"

"Yeah. They weren't joking about that."

I'd seen enough thugs and psychopaths in my time. Gotten to know a few of them, like Scythe and Vincent, really well. This life attracted men who liked to kill. So Grayson's "revelation" wasn't really much of one. "You think they'd want to help us?"

"Is there a chance they'd get to kill someone?"

"I really fucking hope so."

Grayson just shook his head. "They've been calling themselves the murder squad lately, so I think they'd be in."

"That's dark."

"They're dark sorta guys. They kinda make you look morally gray instead of morally black."

"Not sure if that's a compliment or an insult." But I needed help in whatever way, shape, or form I could get it. "Can you get them on board?"

Grayson nodded. "They owe me more than one favor. They'll be in."

I studied the doctor. "You're odd sometimes, you know? In an interesting sorta way."

Grayson grinned. "Was it my ball sack in your face that piqued your interest?"

I choked.

Chaos turned to me slowly, barely concealing his laughter. "Want to tell me what that's about?"

"Not even a bit." I shoved Grayson as I stalked off toward my bedroom. "You're all getting a little too comfortable around here. Can we go back to when you were just a guy I used to work with?"

"But then you'd never get to see my ball sack again."

He and Chaos dissolved into laughter, which slamming my bedroom door did nothing to cover.

And they called me the asshole.

19

HAYDEN

I woke up the next morning with Kara in my bed, but when I rolled over to reach for her, I found there was a squirmy girl in between us, staring up at me with big eyes.

I squished her a little, pretending I hadn't seen her. "This mattress is awfully lumpy!"

Kara and Hayley Jade both giggled.

"Hmm. And it makes noises!"

More laughter as I wriggled around, acting as if I was trying to be comfortable with her in the way. She tapped me on the chest, getting my attention.

I pretended to see her for the first time. "Where did you come from?!"

She just grinned and pointed at the wall in the direction of her room.

I kissed the top of her head. "But you thought my bed was better, huh?"

She shook her head.

"No? Didn't have anything to do with me having a TV in here then?"

She shook her head once more.

"Was it maybe because your mommy was in here?"

Kara's soft, sweet smile was like sunshine on a rainy day when Hayley Jade nodded yes.

Kara slipped her arms around her daughter, and both of us covered the little girl in kisses, while she squirmed to get away.

Eventually, she got bored and wandered out to the kitchen where someone was making a racket and would no doubt get her whatever she wanted for breakfast, even if that something was ice cream. She had everyone here wrapped around her finger, and I was no different.

Kara watched her go and sighed.

"You don't have to come today, you know? Nobody would think any less of you if you stayed just to be her mom. We have Kyle to show us where to go once we get inside Ethereal Eden's gate. There's no pressure on you here at all."

"I know. But I can't stop thinking about Jacqueline. About what they might be doing to her. If you all go in there, guns blazing, she's going to be terrified and fight you every step of the way. If I sit here, I'm just going to develop an ulcer. I need to come. I need to face it all. I can't keep running and I need to be there for her. We need to end this once and for all."

I nodded. I was no different than Hawk. I would have preferred her to stay here where I knew Fang and War and a couple of the other guys would stay behind to watch over everyone. Behind the Slayers' gates felt like the safest option right now, not driving ourselves for hours, right into a situation that might be a one on the danger scale...

But was more likely going to be a ten.

I didn't need to have met Josiah in person to know he wasn't going to give up easily. He wasn't going to let us just walk in there and bring back any woman who didn't want to be there, which was Kara's aim.

I was scared she was going to be bitterly disappointed. But if we got Jacqueline out, that was the main thing.

Even if Josiah wasn't doing anything else, taking photos of her like that, using them to attract the sick fucks who liked that sort of thing, meant she was in grave danger of so much worse.

That couldn't be ignored. Not even for another day. We were leaving and not coming back without her.

Thirty minutes later, Kara hugged Queenie and Hayley Jade goodbye. Queenie left to take Hayley Jade to school, Hawk already having drilled Queenie on all the security procedures that needed to be followed for him to feel like Hayley Jade was safe away from him. I waved at the kid until her face disappeared from view. My heart was torn in two, half of it here with her, the other half beating for her mother who needed me more, at least for today.

The quicker we left, the quicker we could get home. "Let's get this show on the road. We've got a very long day of driving, and probably an even longer night ahead of us once we get there. We all good?"

Everyone nodded. Ice and Aloha went to their bikes. Grayson's murder squad had brought a van that the five of them piled into. Scythe or Vincent, I had no idea which, drove a black Jeep with Kyle riding shotgun.

Hawk, Grayson, Kara, and I had decided to take the Slayers' club van, since it had enough seats to bring home Jacqueline plus anyone else we could get out.

We all rolled out of the Slayers' compound in a single file of vehicles, with a heavy somberness in the air that was reminiscent of going to war.

That's exactly what it felt like, right down to the guns in the black duffel bag at Hawk's feet, that I didn't want to use, but knew we'd probably have to.

I took the first driving shift, but it was a quiet one, all four of us lost to our thoughts. I rested my hand on Kara's leg beside me, rubbing it while she stared out the window. Hawk slept in the back, and the *click-clack* of Grayson's laptop keyboard could be heard above the soft music playing through the speakers.

"What if we can't get her out?" Kara asked quietly.

"We will."

"She might not come willingly, even with me there. I think she wanted to come when we left the first time, but if Samantha and Naomi have been in her ear, telling them what a wicked woman I am for leaving, and how my sins will rub off on Jacqueline if she associates with me, then she might be too scared. She's just a kid."

"We can't leave her there. She's being abused."

"I know. No matter what happens, what she says or does, you have to promise me we're bringing her home."

I glanced over at her to find her staring at me. There was nothing else for me to say. "I promise."

We stopped a couple of times for food and bathroom breaks, but the entire day was more of the same. Filling up the van while Vincent and Whip quizzed Kyle on every detail of the compound. Hawk and Ice checking the guns, making sure everything was loaded and ready to go if we needed them. Kara scratched at her arms absent-mindedly, the way she had the tendency to do when she was stressed, until I walked her into the gas station and started putting all her favorite snacks in a basket.

"I can see what you're doing." She tugged at the sleeves of her sweatshirt. "Stress eating isn't a productive way to pass time either."

I grinned at her. "Who says any of this is for you?"

A little smile crossed her lips. "You're cute. You don't even like Doritos."

"But you do. You're going to rip a hole in your arm if you keep scratching it like that. Eat the chips, Kara. Or do sudoku. Or scroll your phone. I don't care. But I'm also buying duct tape and will tie your hands behind your back if I have to."

She laughed. "So everyone we pass on the highway reports you as a kidnapper?"

"I'll just explain to the cops that after you rejected all my other offers, it was tie you up or park on the side of the road and distract you by making you come. Somehow, what with the indecent exposure laws, I think they would choose tying you up too."

She plucked the bag of chips from my hand and then pulled a scarf from a rack that also held ladies' sunglasses and hats. She waved it in my face so the material skated across my cheek. "I prefer something soft and silky when I'm being tied up, thank you." She winked and went to put the scarf back.

I plucked it from her fingers. "I'll take that then."

She stopped. "I was joking."

I put my lips to her ear and kissed the spot just below

it. "I don't think you were. I'm buying this. And after all of this is over, I'm going to buy at least three more and tie you to the first bed I can get you on."

Despite her protests, there was a quickening of her breath. "I shouldn't find you this attractive in the middle of a run-down gas station."

And I shouldn't have been thinking about sitting her up on the counter, spreading her thick thighs, and sinking my cock into the warm, wet heat in between. But I was.

The tension between us rose thick in the air, despite the setting. It was the same gut-wrenching pull I always felt when she was around. An attraction I could never explain with words because I was sure no one had ever felt so strongly about another person.

A horn honking from out by the pumps caught my attention, and Grayson waved us over from the driver's seat, clearly anxious to get moving.

The moment shattered. I put my arm around her neck and hauled her in tight. "I'm down for sharing you, you know I am. But did you have to pick a doctor who clearly likes to run on a schedule?"

Kara smiled gently, staring out at Grayson who had methodically checked the tire pressure, fuel levels, and windshield wiper fluid at each stop. He'd mapped out the route we were taking with notes that had been emailed to all of us the night before.

Not that half the guys had bothered to read it. Grayson stuck out amongst the rest of us like a sore thumb, and we all knew it.

Despite that, I liked the guy. He'd saved Kara's life, and that had earned him my respect.

But it was the way Kara looked at him that had really cemented his place here. The way she laughed at his stupid jokes and balloon animals. The way her gaze lingered on him instead of her textbooks when they were studying. The way she might not have been willing to admit to herself she was in love with him, but she lit up every time those words fell from his lips.

I opened the passenger door for her, and she got herself up into the van, Grayson leaning over the center console to kiss her.

I got in the back with Hawk who was sprawled out across the back bench seat. I debated taking the row in front of him, but then he moved his leg, making room for me, and so I took up the seat at the opposite end of his bench, leaving one free in the middle of us so we both had a bit of space.

Grayson started the van and turned up the music, singing along with the radio. He was in an oddly good mood that I suspected was fake and an attempt to lighten the vibe that had been darkening with every mile we passed.

Kara joined in, and Hawk nodded at them approvingly but kept his voice low enough only for me to hear. "He's keeping her distracted. That's good."

I wholeheartedly agreed. "Whatever keeps her from scratching her arms raw."

"You like the guy?" he asked after we'd both watched them for a while longer.

"Are you asking if I like him as a friend or if I like him for Kara?"

He shrugged.

He didn't need to answer. All Hawk ever did was

consider what was good for Kara and Hayley Jade. He stared at Grayson and Kara singing along in the front seat, happy smiles on their faces, and being silly in a way I couldn't imagine her being with either me or Hawk. We weren't built like that. Maybe we'd seen too much to ever be that carefree or maybe we just weren't wired that way.

But there was no doubt in my mind that Grayson gave Kara something Hawk and I couldn't. That was why her being with the three of us worked. Each of us providing something different to her, not one of us trying to fulfill her every need and failing because it was impossible for anyone to be everything.

We all needed a village. I'd spent my whole life searching for that. My mom had been amazing, but my brother had been ripped from my life when I was a kid and my father had never been around. I'd joined gangs, looking for that sense of community my mom, great as she was, hadn't been able to give me alone.

I'd finally found it here, with Kara and Hawk, and I wasn't arrogant enough to think we were all she needed. She needed Grayson too. Hawk and I were too intense. Gray was the one who made her laugh.

I nudged Hawk with my knee. "He's about to walk into a war with us with about as much experience in this sort of thing as a chipmunk."

"He's a weak link."

I stared at the way he kept looking at Kara, sneaking little glances of pure adoration from the driver's seat in between watching the road and checking his map. The side of his neck still held the faint tinge of purple from the bruises he'd developed after being strangled half to death. I shook my head. "He's not. He might not have spent half his life running with gangs, but he's willing to die for her, just the same as we are. That makes him just as deadly, even if he doesn't have as much experience with a gun."

Grayson had proved himself once. I wasn't going to make him keep doing it over and over, and I really hoped Hawk wasn't either. That was the sort of thing that would distract us and tear us apart. The exact opposite of the united front we needed to be right now.

To my relief, Hawk settled back against the seat and blew out a long breath. But his shoulders were stiff, and we had hours more on the road. His agitation was contagious, practically palpable in the air. I could feel it seeping through my clothes, sinking into my skin, infecting me as much as it was him.

I didn't want Kara sensing it. Didn't want her to think we were anything but one-hundred-percent confident about how this was going down.

Hawk needed to chill the fuck out and get out of his head.

I reached over and undid the button on his jeans.

He glanced at me warily and then watched me lower the zipper on his fly. "Seriously?"

"You gonna stop me?"

Hawk sniggered and lifted his hips, tugging down his jeans. "Not for a fucking second."

Smug prick. But I liked he wasn't protesting. The windows in the back had a darker tint than the ones in the front. Not completely impenetrable by any means, but they did give off an illusion of privacy from prying eyes on the road outside.

They'd do nothing to stop Grayson and Kara getting a

free peep show, but the thought of Kara watching me blow Hawk only made me hotter. I took out his cock and stroked him until he was hard, and then I leaned over and put my mouth around him.

His hands fell instantly to the back of my head. Not the light scratching Kara was fond of when my head was between her thighs. Hawk's touch was much less thoughtful, all grabby fingers fisting in my hair, his hands trying to control me.

I pulled off and gave him a look.

He laughed and put his hands up. "Fine. Fine. Sorry! Carry on!"

I lowered my mouth over him again, sucking on his knob.

More of the same from Hawk. Him being an arrogant prick and thinking this was his show.

I glared at him again. "You good trying to control everything all of the time?"

"You love it."

He wasn't exactly wrong, but this also wasn't the relationship I wanted with him. I wasn't going to be his bitch. Take his cock whenever he wanted me to.

This was a two-way fucking street, and Hawk needed to learn that. I had every intention of fucking him. Couldn't wait to feel my cock sink inside his tight virgin ass. But we were never going to get there if Hawk didn't let go of his need to be in charge.

That was part of the reason he was so stressed out right now. Because the situation we were about to walk into was unknown. And he had little control over the outcome.

Not that he'd ever admit that. I saw through his bullshit, cocky exterior. I knew he was stressed and scared, and I was just trying to help him. If he wanted to be a dick about it, he could go fuck himself. He was such a bastard.

I was done playing games. "Nah, fuck you. You want to be in control? You can fuck your hand." I shifted back to my side, and slunk down in my seat, tugging a baseball cap low over my eyes.

He could take care of his stress by himself. I didn't fucking care if he worried and stressed himself into an early grave.

Except the thought of him dying had me sick to my stomach. Especially because there was a very real chance of bullets flying when we stormed Ethereal Eden.

I didn't want to lose him.

Not that I was going to tell him that. Cocky bastard wouldn't ever let me live it down if I did.

Hawk snorted. "You fucking mad at me?"

Mad he was still playing stupid games and couldn't just let me in for one fucking minute. Yeah.

He slid across the bench a few inches. "Chaos."

He was pretty much the only person who still called me that. On his lips, I liked it. But sometimes it felt surface level. Like a way of him holding me at arm's length and not admitting I was a real fucking person beneath the persona. The same way it felt when he acted like I was just a place to stick his dick, even though I was sure this thing between us was more than that. "You know that hasn't been my name for a long fucking time."

He paused. "It's habit."

"Whatever."

"Hayden."

I still didn't look up. Didn't have the energy to do this with him right now, while I was battling the realization he'd become someone who mattered to me. Someone I cared about. Someone I might have even loved if he wasn't such a dickhead all the damn time.

I needed a minute to process the feelings potentially losing him tonight was stirring up inside me. I couldn't do that with him yammering in my ear.

His fingers flicked the button on my jeans. Drew down my fly.

I didn't stop him.

He didn't talk.

I lifted my hips but didn't raise my head. Didn't look at him. Was too fucking scared by the sudden swell of feeling inside me. If I looked him in the eye, I might blurt out something dumb.

Like I loved him.

Fucking hell.

Of all the times and places to have a realization about that. This was not it.

I let his mouth wrapping around my cock clear my head. Or maybe it just fuzzed all thoughts right out of existence. I didn't know. Didn't care. But it was better than concentrating on the fact I was just as in love with him as I was with Kara.

Falling for the most emotionally unavailable, still probably a little bit homophobic man on the face of the planet. So fucking fabulous.

But his mouth felt good. There was no denying that. He sucked me slowly, getting me hard, pumping my shaft with his hand and licking my knob while the van vibrations only added to the sensation in the most pleasurable sort of way.

I lifted my hat so I could watch him but kept my hands to myself to prove a point. That I could let him have control. So why couldn't he?

In the mirror on the back of the passenger seat sun visor, my gaze caught with Kara's. A slow smile spread across my lips, liking the way her eyes smoldered with heat, unable to look away from what Hawk and I were doing.

Her shoulders rose and fell too fast, telling me she was breathing too quickly, and the pink creeping up the back of her neck told me this was getting her hot.

I loved she liked watching him and me together.

It only made me wish she was back here with us so I could have my fingers between her thighs, pushing deep inside her pussy and finger-fucking her until she was just as wet as Hawk's mouth was right now.

But I could have the next best thing. "Lift your skirt, Kara."

Grayson glanced over his shoulder at me, gaze dipping to what Hawk was doing, and then went back to our woman.

She was still watching me in the mirror. But she shifted on her seat, pulling her long skirt up so it settled high on her thighs like a mini skirt.

"Put your hand inside your panties. I want to know if you're wet."

Forever willing to please, she shifted on the seat, and her sharp gasp said she'd done exactly what I'd instructed.

"Concentrate on the road. Concentrate on the road,"

Grayson muttered, earning himself a snigger from Hawk, despite having my cock deep in his mouth.

Kara's tiny moans from the front seat told me she was fingering herself, and fuck if that didn't have me thrusting up into Hawk's mouth faster and harder than I ever had before.

To my surprise, he took every inch, until I was practically gagging him with my cock, and still he didn't move or complain. If anything, he worked harder, driving me closer to an orgasm I wasn't even sure I wanted to reach because once I did, it would be over and that felt criminal.

But I wanted to watch Kara come. Wanted to hear her moan. Loved the idea the cars whizzing by outside had no idea what we were doing in here. That somehow made it all the dirtier.

"Angle the mirror so I can see your pussy, Kara. Lay your seat back. Put your heels up on the seat and spread those knees so I can watch you fingering yourself."

I groaned when she did exactly that, laying her seat down so she was out of view of other cars, though the height of the van helped hide her anyway.

It was still a dangerous game to play. If a truck passed us and the driver happened to glance down, they'd see every inch of her beautiful body.

Kara's moan of pleasure made it all worthwhile.

Grayson jerked the steering wheel, making a hard right off the highway onto some sort of access road that felt like it had been paved a century ago, judging by the way the van suddenly jolted and shook as we bounced along.

The walkie-talkie Hawk had brought along crackled

to life, Grayson's murder squad and Scythe questioning where the fuck we were going.

Grayson picked it up and half groaned into the receiver. "We need a minute. Or thirty. Do not follow us."

There was a pause, and then Scythe's sarcastic attitude came over the line. "Be safe now, kids. Or, I guess, don't bother? You can't knock her up twice."

We all ignored him. We'd catch up with the convoy at the next pit stop. Right now, the stress levels were too high, and we all needed a little relief so we could be fully focused when we got there. A few more hours of driving, and there'd be no time for this. No room for the connection we were all desperately seeking.

Grayson had us down some sort of country road in the middle of Bumfuck, Nowhere, nothing but fields, trees, and cows as far as the eye could see. There wasn't even a farmhouse in the distance, and we left the noise of the highway behind, bumping along the dirt road until Grayson parked beneath the shade of some trees and turned off the engine.

Hawk hadn't stopped tonguing the ridges of my cock, and I groaned, partially because he was so damn good at it, and partially from the view of Kara laid out on the passenger seat, her pussy wet and gleaming in the mirror, her sweet fingers rubbing her clit and disappearing inside her body so damn intoxicating I couldn't turn away from it.

I needed to come. Groaned and dragged Hawk's head away so I wouldn't choke him, but he shoved me back, taking me like a pro and sucking me until I couldn't fucking see straight.

My balls drew up, my orgasm imminent. At the last

moment he pulled his mouth away, jerking my cock until I sprayed all over his fist.

My head dropped back on the seat, pleasure swimming through my blood in the most relaxing way that had me forgetting all about the danger Kara was about to be in. I didn't think about it. Just let my brain fizz out, enjoying each stroke of Hawk's hand until my dick couldn't take it anymore and I pushed him away gently.

He caught my gaze, and then slowly he coated his cock in my cum, using it to jerk himself off.

"Fuck, that's hot." I couldn't stop staring at him, the tight grip of one hand on his balls, squeezing himself while the other covered him in my cum.

My dick was so done, sucked so good. But it didn't make the need for him any less.

When he leaned in to kiss me, I devoured him, dragging him in tight and then down on top of me. His heavy weight between my legs had me panting with need, his bare cock rubbing on mine. I needed more than a thirty-second recovery though, so I shifted until his cock rubbed lower, pressing to my ass.

His lips trailed off mine, his stubble scraping across my chin and cheek until he got to my ear. "Hayden..."

We froze.

I squinted.

Both stared at each other.

I'd thought I'd wanted him to say my name, and yet when he did...I realized how badly it just didn't fit.

He huffed out a breath. "That was so fucking unsexy."

"It really was. Felt like you were my schoolteacher or something."

"Oh, fuck off. You're the one who wanted me to be all

romantic and use your actual name. It's not my fault Hayden is about as attractive as a cold shower. Can we go back to fucking now?" He kissed me, and nudged my ass with the slicked-up head of his cock.

I groaned loudly, twisting my head to the side so I could watch Grayson lay his seat right back. Kara climbed over the center console, straddling him and sinking herself down onto his cock.

"Need to see your tits, Kara," I groaned, eyes on her while Hawk filled me so deeply I was sure I would be feeling it for days in all the best ways. He fucked me slow, giving me time to adjust to his body, while kissing my neck and chest, tugging my shirt off so he could lick my nipples while he rode out his pleasure on my body.

Grayson lifted her top, and Kara pulled it off the rest of the way. Her hips rocked sensuously over his lap, her legs digging into the seat belt and the driver's side armrest, but if it was painful, she didn't seem to care. She had her head tipped back, riding him like the fucking goddess she was, all tits and belly and thighs I couldn't get enough of.

Grayson lowered her bra straps and flipped the cups down, exposing her pink nipples, just fucking begging for his mouth.

She beat him to it, though, cupping her breasts, pinching herself between her forefinger and thumb, owning her pleasure.

My dick got hard watching her. Hawk balanced himself with one arm on the back of the seats so he could use the other to stroke my cock into another erection, even though I'd barely recovered from the first.

The combination of the show Kara was putting on,

and him deep inside my body was so good, it was lucky I'd already come once, or I probably would have embarrassed myself.

"Fuck, you're so tight," Hawk groaned, strangling my dick with his fist. "Feels just like this."

He squeezed my cock tight, relaxed, then did it again, jerking me off in a way that was almost as good as Kara's pussy clamping around me.

He thrust in and out, his big body awkward in the small space, but at least we had more room than a car and neither of us seemed willing to stop and take it outside, even if there was no one around for miles.

He groaned, his movements getting erratic, his eyes closing, and fucking me faster, harder, until we were both ready to lose it. I moved his hand away from my cock, not wanting to come again, needing to save that until I could get my hands on Kara.

Her cries of pleasure as she came from riding Grayson's cock echoed around the van. It rocked a little, Grayson coming hard too, burying his face in her tits and sucking her nipple into his mouth.

Hawk fell over the edge a moment later, buried deep inside me. He came with a moan and the noise went straight to my dick.

He pulled out, staring down at me, his breath ragged. His lips found mine, and he kissed me deeply, our tongues in sync.

I throbbed everywhere, could still feel him inside me even though he wasn't. Precum leaked from my tip, and I shifted out from beneath Hawk and leaned forward to lift Kara's chin from where she rested on Grayson's chest. The two of them were a mess of half-discarded clothes and glistening skin, her cheeks flushed pink. "Need you."

"Need you too," she whispered.

I didn't give a fuck it was broad daylight outside. I yanked my pants up only enough I wouldn't trip over them and slid open the back door. Made my way to the driver's side and opened Grayson's door.

Kara was waiting for me, her eyes still hot with need, even though she'd already come once.

She lifted off Grayson, leaving him blissed out on the laid-back seat while I helped her out of the van.

That was as long as I could wait to have her. I crowded her up against the side, put one hand beneath her knee and raised it up, hooking it around the backs of my thighs and opening her up for me to slide right into.

I didn't give a fuck Grayson's cum coated the inside of her thighs and dripped from her pussy. It only made me want her more. I wanted to remind her body she had more than one man who needed to claim her as often as she would allow.

I plunged deep inside her slick slit, filling her, fucking her hard so my pubic bone ground against her clit, giving her the friction she'd need to come all over again.

I gazed down at her sweet face, the big eyes that stared up at me full of love and desire and a connection I couldn't get enough of. What I felt for her was so different than what I felt for Hawk, even though I loved them both.

If I'd said it out loud, Hawk would have made fun of me for a lifetime. But when I was inside her, when her eyes were locked with mine, I knew this was where I was supposed to be.

That she was mine and for the past five years, I'd been walking around, missing half my goddamn soul.

Something changed between us. The attraction and need becoming something more, my heart racing every time I thought about the fact anything could happen tonight when we got to Ethereal Eden. The thought left me in a cold sweat.

"I love you," she whispered, a slight tremble in her voice. "Promise me we're all coming home when this is done. Not just me and Jacqueline. You and Hawk and Grayson too."

I looked away, focusing on the way my cock slid in and out of her body, distracting her by rubbing her clit and pinching her nipples.

I couldn't promise her tomorrow when I knew all too well how quickly it could be ripped away.

20

X

I sniggered at Grayson's van turning off and his instructions not to follow them. Scythe took the words right out of my mouth when he got on the walkie-talkies and gave them shit about it.

Whip shook his head and muttered, "Yeah, because when I'm about to walk into a potentially deadly situation, sex is the first thing on my mind. What's wrong with Gray? Her pussy made of gold or what?"

I scoffed. "Sex is the first thing on every man's mind, at every minute of the day, whether we're walking carefree along the beach or trying to infiltrate some fucking cult, whose members are probably waiting to drown us in holy water." I glanced at the older man, frown pinching between my eyebrows. "You don't think they'll try that, do you? I can't swim very well, and I didn't pack my floaties."

I was pretty sure Whip rolled his eyes, but it was hard to tell because he was steadfastly staring out the window, making sure we didn't crash the van.

He was such a grump. Where was the joy? The excitement about all the killing we were about to do? Yeah, yeah, we'd promised we wouldn't. Innocent people and all that. Blah, blah, blah. But surely one of the cult fuckers was going to step out of line and give me a reason to get my hands dirty.

At least I hoped so, otherwise I could have just stayed home and watched *Jerry Springer* reruns. Man, what a banger that show was. You are *not* the father? Classic TV gold.

Trigger reached his arms above his head and tried to release some of the muscle tension sitting in this fucking van for almost a whole day had created. "Gray's just trying to release some pressure. Leave him alone. Fuck, if one of you had a wet, willing pussy for me to suck right now, I would."

"I did not need that mental image, thank you." Whip checked his mirrors and merged into the next lane to keep up with Scythe in the Jeep and the guys on their bikes.

I shook my head. "He's so pussy-whipped. Have you seen the look on his face every time she's around?"

Trig grimaced. "I've never seen anyone smile so much. Like, do you think his mouth is sore?"

"Has to be." I glanced at Whip. "You ever smiled in your entire life?"

"Not since you came into it."

I sniggered. "Oh, Whip. How I enjoy your dry, dry sense of humor."

Torch flicked the wheel on his lighter a few times, absentmindedly creating the tiny flickering sparks he was so fond of. "Was Gray like this with his wife? I don't remember him being this obsessed with her."

Trig shook his head. "He was nothing like this with Annette. They were both so fucking selfish, so wrapped up in their own shit. They were just arm candy for each other and a warm body to sleep next to at night so they didn't feel lonely."

"But now he's found his true love." I bounced on my seat, needing to expel some energy because I'd been sitting still for hours. "How sweet." So sweet I gagged a little for effect, then grinned. "You ever been in love, Whip?"

"Why the fuck would I tell you that?"

I grinned. "Well, that's a solid yes. What about you, Trigger?"

He twisted to stare out the window.

I raised an eyebrow in surprise. "Seriously? Not even going to give me a yes or no head shake?"

Ace twisted a thin cord around his fingers, his long legs cramped in the small space of the back seat. "You know they aren't going to tell you shit about their personal lives. Would you trust any of us with the details about someone you loved? Hell, look what Trig did to his own sister-in-law? Chopped her up and fed her to the pigs."

Trigger scoffed with a laugh. "That's creative. But why say it like it's a bad thing? If I had fed her to pigs, she would have deserved it. It would have been poetic justice since she hacked shit on me that time I tried to go vegetarian," he grumbled beneath his breath. "Nothing wrong with wanting to save some fucking animals."

"Probably shouldn't tell him about that rooster in Gray's freezer then, huh, Ace?"

Ace shot me a dirty look. "I'm done talking to you for

the rest of the trip. It was one small accidental chicken shooting, and you're never going to let me live it down."

"You yelled, 'Hasta La Vista, baby!' before you pulled the trigger."

"It was me or the rooster, X! The town wasn't big enough for both of us!" Ace crossed his arms grumpily and twisted to stare out the window.

Torch took over where Ace had left off. "I think the point that we're maybe trying to make is we keep our personal lives personal. So why are you even asking about Whip's family?"

They were all so boring. "Because what else are we going to talk about?"

Whip shifted gears. "The weather. The news. Why you told Torch to get that haircut…"

Torch self-consciously ran his fingers through the mullet I'd talked him into getting last week.

I made a face at them. "It's not my fault Torch's ears stick out like Dumbo. Who knew? They were always covered when his hair was longer."

Torch scowled in my direction. "And now I'm not talking to you either. God, you're an asshole."

I shrugged and punched Whip in the arm. "Whip still loves me."

"Whip is going to drive this van off the nearest bridge if you don't learn to read the room and shut up when you're driving everyone mad."

I made a face at him and rolled my eyes. "Whip needs to stop talking about himself in the third person 'cause it's as weird and creepy as that hairy mole on his back…"

The dirty look he shot my way was just straight-up rude.

So was the way none of them answered the next few questions I fired at them.

I sighed, and picked up the radio, pressing the button on the side so I could talk to the Jeep ahead of us. "Hey, Scythe?"

"Yeah?"

"Do you know that ninety-nine bottles of beer on the wall song?"

Without taking his eyes off the road, Whip grabbed his gun and pointed it in my direction. "I swear, X, I will pull the trigger and enjoy every moment of your brains splattering against the window behind you."

I twisted so I was facing him front on. And called his bluff with my fingers pressed against the walkie-talkie button. "Ninety-nine bottles of beer on the wall, ninety-nine bottles of beer..."

Scythe joined in, and we sang together. "Take one down, pass it around, ninety-eight bottles of beer on the wall."

Whip smushed his lips together, his grumpy old man scowl etched deep into his forehead. "I hope Gray has more room in his freezer for dead bodies."

I sniggered. "You love me, Whip. You aren't going to shoot me."

"No, but if you keep singing like that, I might just shoot myself."

21

KARA

I directed the convoy of cars to a side street away from the start of Ethereal Eden's property, not wanting their security cameras to catch us before we'd had time to coordinate the plan.

It worried me that even with Grayson's organizing skills, there wasn't much of a plan to speak of. Kyle and I had both gotten on the walkie-talkies as we'd driven the last hundred miles, trying to explain in as much detail as possible about the layout of the commune, security we knew about, where people were most likely to be gathered, and where my parents' house was. Hopefully, Jacqueline would be sleeping in her bed, ready for us to just pluck her from it and get out of there.

That was what I'd told them over and over. That this place was full of women and children. We weren't going in there to light the place up and send bullets flying.

Nobody was dying on my watch.

Not even Josiah. As tempting as the idea might have been.

Hawk and Hayden had argued with me about that, but I refused to let them spend the rest of their lives in prison for killing him. I wouldn't lose my new family before I'd even truly gotten to love them.

A life in prison was the only future Josiah deserved. One that came with a lifetime of fear and terror at the hands of men just like him.

I wanted him to have the life he'd given to me. And to suffer every minute of it.

Death was too kind a punishment. Too quick. Too painless.

I wondered what the Lord would think of the dark thoughts that tumbled around my head. But if He thought anything other than they were well deserved, then I didn't want anything to do with Him anyway.

"We need guys on the perimeter," Hawk instructed, taking charge of the group. "Someone in the vans, ready to drive if we need to get away quick. We can temporarily ditch the bikes and the Jeep if we have to. The vans will hold more people."

X screwed up his face. "I do not volunteer as tribute."

"Yeah, hard pass on being left behind." Whip cracked his knuckles. "If we aren't killing anyone, fair enough, I'll respect that, but I'm gonna crawl out of my skin if I'm just sitting here waiting while you guys have all the fun."

Aloha pouted at the idea of leaving his bike but was the first to put his hand up for the job that clearly no one else wanted. "I'll drive. But we come back for the bikes if we need to. I'm not leaving my baby here permanently."

Hawk tossed him the van keys. Then turned to Grayson. "You want to drive the Jeep? Make sure your manicure doesn't get wrecked?"

Grayson flipped him the bird. "Not a fucking chance. I'm wherever Kara is."

"Same," Hayden agreed.

They both looked at Hawk, like he might volunteer to be the other driver.

He scoffed. "Yeah. That might happen."

One of Grayson's friends, who I was keeping a wide berth from, even though they were here to help, raised his hand. "I'll do it. I ain't got no death wish tonight like the rest of you. That Josiah guy sounds like a crazy mofo. And really, my skills lie more with fire. I don't think I'm going to be all that useful unless you want to torch the place?" He glanced at me hopefully.

I shook my head quickly. "No. But...thank you for the offer?"

I had no idea how I was supposed to talk to a man as psychotic as Torch. He had crazy eyes, and the constant flicking of that lighter was disturbing.

He gave a little sigh of disappointment but took the van keys and leaned back against it with his arms folded while he listened to the rest of us work through the details.

Hawk pointed at each of us as he talked. "Whip, Ice, Kyle, Ace, and Trigger go in from the far side of the property. X, Scythe, Chaos, Grayson, Kara, and me from this side. We're all heading for Kara's parents' house where we believe Jacqueline will be sleeping, but as two teams in case one is intercepted."

I looked at Kyle. "If your team gets there first, you need to be the one to go in and get her. She knows you, at least a little bit. She'll be terrified if a group of strange men try stealing her out of her bed. I don't want her traumatized any more than she already is." I eyed my guys. "If we get there first, none of you will hold me back from going in that house. No matter what happens. You hear me?"

To my surprise, all three nodded.

A rush of adrenaline filled me.

The last time I'd been here I was terrified for my life. Now I was more scared of losing the people I loved.

Hawk rubbed a hand across the back of his neck, his T-shirt riding up just enough to flash a strip of tattoo-covered skin just above the waistband of his jeans. "If we all have some vague idea of what we're doing, let's go. Keep communications to the bare minimum. Sound is going to travel out here."

Like groups of soldiers, we fell into two lines, figures dark in the deep shadows of the night. I was right in the middle of my group, with X, Scythe, and Grayson behind me, Hayden and Hawk in front of me. I stuck close to Hayden's back and whispered corrections if Hawk started steering us off track. We stuck to the shadows of the neighboring property, the fences of Ethereal Eden gleaming silver in the moonlight and making the place seem more like a prison than a sanctuary.

At the fence line, Hawk kneeled and pulled bolt cutters from his backpack, cutting through the wire to make an opening big enough for all of us to get through.

With every step, my heart beat faster. I was sure, at any moment, we'd trip some sort of alarm. That the floodlights would all turn on, or that the blaring of the siren they'd triggered the night we'd left would give us away again.

But we made it through the outer pastures where the

cows lifted their heads at our approach but let us pass without more than a sleepy moo. I'd given us the more direct route to the house, coming in from the nearest side of the commune, rather than the other side that would take Kyle and his team past the house I'd lived in with Josiah.

I'd planned to come back here and collect evidence that could implicate Josiah in Alice's murder, but now all I could concentrate on was getting my sister, my unborn baby, and the men I loved out of here.

We'd have to find some other way to see Josiah put in jail for the rest of his life. Jacqueline had to come first.

My heart clenched at the sight of the little cabin I'd lived in with Hayley Jade when she was a baby. The one Shari, the woman who'd raised Hayley Jade after she'd been taken from me, now lived in. I moved toward it instinctively, but Grayson grabbed my arm.

"Where are you going? Isn't that your parents' house just up there?"

I nodded. "But there's another woman who needs our help in this cabin."

Hayden and Hawk both stopped and glanced back at us, hearing every word of the whispered conversation because the night was so quiet.

Hawk shook his head. "We don't have that sort of time to waste. The longer we're here, the more chance there is of being caught. I don't like how many vehicles there are over there."

I followed his line of sight, my gaze bouncing across the trucks parked outside every house, and a lot more parked in a makeshift parking lot beside a big barn.

Hawk eyed them all warily. "That's a lot more than

you told us about. Unless Josiah has been buying cars for all the women and kids who live here..."

I shook my head. "Most of us don't even know how to drive. Even those who came from the outside are never permitted behind the wheel. If the women go to town to sell at the market, they're always driven in by one of the men."

Hayden swore softly. "So we need to assume there's more men here than there were. Probably not surprising, after his podcast went viral. It could have brought him a lot of new followers."

Hawk turned to me. "Just Jacqueline right now, okay? She's the target. If we can collect anyone else on the way out then great, but she has to be the priority. Shari is an adult, and she came here of her own free will."

"Not for this life," I whispered. "She didn't come here for this. No one did. He forces her to offer herself to men for sex, Hawk. She's the woman who raised Hayley Jade. We can't just leave her here. Eventually, one of those men will kill her, and I can't live with that. Can you? She's important to our daughter, so she has to be important to us too."

I prayed no one would balk at me calling Hayley Jade ours.

Because I meant it. Grayson might have had more of a friendship with her, and I knew he cared about her deeply. But Hawk and Hayden were the fathers she'd never had.

Queenie was the grandmother I'd always wanted for her. Aloha and Ice the uncles.

She was all of ours.

Scythe turned to Hawk. "We split up. X and I will go

get the woman. You all go get the girl. We meet back here. We came in together. We leave together. Capiche?"

Hawk deferred to me, and I nodded.

I caught Scythe's hand before he slipped away into the darkness. "She's going to be terrified. She'll fight you."

X grinned with a boyish charm. "Don't worry. Women like me. I'll have her happily skipping by my side before you guys even get to your house."

Scythe squinted. "You skip?"

"You don't?"

"I have a five-year-old. Of course I skip. With a rope and everything. Double Dutch champion of the clubhouse, I'll have you know. Totally kicked Queenie's behind, much to her disgust."

"Yeah? I could never get the double unders. Maybe you could give me some tips?"

Hawk glared at both of them like they'd grown an extra head. "Maybe you could both go do what we brought you here for and save your jump rope tips for a more appropriate time?"

Scythe and X both rolled their eyes as they slunk off toward Shari's house, muttering about everyone being so serious all the time and how we were no fun at all.

Hawk blinked, turning his attention back to me. "Honestly, I don't know why we brought them."

Grayson shook his head. "X talks a lot of shit, but he'll get the job done."

Hawk sighed. "Scythe too. They're oddly alike. It's disturbing."

Hayden motioned toward my parents' house. "Let's worry less about the psychopaths who can more than handle their own, and worry more about the four of us getting Jacqueline out without waking up the entire commune."

"Good plan," Grayson whispered back. "This place is creepy as fuck."

He wasn't wrong. I wasn't sure if it was just that it was the middle of the night, and a wind whistled through the trees, creating an eerie sound. Or if it was just the energy of this place, the bad vibes Josiah had created here that somehow lingered even when people weren't around.

Maybe it was the memories of every horrible thing he'd ever done to me in the big house he'd built to show his power and wealth.

A house of horrors I couldn't forget, especially not now, when it was so close.

I wondered if my bedroom was still empty.

Or if he'd found a new wife to torture in my place.

The thought left a sick taste in my mouth. Hayden was right. We needed to get this done and get out of here.

I took the lead, staying low and to the edges of the buildings, but doubling our pace, the beating of my heart now clearing my head and pushing me on rather than leaving me scared and shaking the way I'd been the last time I'd been here

I avoided the creaky porch stair, relieved when the guys all did as well, and waited until they'd crowded around me. "You all stay here," I whispered. "I'll get her and come back down."

"Not happening," Grayson whispered, gaze constantly flickering over our surroundings to the houses next door and the communal area at our backs.

Hawk instantly agreed with him. "Zero chance of you going anywhere alone, Little Mouse, unless Grayson wants to do CPR and restart my fucking heart after I die from the stress of knowing you're in that house unprotected."

I sighed and looked to Hayden to be the voice of reason.

He instinctively knew what I needed, and how to handle Hawk as well. "You two will guard the front and rear entrances while I go in with her." He glanced at me. "I assume one guide is more satisfactory to you? I'll wait outside Jacqueline's bedroom door while you get her, but that's as alone as you're going to get. Deal?"

I nodded quickly. Two of us could get in and out easier than four of us, if they were really insisting on me not going in alone.

I couldn't imagine my own family hurting me.

But then I didn't really know these people the way I'd once thought I did. The people I'd thought they were would have never forced me into marrying a man I didn't love. They'd never have let a stranger take my daughter away from me.

Hawk went to argue, but Hayden put his fingers to his lips. "Your finger is hovering over that trigger like you're just itching for a reason to pull it. This house is full of innocent women and children, and you're not going to be the reason one of them is hurt."

He swore under his breath and then jerked his head toward the door. "Go then."

I twisted the door handle and blinked in surprise. "It's locked. They've never locked the door."

Hawk moved in to pick it. "Josiah's clearly tightening

up their security." He fiddled with his little tool, jimmying it around in the lock.

"Or his people are scared," Grayson murmured. "There are fences everywhere, that should give a sense of security from the outside world. But it won't when the real thing they're scared of is inside these walls."

I stared at him. "What are you saying?"

He shook his head. "If they weren't locking doors before, but now they are, maybe they've realized it's not the outside world they need to be scared of. Maybe they've realized it's Josiah who is the true monster."

Instantly, with that doubt in my head, I wanted to save them all. Storm the house. Wake them all up. Beg them to come with us. It didn't matter what they'd done. They were my family and I loved them. I didn't want them here, living under the black cloud Josiah had created out of what had once been a peaceful, homestead country life.

Like Hayden could read my mind, he gave a silent shake of his head. "We can't risk it. Just Jacqueline."

He always knew what I was thinking. Or rather, could read me in a way nobody else could. That soul-deep connection we'd forged years ago was built on him understanding me, and knowing me until sometimes he knew my heart better than I did.

But he was right. We were reading a whole lot into a lock on the door.

The lock gave a tiny pop, and Hawk twisted the handle, opening the door slowly, his gun pointed into the darkness.

Hayden was right. He couldn't be in here. He was too amped up.

I squeezed his arm as we passed him, hoping the small touch would be enough to calm him.

But I couldn't wait around to see.

We made our way up the stairs on silent feet, me holding my breath, because I was sure if I dared to breathe it would be jagged and loud. We moved fast, Hayden's fingertips grazing my back in a way that might have been distracting anywhere else, but here was just reassuring.

I paused at Jacqueline's bedroom door and glanced back at Hayden, who gave me a silent nod.

I twisted the handle, and we stepped into her room.

I'd half been expecting Josiah to be sitting in her armchair with a loaded shotgun, just waiting for us.

But what we found on the other side was maybe worse.

Moonlight shimmered over glass beads and white satin. A wedding dress, one too tiny to be for any other member of the family, hung from a hook on Jacqueline's wall.

Anger speared through me hot and fast, staring at the gown made for the thirteen-year-old asleep in the single bed, a stuffed teddy bear still clutched in her arms like it was the only protection she had.

Not anymore.

I could feel Hayden vibrating with anger behind me, and I knew instantly that leaving Hawk outside had been the right call. He wouldn't have hesitated in storming down the hallway to my father's bedroom and putting a gun in his mouth.

I knew Hayden wanted to. Even I wanted to. My eyes

burned with hot, angry tears at the betrayal. My father had sold yet another of his daughters.

Was it to Josiah? Was Jacqueline to marry him and take my spot?

I leaned down, sweeping her soft hair off her face.

She looked barely older than Hayley Jade, and my fingers shook with a mixture of adrenaline and fear and anger. "Jacqueline. Wake up. It's me. Kara."

Her eyes fluttered open, then widened in confusion.

Her gaze flickered over my shoulder, and terror filled her expression. She opened her mouth.

I clapped my hand over it before she could make a sound. "Don't scream. He's a friend. He won't hurt either of us."

She shook her head frantically, scooting back on the bed, clutching the covers to her chest.

Hayden's voice was barely a whisper. "Don't say anything. Just listen to your sister. We're only trying to help."

Jacqueline froze at Hayden's command. Then dropped her head meekly.

I didn't like it, but for once the meekness that had been trained into her might be of use. It would have been quicker to just get Hayden to toss her over his shoulder, but we couldn't risk her screaming.

"You're coming with us," I whispered frantically, grabbing her jacket from the back of her desk chair and trying to put it on her. "We know all about what's been happening here. The photos—"

Her head jerked up. Tears filled her eyes then overflowed. "He made me...I'm so embarrassed."

I stopped and hugged her tight, even though I knew

every second we stayed here was dangerous. But she was a child and, in that moment, she needed someone to say it was going to be okay. "You have no reason to be. You're leaving with us and you're never coming back. I have a home. A safe one. Far away from here, and I'll take care of you."

"*We'll* take care of you," Hayden corrected. "But you have to come with us. Now." His lip curled as his gaze caught on the horrifying child-bride wedding dress. "Before Hawk comes up here and sees that and sends bullets flying all throughout the compound. I don't think I can talk him off the ledge again."

I wasn't sure I could either.

Jacqueline tugged on her shoes, but that was all we let her bring. Everything else was left behind, an entire life she'd never see again.

And it couldn't happen soon enough.

We moved down the stairs quicker and more carelessly than we had when we'd gone up them, but suddenly I couldn't get away fast enough. I ran out the front door, Jacqueline behind me, Hayden protecting her from the rear. A light came on in my parents' window, but by then we were already in the shadows, Grayson and Hawk falling in behind us, the five of us moving back toward the meeting place where Scythe and X waited with Shari between them.

I gawked at the gag in her mouth and her hands tied with duct tape behind her back.

I shot Scythe and X dirty looks. "What on earth did you tie her up for?"

X shrugged. "Women normally like when I do that."

We all stared at him, but Scythe was the one who

filled the rest of us in. He held a cloth to his face that was dark with what looked like blood. "She put up a fight. We had no choice."

I stared at him. "She's half your size!"

"Her claws are sharper than Hayden's kittens, and I'm already ripped to shreds from those furballs, so excuse me if I made my life a bit easier with some duct tape. This was me being nice! Normally if someone scratched me like that, I would have carved my name in their skin with my knife—"

Hawk elbowed him. "Not helping your case here, bro."

"They won't hurt you," I promised Shari, connecting my gaze to hers. "I want to take the tape off, but you have to promise me you aren't going to scream."

She nodded quickly, edging closer to me.

I ripped the duct tape from Shari's hands, and she yanked the gag out of her mouth. She glared at X and Scythe. "If you'd just told me you were with Kara, I wouldn't have fought you!"

X glanced at Scythe. "Didn't we say that?"

Scythe paused. "Shit. I don't think we did."

X cringed. "Ooops, our bad. Complaints can be submitted to the head office—"

Gray suddenly stood a little straighter now we'd sorted out the drama. His head swiveled side to side. "Where's Jacqueline?"

I spun around.

She'd been right behind me. But now suddenly, she wasn't.

Panic speared through me. We'd all been focused on

Shari and X and Scythe. Had none of us been watching her?

"There!" Shari pointed to the other side of the communal area.

All I could see of her was her golden hair, flashing in the moonlight, before the shadows swallowed her up again.

"Where the hell is she going?" Gray muttered as we all moved to follow her.

She ran in the opposite direction of her house. Away from all the homes, where people slept. If she was going to alert Josiah of our presence, then she was going the wrong way.

When none of us answered, Shari filled the silence. "She's going to the women's center."

I stopped and stared at her. "Why would she go there? After what Josiah makes her do?"

Shari swallowed hard, not questioning how I knew about that. Details didn't matter now.

She pressed her lips into a tight line. "I don't know for sure, but if it were me, I'd be going back for the hard drive with all her photos on it."

22

KARA

The huge, corrugated iron shed loomed over me, a dark, hulking figure between the trees. It somehow whispered of the evil things that took place inside the walls, and I shivered, despite the thin trail of sweat dripping down my back from running.

"This way." Shari didn't bother to keep her voice down. The shed was at the other end of the main community, well away from the houses we'd been trying to keep quiet around.

Hawk had risked radioing Whip and his team to follow us for backup, even though chasing after Jacqueline had taken us all farther from the getaway cars than any of us really wanted to be.

It didn't matter. I wasn't leaving without my sister, and the guys weren't leaving without me. I followed Shari through the open doorway, eyeing the pin code by the door which clearly Jacqueline had known in order to get in ahead of us.

I hated she knew it. That she'd been forced to work

here, lying and scamming people all while being abused herself.

The entire bottom level of the shed was filled with cheap desks that could have been picked up on the side of the road after their owners had considered them trash. There were a few office chairs, but it was mostly hard stools or unmatching dining table seats pushed neatly beneath each desk. Desktop computers or laptops sat at each workstation, along with thick booklets that looked like movie scripts.

Shari saw me glance at one. "They're the lines we're supposed to feed the targets. He and Onith created them to streamline the whole process." She turned away. "You don't want to read the things in them."

I couldn't stop myself from opening one. The lines on the page were familiar. The same ones Alice had used in the beginning of her texts to Golden. I flicked through the pages, noticing where she'd gone off track, the conversation turning personal and their true feelings playing out, script clearly forgotten. But that didn't stop my eye from skimming farther along and balking at the things Josiah had these women saying to unsuspecting targets. Each page got worse and worse. I shut it quickly. "Let's just get Jacqueline and get out of here."

She nodded, pointing to the mezzanine level. "She'll be up there, probably. In Josiah's office."

I headed for the stairs, but Jacqueline appeared at the top of them, holding a small hard drive. Her eyes gleamed with determination. "I've got it. I can't do anything about the photos already out there in text chats. But I have all the originals. And so much more."

Relief at just the sight of her filled me. I rushed up the

stairs as she ran down them, and I enveloped her in my arms, hugging her tight. I didn't know what she meant by so much more, but I prayed it would be enough to get Josiah arrested. "Clever girl."

She trembled in my arms. "They're making me marry him, Kara. I can't."

I grabbed her by the shoulders and shook her just a little, hoping to get through the terror taking hold of her now she'd done what needed doing. "Who? Who are they making you marry?"

I had to know. Maybe already did, somewhere deep inside me, but I had to hear her say his name.

"Josiah. Please. We need to get out of here. If they catch us—"

"They won't." I refused to believe any other alternative. But that didn't stop the bile churning in my stomach.

Josiah was never going to stop punishing me. Marrying my baby sister was just the latest in a long line of cruel moments.

I caught Shari's hand at the bottom of the stairs, and Hawk glanced at me, a silent question of, *we good to go?* on his face.

I nodded.

I just wanted this to be over. Wanted to be back in my bed, safe with my sister and my daughter on either side of me.

"Well, that was too easy." X practically pouted, wandering through the maze of office equipment. "Saved the day without even breaking a sweat. No knives. No bullets. I could have done this in my sleep."

Scythe stopped and stared at him.

Hawk practically growled. "You did not just jinx us by saying this was easy?"

Scythe took a knife from a holder around his ankle, and then a gun from the back of his jeans, while shooting X a dirty look. "Seriously, bro. That's like, rule number one. You never say it's too easy. You're just asking for shit to hit the fan."

X scoffed, practically waltzing to the exit. "You guys are as bad as my old man. He used to say superstitious crap like that too. It's rubbish. Nothing is going to happen. We're in the middle of Bumfuck, Nowhere surrounded by Jesus lovers. What are they going to do? Pray for my soul? Joke's on them. I don't have one."

Scythe glanced at him warily. "Or they surround the place, guns drawn, trapping us all inside, forcing us to shoot our way out."

X paused at the doorway, the first one to make it that far, and then ducked to the side. He turned wide eyes on Scythe. "Wait, did you peep? It's cheating if you knew that because you peeped!"

We all stared at him.

He rolled his eyes. "Okay, fine! I shouldn't have said anything! But can we deal with the group of men currently surrounding the building first? THEN you can have your I-told-you-so moment?"

All the guys groaned.

But all I could see was Josiah standing outside the door, dressed all in white, like a ghost in the darkness.

A tremble started in my fingers, but Grayson slid his hand around mine. "This isn't the same as when you escaped with Hayley Jade and Alice."

"It feels like it."

Josiah had always made me feel like I couldn't hide. Even in the middle of the group I'd brought with me, shrouded by darkness, he knew I was here. I could feel it. His gaze pierced through shadows, furniture, and bodies, straight through my heart.

"I'll die before he lays so much as a finger on you," Hayden whispered, stepping in close, his big body moving in front of me and going shoulder to shoulder with Hawk so I was shielded from my husband's stare.

But I knew if I was ever going to move past this, I had to be the one to face my own demons.

"Kara... My beautiful wife. I know you're in there. Aren't you going to come out and say hello to your husband?"

His voice sent shivers down my spine, the painful kind you got when you were cold to the bone and anything touching your skin hurt. They felt too much like his fingers, pressing and prodding cruelly at my skin, holding me down, taking what I didn't want to give.

"If he says your name one more time, I'm going to cut his fucking tongue out with Scythe's knife." Hawk gripped his gun a little tighter. "Then feed it to him."

But this was my fight. Not his. "Let me through."

All three men around me stiffened.

None of them moved.

"He has the building surrounded." Scythe ignored me, quietly checking through small windows that I realized Hawk and Hayden had herded us away from. "I can see at least eight guys." He flicked something on his gun. "It's fine. I can take out that many."

X shook his head. "Nope. I count more like twenty. And those look like semi-automatics."

"Well, that's not fucking ideal, then, is it?" Scythe perched on the edge of the desk with a sigh. "Fun wreckers."

"Kara..." Josiah's taunts came again. "I'm going to count to three, and if you aren't out here by then, I cannot be held accountable for what my men might do with the threat you've brought to our holy lands."

Gray turned the knob on the walkie-talkie almost all the way to silent and quietly gave Whip and his team the lowdown on what was going on.

Whip's deep voice came back, barely audible above the heavy breathing of the people around me. "We're coming but we lost Ice temporarily and had to go back for him. Stall them. We're probably fifteen minutes out."

"One..." Josiah called from outside the building, beginning the countdown he'd threatened.

X cracked his neck. "So as far as I can see, our options right now are, sit here and get shot. Run, and get shot. Shoot them, and..."

"Get shot?" Hayden asked dryly.

X grinned. "Hey! How did you know I was going to say that?"

"Not exactly the greatest options." Grayson palmed the gun Hawk had given him to use. "We don't have time to wait for the others to get here. We're out of options. We're going to have to fight. X is right."

I clenched my fingers into fists. "No. He's not. And there is an option you haven't considered."

Everyone turned in my direction.

"You trust *me* to get us out of this alive."

X lowered his voice and whispered to Scythe, "Maybe she has one of those machine gun bras..."

"That would be insanely cool," he whispered back.

We all ignored them, my gaze solely on my men. "Do you trust me?"

I'd trusted the three of them with my life more than once. Now I needed them to put the same trust in me.

None of them seemed very happy, but all three nodded without hesitation.

"Then follow my lead." I glanced at my youngest sister, shielded by Shari's protective arms, and prayed like hell this would work.

If it didn't, we were all dead.

I moved to the edge of the doorway. "Husband. Please. We wish to seek your forgiveness."

"Like hell I do," X muttered, only loud enough for the rest of us to hear.

Hawk shot him a look. "Just do what she says. She knows him better than any of us do, and we ain't fucking all dying here tonight by getting in a shootout we can't win."

I waved a hand at them, as Josiah's deep, arrogant chuckle echoed through the night. "You expect forgiveness? After everything you've done? You came onto my holy lands and brought men wearing the Devil's insignia on their backs."

Actually, it was only Hawk wearing a club jacket with the Slayers' logo on the back, but Josiah was dramatic to his core, forever in the middle of the constant show he put on for his disciples. He loved the attention. His arrogance thrived on it.

And that was exactly what was going to get us out of this.

Taking a deep breath to calm the shaking in my

limbs, I stepped out from the safety of the building. For the first time in months, I faced off with my husband.

It was the first time ever, really. Because I had never dared to openly stare at him the way I did now. I'd spent years staring at my feet in his presence, trying to be the meek, obedient woman he expected me to be.

I never wanted to be her again. And yet I dropped to my knees on the hard ground, small rocks digging in as I knelt before Josiah.

I couldn't bring myself to look away, even though it was expected. I stared him in the eye, hating him with every fiber of my being. "I have been a disobedient, foolish woman." The words scalded my tongue, poisoned the air around me as I spat them out, hating every one but saying what needed to be said. "Let them go and I'll be different. Better. I'll be whatever you want me to be."

Josiah laughed from his position on the hill above me. "You always were a stupid woman. I don't want you, Kara. Didn't you hear? You've been out too long. Tainted by the sins of other men. Your sister is set to be my wife a mere three days from now. You've been replaced. Jacqueline! Get out here and see what happens when a wife of mine disobeys me."

My fingers clenched into fists at my side. Jacqueline and Shari slowly followed me out into the night and knelt either side of me, their gazes firmly on the dirt, their hands tucked behind their backs in the subservient position we all assumed while kneeling in front of the altar at church each Sunday.

A desperation rose inside me, fueled by the sick leer in Josiah's eyes when he looked at Jacqueline. "That doesn't need to be." I distracted him, pulling his attention back to me. "I have returned to take my place at your side. These men I bring with me, they will kneel beside me and allow you to wash away their sins so they, too, can be good men of the Lord."

The seconds ticked by too slowly. Each one spanning a lifetime and fueling the realization that Whip and the others wouldn't get here in time to be any help.

Josiah cocked his head to one side as Hawk, Grayson, and Hayden came out of the shed, their hands up, and knelt either side of Shari and Jacqueline. A moment later, Scythe and X did the same, quiet but clearly not happy.

All of their hands were empty. I had no doubt they'd stashed their guns somewhere beneath their clothes, and I felt sick when Josiah's men moved in and patted the guys down, removing any weapons they found.

Josiah's gaze stayed hot on Jacqueline. "There she is. The bride-to-be."

To my surprise, Jacqueline lifted her head. "I'll never be your wife."

Shari gasped from beside me, and there was a rumble of disapproving words from Josiah's men. Sun was starting to rise at the back of the shed behind us, casting a little light across the sharp planes of Josiah's face.

His expression filled with fury.

"See? She's a child," I begged my husband. "Barely thirteen years old. She's not old enough to be your wife. Not yet. Take me back. Let me train her for a few more years until she's old enough to make a good wife for you."

"You know nothing about being a good wife, you fat, useless bitch. You couldn't even give me a son. Your one responsibility, and you couldn't even do that. Instead, your sister will. She will give me all the sons I desire until her body is as wasted and useless as you are."

I shook my head. "No."

It was a mistake. I knew it instantly, and so did Josiah. He'd seen a weakness.

Seen yet another way to make me pay for the embarrassment I'd caused him.

"Get up here, wife-to-be."

I grabbed for Jacqueline, but Onith, Josiah's second-in-charge, stepped forward and knocked me to one side.

One of the guys let out a growl but was instantly met with a gun to his head. I could practically feel the tension radiating from them as they battled to stay on their knees and do nothing.

Josiah dragged Jacqueline across the uneven ground and placed her at his feet.

We couldn't help her now. Josiah's men had all moved in tight around our group, weapons drawn and pressed to the backs of each of our heads.

But Josiah's hate was aimed solely at me. He grabbed Jacqueline's hair, controlling her with it. "Kneel properly for your Lord and Savior, woman! Did your mother teach you nothing? Are you as useless as your bitch of a sister over there?"

Jacqueline struggled, tears streaming down her face. But at least there was no gun to her head, like the rest of us. At least she would be alive while our bodies lay in a pool of blood and dirt.

I'd thought I could do this. Thought I could save us all.

I'd been wrong.

Josiah's cruel eyes focused on me. "I don't need you to

teach her how to be a good wife. That is something only a man can teach a woman. Maybe I'll start now. Right here. While you watch what your disobedience caused."

No.

He reached for his belt, undoing it with one hand, the other never leaving my sister's hair, even though she fought him every second.

"No!" I screamed.

He undid the drawstring and let the loose white pants fall at his feet. His long shirt covered him, but his hand went beneath, and I just knew he was stroking his cock, getting himself hard.

I only had one card left to play. One I hadn't wanted to show, because the thought of it left me in a cold sweat.

But I wouldn't let my sister suffer the same fate I had. Tears rolled down my face, and I clutched my belly. "Stop. Please, Josiah. I'm pregnant. It's your baby. I've been pregnant this whole time."

It distracted him long enough for him to loosen his grip on Jacqueline's hair. He stared at me, his face a mixture of shock, and then smug pleasure.

Then a sweet, sweet pain, as Jacqueline drew the gun from the back of her pajama pants and pulled the trigger.

23

KARA

"And then, boom! Little Jax just went and blew Josiah's balls off!"

I glanced over at X, busily telling the police his version of events, while the officer's face paled in the early morning light, and he crossed his legs like his own personal area might need protection from the barely five-foot child sitting with two other officers and a blanket wrapped around her shoulders.

I sat beside her while we told the police everything in a much less dramatic fashion.

Well, almost everything.

We didn't mention how Whip and his guys had all turned up at pretty much the exact same time Jacqueline had pulled the trigger point-blank at Josiah's crotch. How the shock of seeing their messiah lying on the ground bleeding had given us the upper hand to take control of the situation, all of Josiah's men disarmed and herded away into the night along with all the weapons.

Except the one gun Jacqueline had used to make sure

Josiah could never hurt another woman the way he'd hurt me.

Ice and Kyle had stayed behind with us. I didn't know where Whip and Trigger were taking the rest of Josiah's guys. I doubted it was anywhere good. I'd heard the guys mumbling about not having a pile of bodies here when the cops arrived.

I'd been scared of innocent women and children getting hurt. Hadn't wanted people I loved to go to jail for murder. But Grayson had given Whip a nod, clearly telling him to take care of the situation, and I hadn't had it in me to argue.

It had been me who'd called the police.

Because even when Josiah lay bleeding on the ground, it didn't feel like enough.

It had been me who'd administered first aid, slowing the bleeding while Josiah howled on the ground until an ambulance arrived.

"He needs to spend the rest of his life behind bars. Search that building, you'll find everything you need as proof of fraud and child pornography," I said to the police officer shakily, watching the paramedics try to stabilize Josiah before they could move him. "Please save him," I called out to them.

The police officer paused, shaking her head and mumbling, "You're a bigger woman than I am. I'd want that mofo in the ground." She cringed then glanced at me. "Don't tell my superiors I said that. Please. Men like him, I just..." She squeezed her eyes closed and shook her head, swallowing hard.

I squeezed the officer's fingers, telling her silently I understood.

One abuse victim could see it in another.

For Jacqueline's sake, I didn't want him to die. Having the knowledge you were responsible for another person's death, even one as evil as Josiah, wasn't something anyone should ever have to feel.

But some darkness inside me just wanted him to suffer in prison for the rest of his life. Where I would know that his every minute was miserable, the same way mine had been every second I'd been his wife. Death would be too kind a fate for the things Josiah had done. He didn't deserve the easy way out his friends would receive at the hands of Grayson's murder squad.

The paramedic shot something into Josiah's arm that calmed his howling long enough for them to get pressure bandages on his wounds and him loaded onto a gurney. The legs folded up as they pushed it into the back of the ambulance, and one paramedic climbed in beside him, the other readying to close the doors.

"Wait!" I broke away from the officer interviewing me and hurried to the back of the vehicle.

The paramedic stopped me, but it didn't matter anyway. Everything I'd wanted to say to Josiah was drowned out by his drugged-up, barely coherent ramblings.

"We will all be judged at the feet of the Lord, our souls melded to our earthly bodies until the ring of fire is crossed. Repent! Repent! The Lord demands your souls be cleansed with fire and rain and blood. Repent! Repent!"

I couldn't even get a word in amongst his verbal diarrhea.

For a man filled with so much natural charisma and

charm that he'd managed to form a cult, what was left of him at the end of the day was nothing but a raving lunatic who I might have actually felt sorry for, if he hadn't deserved everything he had coming.

Hayden moved a phone away from his ear and let out a wolf whistle that cut through the bustle of the scene. "All interviews end now, until our lawyers are present."

One of the older officers frowned at him. "That's not how this works, son."

Hayden simply held the phone out. "You can explain that to my brother."

I let out a slow breath. I knew Hayden's brother, Liam, was one of the best lawyers in the state. We'd met years ago, just after Hayley Jade was born, and I'd never forgotten the calm demeanor he'd handled everything with.

It was clear nothing had changed. The officer listened while Liam barked orders down the phone, and eventually the officer made a face.

He gave the phone back to Hayden. "We've already got statements from Jacqueline and Kara. But according to your lawyer, we'll be finishing these interviews at the station with him present. He tells me he's flying his whole team in today to take care of this." He lowered his voice to a mutter, but I still heard it. "Won't that be fun."

It sounded like he thought it would be anything but.

The police made shooing motions at us. "Go then. We have more than enough details to track you down should you decide to skip town before we're done investigating. We need to process this crime scene."

"They won't find anything other than proof Josiah is a perverted freak," Scythe said quietly from behind us.

"Nothing?" Hawk asked beneath his breath. "You sure? If I have to make a scene so you have more time—"

Scythe rolled his eyes. "Don't be insulting. You know I don't miss things. Jax has a clear-cut case of self-defense which will never go to court anyway, after they see all the fucking shit on those computers." He shuddered then looked at me. "You sure you want him in jail? 'Cause he deserves a bullet."

I nodded at the deadly man who loved Bliss so sweetly it was hard to believe he was the same person I'd seen rubbing her feet just two nights earlier.

He didn't seem happy with my decision, but he respected it. "If he doesn't get life, I've got friends inside who'll pay him a visit and make him wish he had."

"That seems fair."

Hawk grinned and wandered over, shaking his head. "Rebel will be proud of the two of you." He tousled Jacqueline's hair. "Little Jax is even more badass than her eldest sister. Rebel totally lost her title as the biggest baddie in the family."

Jacqueline grinned at his praise.

He glanced at me. "Apart from you, of course."

I laughed at his pathetic attempt at saving my feelings. It was unnecessary. I wasn't ever going to be a badass. I wasn't my sister with her love of knuckledusters. And I doubted I could have even been as ruthless as Jacqueline had, pulling that trigger.

I glanced at her. "How did you get that gun anyway?"

She grinned over at Grayson, her fingers still trembling, though I suspected that might have been more from leftover adrenaline than fear now. "He gave it to me."

I raised an eyebrow at him. "You gave a thirteen-year-old a loaded gun?"

He shrugged. "Simple psychiatry, really. People think men do things to impress women, but often it's the exact opposite. Men like Josiah only care about impressing other men. Everything they do is designed to make themselves appear bigger, stronger. Like the alpha male of the pack. I knew as soon as I walked out there that they'd frisk me and all the other men. We'd be perceived as a threat that the alpha needed to deal with.

"But I also know how Josiah has underestimated you every step of the way. I figured he'd probably be even worse with a young girl like Jax, and she wouldn't be considered a threat who needed to be searched. I tucked the gun into the back of her pants, beneath her jacket, right before she walked out of the building to kneel beside you."

I couldn't help but smile at the nickname they'd all adopted so quickly. After what she'd done here this morning, my sister definitely needed a stronger-sounding name than Jacqueline.

It was weird how in seconds, she'd transformed herself in my eyes from a little girl with pigtails to the badass Hawk had pointed out. She really was a lot like Rebel, and I was glad for it. I didn't ever want her to be taken advantage of the way I had. I'd had to learn the lesson the hard way and more than once. But I didn't want that for her.

I also knew I could be strong in my own way. It didn't have to be in the same way they were.

Hayden put his arm around my shoulders. "Let's get out of here. Liam's receptionist booked us a block of rooms at a motel in town. More than we need. Deliberately. So we have accommodation for anyone who wants to leave this place."

I widened my eyes at him. "Seriously?"

He nodded. "I don't know what comes after that, but for tonight, we take anyone who wants to come with us."

I glanced over at Jax. "Josiah isn't coming back. His inner circle won't be either. No Onith or Jed or Merle." I squeezed her fingers, listing out Josiah's closest allies. "That doesn't mean it's safe here though. There's space now for new leadership, and depending who steps up to take it will determine how you all live. I know this is the only life you know, and I don't want to take away your choices if there's a chance you could be happy here, but I want you to come with us. Live with me. Be part of our family." I glanced up over her head at my three men standing behind her. "It's a pretty special one."

Her eyes filled with tears, but she nodded quickly. "I want to come. Please don't let them make me stay."

I hugged her to me fiercely, a protective parental feeling coming over me. "They wouldn't dare."

The spark of anger inside me that had lived there ever since my parents had married me off to Josiah, without so much of a hint as to what was happening, burned a little brighter. We hiked back to the main communal area, where police officers held the community back.

"Louisa Kara?" A woman gasped.

I raised my head, gaze meeting the narrowed, dark eyes of Camilla, Josiah's second wife. A woman I'd lived with for years who had never once lifted a finger to help me, even though she knew exactly what her husband had done to me night after night, day after day, right beneath her nose.

She pushed through the crowd. "What have you done to him? I saw the ambulance! Is he hurt?"

"Yes." It was the truth. "But I'm sure, like the cockroach he is, he'll bounce right back."

"How dare you speak of a Lord's messenger like that! You truly are the wicked woman he claims you to be."

I rolled my eyes. "And you're cruel. But you're also brainwashed, so I'll overlook it and hope that one day you'll see who the truly wicked one was." I raised my voice, directing my attention to those who were left. Josiah's other wives and their children. Kyle standing with his parents. So many faces I didn't know, many of them women but men too, newcomers who hadn't been here when I'd left. "Josiah isn't coming back. Ever. So you all have a choice. Stay or leave. I'm making the offer to each and every one of you here. If you choose to leave, we'll help. We have motel rooms for the next couple of nights, and after that we'll work something out. You won't be alone."

I stared around the crowd. Taking in each face, the scared expressions, and the hushed whispers. I wasn't surprised when the only people who stepped forward to leave with us were Shari and Kyle's parents.

But it didn't break my heart any less.

There was no easy way to convince them. They had to want more than this life. If they were too scared to try, the way I had, then that was their right. All we could do was hope that whoever of them stood up in Josiah's place would turn Ethereal Eden into a community these people could be proud of. One that shared grown food and took care of each other.

One that did away with a fake religion that had torn them apart.

That was my only hope for them.

I turned and walked away, holding tightly to my sister's hand. At our old home, we let ourselves in, Hawk, Hayden, and Grayson right behind us. This time, I didn't try to stop them.

My father stood across from the doorway, his arms folded across his chest and an unhappy frown pulling at his mouth. His eyes flickered to the blood still sprayed across Jacqueline's pajamas, and then back to me. "Louisa Kara, what have you done?"

I glared at him. "What you should have a long time ago. Protected my family."

He blanched, and I moved to push past him. "We aren't staying. I'm taking Jacqueline...Jax...with me."

"Like hell you are." Dad reached for Jax, but before even one of the guys could stop him, my mother stepped in between.

Her eyes blazed. "You'll let her go."

Her words weren't directed to me for once, but to my father.

He squinted. "What? You want her to leave? How many daughters do we have to lose?"

My mother shook her head, her eyes filling with tears. "How do you not realize we already have? Alice died trying to escape this place. The moment we allowed Josiah to marry Kara, we lost her. And now you've done the same thing to Jacqueline."

"Marrying our leader is an honor!" he yelled. "I was looking out for them!"

But my mother was having none of it. She shook her head. "I believed that with Kara. I really did. She was a grown woman with a child, and she needed someone to care for her. Provide for her." She shook her head sadly at her husband, staring at him with barely concealed hate. "But then you made the same deal for Jacqueline. Who is neither a woman nor a mother nor in need of a man to take care of her."

My father's cheeks blazed red. "She's old enough. Women got married at her age all the time in my parents' generation."

It was then I realized how far he'd sunk. He'd been a different man once. One who'd put us on the backs of ponies and led us around on them. One who'd taken us into town and bought us ice cream. Even as little as five years ago when Rebel had lost her mom, he'd been different.

But a lot had changed. I no longer recognized the man he'd become.

"She's thirteen years old!" Mom shouted, startling us all. "Thirteen! And you sold her to a monster so you'd have his ear. Something he promised you when you gave him Kara, that he never delivered on. When are you going to wake up and realize that man doesn't give you an ounce of respect and never will!"

My father's eyes darkened, his tone threatening. "The Devil has a hold of your tongue."

Hayden ran his across his teeth. "Watch your mouth, old man. From where I'm standing, it seems a whole lot more like she's just telling you the truth."

I might have fallen in love with him just a little more in that moment, watching him stand up for a woman he didn't even know.

My mom grasped my hand and pressed her fingers into my palms. "Take her. Give her a good life away from this place. Love her like she's your own. Please. She isn't safe here, I know that."

I squeezed her fingers back, knowing this woman hadn't always done right by me. But willing to forgive her anyway because that was the sort of person I wanted to be. Not someone who held on to hate and negativity.

Those things ate away at a person like cancer, and I already had enough hate for Josiah and his men.

"Come with us," I begged her. "You don't have to stay here. Naomi and Samantha—"

My mom shook her head. "I need to stay for them. They'll never leave. This life is all they know, and they aren't like you and Jacqueline. They don't have adventure in their souls."

I didn't think I did either. But maybe I had once. Back when I'd first left, full of confidence about finding my place in the world.

It had beaten me down, changed me, but maybe I could get some of that back. For Jax. So she didn't lose that spark the way I had.

I let out a breath and put my arms around my mother, drawing her in tight and fast. But I held her long enough to whisper, "If you ever change your mind, you'll always have a place with us."

It was more generous than she deserved, and I think she knew it.

She pulled away, wiping at her eyes. "I'm so sorry."

I was too.

Hayden, Grayson, and Hawk all glared at my father, just silently daring him to say a word as Jax and I ran up the stairs and packed the few meager belongings she wanted to take with her.

We walked out of Ethereal Eden, my sister and Shari at my side, and the three men I loved at our backs.

24

KARA

"Hop. Hop. Both feet. Hop," Grayson coached, while Hayley Jade made her way across a hopscotch grid I'd drawn onto the concrete patio at the compound.

She coordinated her limbs into the combination of moves required to play the game, pigtails bouncing, Grayson teaching all three girls at once.

I watched from the edge of the concrete, absentmindedly doodling chalk flowers and leaves, and just enjoying the sounds of my child, my niece, and my sister playing together.

Remi tugged Jax's arm. "Hayley Jade wants you to come play Barbies with us. Do you want to?"

Hayley Jade hadn't said a word, but it was clear from the way she nodded and the excitement in her eyes that Remi was right. She and Hayley Jade had developed a strong bond, and even without speaking or signing, Remi was empathetic enough to pay close attention to everything Hayley Jade did. She was a lot like Fang in that respect. Quietly watching, making sure everyone around her was taken care of.

Jax, despite being years older than both girls, nodded. "Sure. Let's go inside." Then she paused and looked over at me. "Unless there's something you want me to do? I could prepare dinner? It's getting late. Or clean. Or do some laundry?"

I got to my feet, brushing the chalk dust off my hands. "You're already doing what you should be doing."

She glanced over at the hopscotch game they'd abandoned. "I'm just playing."

I put my arm around her neck. "Exactly."

"I'm too old to play."

"Says who?" Grayson hopped his way backward down the hopscotch grid to land at our feet. "I didn't hear anyone giving you a hard time. The girls are loving having their aunt here to entertain them." He grinned at her. "We gotta get you up to speed for the next family day at the club. Hopscotch is one thing, but I hear Scythe is Double Dutch champion, and I have my eye on his crown." Grayson cocked his head to one side, studying Jax like a coach would his star athlete. "Maybe ring toss is more your thing? Strong arms. I think Kian has the title for that one, but I reckon you could take him."

She raised one shoulder. "At home, I always had chores..."

I squeezed her arm, hating she hadn't been able to have a childhood. "You'll have them here too. Don't worry, you aren't getting off scot-free. But you get a few days' grace after what you've been through."

Most thirteen-year-olds would have been too old for Barbies and would have found their two little nieces irritating, but Jax had spent her entire childhood acting like an adult. So when she scurried off to sit on the floor of the bedroom she was currently sharing with Hayley Jade and let the two girls use her as a mountain for their dolls to climb, all I could do was smile.

Grayson wrapped an arm around me. "Want to play hopscotch?"

I twisted in his arms and peered up at him over my shoulder. "Seriously? Do you also plan to take the hopscotch title from Lexa? You do know she's only five, right?"

He chuckled, nuzzling his face into the side of my neck. "Actually, I just wanted to watch your boobs bounce."

I rolled my eyes and pushed him away, right as a commotion kicked up in the common room. Everybody shouted at once, and Grayson and I both paused, peering through the doorway to see what was going on. Everyone was in the main living area, staring at the big-screen TV.

"Kara!" Rebel bellowed. "You better get in here."

"That can't be good." I pulled away to link my fingers between Grayson's. I led him inside to join the group gathering around the TV. "What's going on...?"

All Rebel did was point.

A still image of Josiah's face filled the screen, and a newscaster's voice came through the speakers. *"Breaking news this hour of a police raid on a religious cult in Texas known locally as Ethereal Eden. Their leader, John Gooseman, known to his followers as The Prophet Josiah, is tonight in custody after police descended upon a property and seized extensive evidence of fraud and child pornography."*

Hayden whistled under his breath. "Can't believe the media is only just catching on to this."

The newscaster carried on. *"It's believed police had suspicions Gooseman was involved in the murder of Alice Churchill, a former group member who was murdered in a city alley earlier this year. Gooseman was transferred to Saint View Maximum Security Prison after he was released from medical custody, to be questioned further on the murder by local detectives running the case. Police say he has now been cleared of any suspicions relating to Ms. Churchill's death. The case for her killer remains open, and detectives are now searching for other suspects."*

I scratched at my arms nervously, staring at my husband's eyes, cruel even in a photo. They'd picked one that truly made him look like the lunatic he was, with his hair sticking up in every direction and his lips twisted in a snarl of anger. I didn't know where they'd gotten the photo from, but it was a nice portrayal of the evil man I knew him to be.

"Turn it off," I mumbled. "I don't want to hear any more about it."

I turned away and wrapped my arms around myself, reminding my triggered brain I was safe, my girls were here, and Josiah was where I wanted him to be. Behind bars.

He'd never get out of prison. Hawk and Scythe had already promised, if there was even the slightest hint that he'd be up for parole, they'd have someone kill him in jail.

I wouldn't feel an ounce of remorse if that's what it came to.

"You okay?" Grayson asked softly.

I shook my head sadly. "No. Not really. I'm glad he's in jail, of course. It's what I wanted. But if the police don't think he was involved with Alice's murder, then it has to be the man she was talking to online. Right?"

Hayden moved in on my other side, catching the end of the conversation. "They have the text messages from Kyle's phone now. We've given them everything. At least they're looking in the right place. We've done all we can do. We just have to let them do their jobs."

"It just doesn't feel like enough. The police said it could be months before they can get access to that app's data and that even if they can, there's every chance the killer was smart enough to conceal any traces of a trail that could lead back to him."

Grayson pressed a kiss to the top of my head and just let me breathe in his arms for a moment, until my muscles relaxed enough that I wasn't going to break out in trembles. He cleared his throat, eyeing Hayden, and then gazing back down at me. "Maybe it's time we organized a funeral."

During one of the numerous interviews we'd done with the police over the last week, we'd been informed Alice's body was finally being released, and we could now put her body to rest.

It had been both a relief and a burden, one I hadn't been able to deal with for the last few days while I took care of my traumatized sister and made sure she felt safe and happy in her new home.

But Grayson and Hayden were right. I needed to put Alice's death behind me so I could move on and be fully present for the people still here. Being distracted all the time, thinking about those messages and the man who'd sent them to her wasn't getting her murder solved or doing anyone any good.

It was time to say goodbye to her and make my peace with knowing we might never know who had killed her. At this point, I wasn't sure it would make a difference anyway. It wouldn't bring her back.

I nodded and then got to my feet, crossing the room to where Rebel was perched on the arm of a couch, shaking her head at the TV screen still going through the details of Ethereal Eden's history and how a man name John Gooseman had managed to brainwash at least a hundred people into thinking he was some sort of portal to the Lord.

It sounded so stupid when they put it like that. So simple it was nearly impossible to believe anyone had fallen for his lies.

But nobody could judge us unless they'd been there. Josiah was a master manipulator, a sociopath who could lie straight to your face without feeling an ounce of remorse.

I refused to be made a mockery of.

I leaned over, picked up the remote, and turned the TV off.

Everyone looked to me, a position that would have had me crumbling in on myself not all that long ago and staring at my feet, my voice stolen by fear and shame.

Not anymore. "I want to organize a funeral for Alice."

Rebel reached for my hand and squeezed it. "I'll help."

"We all will." War had his baby son asleep on his shoulder. He rubbed his tiny back absentmindedly.

"Whatever you need us to do, Kara, just let us know. We're all here for you."

I smiled at him, forever grateful for his kind heart. He hadn't even blinked when we'd arrived back from Ethereal Eden with Shari, Kyle's parents, and Jax in tow.

He'd simply opened the gates and made room in his family for all of us. Kyle's parents were down in his cabin with him for now, until more could be built, or they found a place of their own nearby. Shari had taken my room, since I had places in both Hayden and Hawk's beds. If Grayson stayed, we were all in the one room anyway, not doing much in the way of sleeping.

War had already started making plans for more residences within the compound. They had more than enough land to make room for everyone, and I could see the pride in War's eyes when he looked around at the safety he provided for those who needed it most.

I thanked him. "I think it would be best for a funeral home to sort out the details of the burial. But..." I cracked a little smile. "I think Alice would have hated if her funeral was just a solemn, gray occasion. Josiah never believed in celebrating a person life after their death. He said it served no purpose and drew attention away from praying for the living. We only had a burial ritual so our souls could enter Heaven to eventually be reborn."

"Pfft," Rebel scoffed. "What about celebrating the fact they were alive? Having time to grieve as a community? Sharing embarrassing stories about them now that they're not around to protest?"

"And getting drunk!" Aloha shouted, raising the beer bottle he'd been sipping on.

I chuckled, instinctively knowing he and Alice would

have gotten on like a house on fire if they'd ever had the chance to meet. It still hurt my heart she'd never got to see this. Me and Hayley Jade happy. Settled. In a home with people who loved us. Who would have loved her too.

I felt myself slipping into grief and anger again, but this time I pulled myself out, not wanting to linger there. "I know most of you didn't know her, but—"

"Doesn't matter. She's family." Aloha winked at me. "So we're going to throw her the party of the century. One so fucking big and loud she'll hear it from wherever the fuck Heaven is."

I laughed when everyone else cheered. Hayden grabbed a notepad from the table and started jotting down ideas for food.

Queenie stole a piece of paper from his notepad and took a pen from her huge, messy bun. "What sort of music did she like? I'll put a playlist together."

"I don't think she would have known any popular music." I cringed, hating she'd never really gotten to have that simple pleasure. "Just pick whatever your favorites are."

"Cardi B it is then!"

I didn't know what a Cardi B was, but if it made Queenie happy then I was sure I'd love it too.

Hawk called out to Hayden. "Toss me my phone. I'll call Ice. Tell him to be back from the Louisiana chapter in time and to bring back some of that rum from the distillery they have there. He can organize flowers too. He used to bang a girl from the flower shop."

War glanced over at the mention of the Louisiana

chapter. "Is he still there? What the fuck is taking Riot so long to get those guns he owes us?"

Hawk shook his head. "I dunno. Ice has been waiting around there for a week. Riot is just wasting all of our time at this point." He punched something onto his screen, presumably bringing up Ice's phone number, and held the phone to his ear, waiting for Ice to answer.

War pressed his lips into a hard line. "Tell Ice to tell Riot that he'll be dealing with me rather than my prospect if Ice isn't back on the road with those guns in time for the funeral. Riot can pay for the rum as compensation for wasting my fucking time, so tell Ice to buy a fucking lot of it."

"You know it." Hawk turned away to take the call somewhere quieter.

Everyone found themselves with something to organize, pitching in, leaning on their strengths and contacts, coming together as a family was supposed to.

Rebel nudged me with her hip, her hands resting on her growing baby bump. "I got Queenie to add some Paramore to her playlist."

I tried to smile at the mention of Rebel's favorite band. "I would expect no less than three songs."

"Good, because I picked five."

I loved that. "Perfect."

Her smile fell away. "It gets easier. With time. The missing them."

I breathed out slowly, sure she meant Alice, but it wasn't just her I felt like I was saying goodbye to. It was my sisters left behind, and my parents as well. "I hope so. I just wish Mom had come with us. Naomi and Samantha too."

"It's okay to let them go, you know? Not just Alice, but your mom and sisters too. You did everything you could. Their decisions are theirs. You aren't responsible for saving them."

"I know."

"But you wish you could have saved them anyway?" She sighed. "Honestly, I don't know how I ended up surrounded by so many people with savior complexes. You fit in well here, you do know that, right? You're all a danger to yourselves. Your New Year's resolution should be to be more selfish. You know there's a cake in the refrigerator? You could just go eat the whole thing and not share a bit."

I hid a laugh. "But I'd feel awful nobody else got to enjoy it."

She rolled her eyes. "You're proving my point. Sometimes it's okay to eat the whole cake."

I squinted at her. "Wouldn't that give you a really bad stomachache? I think I'd be vomiting for days."

She screwed up her face, considering it. "Okay, I think my metaphor got a little off track. Vomiting was definitely not the point."

"What was?"

"I really don't know. This pregnancy has turned my brain to mush. Or maybe it's the having four kids under five? I don't think I've slept more than two hours at a time since the twins were born."

I reached out and put my hand on her belly. Instantly, her little baby gave my hand a solid kick, trying to remove the weight. I grinned. "I can't wait until I can feel mine."

"I'm just jealous you aren't sick. Why did I get a baby

still making me vomit well past first trimester?" She paused, suddenly cringing.

I grimaced. "You thinking about puking right now?"

"I think it was all the talk of cake." She clapped her hand over her mouth and hightailed it toward the bathroom, shoving bikers out of the way as she went.

I followed after to hold her hair back.

Because that's what true family did.

25

HAYDEN

I woke in the middle of the night, sandwiched between Kara and Hawk, all three of us still bare-ass naked from fooling around earlier. I blinked in the darkness of my room, trying to work out what had woken me, but my brain was still fuzzy with sleep.

"Answer your fucking phone already." Hawk fumbled on the bedside table next to him until he found the offending device and dropped it onto my chest.

I picked it up and blinked at the blurry screen, trying to make out the time, but got sidetracked by Luca's name flashing obnoxiously.

"Shit." Instantly more awake, I scooted to the end of the bed, yanked on some boxers, and replaced the covers over Kara's shoulders.

Hawk rolled into my spot, pulling her tight against his chest and spooning her from behind.

I let myself into the dark, quiet communal room. Everyone was still asleep, and it was almost pitch-black. But I'd lived here long enough now that I instinctively knew where all the furniture was. I sank down onto the cracked leather couch without bothering to turn on the light.

"What?" The greeting came out short and snappy, my entire body already on alert because Luca calling at this hour of the night couldn't mean anything good.

Luca didn't even say hello. Just barked an order down the line. "I need you."

Oh, fuck him, calling me like I would just drop everything to come to his beck and call at two in the morning. "Don't care. I'm going back to bed."

"Hayden, please."

I paused at the crack in his voice.

I was pretty sure I'd never heard Luca say please in the entire time I'd known him. Asking nicely wasn't in his personality. There was never any room for refusal. He just demanded what he wanted, and ninety-nine-percent of the time, he got it.

He certainly never showed any emotion.

"What's wrong? Is it Sinners?" I'd only left there a few hours earlier. My heart rate picked up as I mentally tried to remember if I'd switched off every gas burner and set the alarms.

"I'm at the hospital. In emergency. I won't be here long, but I need you to come down. Please." He ended the call before I could ask any other questions.

I swore under my breath and contemplated just going back to bed, but the kernel of worry inside me would keep me awake, I just knew it.

Luca had been off the last time I'd seen him. Upset over his underage sister's marriage, and things had clearly been strained between him and his father.

It was the knowledge I was probably the last person he'd call if he had any other options that had me flicking the flashlight on my phone on and sneaking back into Hawk's room to grab my clothes and boots.

I kissed Kara's cheek softly, and she stirred, but I murmured softly in her ear, "I have to go out for a bit. Go back to sleep."

She mumbled something but nodded, and I slipped out of the room. The other day when we'd been planning Alice's funeral and memorial, I'd left a notepad and pen on the big communal table. I paused, jotting down a note that told them where I was going.

Couldn't be too careful with Luca. Being summoned to his hospital bedside could end in any number of ways, and if I didn't make it back for whatever reason, at least they'd be able to give the cops a starting spot.

The thought didn't leave me particularly warm and cozy. For half a second, I thought about taking one of Hawk's guns with me, but what the fuck was I going to do with one of those in the middle of a hospital filled with sick people and kids? Not to mention the fact I'd never get it past all the new security measures the hospital had installed after what had happened to Kara.

I drove into town, cursing myself for being this stupid. I tried talking myself out of it, the warning in my head practically a siren, but my fingers held the wheel steady, and my foot stayed on the gas until I was walking into the emergency room like the complete sucker I knew I was.

Gray was here somewhere tonight, taking on an extra overnight shift when one of his patients had taken a turn for the worse and was in the middle of an involuntary psych hold. But I hoped that wasn't anywhere near the emergency room, because whatever was happening with Luca didn't need to involve my family.

I blinked at feeling protective over Grayson. That had snuck up on me, maybe somewhere between him saving Kara's life and realizing he'd watched YouTube tutorials on how to French braid Hayley Jade's hair. He was terrible at it. Her hair had looked like a rat's nest when he'd given his newfound skills a whirl, and Hawk had made jokes about this being why he wasn't a surgeon getting paid the big dollars.

But I'd seen Hayley Jade's face as she'd checked herself out in the mirror. She'd been absolutely thrilled and had been Grayson's little shadow for the rest of the evening, following him around, gazing up at him with big, adoring eyes.

I doubted anyone else had noticed, but I had.

I entered the hospital and pushed all thoughts of my family aside. I couldn't think about them right now. Luca could be your best friend if he wanted to be. Or your worst enemy. I never knew which one I was going to get until the moment I saw him.

I paused at the reception window and spoke to the woman on the other side. "Where can I find Luca Guerra, please?"

She tapped her fingers across a keyboard, then shook her head. "No one here by that name."

I sighed and pulled out my phone to call him, having no idea what sort of alias he might have used and no desire at this time of morning to try guessing.

The woman interrupted me before I could make the call. "We do have an Isabella Guerra, though, with Luca Guerra listed as next of kin."

I frowned. "Okay. That'll work, I guess. Can you tell me where they are?"

"Are you family?"

"Sure."

The woman looked too tired to argue.

"She's been moved to the private ward. They don't have visiting hours, so I guess you're free to head up there if you want to. Floor three. Bed 327. Elevators are just behind you."

I thanked her and made the short ride up, trying to make any sense of what was going on here.

But by the time the doors opened and I found Isabella's room, I still had no idea what was going on. I knocked quietly on the open door, the room warm with a soft, rhythmic beeping coming from a machine attached to the teenage girl lying in the bed.

Luca sat on a chair, his arms folded on top of the mattress, his head twisted to one side while he watched over his sleeping sister. "She tried to kill herself."

I leaned on the wall. "This is the sister your dad married off to that old prick you brought to the restaurant the other week, right?"

He finally lifted his head to look at me and nodded.

I had to fight to keep my expression neutral. I'd never seen Luca so wrecked. He had dark circles beneath his eyes, his normally neatly styled hair stuck up at all angles. There was no sign of his trademark suits or even the gym gear I'd seen him in once or twice. He wore a plain white T-shirt and a pair of gray sweats I suspected might have been his pajamas.

"Is she going to be okay?"

Isabella didn't wake at our hushed conversation, but

even in sleep her forehead was lined in a way no girl her age should have been. She should have been at school. Or cheerleading on the sidelines of a football game.

Not lying in a bed with a rock on her finger the size of Texas after having her stomach pumped.

"Doctor says yes. He wants her to stay for twenty-four hours of observation, but she can't. I've got my guys downstairs, my bags packed." His gaze met mine. "I'm taking her and running. She's not going back to her fucking husband while I'm still breathing. I'm not fucking losing her."

"I would do the same."

He held my gaze for a moment, then nodded, pushing to his feet and putting his hand on Isabella's shoulder. "Hey, Is. Wake up. We need to get going."

The girl blinked sleepily, but I was still confused as to why I'd been summoned. It wasn't like Luca and I were friends and he just wanted to say goodbye.

Isabella sat up groggily, and he pulled a sweatshirt over her head, like I would have to Hayley Jade.

He glanced around, clearly searching for her shoes, and I toed them toward him from beneath the end of the bed.

He crouched to pick them up, and when he straightened, he held his hand out to me. "Sinners is yours. I've already told my lawyers to sign over the entire business to you. You'll get the paperwork in the next few days."

I widened my eyes in surprise, but instantly, suspicion followed. Because nothing ever came from Luca without a price. "What's the catch? The whole business is in my name, but I pay you ninety-percent of the profits off the books?"

Luca's eyes hardened. "No. There's no catch. You can't send me any money. Or try to contact me. I need there to be zero trace if I'm going to get her away safely before her husband and my father find out."

I stared at him, some deep-rooted part of me understanding what it was to suddenly be the father figure for a child who needed you. Recognizing this was him doing exactly what I'd taunted him with last time I'd seen him. I'd told him he needed to man up. Take responsibility for his actions and be someone he could be proud of.

He'd claimed he didn't have the luxury.

But apparently now he was doing it anyway. For his sister.

He sniffed with a shrug. "Sinners was always supposed to be yours anyway. I only bought it to mess with your head."

We both knew that wasn't exactly true. He'd enjoyed building that business. I'd maybe even enjoyed having his guidance. At least I had when he hadn't been trying to force me to do illegal shit for him.

"Where will you go?"

He grinned, helping his sister off the bed now her shoes were on her feet. "Who knows? Anywhere Is wants to go, I guess."

She raised her head and stared up at her older brother. "Seriously? Even Str—"

Luca put a finger to her lips. "If you tell him we'll have to kill him." He gave me a solemn nod. "And I'd rather not hurt this one."

The two of them shuffled to the door, Isabella wincing with each step and clutching her stomach but determined to leave anyway. I stood watching them, trying to wrap my head around owning my dream business. Not just a shitty ten-percent share. But the entire thing.

Luca glanced back over his shoulder. "Chaos?"

"Yeah?"

"Be careful of my dad, okay? He'll come looking for me when he realizes both Is and I are gone. Sinners, along with all my other businesses, will be the first places he tries."

He disappeared around the corner.

Leaving me wondering if a gift from Luca Guerra was ever something actually good, or if it was just a nightmare waiting to happen.

26

HAWK

I'd been to too many fucking funerals. My parents'. War's old man. Brothers within the club who hadn't been as lucky as I had so far. I'd stood amongst their gravestones, throwing dirt on top of caskets, detached from the scene and already mentally planning the drinks I'd consume as soon as the priest was done rambling with their everlasting-life bullshit I'd never believed in.

But this one was different. Alice's funeral had been so long coming, and the words the priest said actually mattered to Kara. She might have left Josiah's bullshit behind, but her faith in something bigger than us hadn't completely disappeared. Burying her sister meant more than just a formality we had to get through so we could go get drunk afterward.

It needed to be perfect. I'd spent days trying to think of every little thing that would make it better, trying to make sure she had everything she wanted, right from flowers to music to food.

Everyone had pitched in and helped where they could, and it was clear to me I wasn't the only one who'd wanted to do this right for her.

It wasn't just me and Chaos and Grayson who loved her. That much became evident day by day as everyone came together to make this funeral exactly what Kara needed it to be.

Closure on her old life. And the true beginning of a new one.

Around me, our friends got off their bikes, or climbed out of their vans and cars, leading kids and significant others across the graveyard to where Alice's casket sat raised above an open grave. Kara had chosen not to have a ceremony in the church up on the hill, but an outdoor memorial, in the warm midafternoon sun.

I pulled my tie from my pocket and put it around my neck, fiddling with the stupid thing and wishing I hadn't brought it. I'd practiced tying it with the help of a YouTube video the night before and thought I'd had it down, but staring at it hanging loosely around my neck now, I was pretty sure Hayley Jade could have done a better job.

I yanked it off again, frustrated with myself and uncomfortable in the too tight button-down shirt that vaguely itched my arms. "Should have just worn my club leathers and jeans like everyone else," I muttered. "So fucking stupid."

"Not stupid." Gray stopped at my side and held his hand out, palm up.

"What?" I snapped, the back of my neck hot at him hearing me talking to myself. "Odd time for a high five."

He rolled his eyes. "Give me your tie."

I glanced at him warily. "Not if you're going to put it around my neck and get all up in my face tying it for me."

Grayson plucked the tie from around my neck. "Why? Scared I'll kiss you while I'm at it?"

"I wouldn't recommend trying it."

"You kiss Chaos."

"Doesn't mean I want to kiss you."

He chuckled, making a show of putting the tie around his own neck and twisting it around his fingers into a neat knot I would have never in a million years been able to achieve, even if I'd had the YouTube tutorial in front of me every time.

"Don't worry. I have no interest in kissing you either. Doesn't mean I can't help you though. Friends do that." He loosened it, pulled it over his head, and then held it out to me, asking silent permission to fit it over my head.

I nodded. "Thanks."

"You aren't big on suits, huh?"

"Is it that obvious?"

He tugged one end, and the knot magically slid up to sit perfectly at my throat. "Only because you look about as comfortable as patients do when you have to check their prostates."

I took over the fitting of the tie, straightening it so it hung neatly down the center of my chest and then shoved my hands in the pockets of the dress pants I'd bought the day before. Hadn't even washed them yet because I was pretty sure there wasn't an iron at the clubhouse, and I didn't want to lose the neat front creases the store had pressed into them. "I just wanted everything to be perfect for Kara."

He spotted her standing close to the grave. She talked

with Bliss and Rebel, their kids all occupied by War and Fang letting them run off energy in an open space where they wouldn't step on graves. A bunch of nurses from the hospital had come, as well as Chaos's brother, Liam, and his family. All of the club had turned up, from prez to prospect...

I swore under my breath.

Grayson glanced at me. "What's wrong? Everything is fine."

"Ice isn't here."

"Is that a big deal?"

"Only if anyone wants to drink after this. I had him organizing all the alcohol."

Grayson elbowed me. "Stop. This whole thing isn't on your shoulders. I'm sure he'll be here. And if he isn't back at the clubhouse with the alcohol when we get there, then who cares? We'll go buy more."

I breathed out a slow breath, knowing that was true.

"It's not your job to make everything right for her, you know."

"But I want to."

"Sometimes, I do too. But what she needs right now is you. Me. Chaos. Not alcohol or your tie to be straight."

"It's really annoying when you do your shrink thing and think nobody will notice."

"Am I right though?"

"Nobody likes a know-it-all, Gray."

He laughed and nudged me with his shoulder. "Come on. Let's get this thing done so we can go drink..."

I stared at him. I'd literally just told him that if Ice hadn't made it back from Louisiana then there was nothin' to drink.

"The pop and juice boxes we bought for the kids." He rubbed his stomach. "Mmm, delicious."

I huffed. "Your jokes are as bad as your glove balloons, you do know that, right?"

He took a blue medical glove from his pocket and waved it around in my face. "Need me to make you one? It'll turn that frown upside down."

"I'm going to push you into that open grave if you don't stop."

But I was battling back a smile as Gray put his stupid glove away, and I was saved the torturous squeaking of his latest attempt at creating a bear or a moose or fuck knows what else.

I'd buy him a proper set of twisting balloons and an instruction book for his birthday.

At the edge of Alice's grave, I stood shoulder to shoulder with Gray and Chaos, Kara holding Hayley Jade's hand just a step in front of us. I stood so close my chest brushed her back, and my fingertips rested on Hayley Jade's head, needing to be touching her, just in case she got distracted and moved too close to the gaping hole in the ground.

It sent flashbacks of pulling Kara from the earth after she'd been buried alive, and Hayley Jade stared up at me curiously, as if she could sense my tension.

I forced myself to relax and stroked my fingers across her little forehead instead, sweeping the hair back off her face.

She smiled so sweetly, it was all I could do not to

sweep her up in my arms and hug and kiss the shit out of her.

"Love you," I signed to her silently, not wanting to interrupt the priest saying blessings over the coffin while two men from the funeral home lowered it into the ground.

My stomach lurched as it sank toward its final resting spot.

This had to be so much worse for Kara. I couldn't help myself. I put my arm around her from behind, drawing her close against me.

She sank back, like she needed the touch just as much as I did, her body trembling. "I hate the smell of fresh dirt," she whispered, only loud enough for me to hear.

After that night, I did, too. Which was why I'd made one request of the priest.

The coffin hit the bottom of the grave and he motioned for me to go ahead.

I took out the little slip of paper where I'd written down what I needed to say because, even though it was only one sentence, I'd known I would fuck it up or sound dumb if I just tried to wing it. I unfolded it and raised my voice enough that everyone could hear. "Instead of throwing soil, I'd like to invite each of you to come forward and take a flower to place on the coffin instead."

Kara blinked and stared up at me. "Really?"

I shoved the paper back in my pocket and leaned down to kiss her mouth. "I didn't want you having to put your fingers in the soil. And from what I've heard about Alice, brightly colored flowers seemed more her style anyway."

Kara's eyes got misty, but she smiled through her tears. "She would approve, I'm sure of it. Thank you."

I twisted, searching for the basket of flowers, but it wasn't at the priest's feet like it was supposed to be. I swore low under my breath, realizing drinks weren't the only thing I'd asked Ice to take care of. He was also in charge of picking up the flowers from the girl he knew at the florist. "Please tell me Ice is here somewhere by now?"

Everyone looked around, until the new prospect—Collins? Colingwood? Something stupid—cleared his throat. "He's not here. I think he's running late..."

Irritation bubbled up inside me. The ceremony was nearly finished. He wasn't just running late. He'd fucking missed the whole thing.

He'd had one fucking job. Fine, two. But neither of them should have been a big deal. I'd only given them to him because I'd been so busy coordinating everyone else and making sure it was absolutely perfect for her. Hell, he could have outsourced to the other prospects, but he hadn't even bothered to do that. He'd just not bothered to even turn up.

As usual, Ice couldn't do the simplest of tasks without irritating me.

Kara put her hand on my arm. "It's okay. The thought still counts."

I didn't want to lose my shit here in the middle of the funeral. But I was more than just angry. I was disappointed. And sad. I might not have known Alice, but Kara had, and the sorrow and grief emanating from her just broke my fucking heart.

All I'd wanted to do was make her smile. I hated I hadn't been able to. "I'm sorry."

Chaos leaned his arm against mine, his presence calming something inside me just from having him close. Silently, his fingers laced through mine, in front of everyone.

I didn't stop him. Didn't even want to. Didn't care if everyone knew we were a thing. Not when I couldn't even deny it to myself.

The priest cleared his throat. "Okay. Well. If we aren't going to do the soil or the flowers—"

He paused when Hayley Jade darted past him, a blur of dark-blue dress and flying hair.

"Hayley Jade!" I shouted, lunging for her, terrified she was going to slip and end up sliding down on top of the coffin.

But Kara grabbed my arm. "Wait. Let her go."

Against every feeling inside me that screamed to run after the little girl, I stood still, because Kara had that effect on me. As much as she might have liked me telling her what to do in bed, the moment she gave a command outside it, I had no desire to do anything but follow.

But I wasn't taking my eyes off that kid.

My kid.

She ran to the edge of the graveyard, where the manicured lawns gave way to trees they hadn't cut down yet to make more room for new burial sites. The grass grew long between the trees, wildflowers sprinkling color throughout.

Hayley Jade stopped, crouched, and picked a handful of them.

A tiny smile grew across my face as she ran them back to us and held them up to me.

I knelt in front of her. "You're pretty clever, kid."

She nodded, like she'd been told that a time or two before.

"Girl knows what she's doing!" Queenie called out loudly from somewhere behind us. "Come on, y'all." She led the group to the edge of the trees, and one by one, everyone spread out, collecting as many of the wildflowers growing there as they could find.

I passed some of the bouquet Hayley Jade had picked to Kara, Chaos, and Grayson, and when the rest of the group returned and took up their places, I took Hayley Jade's hand and led her to the edge of the grave.

Together we tossed in our flowers, watching them land on the polished wood coffin.

Hayley Jade waved sadly at the flowers, and I led her away, circling around to the back so everyone else could have their turn. Chaos, Kara, and Grayson all approached together, everyone else lining up behind them. One by one, our family and friends covered the coffin in the wildflowers until there was none left.

The priest finished his blessings and went back up to his church. Rebel hugged Kara and said she'd see us back at the clubhouse for the party. Madden whined at Rebel's feet, and Lavender was crying in Vaughn's arms at the edge of the group, her eyes tired and her face screwed up in an angry scowl.

Rebel cringed at her cranky daughter, but her words were for her sister. "We're all going home for quick naps, but we'll be over at the clubhouse soon."

Kara thanked them for coming, and they disappeared into the crowd.

War and his family approached, Bliss hugging Kara and War clapping me on the shoulder. "It was a good thing you did, with the flowers. Thoughtful, some might even say. Others might speak of how very unlike you it is."

I raised an eyebrow at him. "Where you going with this?"

He grinned. "Others, not me of course, might even call you pussy-whipped."

I gave him the middle finger. "Fuck off."

He clapped me on the shoulder. "You gave me so much shit about Bliss and Scythe. And now you're doing exactly the same fucking thing. Holding hands with a guy while your other arm is around your girl."

"You noticed that, huh?"

"Everyone did. And I don't think you care."

I didn't. "How long until you get over that?"

War slung his arm around my shoulders. "Oh, there's no getting over it. I'm going to be paying out on you for years to come. I haven't even scratched the surface of the shit I'm going to give you. So, you a top or a bottom?"

I shoved him away good-naturedly, knowing I deserved it and more. And honestly, not even minding that much.

The roar of a motorcycle had us all pausing and looking over as someone in full leathers and a full-face helmet kicked gravel up on the barely-there road that snaked through the cemetery.

The engine cut out, and he got off his bike, pulling off his helmet.

Ice looked like shit, his hair a mess, his eyes red-rimmed like he was hung over or high.

Anger swirled inside me as Ice's gaze landed on me and he started making his way through the crowd.

"Easy," War warned beneath his breath, jokes about the reverse harem I'd found myself in put aside. "Kara doesn't need you getting in a fist fight right now."

I breathed out slowly, knowing he was right.

Everything had turned out okay in the end.

But that was real hard to remember when it was clear Ice had gone on a bender instead of doing what he was supposed to do.

He stopped in front of me. "I'm so fucking sorry. I know I forgot the flowers."

I didn't say anything. What was there to say? If I opened my mouth, I was probably just going to make things worse. It wasn't even just about the flowers. It was about the fact I'd asked him to do something important and he'd decided going out and getting lit was more important.

"Where have you been?" War asked, clearly no happier than I was.

"At the Louisiana club. I only just got back into town. Drove all night."

War shook his head. "Your business there was done days ago, so that ain't gonna fly. You just stayed to party, that about right?"

Ice didn't say anything. But War took his silence as confirmation. "You're supposed to be Kara's friend. You should have been here for her. But you'd rather be with Riot and his boys than with me and mine when we needed you. That how it goes? You want to patch in with Riot and his crew?"

Ice shook his head.

War's face twisted into a scowl. "Don't lie to me. Riot

called me this morning and said you'd asked him to join the Louisiana chapter."

I blinked. War hadn't said a word to me about that, though fuck knows I'd been run off my feet this morning and hadn't had a chance to talk to him before now. "What the fuck? Why the hell would you want to do that for? You know the shit they're into!"

Ice's face paled. "He said he wouldn't say anything…"

"Yeah, well, that's what you get for trusting Riot. He's not exactly known for being honest." War sounded tired. "This needs to be discussed in church. Not here, where people are grieving, and the sight of your face pisses me off. We'll talk about it tomorrow. Or the next day. Or whenever the fuck I feel calm enough to deal with it."

Ice nodded and turned away, slinking back to his bike and pulling on his helmet without talking to anyone else.

War sighed as Ice rode away, everyone staring after him. War reached over for Kara, touching her arm gently to get her attention. "I'm really sorry about that."

She shook her head. "No. It's okay. I understand it's club business."

He nodded. "Can I borrow Hawk for just a minute?"

"Of course." But Kara's big eyes were full of worry.

I gave her a reassuring nod and then turned to Grayson. "Can you take her home? I have my bike and I won't be far behind."

"Sure."

War dropped a kiss onto Bliss's mouth, whispered something in her ear, and then she walked away with the rest of the club, everyone making their way to the parking lot.

When it was just me and War left by the gravesite, he sighed. "We've fucked up with Ice."

I screwed up my face, not wanting to admit it, but he was probably right. "We should have patched him in earlier, shouldn't we?"

War shoved his hands in the pockets of his dark denim jeans. "He fucked up today. There's no doubt in my mind about that. Both with not being here when he was supposed to. And in asking Riot to make him a member. But I feel like we pushed him into it."

"It's not all on you. Your whole life has changed in the past five years. This club isn't your number one priority anymore."

"I'm the prez. I should have been leading better. Making sure he was getting somewhere, building that trust with him so I felt comfortable patching him in."

I shook my head. "Nah. It falls on me. I'm supposed to take your spot when you aren't around. But I've had my head in the fucking clouds, dreaming about doing anything but Slayers' shit."

War glanced at me. "The paramedic shit, you mean? That's what you've been thinking about?"

I shrugged. "It's all I've really wanted to do for years. My heart ain't in this life. I love this club. And I love my brothers. I don't want to leave. But I want more."

War gave a little laugh. "All I've been doing for years is raising babies. And it's the best thing I've ever done."

I choked on a laugh. "Our old men are rolling over in their graves right now, aren't they?"

He shrugged. "Probably. But fuck them. They were assholes anyway. There's nothing to say we can't run this club the way we want to. We don't have to run it the same way they did."

I breathed out slowly. "So what are we saying here? Are we out? Are we shutting down the club?"

War recoiled like I'd slapped him. "Fuck no. That club is family for the people who live there. Queenie and Aloha. Ice. The girls. There'll always be the Saint View Slayers. But maybe we're just different now. Maybe we're more of a..."

I widened my eyes at him. "If you say we're a Sunday social club, who just ride out to pretty places to look at the scenery, I'm going to have to kick you in the balls."

He sniggered. "We'll work it out. But I think the first thing we need to do, despite the fuckups he's made lately, is patch Ice in."

I rolled my eyes, but I knew he was right. "Fine. We can announce it at the wake tonight once everyone gets there. But not Colon."

"Who?"

"The other prospect. I still need at least one of them to torture."

"I don't think that's his name."

I shrugged. "Close enough."

27

ICE

I couldn't fucking breathe. My leather jacket that normally fit like a glove was suddenly too tight, and I ripped it off, balling it up in my hands, only to have the Slayers' demon staring up at me.

My eyes watered at the sight of it. It was so familiar now, after wearing it almost every day for the past six years. I'd longed to wear it for years before that as I'd watched the club roll through town with War's dad in the lead position.

I'd wanted to be a part of it so badly. Thought all my dreams had come true the day Army had said they'd take me on as a prospect.

But that prospect patch had sat beneath the demon for years and years, and I'd had to watch Riot patch in new members, who'd only done a quarter of the time I had.

While War just kept saying my time would come, and Hawk gave me shit every time I fucked up.

I wiped angrily at my eyes, hating I was as weak as

they thought I was.

I shoved the jacket in the trash at the entrance to Saint View Prison. I'd never wear it again. I'd been stupid enough to waste years waiting for them to accept me, when they'd clearly never had any intention of doing so.

I went to the reception, gave my name, and asked to see a prisoner.

The guard in uniform tapped her nails across the keyboard and studied the screen, confusion creasing her brow.

I cleared my throat. "He's only been transferred here in the last day or two, I think. Might even be in the infirmary? He was brought here straight from the hospital."

"How do you spell the last name again?"

"Gooseman. G-o-o-s-e-m-a-n. John."

The wrinkles on her forehead smoothed out. "Oh, of course. I had it as M-E-N. It looks like he's in a regular cell, so he is entitled to visitors. He needs to agree to see you though. I need your full legal name, please."

I cleared my throat, forcing the full name I hated out of my mouth. "Alexander Key. Tell him he doesn't know me. But he'll want to speak to me."

She raised an eyebrow but waved me off toward the waiting room.

I slunk down in a hard plastic seat and stuck an AirPod in one ear, leaving the other out so I could hear if the woman called my name. I pulled my phone from the pocket of my jeans and scrolled to the podcast app, sighing at the line of check marks against each episode title, indicating I had no new episodes to listen to.

There'd been nothing new since Josiah had been arrested. I'd already listened to all the older episodes at least twice each, but I randomly picked one anyway and let Josiah's familiar voice fill my ear.

My heart rate lowered with every word, and the feeling of calm I always got when I listened to his teachings was a relief after the bitter disappointments of the last couple of days.

The last few months, really.

Nobody ever kept their promises. Not Riot. Not War or Hawk. Not every foster parent who'd promised to adopt me but then picked a cute little baby instead of the gangly preteen who nobody wanted.

Not Tulip.

Alice.

Her betrayal was the one that had hurt the most.

"Alexander Key?" a guard standing by the door called.

I stood quickly, shoving my headphones in my pocket. "He agreed to see me?"

The man nodded. "Yes. But he hasn't earned the right to visitation in the main room. You'll have to make do with the phones. Booth seven, right down the end."

"Thank you."

I didn't care how I got to talk to Josiah. Just that I did.

Nerves shook my fingers as I approached, and I gave myself a mental slap in the face, trying to be cool. I didn't want to come across as some sort of groupie, all starstruck and unable to speak clearly when face-to-face with a celebrity.

I sat in front of the thick, clear screen, scratched and nicked and smudged with fingerprints. An old-school phone with a cord hung on a hook to my right. A door on the other side opened and a guard led the prophet into the room.

Despite myself, my heartbeat picked up, racing fast. My leg bounced like it had a mind of its own.

Josiah scowled at the guard, saying something I couldn't hear, and limped toward the booth, walking with the slow, shuffling movements of someone who'd been recently injured. His lips moved in rapid succession that could have been curse words as he sat and stared at me.

He didn't look like the pictures I'd seen of him on the Ethereal Eden website. I was used to seeing him all in white, his hair long, beard neatly trimmed. It was a stark difference from the bright-orange jumpsuit with black numbers and letters stamped across the front of it. His long hair was greasy and unkempt, scraped back into a messy ponytail with strands falling loose everywhere.

I picked up the phone warily and put it to my ear.

A second later, Josiah did the same.

"Who are you?" he asked.

He might have looked almost like a different person, but his voice was one I knew. One I'd listened to weekly ever since I'd first heard about Ethereal Eden.

My nerves drifted away. "Alexander...Just Xan, really. Xan Key. You don't know me."

"Clearly."

"But I know you. I've listened to all your podcasts. I have for a long time. I have to tell you how seen and heard I feel every time you have a new episode..." I trailed off at the bored expression on Josiah's face.

His eyes suddenly sharpened, and he leaned forward, closer to the glass that separated us. "What's that tattoo on your forearm?"

I blinked and gazed down at the arm resting on the little desk in front of me. I had a Slayers' tattoo there that

I'd gotten years ago when I'd first been accepted as a prospect. I held it up so Josiah could see it.

"You're a Slayer?" He sat back, at least as far as his cuffs would allow. "Well, you suddenly got a whole lot more interesting."

I mentally berated myself for not leading with that. The prophet had no time to indulge in compliments and flattery. They were the Devil's work, making women vain and men arrogant. I should have known better. "I came to warn you to be careful. To watch your back in here. The Slayers have it out for you. If you aren't sentenced to life, they're going to have you killed."

I knew every word was being recorded, but I didn't care if I threw the Slayers under the bus. They'd already mowed me down with it, so they could feel the pain of betrayal the same way I had today when I'd realized how stupid I'd been to ever think they'd let me truly in.

Josiah seemed like he was pondering that for a moment, and then he nodded. "I appreciate you bringing me this information. You said you were a fan of mine?"

I nodded quickly. "I've been listening for a year or so. Every episode."

"And yet you never came to join us at Ethereal Eden? Why not?"

Embarrassment heated my cheeks. "I wanted to. Tulip made it sound so wonderful at first. A place where all were accepted for their true selves."

Josiah nodded. "That's what Ethereal Eden is, Xan. A haven for those who have been rejected by regular society. I wish you'd come to me. I could have saved you the pain I see in your face right now."

I swallowed thickly, wishing I'd done things differently too. "But the more I got to know her, the more she changed her story. She was tainted by evil; I know that now. Her mind and her tongue slowly poisoned against the Lord. She lied to me all along, saying she wanted to marry me. Have a family with me. But when I said I would come there so we could be married, she told me not to. Told me she was leaving the flock and turning her back on the one true religion."

He shook his head. "Tulip..." He screwed up his face, and then the lines in his forehead smoothed out. "Alice."

I nodded.

"She took my wife and child with her. Did you know that, Brother Xan?"

A warm flood of acceptance filled me at him calling me brother.

It was all I'd ever wanted from the Slayers. Why I'd joined them in the first place. Because they were brothers. Family. They'd promised to make me a part of it.

But clearly, they'd lied as much as Alice had. They'd all filled my head with hopes and dreams of a better future, one with people who loved and cared for me.

And they'd all taken it away with their lies.

I twisted my fingers around the phone cord. "I know. Kara and Hayley Jade. I've tried to bring them back to you. Both of them."

He cocked his head to one side. "How?"

I knew I couldn't admit what I'd done. Not here, with every word being recorded. So I quoted one of my favorite teachings back at him, one I had held on to, analyzing it my mind regularly until it had become a sort of mantra I knew word for word. "Women need to be reborn when they have sinned. They need to prove their worth. Prove that the evil can be leached from their souls."

I implored him with my eyes to understand that I had tried but only succeeded once.

When I'd put a cord around my sweet Tulip's neck in a city alley and pulled it tight, cutting off her oxygen, and watching the sins release from her body as her lips turned blue.

But I had failed with Kara. Failed by putting her in that box and burying her. I should have just made it fast, like I had with her lying sister. I'd wanted Kara to hear the Lord's words when she died, so her soul would be cleansed and reborn. But all I'd done was give the evil inside her time to connect with the evil in Hawk and Chaos.

A small smile spread across Josiah's lips. "You did well, child of God."

I bowed my head and fought off the pride at his praise, knowing it would be a sin to feel it but struggling not to. "Thank you."

"But you can do more. You must if you are to lead the movement to rebuild Ethereal Eden in my absence. My wife's soul needs to be reborn. And my daughter, she needs to be brought back to her people."

I lifted my head quickly, widening my eyes. "Lead... You would accept me? Even though I have failed?"

He put one hand to the glass. "Of course, my child. Like I said earlier, all are accepted at Ethereal Eden. You are already one of us. A child of God."

Tears pricked at the backs of my eyes again.

It was the acceptance I'd wanted Army or War or

Hawk to give me for so many years. An acknowledgement that I was part of them. That I was family.

And yet they never had. They'd held it just out of my reach, toying with me like a stupid kitten that knew no better.

They were the stupid ones. I'd hedged my bets. I'd found others who would accept me, even when they hadn't.

Hawk and War had berated me for every little mistake I'd ever made.

Josiah hadn't even punished me for failing to kill Kara. He'd opened his gates and accepted me.

And told me to try again. I saw his instructions there in his eyes.

"I won't fail again." I swore the promise with every fiber of my being.

"The Lord is pleased with you, Brother Xan. He will reward your obedience and commitment."

The bored-looking guard rolled his eyes and tapped his watch. "Time's up."

My upper lip curled at his arrogance and the evil inside him that had him dismiss Prophet Josiah's words as rubbish.

The guard was just like the men at the club. Their evil souls protecting the evil in Kara's.

They all needed to be reborn in the Lord's image.

They just didn't know it.

But I did. I would show them the way.

And when they were reborn, I'd welcome them into the Lord's embrace. I'd accept them the way they'd never done for me.

28

HAWK

The clubhouse was the fullest I'd seen in a long time. People seemed to have come out of the woodwork, filling up the parking lot with almost as many cars as bikes. We pulled chairs from everywhere we could and got out picnic blankets for the kids, not that any of them were sitting on them. They were too busy running around and playing on the equipment.

Music played loudly across a portable speaker Queenie had brought out, and after a couple of rounds of drinks, she'd dragged Hayley Jade onto a makeshift dance floor and was spinning her around, the two of them laughing hysterically.

There was a party vibe in the air, one that had Kara smiling from ear to ear at the edge of the crowd, taking it all in.

I dropped a kiss on her shoulder as I passed, my arms loaded up with beer we'd had to run into town for after Ice hadn't shown. "Happy?"

She nodded. "Very. This is exactly what she would

have wanted. Fun. Laughter. Friendship. Family." She gazed up at me. "Thank you."

"What for?"

"For today. For every day. For letting Hayden and Grayson in. For accepting me. For loving Hayley Jade."

She smiled, staring at something, and I followed her line of sight to Grayson, who'd jumped onto the dance floor. He hadn't gone back to his place in between the funeral and the party, so he had his dress shirt half unbuttoned, cuffs rolled to his elbows, and his tie around his head like Rambo.

I screwed up my face at the man who was supposed to be a serious, responsible doctor. "You sure you want to thank me for that one?"

She lifted a shoulder, her small smile reaching her eyes. "I kinda love him."

"Is it the bad dance moves?"

She giggled and twisted to look up at me. "Maybe. But I love you for a whole different set of reasons."

I snuck a hand down her waist and over her ass to grab a handful. "Yeah? It's for all the hot sex, right?"

To my surprise, she moved in closer, so her hand brushed over my cock, and her eyes held a glint of mischief. "Absolutely. But also for how you love people."

Awkward embarrassment crept up my neck. "Don't get too excited. I love you and Hayley Jade. That's it."

"Liar."

I knew what she was getting at. I just didn't want to admit it. "Fine. I love War and Rebel too. Though War's full name is ridiculous, and Rebel is stupidly short and never shuts up." But even as I said it, my gaze wandered around the yard, searching for Chaos.

Even I couldn't deny the way my breath faltered at the sight of him with one of his nephews on his shoulders, a beer in one hand, and holding on to the kid's legs with the other. He and Liam were deep in conversation about something, but it didn't seem like a serious one. Like everyone else, their smiles were wide and there was a lot of laughter.

She nudged me gently. "Have you told him yet?"

I glanced down at Kara. "That I love him? Do you even know me at all? I'm not telling him that."

She shrugged. "You should. He loves you too."

"Doubt it." Sex was one thing. Attraction, sure. Chemistry? Had it in bucketloads. But telling him I fucking loved him was dumb.

I wasn't saying it.

But I could show him. Maybe.

Ah fuck. This was a bad idea. Except now that it was in my head, it was suddenly all I could think about.

Kara nudged me. "Nobody is hanging out inside. If you two want a minute...or thirty." She tried to hide a knowing smile, like she knew exactly what I was thinking about.

I raised an eyebrow at her being all fucking cute and cheeky. "You going to come with us?"

She was still gazing at Grayson. "No. I have someone I need to say 'I love you' to as well." She pressed her tits against me and lifted up onto her toes. "Later, though... after the party..."

I tilted her chin up to capture her lips, kissing the fuck out of her because the thought of getting her clothes off had me hot. Her nipples were hard through her shirt, begging me to pick her up caveman style and carry her to my bed.

Which I was so doing once there weren't people wanting her attention every few minutes.

She practically skipped off to join the dance floor, Grayson grabbing her with a wide smile so full of devotion, even I couldn't help but smile at him. He spun her in a circle and dipped her low, pressing his mouth to hers.

Fine. They were fucking cute. Whatever made her happy was all I cared about it. I left them holding hands with Hayley Jade and edged around the dance floor, refusing to get pulled in, even though Queenie did her best.

Some things might have changed with me, but dancing wasn't ever going to be one of them. Unless it was of the naked, horizontal kind with Kara writhing beneath me.

Liam grinned at me when I stopped beside them and held his hand out for me to shake. "How you doing, Hawk?"

I took his hand. "Good. Sorry to interrupt. But can I borrow your brother for a few minutes?"

Liam's brow furrowed. "Of course. Everything okay?"

Fuck, was I being that obvious? Shit. My palms were sweating, and I could tell I was breathing too fast. Not to mention being too polite. Since when did I say things like, "sorry to interrupt?" I swallowed hard. "Yeah, good. Thanks."

I wanted to groan, but Chaos lifted the kid from his shoulders and handed him back to his brother.

I turned on my heel abruptly and threaded my way through the crowd into the clubhouse, which was indeed empty of bodies, everyone making the most of the warm evening and the lingering sunset.

I headed straight for my bedroom, and Chaos followed, kicking the door shut behind him.

He leaned back on it, studying me. "What's wrong?"

Nerves were getting the better of me, and so I blurted out the first stupid thing that came to my head. "Nothing. Just wanted to get my dick sucked."

He raised an eyebrow, like he knew that wasn't the truth, but I couldn't stop the hammering in my heart. I needed something else to focus on.

He stepped in close, his mouth a mere inch away from mine and breathed out slowly. "Then ask me nicely."

I wasn't doing that. Instead, I undid the button on his jeans, and then the zipper and slipped my hand inside his underwear, needing to touch him.

I dropped to my knees, yanking down his pants and underwear and fitting my mouth over his cock.

He was warm, the taste of him now familiar, and I sucked him as he toed his shoes and socks off and stepped out of the puddle of clothes. He leaned against the door, one hand coming to the back of my head and resting there gently while I tongued his shaft and snuck my hand between his legs to cup his balls.

I moved rhythmically, plunging down over his cock and then drawing back, taking him fully to the back of my throat and then withdrawing right to the tip. My heart rate calmed with each suck and lick, my breathing slowing until my dick was as hard as his. All my thoughts turned to the need building inside me, while Chaos's precum beaded on my tongue.

This was easier than feelings I didn't want to have.

He helped me to my feet, and I pulled his shirt off with one hand while reaching behind him to lock the door with the other. I kicked my shoes and socks off, following him to the bed as he got on it and twisted onto his side, rummaging through the top drawer of my bedside table until he came up with a bottle of lube. He lay back on the pillows, watching me with heated eyes, one hand lazily stroking his cock, keeping himself hard while I got undressed.

I got my jeans off, yanking them down. And then my shirt hit the floor somewhere beside his and I was crawling across the bed to him, settling between his muscled, tattooed thighs. I stared down at him, all fucking abs and biceps and golden skin. His chest had the lightest dusting of hair, with a darker trail that ran from beneath his belly button to the thatch above the base of his cock.

He squirted lube onto his fingers and then reached for me, getting it over my cock, slicking me up so good it had me groaning in pleasure. I lowered myself down on top of him, rubbing all up on his dick and lowering my head to kiss him.

I plunged my tongue into his mouth, thrusting slow with my hips, nowhere near penetrating him, both of us writhing together, getting off on the feeling of skin on skin and the pure attraction I couldn't ignore when we were naked together.

Our movements became frenzied, our kisses deeper, harder, less gentle, more demanding. Chaos bent his knees, raising his hips, forcing my dick lower, grazing against his taint and then between his ass cheeks.

We groaned at how close we were to where we wanted it. I nudged his entrance with my tip, wanting so fucking badly to just push inside and fuck him until we both came.

But I'd come in here for something else.

I leaned down and kissed him hard, moving every inch of our bodies together so I had the best leverage when I flipped our positions, rolling us so he was on top and I was laid out beneath him.

I reached between us, gripping his cock and guiding it to my ass, making it clear what I wanted.

He blinked, surprise clear on his face. "Hawk..."

"Don't say dumb words. Just fuck me." I swallowed down the nerves. "And kiss me. Don't stop kissing me."

He lowered his mouth to mine. "You sure?"

I only kissed him harder, raising my knees and hips the way he just had for me and groaning softly when the tip of his cock found my entrance. He was slick with lube from me rubbing against him, but he squeezed the bottle again anyway and pressed his hand between us, stroking my taint with the cold liquid, then lower to give the same treatment to the spot I wanted him most.

He thrust his tongue into my mouth, kissing me hard and fast, spinning my head in dizzying circles that only fed the pleasure inside me. His slow thrusts teased my ass, opening me up just the tiniest bit each time he prodded me there, my dick getting all the delicious friction from being between our two bodies.

He teased me, going slow, until I was writhing beneath him, need building inside me, a desperate ache to feel him there, to have him deep inside me, our bodies connected in a way I couldn't stop thinking about. I rocked my hips, trying to get more, desperate for the feel of him.

"You feel so fucking good," he muttered against my lips. "Your ass is so tight I'm going to come the moment I get inside you."

He drew back to stroke my cock, and I wanted to scream in frustration at how close he'd been, and yet, now he was making me feel good in a whole different way. I threw my head back and groaned, jacking my hips up, thrusting into his grip, abs flexing, fingers bunching into the sheets as I fought back my orgasm, not wanting to come.

He prodded my ass again, the added sensation maddening, bringing me right to the edge of an orgasm I could barely keep a grip on.

He kissed my neck, bit me there just enough I knew it'd leave a hickey, one I'd fucking wear with pride because I wanted his mark on me just as much as I wanted mine on him.

My head spun. My breathing was too fast. I just wanted him to fuck me so I could come.

I caught his gaze, ready to demand the orgasm he'd been taunting me with.

But the words that came out were soft. Gentle. And not at all what I'd planned.

"I love you."

He paused, but then grinned, like I'd said the funniest fucking thing. "Did you just say you love me?"

Embarrassment crept up my neck. "No."

He snorted on his laughter, but then it died, and he brushed his lips over mine. "Yeah, you fucking did."

I shrugged.

He turned the kiss deep again, focusing more on kissing me than fucking me, and I couldn't help the way I grabbed the back of his head, holding him to my mouth, needing every stroke of his tongue against mine, every bit of connection, every head-spinning moment of devouring him. Because whether he laughed at me or not, there was nothing I could fucking do about the way I felt for him.

I could take back the words, but there was nothing I could do about the feeling. About how I needed him. About how the thought of losing him or Kara left me so damn breathless I was sure it would kill me.

"Hey," he murmured, pulling back.

His gaze caught mine. His voice softened. "You ready to hear how I love you too? Or am I going to get punched in the face for it?"

I scowled at him. "I wouldn't do that."

He gave me a deadpan stare. "Oh really?"

"I wouldn't do that, *anymore*."

Chaos just rolled his eyes.

"You gonna fuck me or we just gonna lie here whispering I love yous like fucking saps? And by the way, don't expect me to go around wearing rainbow flags and telling everyone we're boyfriends or some shit, okay? I'm not fucking doing that—"

His dick pressed inside me in one full, sweet thrust that ate the words right off my tongue. My entire body tensed at the deep, foreign thickness inside me.

"You okay?" he asked quietly.

With that one question, all my bullshit disappeared, taking all the walls I'd put up between us with it. "I'm good. Just go slow."

He nodded, lowering his head to kiss me again, just like I'd asked him to.

He moved slowly in and out of my body, his kisses gentle, a distraction while my body adjusted to the feel and my brain let back in every pleasure he'd been building. I breathed as he moved inside me, raising my hips and ass so we rocked together, him hitting me at just the right angle to bring that budding orgasm back to life.

I groaned, raising my head to kiss his neck, his shoulder, and biting down there when he filled me so perfectly and stars danced behind my eyes.

"You're so fucking tight," he groaned. "I need to come."

I did too.

With his muscles flexing and one hand wrapped around my cock, he jerked me in the same timing that he thrust into my body. He built us both up until I was practically mewling for him to just give it to me, begging him to fill me, needing him to come in me, so I could come on him.

My body adjusted; he picked up the pace, moving faster and faster until I couldn't hold on another second. I closed my eyes, arched my back, dropping my head into the soft pillows, and let the orgasm rip through me.

Chaos came with a groan, buried deep inside, my cum spilling over his hand and landing between us.

He pumped in and out of me a few more times, each one a torturous pleasure that had me begging for more even though I knew all too well that neither of us could handle another round.

He collapsed, his dick going soft inside me, neither of

us giving a fuck about the sticky mess of pleasure between us.

"Gonna fuck you just like that again," he whispered dirtily in my ear. "But while you're dick-deep in Kara's ass and Grayson is in her pussy."

I groaned, biting his shoulder, the image of the four of us sending quivers of need through every muscle in my body. I rolled over, catching a glimpse of the dark sky outside, the sun having set at some point while we'd been preoccupied. I knew people would be starting to wonder where we were and we should get back out there, but I couldn't do any of that when he was talking dirty in my ear and my dick was getting hard again.

"I—"

Whatever he'd been about to say dried up on his tongue as screams from outside ripped through the night.

29

ICE

THIRTY MINUTES EARLIER

Fang gave me a disapproving glare as I stopped a rental van in front of the Slayers' gates. The big man's deep scowl was nothing I hadn't seen before. It scared the fuck out of most people, me included, when I'd first joined the club. But I'd come to realize he was actually one of the nicer guys here.

At least he didn't lie and promise me things he'd never had any intention of following through on. Like Hawk and War.

I gave him a nod as a greeting.

He didn't return it. "Where the fuck have you been? Hawk and War were looking for you earlier. They have something they need to discuss with you."

"What?"

Fang stared at me. "I ain't the prez. Not my place to say."

I didn't know why I'd bothered asking. I already knew. I was surprised my bags weren't already packed and waiting for me at the gate. Surprised they were even giving me the courtesy of telling me to my face that I was out.

Anger boiled inside me, hot and uncontrollable every time I thought about Hawk's smug expression and War's condescending frown. Both of them judging me for every little thing I'd done wrong.

They didn't get to do that anymore. The Lord was the only one who could judge my sins.

Fang glanced at the van. "Where'd you get that?"

I shrugged. "My bike broke down in town. Borrowed the van from a friend so I could get the bike back here without calling a tow truck or for one of you to bring a club van down."

Fang nodded. "Go on then. Prez is already gonna be pissed you're so late. Don't make it worse by fucking around out here."

I got back in the vehicle, driving it through the gates and watching them close behind me in the rearview mirror.

"Sinners must be reborn to cleanse their sins," I muttered at Fang's figure getting smaller in the reflection. I waited until he was out of sight, driving the van slowly down the unpaved driveway toward the clubhouse, trees and shrubs either side of me lit up with golden hues while the sun sank.

I steered the van off to the side of the driveway, well before the parking lot or the clubhouse came into sight.

Right next to the dating app I'd first met Tulip through, my phone home screen had a surveillance app. It was one I used daily while sitting on the front gate, bored out of my brain, watching for dangers that almost never appeared. Security cameras had been strategically placed around the perimeter and throughout the compound in key areas. There was no sound, but the camera by the front door of the compound showed that's where everyone was. Kids playing on the lawn. Adults sitting around drinking or talking or dancing.

The Lord had brought them together like that, I was sure. Grouping them to make what needed to be done easier.

For the first time in years, my head was calm and my eyes clear. I had a purpose. I knew what had to be done. Josiah had given me that clarity I'd been seeking in all the wrong places.

There was no camera monitoring this part of the driveway or the woods either side. I double-checked the app, making sure I couldn't be seen.

Nothing on the screens.

I just had to hope Fang hadn't noticed my van hadn't made it all the way down to the parking lot. I paused for a few minutes, waiting for his voice to come over the walkie-talkie and ask if I'd gotten lost or something, but there was nothing but silence.

A small smile tugged at my mouth. The Lord had my back. I was pleasing Him, and He was making my steps easy. I put my AirPods in my ears, hit play on another of Josiah's episodes, and let his words fuel my steps, each one bringing my soul closer to the salvation I so desperately needed.

There was no bike in the back of the van. A lie that had fallen so easily from my lips now that I was back here, with the demons from Hell on the gates and men who did their bidding within.

I was a sinner too. I knew that. I'd been led astray as easily as Kara.

As easily as Tulip.

I put one of the large containers in the back of the van into a backpack, strapping it to my back, ignoring how heavy it was and the way the liquid inside sloshed around. Hefting the other two containers out of the van, I set them down in the dirt, fitting funnels to their openings so the fuel inside wouldn't dump out all in one spot.

The sounds of the party were loud and filtered across the early night air as I slipped into the woods, leaving a trail of clear liquid on the ground behind me.

I stomped through the undergrowth, not bothering to be quiet or careful because the music covered my footsteps and the greenery was too thick here for me to be seen.

I knew exactly how close I could get to the clubhouse before I could be seen by the surveillance system.

I didn't need to be close.

Not yet.

I moved quick, making a wide circle around the group, stomping through the trees with Josiah's encouragement in my ears, his words all fitting together so perfectly it was like he'd created them just for me.

The gasoline in the two hand containers ran out quicker than I thought it would, and I swore beneath my breath.

But I couldn't use the container on my back and I had no others.

It would have to do.

I stepped away from the trail of accelerant, wiped my

hands off on a rag, and then fished a tiny box out of my pocket.

The match scratched against the side, the little flame lighting up the end instantly.

I tossed it to the trail of liquid, eyes widening when the flame whooshed along the fuel, lighting up a wall of flame.

I waited for them to notice.

Three.

Two.

One.

The first scream pierced the night air, sounding exactly like the Devil escaping the souls who had him trapped.

30

KARA

A FEW MINUTES EARLIER

I had two left feet, but even I could handle swaying slowly in Grayson's arms, smiling up at him while he repeated a joke Hayden's nephew had just told him.

I laughed when it was clear from his expression that he'd gotten to the punchline, even though it honestly wasn't funny. The happiness on his face was all I cared about.

He pulled me a little closer, until my chest was pressed to his and his arm snaked around my back, holding me tight. "Telling you bad jokes, while slow dancing to fast songs, might be my new favorite thing to do."

"Mine too."

"You seem happy."

I twisted my fingers in his shirt. "I am. I've needed this closure. Needed to let her go so I can move on."

He kissed my forehead softly, his lips lingering. "Good."

Smoke tickled my nose, and I wrinkled it, Grayson making the same face and twisting us away from the grill Aloha was handling with an apron tied around his solid middle.

But the smoke didn't get any better. If anything, it got worse.

Grayson paused.

I glanced up, following his line of sight.

It took a good second for me to understand what I was looking at. That the glowing red and orange in the woods was no longer the setting sun.

The sun was gone.

But flames flickered through the trees.

"Fire!" Grayson shouted.

Someone screamed, and then another. Until screams cut through the night, terrifyingly real, even though I was frozen to the spot.

People shouted, and Gray put his phone to his ear, barking down the line at a 911 dispatcher.

"Hayley Jade!" Her name came out as a hoarse shout, and I spun around, searching through the group for her.

Kids and adults alike ran everywhere, food dropped in the process of everyone trying to find their families and War trying to herd everyone back from the danger.

Hawk and Hayden came sprinting out of the clubhouse, both of them shirtless, their jeans undone, boot laces trailing on the ground, but Hayley Jade wasn't with either of them.

"Jax! Hayley Jade!" The scream hurt my throat. I stumbled desperately, nearly tripping over a chair that had been knocked over.

"I've got her, Kara!" someone shouted behind me.

Relief flooded through me, catching sight of Hayley Jade being guided back with the other kids by Queenie and Jax.

"The firefighters are twenty minutes away," Grayson muttered, staring at the flames gaining traction by the second.

Hayden surveyed the scene. "There's nothing behind us but more fuel for it to burn."

Grayson nodded. "If it really gets going, it'll be quick. Outrunning it with all those kids..."

My heart sank.

Hawk swore under his breath. "There's a lot of us. We can put it out if we move fast."

Terror gripped my throat. But there was no other way. We were on our own. Too remote to wait for help.

Hawk sprinted for the garden shed, pulling out a shovel and then running for the flames. Hayden and Grayson followed a moment later, the three of them sprinting toward the danger with nothing more than garden tools as weapons.

Hayden glanced back at me, shoveling dirt on top of the flames to snuff them out. "Stay with Hayley Jade!"

But it was clear to me, even as the rest of the Slayers joined the fight, that we needed more sets of hands than just the men. I looked around frantically, spotting the heavy cloth grill cover.

I caught Queenie's eye, and neither of us had to say anything. I knew she'd protect those kids with her life. Bliss pushed Ridge into Rebel's arms and shouted for her to go with Queenie and the kids.

Rebel seemed like she wanted to argue, but she was

heavily pregnant, and Bliss didn't stop to see if she agreed or not.

And neither did I. There was no time for arguing. Or discussions. Or negotiations over who would stay behind and who would go to the flames.

The men didn't get to be protective.

We needed everyone to fight.

We all knew it.

I picked the cloth covering up and ran toward the flames, coughing into the thicker smoke. I hit the nearest flame with the bag, smothering it, and then again. And again.

Around me, my family did the same. Bliss had found a blanket and had taken up a spot beside me, beating back the flames the same way I was. Others dug up dirt to throw onto it. Heavy motorcycle boots stomped out what they could.

The two kitchen extinguishers Hayden had insisted on installing when he'd first started cooking here made the biggest dent in the flames, but we hit back with whatever we could find.

Smoke got in my eyes. The heat from the flames burned.

But by the time sirens rang in the distance, the fire was out.

Cheers went up as Hawk stomped out the last ember. Soot and dirt streaked his torso and face.

Grayson strode through the trees, gaze running all over my body when he found me. "Are you hurt?"

I shook my head quickly, and he nodded once, giving me a lingering look like he wanted to stay, but we both knew he needed to see if anyone was injured. Down the line, Hawk's gaze met mine. I gave him a quick nod, telling him I was okay, and then he turned away to help Aloha with a burn on his hand.

War and Nash helped Bliss to a seat, all three of them coughing. Gunner slumped beneath a tree, some of my nurse friends from the hospital going to him to take his pulse.

I stared at the scorched ground, fingers shaking, but I couldn't stay another second. I needed to get to Hayley Jade.

Ignoring all the parts of me that hurt, I turned and ran, following the lay of the land, knowing the kids had to be down here somewhere.

"Kara."

I stopped.

Ice was coming up the hill with Hayley Jade in his arms. Her eyes were red and her cheeks streaked with tears, but she didn't appear to be hurt. Relief flooded me and I ran to them, reaching for her.

He twisted away, not letting me take her.

"What are you doing?" I tried again. "Ice, give her to me." But this time, when he twisted out of my reach, I saw the gun in his hand, pointed right at Hayley Jade's stomach.

It wasn't unusual for one of the guys to have a gun. But Ice had never been so careless with one around Hayley Jade before. "Ice! Your gun!"

He glanced down at it. "Oh, sorry."

But when he moved it from pressing against Hayley Jade's stomach and very deliberately pointed it at me, his voice was as cold as his road name. "Josiah says hello."

31

ICE

The fire had worked beautifully as a distraction so I could get in and get Hayley Jade. I hadn't counted on Kara fighting the fire with the others. I'd thought she'd run, or that Hawk would have forced her back. So that had slowed me down a bit, but in the end, it hadn't mattered.

I'd found them both.

Now the cleansing ritual could begin.

I was so foolish for not understanding Josiah's words earlier.

The night we'd gone to Ethereal Eden, when I hadn't been able to save him, he'd preached of a ring of fire as he'd been loaded into an ambulance.

He'd been speaking to me. I knew that now.

I hadn't had enough gasoline to save everyone's souls like I'd wanted, but I knew Kara's and Hayley Jade's were the most important. She was Josiah's wife. Hayley Jade was his child. The Slayers had never deserved them.

They'd tricked Kara, lured her away from what was good and right. I saw that now, but I couldn't save them all.

I would bring her back to the flock. Would return her to the Lord.

Josiah would accept me. Reward me for doing the Lord's work. Take me beneath his wing and give me the family I'd always wanted.

The one Tulip had promised before she'd ruined it all.

My head hurt. My brain pounded against my temples, my physical body, ruined with sin, now trying to stop me from what was right. What needed to be done.

One good thing about Hayley Jade not speaking was that she stood there silently, watching while I shoved a rag in her mother's mouth and put a thick piece of tape across it, holding it in place. Tears streamed down the girl's face, but she didn't move. Didn't utter a sound.

Kara struggled against my hold, trying to communicate with Hayley Jade, but one swift hit to the head from the butt of my gun had her quieting down. The fight went out of her, and her eyes fluttered. I pulled the cord from my backpack, wrapping it around her wrists tightly like handcuffs. I stared down at the familiar rope, remembering the last time I'd used it. I liked the symbolism. "Same thing I used around Tulip's neck," I mumbled to myself.

Kara's head snapped up, her eyes widening, full of fear.

I shook my head at her. "Don't worry. I know what I'm doing this time. I won't mess up again, like I did when we buried you."

Her body trembled, but she stared at Hayley Jade,

trying to say something, but the gag in her mouth and her bound hands did their job. Which was good, because I needed to concentrate.

I dragged Kara farther up the hill, loving the way Hayley Jade just followed along like a little lamb trailing its mother. I glanced down at her. "You're a good woman of the Lord, Hayley Jade. Doing exactly as you're told. Josiah will be so pleased."

I frowned when she didn't acknowledge my praise.

She just cried those silent tears and tripped over her own feet, stumbling across the rough terrain, dodging trees as she tried to follow Kara up the hill.

"Keep up!" I snapped at her.

She moved a little faster. That pleased me.

Shouts came from the area we'd just left.

They'd probably found Queenie and Rebel then. I'd pistol-whipped the older woman hard enough to knock her out. Rebel was normally feisty, and I'd thought she'd put up a fight, but as heavily pregnant as she was, she hadn't been quick enough to stop me. I'd left her sitting on the ground, gagged with her hands cable-tied behind her back.

Then told the kids there was a sniper in the woods, ready to kill them if they so much as uttered a sound.

Another lie the evil here brought forth in me.

Kara's name was shouted through the night air by a dozen different voices. Chaos's, Hawk's, and Grayson's mixing amongst others.

A trickle of worry made its way down my spine, but I sucked in a deep breath and reminded myself I needn't fear. God was showing me the way.

My van wasn't much farther. Once we got there, I'd

drive us back to Ethereal Eden. Cleanse our sins with fire. Then take my spot as Josiah's right-hand, as he had foreseen.

The clubhouse loomed. I just needed to get past it. Get a little farther up the hill. I peeked around some trees. Hawk, Hayden, and Grayson all stood in the middle of the clearing, their panicked expressions so typical of men with no faith. No trust that the Lord knew what was best for them.

I knew I was on the right path. I could wait. They wouldn't stay there long. They'd disperse, searching for Kara.

Kara noticed them, and I clapped a hand over her mouth so even her muffled cries couldn't be heard.

The fight in her body didn't last long, and I whispered soothing words in her ear, reminding her the fatigue she felt right now was the evil leaving her body.

"Kara!" Hawk shouted.

Footsteps drew closer, each one cracking twigs and crunching over dead winter leaves. "Kara!"

That was Chaos. But from the rumble of low conversation between shouts, he and Hawk weren't alone.

Kara thrashed in my grip, though the hit to the head had clearly disoriented her. I pulled on her bindings, watching the cord cut into her skin. "Stop or I'll kill Hayley Jade right here, right now. You'll give me no choice. And then her soul won't be reborn, and she'll rot in Hell for all eternity. Is that what you want for your daughter?"

Kara stared at me like I was some sort of monster. When all I was trying to do was help her. I held her tighter and glanced at Hayley Jade. She blinked up at me with huge, scared eyes. I shook my head, finger to my lips, reminding her to stay quiet.

Chaos's shouts grew near. "Kara! Hayley Jade!"

Hayley Jade's gaze darted to Kara's.

And then she ran.

She lurched out of the bushes, sprinting for the three men heading toward us.

I knocked Kara off her feet, shoving her down, and lunged after her daughter, rage coursing through me.

"Hayley Jade!" Hawk ran toward her, his big strides closing the gap between us fast.

But I was quicker. Smaller. I didn't have any of the bulk Hawk and Hayden had.

I caught Hayley Jade around the waist, lifting her off the ground, her feet kicking the air, her fingernails scratching at my forearms as she tried to get to the three men her mother had been whoring herself out to like a common slut for months.

I backed up to where I'd left Kara, her head bleeding, her eyes unfocused.

Hayley Jade screamed, her high-pitched squeal piercing through my ears. She reached her arms to them, her fingers twisting in the secret sign language Hayden and Kara had been teaching her. "Daddy!"

Hawk, Chaos, and Grayson all stopped.

Even I was surprised by the ragged sound of her voice.

Hawk's face crumpled, and he stumbled forward, reaching for her. "Ice. Give her to me."

I pointed my gun at him. Idiot wasn't even armed. Wasn't even fully dressed, his bare torso streaked with soot and dirt.

Now he knew what it felt like, to feel small and useless. Incapable.

"Daddy," Hayley Jade sobbed again, her voice stronger this time, her fingers still making that same sign.

Chaos looked like he wanted to vomit. His gaze trained on her hands. His voice was wobbly when he finally turned to me. "What are you doing? You're scaring her. Let her go. She's just a kid."

I took a few more steps toward where I'd left Kara.

Hawk's bleak expression morphed into anger. "Get your hands off my daughter. I swear to God, if you've hurt her—"

He lunged for me, but again I was quicker. And now I was pissed off. I shot a single round into the air. Then lowered the gun to point at Hayley Jade.

"Stay back."

Grayson held his hand out, blocking Chaos and Hawk from advancing any farther, but his gaze was trained on me. "Okay. We're not coming any closer. Let's just talk, okay? What do you want? You have to want something, right?"

I tried to keep the tremble out of my fingers. "It's not what I want. It's what the Lord wants. What I must do to enter His kingdom! Prophet Josiah has foreseen it!"

Hawk blinked. "Prophet...you're with him? You've been with him this whole fucking time?"

Anger coursed through me. "I was with you! I did everything for you! All the chores! All the shit jobs! Anything you asked of me! But it was never enough, was it? Never enough to get you to accept me."

Hawk shook his head. "We've been waiting for you all afternoon. War and I decided to patch you in."

I froze. "No. You're lying. Just like Tulip lied."

Hawk screwed up his face in confusion. "Tulip? What the fuck is Tulip?"

But Grayson swallowed hard. "Tulip was Alice's code name on that app we found on Kyle's phone, remember?"

Chaos's head snapped up in horror. "You're Golden? You're the man she was texting?"

Hawk screwed up his face in confusion. "No. That man said his name was Xan. That's not your name."

I stared at Hawk, a seething anger rising inside me that, even after five years of being here, waiting on these men hand and foot, not one of them had bothered to try to get to know me, even at the very base level. "Isn't it? What's my name, Hawk? My real name?"

He scrubbed a hand over his face. "I don't fucking know, okay? Is that what you want me to say? That I'm a prick who never bothered to ask? You aren't a special fucking snowflake, Ice! I'm a prick to everyone! I don't know anyone's real fucking names! Gunner has been with this club since I was a kid, and I wouldn't have a fucking clue what's written on his birth certificate. I never asked because who you were before you joined this club doesn't matter. You were some street trash no-hoper, right? Most of the guys were! Did you want me to remind you of that by asking about your messed-up childhood or the parents who didn't give a fuck about you?"

"It's Alexander," War said quietly, coming up behind Hawk, his gaze steadily trained on me. "Your name is Alexander. Xan for short, I guess."

Hawk hadn't been wrong. I hated the name Alexander. It only reminded me, that at some point, I'd had parents who'd given me that name. And then they'd decided they didn't want me enough to keep me not long after.

Grayson fixed his stare on me, his expression unchanging, though I saw the flicker of something in his eyes.

"What do you want?" he asked again.

I laughed bitterly. "What do I want? I want to walk out of here and take Kara and Hayley Jade back to Ethereal Eden where they belong."

Grayson's voice was eerily calm. "You know we aren't going to let that happen. So let's talk about what else you want. Because there has to be more, right? You didn't just kill Alice for no reason."

The lump in my throat rose swiftly at the mention of her real name. I couldn't say it out loud. "Tulip was a liar. She said we were going to be a family. Her and me. That I'd come live with her at Ethereal Eden and be blessed by the Lord."

Kara finally got the tape free from her mouth and spat out her gag. I didn't bother trying to stop her. She was bleeding, a crumpled mess on the ground. She couldn't hurt me.

But her gaze burned mine. "You were a victim of Josiah's scams. Alice met you on that dating site and told you all about Ethereal Eden and how wonderful it would be for a man like you. A man who didn't fit within the norms of society. A man who wasn't accepted anywhere else. You had the Slayers, but they weren't patching you in, so you were vulnerable. Exactly the type of man Josiah targeted."

I shook my head, despite knowing in my gut that every word was true. It didn't matter now.

Kara continued, "I read every single word of those texts. You never told her you were a biker."

"Why would I? I'm nothing to this club. Nothing more than their errand boy." Heat burned the back of my neck just thinking about admitting my lowly status to a woman I'd wanted to build a life with. The very thought of her knowing what a loser I was then was mortifying. "I never lied to her. Just kept parts of myself private. But she lied in every message. Every single one."

Kara's bottom lip trembled. "Except she didn't. At some point, Alice developed real feelings for you. I saw the scripts she used when we went to save Jax. She'd used them almost word for word in the beginning, introducing you to Josiah's teachings. Drawing you into his web. Until you told her about how you like art and how you like to bake. Until you complimented her and made her feel important enough that she switched to using Kyle's phone so she could talk to you more."

Bitterness sat hot on my tongue. "I was going to come to her. I wanted to. I knew I was never going to be accepted here."

Kara's expression morphed into one of understanding. "But then we left."

Hayley Jade had gone quiet in my arms, and my fingers shook, still holding the gun at her back, knowing I couldn't let her go. Couldn't let my guard down for even a second or their evil would overcome me and I would cave into the alluring pull of the Devil. "Evil had gotten into her soul. She was supposed to be my wife. Good and obedient."

Grayson nodded. "So you killed her. You lured her out to a nightclub. Teased her with the promise of freedom.

And then you put a cord around her neck and tightened it until she couldn't breathe."

He didn't understand! Nobody did. "She needed to be reborn. To be cleansed of her sins. I did what needed to be done!"

Grayson wasn't finished. "And then you did the same thing to Kara, burying her alive."

"When she showed up here, at the clubhouse, and I found out she was Alice's sister, I realized the Lord was showing me the way. She's poison. She poisoned Alice. Drew her from the safety of Ethereal Eden with lies and evil words."

I pushed Hayley Jade at Kara and stood behind them, my gun never wavering. It was the only thing keeping the others at a distance. I knew that.

I eyed Hawk and reached over my shoulder to unzip my backpack. "If you so much as move an inch, I'll pull this trigger and end them now. Their eternal damnation will be on your shoulders. Alice's is on mine. I didn't know how to cleanse her soul properly and I let anger get the best of me. But I know better now. Josiah has shown me the way."

I raised my gaze to the sky and repeated the words imprinted on my brain ever since I'd heard Josiah speak them as he'd been loaded into the ambulance at Ethereal Eden. "We will all be judged at the feet of the Lord, our souls melded to our earthly bodies until the ring of fire is crossed. Repent! Repent! The Lord demands your souls be cleansed with fire and rain and blood. Repent! Repent!"

I took the final container of gasoline from my backpack with my free hand.

Then turned it upside down, dumping clear liquid all over the two females at my feet, as well as myself.

Kara screamed; clutching Hayley Jade close as the liquid poured down over all three of us.

Hawk let out a bellow of rage. Grayson and Chaos both lurched forward, only to be grabbed by other members of the club who I hadn't even noticed surrounding us. Smoke still hung in the air; the darkness only brightened by the lights from the clubhouse that barely reached the circle of accelerant I'd made around us.

I pressed the gun down on Hayley Jade's head hard enough she cried out, reminding everyone who was in control here. The rush of power sped through my veins, adrenaline pumping my heart faster than it should have now that the moment was here.

I needed to get this right. Needed for us to be delivered into His holy embrace. For my sins to be forgiven. I stepped forward. Raised my arms, a lighter clutched in one hand.

With a single flick of my thumb, I lit up the night.

32

HAWK

Flame erupted in the blink of an eye.

Grayson and Chaos reacted almost as quickly, both of them diving for Kara and Hayley Jade. Screams rang out around me, people rushed everywhere.

All I could do was stare at Ice, while flames engulfed his body.

He dropped his gun, screaming in pain, the gasoline fueling the fire until he was a walking inferno.

"Get the kids out of here!" War roared, standing beside me, the two of us watching Ice burn while he screamed in sudden agony.

I dragged my gaze away from the horrific sight and down at Chaos, Grayson, Kara, and Hayley Jade. My stomach plummeted, bile rising in my throat. "Are they hurt?"

They were both drowned in gasoline, their eyes red, and their skin had to sting, but I couldn't see a burn on them. Grayson turned Hayley Jade around, covering her ears and eyes.

Chaos held Kara in his arms, dragging her away from the flames. "He'd stepped away enough that the trail of gasoline was broken. The flames didn't get to them."

"It burns!" Ice screamed, limbs flailing as he tried to put out the fire he'd created. "Kill me!"

His screams pierced through the night, churning my stomach.

There was no more talk of the Lord or Josiah or rebirth.

There was nothing left but a burning man in utter agony.

He'd tried to kill my woman. My daughter. And for those sins, I couldn't pick up the gun to do as he'd asked. "Only the prez can shoot within the clubhouse gates."

The acrid stench of burning flesh filled the air, and I covered my mouth and nose with my arm, coughing as the disgusting smell permeated everything.

War picked up the gun. Pointed it at Ice, who'd collapsed on the ground.

But he was too late.

Ice's cries quieted.

He stopped moving.

War shook his head, emptying the weapon of bullets and throwing it into the flames with him. "Enjoy your eternal life, Ice. I don't think it's going to be behind pearly gates. Say hello to Josiah when he gets there."

The media caught wind of Josiah's death by the next evening. I sat in Hayley Jade's hospital room while she played on her iPad, fingers moving deftly across the screen like she'd owned one all her life.

I stared down at my phone and the massive headline that read: *Cult Leader Found Dead in His Prison Cell.*

I flashed it at Chaos on the other side of the room. His eyes flicked side to side while he read it and then nodded. "Your guys work fast."

I wasn't sure if it was one of our guys in the prison who'd been the one to repeatedly shank Josiah and leave him bleeding out on the concrete floor of his cell, or if it had been someone Vincent and Scythe knew from their time inside.

Either way, I didn't care.

Only that dickless Josiah was now six feet under, his eternal fucking soul sold to the Devil to do as he pleased.

I fucking hoped he got exactly what he deserved.

It didn't feel like a victory though. Ice's screams for me to kill him echoed over and over in my mind, guilt swirling inside my belly.

I'd already vomited twice in the last twenty-four hours. I was pretty sure I wasn't done.

Chaos snapped his fingers at me. "Stop it."

I screwed my face up at him. "I didn't do anything."

"You're blaming yourself. I can see it."

I sighed heavily, glancing at Hayley Jade, but she had her headphones on and was fully engrossed in whatever YouTube video she was watching. "If I'd just patched him in earlier..."

"Fine. Let's talk that out. Why didn't you?"

I shrugged. "I don't know. Something always felt off. The others wanted me to, and I kept finding reasons not to. But maybe if I'd just patched him in, given him the family he so clearly wanted..."

Chaos sighed. "He was messed up long before you came into his life. It's not on you."

Grayson had confirmed it, finding hospital records for Alexander Key, detailing a long history of mental illness, ranging back to when Ice had been committed for the first time at barely twelve years old. We'd found empty bottles of pills in his room at the clubhouse. Antipsychotics that hadn't been refilled in the past few months.

He'd been spiralling for a long time, and none of us had seen it until it was too late.

But it didn't matter what anyone said.

I'd always hold guilt over it.

That was my cross to bear. One I doubted I'd get over anytime soon.

But I would put it aside, bury it deep, because the people I had here were more important than the dead.

I leaned over and pulled Hayley Jade's headphones off and grinned at her. "Say elephant."

"Elephant," she chirped back happily.

Chaos grinned at the game we'd been playing ever since Hayley Jade had been brought here for observation. Which mostly consisted of us getting her to say random words, just because we were scared she might stop talking if we let her stop for too long. "Say spaghetti."

She twisted her legs up beneath her and bounced excitedly. "Too easy. Spaghetti."

I leaned back on my chair and folded my arms. "Say pterodactyls are the best dinosaur."

She made a face at me, her cute nose scrunching adorably. "But they aren't. T-Rex is."

I chuckled, just loving the sound of her voice. "Say Daddy again then."

She rolled her eyes. "I already said it about one hundred million billion times!"

I leaned in, kissing her soft cheek. "Don't care. Say it again."

"Daddy. Daddy. Daddy." She looked at Chaos and silently signed, "Dad, make him stop."

I ruffled her hair. "Excuse me, short stuff. I understood that!"

She giggled. "Oops."

In the space of an instant, in the terror of a moment I wished she'd never had to see, she'd started talking again.

And I'd become Daddy.

Chaos was Dad, though she signed it more than she said it out loud.

Grayson stuck his head around the door, and Hayley Jade's face lit up. "G-Dog!"

I battled back laughter, and Chaos sniggered.

Grayson came in and high-fived Hayley Jade, but even he chuckled. "I know we said we'd try out G-Dog, but I don't know if I'm feeling it. I think it might be too cool for me."

Hayley Jade nodded seriously. "It's *definitely* too cool for you."

He laughed. "Thanks for agreeing. I think. Maybe we should try something derivative of my first name. Fred, maybe?"

Hayley Jade screwed up her face. "No. Definitely not Fred." She grinned. "What about Freddie Spaghetti?"

Grayson nodded slowly, pretending to think it over. "That does have quite the ring to it. Let's try it!" He fist bumped her this time, the two of them dissolving into laughter. He moved his hand around, making her chase it with her wobbly, noodle-like fingers.

We were letting Hayley Jade lead in what she called us. Chaos and I had been given parent titles, but it was clear the way she felt about Grayson, at least for now, was different. They had a fun uncle/niece sort of relationship going on, one that was bringing Hayley Jade a whole lot of fun and happiness while she waited to get out of the hospital. Kara was in another section, taking care of a small burn we hadn't noticed until we'd got here.

"You okay?" I asked Grayson, standing to meet him in the doorway as Hayley Jade babbled to Chaos about whatever it was she'd been watching on her iPad.

He dragged his gaze away from her, a smile still on his lips. "Yeah, of course. Why?"

I shrugged but then answered honestly, "It would fucking kill me to hear her call another man Dad or Daddy and not me."

Grayson shook his head. "You and Chaos have a different sort of connection with her. You're her parents." He grinned. "Wait 'til she's a teenager and hates your guts. While I'm still the fun one she loves." He smiled at the little girl fondly. "I love her. Don't get me wrong. I'd lie down on train tracks for her, and for Kara. But I can meet her where she's at. I don't need her to call me Dad to love her like she's my own. Dads come with all sorts of titles. Maybe mine is Freddie Spaghetti."

"I'm still rooting for G-Dog, personally."

A voice spoke up from behind us. "Beep-beep. Is there room for one more at this party?"

I glanced over my shoulder at Kara, freshly showered, wearing clean clothes we'd brought up for her, a white bandage on one leg the only evidence of the fire that had tried to claim her life the day before.

Grayson slipped straight into doctor mode. "What did the burn unit say?"

"To come back to have it redressed and that I'll probably have some scarring, but it shouldn't be too bad."

He nodded. "Good."

"And the baby?" I asked.

She smiled up at me. "Baby is clearly made of tough stuff. He's doing well."

All three of us stared at her, but it was Hayley Jade who got words out first. "I'm having a baby brother?"

Kara nodded. "They said it was still a bit early to tell for sure, but that's what they think!"

Hayley Jade cheered and did a happy dance on her bed that had it squeaking and rocking on its wheels.

Kara glanced around at the three of us. "Do any of you want to have some sort of reaction?"

Grayson got his hands on her first, sweeping her up and spinning her around until she laughed. "Shit, a boy? Seriously? Okay, so hockey. Obviously. But also ballet, because flexibility is important, and I don't want him thinking that dance is only for girls."

Chaos pulled her from his arms and down on his lap. But his laughter was for Grayson. "The kid probably hasn't even grown feet. You can't put him in skates yet."

Hayley Jade's eyes went big. "The baby has no feet?" Her face twisted into a mixture of awe and horror.

Grayson sank down on the bed with her and started explaining all the different stages of fetal development and assuring her her baby brother would indeed have feet and the little buds he currently had would grow.

Chaos snaked his hand into the back of Kara's hair and tilted her head so he could capture her lips. "A boy is going to be very fucking cool."

She clutched his arms, nodding as she smiled against his mouth. "I can't wait."

I dropped down on my knees in front of her, not caring about the hard linoleum floor, just needing to get my hands on the swell of her belly. It was only a tiny bit different than normal, but it was enough to be noticeable to me. "He's seriously in there."

She put her hands over the top of mine. "He is."

It was so fucking weird to think about. That she had this whole other little person inside her who might very well look like me. "How does everyone feel about the name Eagle?"

I kissed Kara's belly as the sounds of their protests filled the room.

Maybe Falcon then.

33

KARA

For the third time that day, Rebel dragged me into an underwear store. Bliss wasted no time, bypassing the racks of everyday T-shirt and sports bras and headed straight for the back of the store where they kept the sexy stuff.

My cheeks heated as they tossed scraps of barely-there lace at me, and I just tried to keep up, sorting through each one, giving big fat nos to all of them.

Rebel shoved her hands on her hips, her heavily pregnant belly jutting out in between. "Kara, this baby is going to be graduating college before you choose something. It's just underwear. You'll be smoking hot in any of it."

I rubbed my hand over my own belly, though I didn't have the obvious pregnancy bump my sister did. Yet. "I just want to look a certain way. Not..."

"Like Hawk's Little Mouse?"

I shrugged. "I like when he calls me that now. It's sweet."

"It's degrading, and Hawk is a pig. Mostly."

I shot Rebel a look. "Says the woman whose man still calls her Roach."

Rebel got a dreamy expression on her face. "But it's so hot on Vaughn's lips."

Bliss screwed her face up. "Okay, enough, you two. It's not degrading if you like it. And you clearly both do. You weirdos."

Rebel raised an eyebrow at her. "Should we start on the whole 'baby girl' thing? I don't think War even remembers your legal name."

Bliss smiled at just the mention of her man but then clapped her hands. "Let's focus on the task at hand, shall we? Sexy underwear for Kara's photoshoot."

I bit my lip. "This might have been my worst idea yet. And I'm not sure taking some sexy selfies really counts as a photo shoot."

Bliss shook her head, holding up some sort of outfit that pretty much only consisted of straps and buckles. "No, I totally get it. You're going to be as heavily pregnant as your sister before too long, and then you're going to have a newborn. Get all the hot sex now while you're in that second trimester horny stage. Enjoy it. Let us live vicariously through you by giving us all the details afterward. I'm pretty sure Ridge is never going to learn how to sleep through the night, and we're all too tired to even think about getting some naked fun time in."

My eyes bulged as she shook the strappy garment in my direction. I pushed her hand away. "Definitely not that one."

Bliss shrugged and then threw it toward the cashier,

giving us a wink. "He's gotta learn to sleep through the night eventually, right?"

Rebel sniggered at her bestie but then paused, her fingers on a baby-blue teddy. Lace flowers covered the underwire cups of the plus-size garment, but the rest of it was see-through, with only the odd bit of embroidery as decoration. Laces wound their way up both sides, decorative more than functional, but sexy, nonetheless. She held it out to me. "Kara..."

I touched it gently, loving the soft silky texture of the material.

A tiny voice in the back of my head reminded me it would show off all the areas of my body I was conscious of. There would be no hiding my belly rolls or the cellulite on my thighs and ass.

But a little smile tugged at the corners of my mouth just thinking about slipping into it and the expression on Grayson's face when he opened his phone at the hospital and found a photo of me in nothing but lace. Hayden would get his while he was at a family function with Liam. And Hawk was studying for his GED at the clubhouse. The thought of him staring at my photo while surrounded by all his brothers had heat racing down my spine.

I took the outfit to the register and paid for it proudly, not hiding it away like some shameful secret. I used money I'd earned from my job at the hospital, the thrill of having my own money and standing on my own two feet never getting old.

When Rebel dropped me off at Sinners an hour later, I sucked in a deep breath, letting myself in via the security door in the back that led straight into the maze. I'd phoned ahead and whispered down the line to Chloe, Hayden's maître d' of the night, what I was planning, and she'd verbally high-fived me and said she'd keep the staff out of there. I'd have the place to myself until later, when it would open to the public.

I hadn't decided whether I'd be staying for that or not yet.

It was early for a Saturday night, the maze empty but already set up for later, when couples finished their meals and went searching for a little dessert. Sultry music played over speakers. The lights were dim and cast a reddish-pink glow that bounced off the black walls, beds, chairs, and sex toys.

I snuck into the changing rooms and, taking a deep breath, reminding myself I wanted this, I stripped my clothes. I showered, dried my hair, put on some simple makeup from the kit in my bag. I wasn't very good with it, but I liked the way the mascara made the color of my eyes pop and the glossy red lipstick drew attention to my mouth.

My fingers trembled when I put on the teddy, but when I looked in the mirror, I was pleasantly surprised by the reflection that stared back at me.

I was no skinnier than I'd been when I'd first arrived in Saint View. In fact, I think I'd probably put on a few pounds, courtesy of Hayden's cooking. Or it might have been the pregnancy. But I tried to see myself through the lenses of men who'd spent months building me up, not just with words, but with actions. I couldn't go anywhere without one of them touching me, taking me into their arms and whispering in my ear how beautiful I was.

Amber had actually asked me once if I got sick of it,

but I'd quickly assured her that after a lifetime of being starved of affection, I wanted their touches as much as possible. That each of them made me feel like a queen in a different way, and somehow, between the three of them, they fulfilled every part of me that had ever gone begging, starving, or neglected.

In their arms, I felt whole again. At peace.

And even a little bit sexy.

Grayson's shift would be finishing soon, and Hayden's family commitment was supposed to have just ended. Hawk was always ready for a study break.

I just needed to send them an invitation to the party they didn't know we were having. A ripple of excitement tingled across my skin. This was bold and brave, and it didn't really feel like me. But I liked it. It felt like the woman I was becoming, now that I was no longer scared all the time. It was one I wanted to try on for size.

I wandered into the maze, setting down my phone on a bench and turning on the camera's self-timer. If Rebel and Bliss hadn't had kids and men of their own to go home to, I might have asked one of them to stay and be my photographer.

But my snatch was on full display, and I was already getting horny, just from walking around like this, so maybe it was better I was alone.

I posed myself demurely, perching on the edge of a bench, feeling incredibly silly, and then checked the photo.

I frowned at it. My legs were closed. I had my arms covering my belly. Apart from the fact I was wearing lingerie that barely contained my breasts and there was an array of sex toys in the background behind me, I could have been sitting on a church pew, taking a photo for my parents.

Not exactly the vibe I was going for. I set the timer again, but this time, I opened my legs wide like the women in the inspiration photos I'd saved to my phone. Arched my back. Threw my head back and parted my lips, closing my eyes, the way I did when I rode one of their cocks.

Heat warmed me just thinking about having one of them beneath me.

And when I looked at the photo, my mouth dropped open.

I suddenly saw myself the way they saw me, and my eyes watered. I wasn't perfect. My breasts didn't sit high and perky. My skin wasn't blemish-free. I didn't know how to edit the image to make all the little lumps and bumps disappear.

But I didn't even want to.

I saw what they did.

Saw a woman who no longer wanted to hide away, even if she did like her man calling her "Little Mouse." Saw the woman who'd spent time in therapy, talking through every trauma I'd suffered. I still had a long way to go, but every session brought me closer to the woman I wanted to be in the future.

In that photo I saw the evidence of my self-confidence blooming. And it seemed only right I share it with the three men who'd helped me discover that side of myself.

I threw the image into our four-way group chat and then nervously tossed my phone aside, too scared to even peek at it.

But the message tone dinged almost immediately, and then again and again.

I couldn't help but sneak a glance at it.

Hayden: *Holy shit, Kara. You're so fucking beautiful. Send more.*

Hawk: *Fuck.*

Hawk: *Where are you? I'm already out the door.*

Grayson: *Good thing I'm at a hospital. I need reviving.*

Hawk: *You can't send a photo like that and then not tell me where you are,* Little Mouse. *An address. Now.*

Hayden: *She's in the maze at Sinners. I can tell from the background. I'm on my way.*

Grayson: *Leaving now too.*

Hawk: *Don't you have another thirty minutes left of your shift?*

Grayson: *Eh. I'll quit. Didn't really want to be a doctor anyway. We'll call all those years of med school and residency a fun side quest.*

I giggled at their messages and found a few other places around the maze to pose, dropping each image into the group chat without saying anything else.

My heart pounded when the main door to the maze opened, letting in a quick rush of light and noise. I scuttled deeper into the maze, my heart rate picking up at not knowing which one it was. "Don't say anything," I called out. "I'm waiting for you at the glory holes."

A groan was all that came back, though I couldn't tell from that noise alone which one of them it was. It didn't matter. That was part of the fun. My core throbbed as I knelt on the leather pads that covered the hard concrete floor, and waited, straining my ears for the sound of his footsteps.

My breath quickened when I heard them pass behind me and then circle around to the other side of the wall. I didn't peek at who it was. I didn't want to know. There was no fear it might not be one of my guys. I trusted Chloe to keep me safe and not let anyone back here for the first hour, so I could have this time alone with them.

He undid his zipper, and there was a rustle of clothing being removed on the other side.

Some of the holes on this wall were big enough only for a dick to fit through and designed to be lubed up and a tight fit. But others were larger, so the man could see the lips of the person on the other side. They even had chin rests, and handles either side, to make gripping the wall easier. I closed my eyes and dropped my chin onto one, trembling with nervous anticipation as my fingers closed around the handles.

The first touch of his dick to my lips had me almost self-combusting. My lips parted like they had a mind of their own, and he pushed his way inside my mouth, stretching me wide around him.

I instantly knew it was Grayson. His taste and size were so familiar now, after spending months in bed together, having sex in every way he could think of, and exploring each other's bodies until I knew every part of the man I'd fallen so hard for. I moaned at the feel of him sliding on my tongue and mourned the loss when he pulled out, only to thrust back in.

It was a strange feeling not to be able to see him, but the little groans of pleasure from his side of the wall told me he was getting off on this as much as I was.

"Finger your pussy, Kara," he groaned. "Get yourself

as wet as your mouth. They're going to need to fuck you as soon as they see you on your knees like this."

I dropped one of the handles, desperately spearing my fingers between my thighs. The silky, sheer material covering my pussy was too soft to resist. I rubbed it over my clit, moaning around his cock, letting the vibrations drive him higher.

I was vaguely aware of the door opening again, but I was too lost to the sensations of Grayson in my mouth, my fingers on my clit, to pay it any attention.

It wasn't until fingers trailed down my naked spine that I realized one of the others had found us.

"Close your eyes," he whispered.

I relaxed into the darkness, torturing myself with slow rubs until strong fingers brushed mine aside and took over the job.

Pleasure spread as the man fit himself behind me, his bare thighs brushing the backs of mine. He stroked one hand through my hair, fingernails scratching gently over my scalp while the other slipped beneath my teddy to push between my folds.

Grayson went deeper, faster, thrusting into my mouth until his pants and groans were audible above the sexy music. "Gonna come, Kara. Need to come between those pretty red lips. Fucking hell."

I swallowed him down eagerly, taking every drop across my tongue, the taste of him only heightened because I had my eyes closed.

He was barely done when the man behind me lifted me to my feet and pushed me up against the wall I'd just been leaning on. He lowered his head and kissed me hard, his naked body strong and solid on mine.

Hayden. No doubt about it. I knew as soon as my fingers touched his skin. As soon as his lips were on mine. He kissed like no other man, slowly, deeply, that connection between us sparking like crazy, even when I couldn't see him.

I didn't need to, because whatever it was that had always drawn me to him wasn't physical. It was his heart I loved. His soul.

But it was his body that brought me to orgasm each night, neither of us ever able to get enough of the other.

"You look so fucking beautiful," he groaned. "On your knees in my club, taking cock like that. Fuck, Kara." He was frenzied, his kisses turning rough and fast, his fingers touching me above my underwear, beneath it, my nipples, my clit, my pussy, my ass.

He was everywhere but never for long, each part of my body lighting up beneath his touch and then left craving more as he moved on. I grabbed at him just as much, needing his dick inside me, desperately wanting to be filled. But he caught my hands, drawing them up the wall, pinning them there in one of his so his other was free to torture me in the best way.

Something pressed between my legs. Something thick and solid, sliding aside the silk to slick through the moisture at my core.

Hayden switched on the vibrator, and then it was inside me, filling my aching pussy.

I moaned, thrusting my hips, taking the toy deep and feeling every vibration right to my core.

He'd used toys on me before. They all had, but it felt different this time. All my senses heightened because I couldn't see.

"Look at you, Little Mouse. All tits and ass and red lips I want to fuck."

I twisted my head toward Hawk's voice. I hadn't even heard him come in. But knowing he was here, watching what Hayden was doing to me, only turned me on more.

"Grayson," I moaned.

"He's here too, hard as a fucking rock again, even though I can still taste him on your mouth."

Hayden kissed me again, and I couldn't hold on to myself any longer. Not when his kisses spun my head, his big body covering mine, and a toy vibrating inside me.

I splintered apart, clenching around the toy, my body trembling with pleasure.

I hadn't even stopped shaking when Hayden swapped with Hawk. He lowered his head to my neck, kissing me there, sucking and licking my skin, until his lips moved to my ear. "That fucking lingerie is killing me, Little Mouse. It was all I could think of while I drove over here. But now I just want you out of it."

He fit his fingers beneath the shoulder straps and drew them down my arms. The cups fell away from my breasts, and a moment later, the lacy teddy was somewhere on the floor. His fingers traced over my skin, tantalizing every inch with featherlight strokes.

The doors opened again. More voices. More noise.

My eyes flew open. What time was it? Was the maze open to the public already? Surely my hour hadn't passed?

"I want to tie you up," Hawk groaned into my ear. "Want to fuck you in every hole. Watch Gray and Chaos take you at the same time. Fill you up so fucking good you scream our names."

I could barely breathe. I wanted that so bad. Every part of me aching to be theirs. But the thought of an entire club seeing me like this...

It was both hot and terrifying.

"Blindfold me."

Grayson picked up a silky piece of cloth sitting with the sex toys and wrapped it around my eyes, plunging me into darkness once more.

"Nobody but us will touch you." Chaos moved in behind me, kissing my shoulder.

I trusted them to keep me safe. They might have been willing to share me with each other, but that was as far as the agreement went.

Hawk kissed me hard, holding the back of my head and walking me backward. I wrapped my arms around his neck, soaking in the familiar feel of his naked body, my heart rate dropping back to normal, even as he fit silks around my wrists and raised them above my head, hooking them onto something hanging from the ceiling that held me there in place without the support of a wall or other structure behind me.

He knelt at my feet and put his face between my thighs, sucking and licking my pussy while fitting the same soft silks around my ankles. There was a solid spreader bar between them that prevented me from closing my legs.

Not that I wanted to.

At least not until voices I didn't recognize drew closer, and I started thinking about who might be watching me, staring at my naked body, judging my heavy breasts and fat thighs.

Grayson stepped in behind me, snaking an arm

around my middle and grabbing a handful of my breast to squeeze my nipple. I relaxed into his touch. At the feel of Hawk between my thighs, I was dripping with arousal, aching to release an orgasm he was building inside me. The voices around me were still there, but they faded into the background with every touch from my men. Every whispered word of how beautiful I was, every encouraging murmur about how each man there wanted to be them, had me preening beneath their praises until all I could do was concentrate on not self-combusting.

"Need to be inside you, Little Mouse." Hawk got up onto his feet and circled his arm around my waist. He stepped inside the triangle made by the bar and my legs, and then hoisted me up into his arms.

He supported my weight, holding the backs of my thighs, doing all the work to maneuver me down to impale me on his cock.

We both groaned loudly when he found his mark, sinking deep inside my wet channel. Grayson moved in behind me, dick moving between my ass cheeks as I was sandwiched between them.

"I want you both," I moaned, reaching one arm back for him, wanting to please him. But also desperate to increase the building need inside me so I could get over the line and come again. I burned with need, Hawk so deep inside my pussy. Bouncing me on his cock so it hit all the right places.

Grayson thrust inside my ass, and I cried out, my pleasure loud above the music and the soft moans of group sex around me.

He held my breasts while he took me from behind, he

and Hawk slowly working out a rhythm, groaning and whispering the praise they knew I needed so desperately.

The sounds of sex around me amplified, more than just the noises the four of us were making.

Hawk whispered in my ear, "They're all getting off on watching you, Little Mouse. Watching Grayson's dick in your ass, while he plays with your tits. Watching me pound your little pussy while Chaos fucks me."

I gasped at his dirty words, embarrassed and turned on by each of them and no desire for him to stop. The moans continued, until they were all I could hear, each one like catnip to my clit, a pounding rhythm starting up there that spread through my entire body until I was wild. "Take my blindfold off. I want to see."

Grayson pulled it off from behind me, and I caught a glimpse of myself in a wall of mirrors.

I let out a rush of breath, staring at my body, the flush of my skin, their hands on every curve, and the roomful of men and women all watching us with nothing but lust and desire and appreciation for the show we were putting on.

"See how much every man in this room wants you, Little Mouse? See how they're fucking but their eyes keep coming back to you?"

I tipped my head back, resting it on Grayson's shoulder, letting Hawk kiss my neck.

"So fucking beautiful," he whispered. "So fucking mine."

He fucked me harder, pumping in and out of my body. He groaned deeply when Hayden thrust inside him, taking him from behind, all four of us joined at once.

Hawk came hard, a shuddering explosion inside my pussy that set off my own orgasm. I clenched around him and Grayson, every muscle inside me spasming until Gray fell over the edge as well.

Two more thrusts, and Hayden bit down on Hawk's shoulder, groaning out his own orgasm against the other man's skin.

My head spun. Or maybe it was the room. I had no idea. All I knew was that we stilled, my body completely boneless. But I didn't fall, because they had me, just like I knew they would. I think I came again, my pussy so oversensitive that every tiny movement from one of them sent new waves of pleasure crashing down over my head, drowning me until my skin was ablaze, an inferno simmering away in my blood.

I was vaguely aware of being carried somewhere, and when I was finally able to open my eyes, I found myself in one of the private bathrooms, a hot shower running, and all three of my men washing me off.

Only to do it all again.

34

X

SIX MONTHS LATER

I rapped my knuckles across the glossy, painted wood door and stared up at the McMansion Scythe apparently lived in. "So freaking fancy," I murmured to myself, poking at the doorbell with a finger. And then a few more times because I liked the way it felt and the *ding-dong* it created somewhere deep in the house.

A woman opened the door and smiled at me, her long auburn hair pulled up in a messy ponytail with bits falling out of it. "Can I help you?"

"Can Scythe come out to play?"

The woman blinked. "Excuse me?"

Oops. Nearly gave away my entire hand too soon. "I meant is Scythe home?"

She squinted at me. "Does he know you?"

I grinned. "Of course! We're BFFs. I'm X."

Her face smoothed out in understanding. "Ah. The new friend from Grayson's support group. He told us about you. Scythe! Door!"

A moment later, Scythe appeared. He kissed the woman on the cheek as she moved back inside the house, and he came out to stand on the doorstep, closing the door behind him. He held his hand out to me. "What are you doing here? Grayson need something?"

I slapped his palm with a grin. "Do you want to build a snowman?"

His eyebrows turned into one crinkly long caterpillar when he frowned at me. "A what? A snowman? It never snows here."

"Come on, let's go and play."

He squinted at me. "You're weirder than I am, you know?"

It was lucky I liked him. His lack of knowledge of Disney songs was truly upsetting. "Come on. Come out with me tonight. I know you want to. I'm only going to do a little killin'." I pulled the knife from the holder on my hip and offered it to him.

He sighed. "Just a little, huh? I told you. I'm out of the game. I only come out of retirement for emergencies."

Pfft. Details, details. "You say that but you're looking at my knife like you want to marry it."

Scythe's gaze lingered on the shiny blade. "Just let me touch it. Just a bit."

I dangled it just out of his reach and took a step back. "Come on. It's not like we're killing anyone who doesn't deserve it. We're cleaning the streets up. Making them a better place for all. This is a community service, Scythe!"

He sighed. "Don't you have Whip or Torch or one of the other guys to go killing with? I've got kids who need bathing, floors that need vacuuming—"

"Entrails that need spilling..."

His gaze dipped to my knife again. He shook his head. "Vincent's gonna kill me, but ah, fuck it. Okay, I'm in. I'm not killing anyone. I'll just watch. Take the edge off. You have any idea how hard it is to just go cold turkey on this shit? Just let me make sure War and Nash are good for kid duty. We gonna be long? I might pick up dinner on the way home so no one has to cook."

"I'll have you home in two hours, tops. I won't even make you do cleanup. You can just do all the stabby fun bits."

Scythe clapped me on the shoulder. "Super generous of you. But like I said, I'm retired."

"Mmm-hmm. If you say so."

"Gimme five and I'll meet you in the car."

I hummed beneath my breath as I jogged back to my car and slid behind the steering wheel. While I waited, I pulled out the list of names Gray and Whip had authorized as targets.

Scythe got in beside me a second later, a glint of joy in his eyes. "That the list? Got anyone good in mind?"

I trailed my finger along the page. "Murderer, murderer, rapist, murderer…ooh! Serial murderer! Don't get too many of those in Saint View." I sniggered to myself. "Well, apart from me. And you. And Whip. Torch. Trigger. Ace. That guy I met in prison…shit, what was his name again?"

"Furlowe? You ever meet him?"

"Short with glasses?"

"Yeah, that's him."

"Good guy. I should tell him about Gray's group when he gets out."

"Pretty sure he's doing five consecutive life sentences."

"Oh. Right. Well, you snooze you lose."

Scythe nodded and sat back in his seat. "So how do you like to work? It's been a long time since I went out with anyone like this."

"You normally work alone?"

He shrugged. "Used to work with my sister sometimes, before she shacked up with a guy."

I crinkled my nose. "Got married and had kids?"

He shook his head. "Nah. I'm the one with all the ankle biters."

"What's that like?"

He grinned. "Pretty fucking sweet. You should try it."

I winked at him. "More of a love 'em and leave 'em type."

Even as I said the words, they didn't quite sit right on my tongue. But I didn't have much choice in the matter. I wasn't like Scythe. I couldn't just give this up. He might have gotten into this life because of some family thing he seemed to have going on.

I'd gotten into it because I had no other choice.

I couldn't ignore the urges inside me. There was no negotiating with them. Only placating them with violence.

But Grayson's group had shown me how to channel it in better ways. He hadn't tried to make me stop. We all knew I couldn't.

For that reason alone, I would never date a woman. Never let one sleep in my bed. I didn't want to kill innocent people, especially women, but that meant keeping my distance from them.

Never being alone with one.

I could fuck one in the middle of Psychos. I wasn't

going to slit someone's throat while they were riding my cock in a room full of people. But getting one alone? No. The temptation would be too great.

I thrust the list at Scythe, trying to keep a grip on the bloodlust that had crept up on me earlier in the day and hadn't eased up. "I don't care which one we go for. You're the guest. Your choice. Just no women."

He nodded slowly, his gaze wandering down the page. "Okay. Any other rules I need to know about?"

I shook my head, concentrating on the road. "Nope. Oh wait. No killing innocents. And no witnesses. It's Gray's one rule. If we get there, and there's someone else in the house, then we leave and come back some other time."

"Or we go hit up a different target on the list?"

I grinned at him. "It's like we share one brain."

Scythe screwed up his face. "I already share mine with someone, so I'd prefer if we didn't."

I chuckled as he directed me to the target's house, and I parked the car right in the driveway, like I owned the place.

Scythe eyed me. "Bold."

I reached between us into the back seat and pulled out an empty pizza box. "Less suspicious than parking on the street. This way the neighbors think I'm a friend." I held up the pizza box. "Or the delivery driver. You coming?"

"Is there actually pizza in that? I'm starving."

"Focus, Scythe."

"Right. Sorry. You lead. I'll follow."

I nodded, and we both got out of the car. I sniggered at the glint of metal just barely poking out of Scythe's sleeve. It was the same place I liked to keep my knife as well. I pressed my wrist against the edge of the pizza box, and the steel of my blade touched cold to my skin, reassuring me I hadn't left it at home.

That had only happened one time, and Whip still gave me shit about it. He was such an asshole. It could have happened to anyone.

Scythe stayed back, sticking to the shadows and out of sight of the doors and windows. While I walked up to the door, channeling my inner pizza delivery guy. I hit the doorbell with the corner of the box.

The door opened, and I recognized the target instantly. Paul Jeddersen. Forty-two. Well known on the streets for abducting and raping women, even though the police could never get him for more than a misdemeanor. The guy was slick, clean, never leaving behind enough evidence to convict.

My skin crawled just at the sight of his clean-cut, suburban dad getup. It was the look that had fooled all his victims into trusting him.

I held the box toward him. "Someone call for a pizza?"

He shook his head. "No. Wrong address."

I pretended to peer down at my phone. "Paul Jeddersen. 1258 Olympic Drive?"

"That's me, but I didn't order the pizza."

He went to close the door, but I shoved the box at him again, preventing him from shutting me out.

"Is there anyone else here who might have ordered it?"

Irritation crept into the man's expression. "No. There

isn't. That's definitely not mine. I don't even like pizza, I'm lactose intolerant."

"Oh damn, you are? That sucks so much. Cheese is the best. Like, it's actually my favorite thing in the world. But it gives you the farts, huh? Or the squirts?"

Behind me, Scythe chuckled softly.

Paul shook his head. "What?"

"Not eating dairy is a crime, Paul. One you just admitted you are guilty of."

The man spluttered, clearly flustered. "Like I told you, that pizza isn't mine. Leave now or I'm calling the police."

I dropped the box, and the game, wedging my foot in the door. "Well, that's rude." I glanced over my shoulder at Scythe. "Isn't that rude?"

"Very unhospitable."

"Agreed. Aren't you going to invite us in, Paul?"

Paul's fear flickered in his eyes. "Who are you?"

The bloodlust inside me surged, pleased by the scent of fear in the air. I dropped my mouth open in mock outrage, playing with him. "First you don't offer us any cheese. And now you don't even know my name?" I tutted beneath my breath as I pushed my way into the room. "But I know yours. And it's not because you ordered pizza, Pauly. Little secret? I already ate that whole thing. And it didn't make me shit myself."

"This is the weirdest killing I've ever been to," Scythe murmured behind my back. "I don't know if I'm hungry or ready to vomit."

But my gaze was too set on Paul to pay Scythe any attention. The red haze the bloodlust stirred up spread through my body, rushing on my breath, priming each of my muscles for the fight and the release I so desperately needed.

But Paul caught his words. His gaze darted between the two of us, and he put his hands up. "I didn't do anything! I swear! I'm innocent!"

I fucking hated when they lied. I dropped the knife down my sleeve and wrapped my fingers around the handle. "You've got one chance to tell us the truth. Admit what you did."

He backed up, knocking over a lamp that went crashing to the floor. "Fine! I did it! I abducted those women. Killed them. I can't help it. It's not my fault!"

I knew all about urges that weren't my fault.

Didn't mean I felt sorry for this prick.

Paul kept babbling. "They were just so tempting. All pretty hair and tits and ass. So easy to manipulate and control."

His hand drifted to his crotch and rubbed it.

"Oh, fuck off," Scythe muttered. "Definitely not hungry anymore. Gag."

Neither was I. There was a reason I never killed women, even though some of them on the list more than deserved it, like Gray's wife and her sister had. The red haze swamped me, conjuring up images of Paul's victims' last moments, trapped and hurt, screaming for their lives, their fear palpable in the air. My heart pounded. In front of me, Paul's image morphed into someone else.

Someone I'd spent a lifetime wanting to kill.

The knife was in his gut before I knew what was happening. Over and over, I plunged it deep into his stomach, his hot blood spurting everywhere, covering my clothes, but I didn't care. It had been too long since I'd seen the flow of crimson coating my blade, pooling on the floor around my victim.

I couldn't stop. My knife had a mind of its own, desperately needing to be used. Each slice of his skin was a rush. Each new wound retribution for every life he'd destroyed.

Blood coated my hands. My clothes. My face. But I didn't stop. I couldn't. Not until the bloodlust had been satiated.

But it never would be. Not fully. I knew that. Killing quieted it for a little while. But it would come back. It always did.

"X!"

I froze with my knife in the air, mid-strike, and glanced over my shoulder at Scythe. My mouth dropped open. "I'm so sorry! Did you change your mind?"

Paul, full of stab wounds, was very much dead on the floor at my feet. I cringed but held the knife out to Scythe with a sheepish grin anyway. "Want to have a turn?"

But his gaze didn't meet mine. He was focused on something just over my shoulder. "So...we have a problem..."

I spun around to follow his line of sight.

A set of eyes stared back at me. Big, blue, terrified eyes, rimmed with dark lashes. Matted blond hair stuck to her face, and ripped clothes exposed her curvy body.

As well as the damage Paul had done to it.

The red haze that demanded blood switched on a dime and demanded something a whole lot different. Lust surged through me at the sight of her full tits and pink lips.

She backed up until she was in the corner of the kitchen, a knife block just to her left.

Her gaze darted to it.

So did mine.

She'd seen everything we'd done. I couldn't let her just walk away. But I couldn't just kill an innocent either. Which category did she fall into? Was she a witness I needed to get rid of? Or an innocent I needed to spare?

Grayson's rules were so confusing!

The woman grabbed a knife from the block and hurled it in our direction.

Scythe and I stared as the sharp blade sailed between us.

The woman screamed, plucking another knife and sending it our way.

Scythe and I scattered. Knives continued to fly.

"Oooh, I fucked up," I shouted to Scythe. "Didn't I? What the hell am I going to do now?"

Sharpened steel sailed past him, just an inch from his head. "Duck?"

EPILOGUE
GRAYSON

*H*elium balloons on strings bounced around in the warm summer breeze. Families sat shoulder to shoulder on white chairs, some spilling over and forced to stand on the grass at the sides. Cheers filled the air as each graduate walked across the stage, proudly wearing their caps and gowns.

"Here she comes!" I whisper-shouted to Hayden beside me.

He put two fingers into his mouth and wolf whistled loudly. "Yeah, Hayley Jade!"

She glanced up at his shout, waved her little hand excitedly, then practically ran across the stage to the school principal, who was handing out their kindergarten graduation certificates.

"This is so over-the-top but so fucking cute," Hawk muttered from the other side of Kara. He pushed up onto his feet when Hayley Jade shook hands with the principal. "That's our girl! Yeah!"

Everyone turned to stare at him, but we all quickly

joined in, hooting and hollering and making fools of ourselves.

Hayley Jade's laughter was infectious as she waved her certificate at us and yelled, "I got my award. Can we go to McDonald's now?"

The crowd all chuckled to themselves, but the four of us grinned like lunatics. The sound of her voice never got old, even when she was chattering a million miles a minute and nobody else could get a word in. She'd spent months more than making up for all the time she hadn't uttered a sound.

We all sat down, and Hayden reached across me to squeeze Kara's leg. "Are we going to have to bribe you with McDonald's when it's your turn to get up on that stage?"

She shook her head. "Not me. I can't wait. Might have to bribe Hawk though."

He screwed his face up. "I'm not wearing a fucking gown and having everyone stare and clap at me. Plus, I have to actually pass the GED before I can even think about enrolling in anything more than that."

I glanced at him while other people's kids continued crossing the stage. "You're not still worried about that? You're going to pass. You studied so much. You both did."

Hayden leaned back on his chair and crossed his arms. "Pretty sure you both studied so much even I could pass it now, just through secondhand osmosis." He paused. "I think I learned that word in one of your study sessions, actually."

Hawk didn't seem convinced. "I've failed it before."

I glanced at my watch. "Only an hour until they release the results and put you out of your misery."

He nodded, but we could all see it was worrying him. An hour at McDonald's watching Hayley Jade run around on a sugar high would probably do him good. At least it would distract him.

Half of Hayley Jade's classmates' families seemed to have had the same idea as us, multiple families all pulling into the restaurant at the same time. I ordered for the five of us while Hayley Jade ran off to the playground with her friends, and Kara chatted with one of the school mom's she'd gotten to know. It was noisy and chaotic, but there was a celebratory vibe in the air I just knew we'd be continuing when we got home and Kara and Hawk's results came out.

It took forever to get Hayley Jade to leave, and when we finally got back to the clubhouse, Hawk paused the van at the gates. Fang ducked his head, so he and Hawk were even heights, and passed over some mail for us to drive down. But his gaze was pretty firmly on Hawk.

"You get your results yet?"

Hawk's huff of nervous impatience was all he got in reply.

Kara answered as she took the mail from Hawk's fingers. "Don't mind him. They've just released so we're driving down now to get our laptops. He's nervous."

Fang hit the button on the gates that set them to open. "You've got it this time, Hawk. Quit stressing yourself into an early grave. And if you don't—"

Haw shot him a look that could have killed.

Fang chuckled. "Right. Never mind. Good luck, Kara."

She smiled at him, taking this whole thing a whole lot better than Hawk was. "Thank you."

I sat back on my phone, scrolling through it while

Hawk steered the car down the driveway, past the blackened trees and shrubs that were still trying to regenerate after everything that had happened with Ice.

He parked the van, Hayley Jade skipping off inside to show her graduation certificate to all the guys. But Hawk didn't move to follow her, like he normally would have. He paced the parking lot, his hands on the back of his head.

"I can't do it. I've failed. I just know it. I'm too fucking dumb for this shit. What made me think I could do this?" He glared at me. "You! You made me think I could. Fucking hell, Gray. You seriously suck. You know that, right?"

I laughed at him, which only made him madder. "I didn't make you do anything. I just encouraged you to have another go at something that's important to you. And you *can* do it."

Hawk wasn't done spiraling. "You don't know that!"

"Actually, I do." I flashed my phone screen at him. "You passed. I looked your results up because I knew you'd be dramatic about it."

He gaped at me. "Seriously? Let me see that." He grabbed my phone, studying the screen and then staring back up at us with huge eyes. "That's my name! I fucking passed!"

He grabbed Kara, kissing her hard, and then planted one on Hayden as well.

I grinned at him. "Gonna kiss me too?"

"Not a chance."

I sniggered. "Manly handshake?"

He shrugged. "How about a hug as a thank you for all your help? I know I only passed because of you."

To my surprise, his tone was sincere, and when he pulled me in for a hug, it was genuine.

"Thanks, Gray. I mean it. For everything. Not just this."

I swallowed hard, surprisingly emotional. But I was actually really fucking proud of him. None of his success had anything to do with me. He'd earned every mark himself and he was going to be a kick-ass paramedic one day.

Just like Kara was going to be an amazing nurse. I grinned at her over his shoulder. "You passed too, by the way. You'll be able to enroll in your nursing program as soon as you're ready."

Hayden whooped and picked her up, spinning her around, while she groaned about him squishing the baby.

He put her down pretty quick, giving her bump a loving rub. "Sorry, little man. But your mom is pretty awesome."

"So are his dads." She smiled at all of us. "What should we do to celebrate? Anything but McDonald's. I'm so full."

Hayden leaned down to kiss her neck. "I have some ideas. Most of them involve multiple orgasms as a way of rewarding you for all your hard work."

You couldn't wipe the smile off Hawk's face. He ran his hands down Kara's back 'til he got to her ass, then kissed Hayden over her shoulder. "I had some similar thoughts of my own."

Kara looked at me hopefully. "Might be one of our last chances before this baby comes along."

I leaned in and kissed her sweet mouth. "Sperm is

supposed to be good for softening the cervix and bringing on labor."

Hawk's eyes lit up, as they always did when we talked medicine. "I read about that! It contains a high level of prostaglandin."

Kara nodded. "Nipple stimulation is supposed to help too."

Chaos screwed up his face. "It was sexy until it wasn't. You guys are seriously ruining this for me."

Kara led him toward the clubhouse. "Let's go inside and I'll tell you all about how when the cervix dilates you can—"

A phone ringing cut her off. It took everyone staring in my direction to realize it was my other phone, the one only my murderous little band of psychopaths used.

But instead of the usual blocked number, it was a video call.

I frowned at it, my heart rate picking up at the change in routine.

"Everything okay?" Kara asked softly.

I forced a smile at her, not wanting to worry her when she was this close to giving birth. "I'm sure it's fine. Just one of the guys probably thinking about going on a murder spree and needing to be talked off the ledge."

Nobody laughed. Not even me. "Yeah. Okay. Not funny. I'm going to take this."

They all nodded, understanding now this was a responsibility I took seriously, both as a doctor and as a friend and brother. These men needed me to keep them on the straight and narrow. Or as much of one as there could be when I was endorsing them killing people.

Keeping it to those who truly deserved it was the only way I could sleep at night.

I waited until my family had gone inside and the heavy front door of the club had swung closed behind them. Then I answered the call.

"Grayson!" Scythe's face filled the screen.

I blinked in confusion. "Scythe? How do you have this number? What's going on? Are you okay?"

"Aw! It's so nice of you to ask. Men don't do that enough these days, do they? We really should ask each other that more."

A crashing thumping noise came from somewhere behind him, and then X's howl of pain.

I widened my eyes. "Was that X?" My stomach sank. "Scythe, are you hurting him? I know he's insanely annoying—"

"Am not!" X shouted from somewhere off-screen.

I blinked, shaking my head and heading toward my car, grateful I'd left the keys in it and didn't need to waste time going inside to get them. "And childish, but if he's pissed you off enough for you to hurt him, then let's just talk about—"

Scythe winced at another crash in the background.

X howled again. "She's trying to kill me, Gray! Help!"

I stopped mid-stride. "She?"

Scythe flipped the phone around.

I peered at the screen and then gaped at the woman throwing kitchen utensils in X's direction while he shielded himself with a fat, hardcover cook book.

Scythe turned the phone back on himself and grinned sheepishly at me. "Some mistakes might have been made tonight."

I sighed, shaking my head as I got into my car. "Send me your location. I'm on my way."

"Will do."

"Scythe?"

"Yeah?"

"Can you try to keep the woman alive long enough for me to get there?"

"Why are you throwing eggs at me?" X yelled in the background. "We could make omelets with those!"

Scythe sniggered, sitting back in a chair like he was eating popcorn at a movie. "I'm not sure it's her you need to worry about."

THE END.

Want to know who the baby daddy is? Or what really happened the night Kara was buried alive?It's all in the free bonus scene on my website. Check the bonus content tab at www.ellethorpe.com

X and the murder squad are back in the next Saint View Trilogy, now available for preorder! While you wait, check out all the other Saint View books listed on the Also By pages at the end of this book.

ALSO BY ELLE THORPE

Saint View High series (Reverse Harem, Bully Romance. Complete)

*Devious Little Liars (Saint View High, #1)

*Dangerous Little Secrets (Saint View High, #2)

*Twisted Little Truths (Saint View High, #3)

Saint View Prison series (Reverse harem, romantic suspense. Complete.)

*Locked Up Liars (Saint View Prison, #1)

*Solitary Sinners (Saint View Prison, #2)

*Fatal Felons (Saint View Prison, #3)

Saint View Psychos series (Reverse harem, romantic suspense. Complete.)

*Start a War (Saint View Psychos, #1)

*Half the Battle (Saint View Psychos, #2)

*It Ends With Violence (Saint View Psychos, #3)

Saint View Rebels (Reverse harem, romantic suspense. Complete)

*Rebel Revenge (Saint View Rebels, #1)

*Rebel Obsession (Saint View Rebels, #2)

*Rebel Heart (Saint View Rebels, #3)

Saint View Strip (Male/Female, romantic suspense standalones. Ongoing.)

*Evil Enemy (Saint View Strip, #1)

*Unholy Sins (Saint View Strip, #2)

*Killer Kiss (Saint View Strip, #3)

*Untitled (Saint View Strip, #4)

Saint View Slayers Vs. Sinners (Reverse harem, romantic suspense)

*Wife Number One (Saint View Slayers Vs. Sinners, #1)

*Torn in Two (Saint View Slayers Vs. Sinners, #2)

*Three to Fall (Saint View Slayers Vs. Sinners, #3)

Dirty Cowboy series (complete)

*Talk Dirty, Cowboy (Dirty Cowboy, #1)

*Ride Dirty, Cowboy (Dirty Cowboy, #2)

*Sexy Dirty Cowboy (Dirty Cowboy, #3)

*Dirty Cowboy boxset (books 1-3)

*25 Reasons to Hate Christmas and Cowboys (a Dirty Cowboy bonus novella, set before Talk Dirty, Cowboy but can be read as a standalone, holiday romance)

Buck Cowboys series (Spin off from the Dirty Cowboy series. Complete.)

*Buck Cowboys (Buck Cowboys, #1)

*Buck You! (Buck Cowboys, #2)

*Can't Bucking Wait (Buck Cowboys, #3)

*Mother Bucker (Buck Cowboys, #4)

The Only You series (Contemporary romance. Complete)

*Only the Positive (Only You, #1) - Reese and Low.

*Only the Perfect (Only You, #2) - Jamison.

*Only the Truth - (Only You, bonus novella) - Bree.

*Only the Negatives (Only You, #3) - Gemma.

*Only the Beginning (Only You, #4) - Bianca and Riley.

*Only You boxset

Add your email address here to be the first to know when new books are available!

www.ellethorpe.com/newsletter

Join Elle Thorpe's readers group on Facebook!

www.facebook.com/groups/ellethorpesdramallamas

ACKNOWLEDGMENTS

There's an ever growing group of people who make these books possible and they all deserve the hugest thank you.

Thank you to the Drama Llamas. You guys make my days fun. If you aren't already a member, it's a free reader group on Facebook where I share all sorts of stuff. Come join us, everyone is welcome. www.facebook.com/groups/ellethorpesdramallamas

Thank you to Montana Ash/Darcy Halifax for writing with me every day and being the best office buddy/work wife ever.

Thank you to Sara Massery, Jolie Vines, and Zoe Ashwood for the constant support, friendship, and book advice.

Thank you to the cover team:
Emily Wittig for the discreet covers and Michelle Lancaster for the photography.

Thank you to my editing team:
Emmy at Studio ENP and Karen at Barren Acres Editing.

Dana, Louise, Sam, and Shellie for beta reading. Plus my ARC team for the early reviews.

Thank you to the audio team:

Troy at Dark Star Romance for producing this series. Thank you to Michelle, Sean, Lee, and E.M. for being the voices of Kara, Hawk, Chaos, and Grayson.

And of course, thank you to the team who organize me and the home front:

To Donna for taking on all the jobs I don't have time for. Best admin manager ever.

To my mum, for working for us one day a week, and always being willing to have our kids when we go to signings.

To Jira, for running the online store, doing all the accounting, and dealing with all the 'people-ing.' Not to mention, being the best stay at home dad ever.

To Flick and Heidi, for helping pack swag, and to Thomas, who refuses to work for us, but will proudly tell everyone he knows that his mum is an author.

From the bottom of my heart, thank you.

Elle x

ABOUT THE AUTHOR

Elle Thorpe lives in a small regional town of NSW, Australia. When she's not writing stories full of kissing, she's wife to Mr Thorpe who unexpectedly turned out to be a great plotting partner, and mummy to three tiny humans. She's also official ball thrower to one slobbery dog named Rollo.

When she's not at the office writing, she's probably out on the family alpaca farm, trying not to get spit on.

You can find her on Facebook or Instagram(@ellethorpebooks or hit the links below!) or at her website www.ellethorpe.com. If you love Elle's work, please consider joining her Facebook fan group, Elle Thorpe's Drama Llamas or joining her newsletter here. www.ellethorpe.com/newsletter